BROTHERS IN ARMS

Also by the author

Four Days in June

JACK STEEL SERIES
Man of Honour
Rules of War

IAIN GALE

Brothers in Arms

HarperCollins*Publishers*

HarperCollins*Publishers*
77–85 Fulham Palace Road,
Hammersmith, London W6 8JB

www.harpercollins.co.uk

Published by HarperCollins*Publishers* 2009

1

A catalogue record for this book
is available from the British Library

ISBN 978-0-00-725357-9

Set in Sabon by Palimpsest Book Production Limited,
Grangemouth, Stirlingshire

Printed and bound in Great Britain by
Clays Ltd, St Ives plc

FSC

© **Mixed Sources**
Product group from well-managed
forests and other controlled sources
www.fsc.org Cert no. SW-COC-1806
© 1996 Forest Stewardship Council

In memory of Sarah Gale, 1965–2008

PROLOGUE

High on the crest of a hill, above the little Belgian village of Eename, barely fifteen miles from the border with France, a tall rider in the distinctive, scarlet coat of an English staff officer, raised his broad frame high up in his stirrups and craned forward over the neck of his mount. Putting a spyglass to his eye, he gazed northwards across the verdant summer countryside and prayed for a miracle and with it a glimpse of his destiny.

Had they been looking closely, any one of the small group of horsemen who had accompanied him to his hilltop vantage point might have noticed the small smile that played across his features and in that instant would have known that they had found their goal.

William, first Earl of Cadogan, Chief of Staff and Quartermaster General to the army of his Grace the Duke of Marlboroough, had been in the saddle since one o'clock that morning, riding at the head of sixteen battalions of infantry and eight squadrons of cavalry. He had marched his little force at double time – some three miles to the hour – the thirteen miles from the town of Lessines, just to the north of Ath, to this spot. Below him and a little away to his left lay the town of Oudenarde, waking from its gentle slumbers, with its tall church, fanciful baroque *hotel de ville* and spreading, star-shaped fort. And pausing now, he wondered whether he had found what he and his advance column had been searching for. Through his telescope, even in the early light and clearing mists, Cadogan could clearly make out on the opposite slope, the small forms of men in pale grey coats and black tricorne hats trimmed with yellow lace as they went about the mundane business of an army in camp. French infantry. The advance guard perhaps of a mighty force which until lately had been preparing to lay siege to allied troops in Oudenarde. Clearly, their awareness of the proximity of Marlborough's allied army had thwarted any such plan and they had moved to a fresh position where they would not themselves become encircled as was so often the case in such a siege. But, from their present behaviour, thought Cadogan, with growing satisfaction, it was clear that they could not believe that Marlborough's men might be perilously close at hand on this brightening summer morning. And that was precisely what Cadogan and his Commander in Chief had hoped.

The town of Oudenarde lay astride the river Scheldt, inundated with wide-ranging marshland, and the most vital element of Cadogan's modest force was the pontoon train with its team of skilled engineers: the means by which the great army of 70,000 men, horses and guns that came in his wake was to cross this formidable natural obstacle. But it was not to Oudenarde that Cadogan now turned his attention, but the wide valley of farmland beyond the river traversed by three streams and enclosed by three low hills.

It was as fine a morning as any of them had seen since the start of this campaigning season and the Belgian fields lay bathed in sunshine. It was, Cadogan guessed some time after eight o'clock on the eleventh day of July in the year 1708. And he was determined that this would be a date that would be remembered for evermore. A day that would be told of in England's schoolrooms for centuries to come. A great day of British victory.

He had his orders. He was to sweep the road from Lessines clear of the enemy and then clear a crossing over the Scheldt. He must lay his five pontoon bridges hard by Oudenarde and form a bridgehead which he would hold until relieved by Marlborough – whenever he might arrive.

He turned to an aide: 'Cassels, ride back to Colonel Harker and tell him to have his pioneers move down to the river as quickly as he can. He must lay his bridges there'. He pointed towards Oudenarde. 'Hurry, man. We've no time to lose.'

As the young officer rode off, Cadogan looked again at the French on the opposite hill and wondered whether an enemy officer might at that same moment be watching him in a similar way and wondering at his purpose. He knew that the French too were spoiling for a fight. And he was aware that at no time in this war had a victory been so keenly needed by Marlborough as it was now.

It had been a dreadful year, spent mostly in sieges. The Dutch had insisted that it was the only way. Marlborough, Cadogan knew, was powerless without Dutch support. Of course, the Duke had not been idle in the last season. Was he ever? He had struck on a scheme to land Prince Eugene in southern France, at Toulon. It had been a bold plan. Too bold – and had come to nought. Yet for once it had not been the Dutch but their ally the Emperor of Austria himself who had forbidden it. It was said that the Emperor wished to sue for peace with the French. To treat with Louis? Cadogan, like Marlborough had been nonplussed. Certainly, now in its sixth year, this war was draining Europe dry, bathing the continent in blood. And to be sure neither of the English Generals wanted further carnage. But it was clear to any man with even the most modest military knowledge that before the French would accept any terms of armistice, a great victory must be won over them.

Then, in July disaster had struck when General Galway's army had been routed at Almanza in Spain and the peninsula all but lost. After Marlborough's triumphs in the Low Countries it scarcely seemed possible. A British-led army put to flight and half its men lost or taken captive. Finally, only a week ago, the vital strategic towns of Ghent and Bruges had been taken by the French. Or, in effect, had been lost to them by the treachery of their townspeople. Here was proof surely of the rumour that the Belgian people were growing tired of the allies and their great English General and would rather revert to French rule. So now, as a consequence of their perfidy, there was a real risk of the allied army's communications and lines of supply being cut with England.

Cadogan broke off from his musings and spoke to one of the men at his side, a portly Colonel with an amiable, florid face: 'Tell me, Colonel Hawkins. What think you of our predicament?'

'My Lord, we are well placed to hold the French here. And, should we manage to engage them, I have no fear that we are equal to the task.'

Cadogan nodded: 'No, Colonel. You mistake me. I am interested in your opinion of the campaign as a whole. You are aware that the French under Vendome have placed themselves behind the Bruges canal: that in effect, despite the fact that tactically we have them, or some of them, in our sights here, strategically they are in our rear. You know too that our intelligence has it from the most reliable sources that an army under Marshal Berwick is marching to join that of Vendome.'

'If that is the case, my Lord, then we must act with all possible speed to engage Vendome. For against their combined strength we would surely have little hope.'

'Quite so. That is Marlborough's intention and that, you perceive is why we are here. It is our task to hold the attention of those men over there and their Marshal until Marlborough can reach us and give battle.'

'And that we shall do, Sir. The plan was well conceived. To cross the Scheldt here, above Oudenarde is such a move as only the Duke could make. This is the stuff of Blenheim and Ramillies. D'you doubt him, my Lord?'

Cadogan frowned at him: 'Would I ever question that man's genius? No, Colonel Hawkins . . . James. Like you I am aware that in placing us here the Duke has taken position not only between the two enemy armies, but between Vendome and France itself. And yet, I am worried. Think of Ghent, James. Consider how easily it gave itself up to the French. What d'you suppose would happen if other towns should follow suit? What then if our army should find itself adrift in a hostile land with neither supply of ammunition nor provisions?'

Hawkins, knowing the full horror of the answer, said nothing. Again, Cadogan peered across at the tiny, pale grey figures busy opposite them and knew that the moment had come to take a gamble. A gamble on which would rest the fate of the entire allied army. There was no sure way of knowing the true extent of the French presence here but something told Cadogan – an instinct born of almost twenty years of campaigning – that over that hill lay the might of France. It must be so, he reasoned. Where else might Vendome be?

Banishing any doubts, he turned to the young officer on his left and spoke in a low, grave, emotional voice in which it was easy to detect the gentle lilt of his native Dublin: 'Cornet Rodgers, take yourself off on a ride if you will back to the Captain General.'

The officer nodded, awaiting his orders.

Cadogan, frowning, thought for another moment, raised his glass to his eye once again and then dropping it quickly, turned again to the man: 'Tell Marlborough that we've found them. That I've found Marshal Vendome, unless I am very much mistaken, and all his army. Tell the Duke that I intend to give them battle within the hour. And, Rodgers, ask his Grace with all possible politeness if he will', he chose his words with care, 'make haste. Oh, and if you wish to escape a scolding, take care to do so quietly. The Duke is not in the best of health a present.'

As the watched the nervous young man ride out of sight, Cadogan turned again to Hawkins: 'Tell me, James, have I done the right thing? Do you think Vendome is over there? You don't suppose that what we see might be merely a detachment. A rearguard, or a recconnaissance? Could I be wrong?'

Hawkins looked at him and smiled: 'My Lord, there is no way of knowing whether you are wrong or right until the French show more of themselves. But in my opinion you are in the right. And more importantly you have done the right thing. You need not fear either for your honour or your reputation.'

Cadogan shook his head: 'I do not fear for myself, James. But for the army and for Marlborough. He has been feverish for some days now. And whatever the physical malaise I know that it is the need for battle that truly trouble troubles him. If I am mistaken; if that is not the French army over there; then we may ourselves be caught in turn . . .'

He was interrupted by the arrival of a breathless Cornet of Dragoons.

Cadogan waved him to be calm, waited while he recovered his composure and allowed the boy to speak: 'My Lord, we have observed a body of French horse advancing down the valley. They appear to be in search of provisions. They have a great many wagons, Sir, and an escort of dragoons on foot. My General asks, should we engage them?'

Cadogan smiled and thought for hardly a moment: 'It's the train, Hawkins. The train of Vendome's army. He's there. We have found him.'

He turned to the Cornet: 'Tell your General that he must engage them. Tell him to cut them up as best he can and see if he can't take a colour if there's one to be had and as many officers as he likes. But make sure that he leaves enough of them alive to take the news of our presence and their disgrace back to their masters.'

This, then, was the miracle he had sought. A means of alerting the battle-hungry French to the fact that they were here. Now he would draw them out, before Vendome was able to choose to wait for Berwick and his secondary army. And then it would be too late.

Hawkins could see it too. He smiled: 'We have them, Sir. You were right and if I know the French they won't be able to help themselves. They'll want revenge for this, good and proper. And I'm willing to wager that Marshal Vendome is still at breakfast. And that when he chooses to leave his table, he'll find half his army departed for the field, eager to regain the honour of France. Thank God.'

'Yes. We must thank God, James. But you'd better start praying to him too. Remember, we have but ten thousand men to hold off ten times that number. And Marlborough still twenty miles distant.'

'Oh, we'll manage it, Sir.'

'I have no doubt that we shall manage it, James. Our troops are the finest in the world. And it's not the odds I fear. The ground too is in our favour. This battle will be all to do with timing. And the first thing we must do is to get those pontoons in place.'

He looked hard back down the length of the column: 'Where the devil is Harker?'

Raising his voice, he yelled towards a group of staff officers: 'Someone find me Colonel Harker and his damned boats.'

He had hardly finished speaking when the first of forty ox-drawn carts heaved into view, laden with its tin-built pontoon boats and the wooden baulks that were to be nailed and lashed across them. A flushed Colonel Harker rode at its head and spurred on towards Cadogan whose nod of recognition was rewarded with a salute.

Now it begins, thought Cadogan. In an hour the boats would be in place. Another and the French would be throwing everything they had at his little force. And then, all they would be able to do was stand and fight, and wait.

ONE

The familiar, acrid stench of smoke and powder drifted with the staccato rattle of musket fire up towards them across the river. Captain Jack Steel, standing on one of the wooden pontoon bridges laid earlier that morning over the river Scheldt, was drawn away for a moment from the spectacle of battle unfolding before him by the sound of laughter.

Looking to the left and down towards the water, he saw three of his men pissing into the river, the pale streams of urine arcing against water and landscape as they competed to be the highest. Steel listened to their laughter and boastful claims and decided to allow them one more moment of innocent fun. For who knew if this day would be their last – or indeed his own? The remainder of Steel's company of Grenadiers, fifty-one men all told, stood and sat at their ease directly to his rear, as they had been told they might. They talked among themselves, not of the battle going on below them, nor of anything to do with the war, but of other things: of women and booty and glory and the various virtues of English porter and Scottish ale. But gradually their diverting conversations were turning thin and more men became silent by the minute.

It was hardly surprising, thought Steel. They had been here for near on two hours now and it was not hard to see the telltale signs of impatience and growing unease that came when death was near. The long march to the guns had taken them sixty miles in fifty hours, some of it cross-country, and now those who chose to stand, drawn to the music of the battle, found themselves reluctant yet compelled spectators looking down on a bloody struggle. There was nothing worse than this for a soldier, thought Steel, save of course death itself, and maiming. Nothing worse than this waiting. For with it came the rising fear that clawed away at your guts and lurked like some evil spirit or canker inside your brain. The knowledge that soon, very soon he reckoned now, they too would be part of that maelstrom of hot lead, cold steel and all too yielding flesh down there in the little valley. And if that moment was to come, then he damned well wished it would come soon.

Steel turned to the men behind him and found at only a few paces distant the company's young, rosy-cheeked ensign, Tom Williams, now aged twenty and no longer the gauche boy he had been when he had purchased into the battalion – Sir James Farquharson's Regiment of Foot – four years ago this summer. Williams had joined the colours shortly before the great victory at Blenheim, Marlborough's first great triumph in which the regiment and in particular Steel's Grenadiers had won renown. Steel had grown to feel an almost fatherly obligation to Williams in that campaign and he felt no less close now, imparting when he could sage advice and reasoned reprimand where necessary.

'Tom, I think that we might fall the men in again now. It shouldn't be too long before we go, by the look of things. But we'd best keep them on their mettle, eh? You might inspect their weapons again. That sort of thing. I want every musket checked and re-checked. And make sure that their bayonets are all well greased. Oh, and before you do that get those three idiots back from the river. Their tackle might just prove too tempting a target for the French, and we don't want to draw enemy fire without good cause.'

Williams laughed. He loved Steel's wry wit and envied him his way with the men. It was the pinnacle to which he aspired. And what better model to have? The ability of this man to combine all the qualities of a gentleman with a genuine empathy with his troops picked him out as a natural leader. Yet at the same time it seemed that Steel always kept an implicit awareness of his own station and their place. In short, Jack Steel was everything that a soldier should be, thought Williams: cool in battle, ruthless and implacable in combat, level-headed, intuitive and pragmatic. Throw into the equation the fact that he was also enviably handsome, and at six foot tall a giant among men, and you had a worthy hero for any young subaltern. This was precisely how Williams hoped the men might see him when he too rose to the rank of captain in command of his own company – if he should manage to survive that long.

He knew that he mustn't think that way. Hadn't the sergeants told him so in his first battle? And Steel for that matter, more times than he could remember. But still he could not banish the dark thoughts from his mind. Like Steel, he knew that if there was any obvious target for the enemy it was sure to be an officer. And, like Steel, Tom Williams was tall for his time. Both men were remarkable in an age when the average height was a good ten inches less. But then these were grenadiers – a company of giants, hand-picked from the regiment and the army as much for their stature as their skill at arms. They were the storm troops of the army, the first into any fight and more than likely the last men out.

Williams turned to the company's senior sergeant, a similarly tall, bluff Geordie with an infectious grin named Jacob Slaughter, whose hard-bitten face told of countless actions and larger engagements. 'Sar'nt Slaughter. Those men there – discourage them from that, if you will.'

He had learnt his style of command direct from Steel, and the coolly laconic order still did not sit quite as easily as he would have liked on his lips. The sergeant smiled at the boy's attempt, confident in the knowledge that Williams could do no better than model himself on Captain Steel, and in turn barked a command towards the clowns on the river bank.

The three men suddenly went quiet and hurriedly buttoned their breeches. Then, turning back towards the company, they scrambled up the muddy slope and returned to the grinning ranks. As they passed their captain, Steel nodded and ensured that they could see his gaze, half disapproving, half amused. As they hurried into rank Slaughter shouted further commands, which were echoed by the other sergeants and corporals of the company. Then, careful to be firm but not too forceful, he began to use the wooden staff of the long sergeant's half-pike to urge the files back into line and dress the ranks, ready for the long-awaited march attack.

Steel knew of course that all their muskets were clean and had been checked. In fact they had been cleaned and checked these past two hours, and at all the halts on the long march that had brought them to this place. He knew too that every man's razor-sharp socket bayonet, newly issued to replace the old plug variety, was slick to perfection with grease so that it would slide smoothly from the scabbard when the time came and slot with ease on the steel nipples at the end of their muskets before slipping just as easily between the ribs of the French when eventually they met them on the field below. But he knew too that in their present condition anything must be done to keep the men's minds off the carnage now so evidently taking place to their front.

Steel stared back into the smoke of the battle. He heard the crash of musketry again and the distant cries of anguish caught on the wind that he knew would also be only too audible to the men. Behind him, as if to affirm his fears, one of the younger recruits to his largely veteran company vomited onto the white-gaitered legs of the man to his front, who, naturally, turned and swore at the youngster and, even though he carried his musket at the high porte, still attempted to swing a punch. Sergeant Slaughter shouted to both of them and, mouthing

12

oaths, went to help the terrified and now mortified recruit to regain his composure and wipe the dribbles of vomit from his scarlet coat. Steel turned back towards the enemy. He would give almost anything now to propel his men into a state of readiness, bursting to be at the enemy. Yet at the same time he wanted to make them feel at ease. It was a hard trick, this balancing act. But, he told himself, hadn't he done it many times before? And didn't he know most of these men like his own family? Better, now he thought of it. He turned to Williams.

'A song, I think, Tom. Let's have a song. Who's the best voice in the company, would you say? Taylor? Dan Cussiter?'

'It must be Corporal Taylor, sir, to be sure.'

'Then Matt Taylor it shall be.'

Steel scoured the ranks for the man.

'Taylor. Where are you? Come on, Matt. Give us all a tune. Sing up above the guns. And be sure to make it a good 'un. "The Rochester Recruit" or something similar.'

Corporal Matthew Taylor, a gangly, bankrupted clerk from Hounsditch and for the last six years, since the start of this war, the company's invaluable and learned apothecary and medical expert on account of his knowledge of herbals, cleared his throat and began to sing in a hearty tenor:

'Oh a bold fusilier came marching down through
    Rochester,
Bound for the wars in the Low Countries.
And he sang as he marched
Through the crowded streets of Rochester,
"Who'll be a soldier for Marlborough and me?"'

As one the company joined in, with the familiar chorus:

'Who'll be a soldier, who'll be a soldier,
Who'll be a soldier for Marlborough and me?'

13

Steel smiled to see how, as ever, the magic worked so quickly on the terrified men. That was the answer, for now at least: the way to kill a few more idle moments. Set them thinking about their beloved 'Corporal John' – John Churchill, Duke of Marlborough, ennobled by the Queen after Blenheim – about how he had won so many great victories for them and how today was sure to be another. Blenheim, Ramillies and . . . What, he wondered was the name of that little hamlet to their front?

'Tom. What's the name of that village?'

'Place called Eename, sir.'

No, thought Steel, that would not do. It hardly had a martial ring to it. Better of course the larger place to their left. Oudenarde. That would look better in the history books and on the broadsheets in the London coffee houses. Blenheim, Ramillies and Oudenarde. Not forgetting Ostend, the lines of Brabant . . .

From behind him, above the singing and the noise from the valley, Steel caught the sound of a loud sneeze, and he had no need to guess from whom it emanated. Henry Hansam, his second-in-command, had found his own cure for the battle-field terrors yet again and was indulging in it as ever before an engagement. Hansam took snuff, and at such times as these in such quantities that his consumption increased tenfold. While in other companies and battalions the men might have advanced to the ring of huzzahs and the beating of drums, in Steel's, for the past six years, the accompaniment to any attack had been embellished with a succession of Hansam's explosive sneezes.

Steel turned towards him. The lieutenant saw him and spoke over the resounding noise of the men's singing.

'Care for a pinch, Jack? Newly arrived consignment from England, via Ostend. Finest Spanish, and I'm reliably informed that it originates from that very shipment taken by Admiral Hobson off Vigo in 1702. Superb stuff. You're quite sure that you won't . . . ?'

'No, thank you, Henry. And no matter how you may press me, and whatever its divine provenance, you know quite well that the day will never dawn when I descend to pushing that filthy stuff up my nose. Drink is my vice. And perhaps a round of piquet or whist.'

'And you only have eyes for one lady now, Jack. The lovely Mrs Steel has all your attention. Gone are the days –'

Steel, laughing, interrupted him. 'Quite so, Henry. All my roving done. A simple life is what I crave. Glory, promotion, riches. The love of a good woman and the company of such men as I am proud to serve with. I ask for nothing more.'

Hansam laughed. 'Well, please yourself. But you don't know what you're missing. Rare stuff this. Very sweet. Fragrant as lavender. Calms the nerves.'

'Sweet, Henry? That muck's as rank as a Holborn sewer. And from the amount of it you shove into your nostrils, I'm surprised you have any nerves left that need to be calmed.'

Hansam smiled and his face contorted as he was consumed by another sneeze, even more violent than the last. Steel laughed again and was pleased to see Slaughter and his men, for all their singing, grinning as they picked up on catches of the officers' conversation. It always made them feel relaxed to see their superiors appear so phlegmatic in the face of the enemy. To keep one's head in battle, as now in the moments before it began, was one of the prime requisites for any officer. An officer, they knew, was bred to such a role. Bred to be a gentleman by birth and by inclination. And with that went a natural confidence. An officer, a real officer, was unassailable, indestructible. And while he might not have been born into any great wealth, Jack Steel, the hard-pressed gentleman-farmer's son from Lowland Scotland, was surely a natural officer in their eyes. Purchased into the army by his former lover, a court lady at St James's and wife of an elderly nobleman, Steel had established a reputation for his sang-froid. Yet behind the façade, if truth be told, there still lurked as unwelcome a heart-freezing terror as afflicted the greenest recruit. Who could not be afraid at such a moment?

Steel cast an eye over the company and beyond his men to the others of the regiment and took in their parade of well-known, unshaven faces beneath their tall mitre hats, the symbol of their elite status, blue and red embroidery emblazoned with gold wire and white lace. The hats, worn only by grenadiers, were designed to facilitate the throwing of the bombs from which they took their name, and they carried those weapons still, even though those unpredictable weapons were used increasingly less often in battle. Each man carried in a black leather case three of the small black metal orbs, named after the Spanish word for pomegranate, which when lit by a fuse and hurled like a cricket ball were still capable of doing damage to an entrenched position and wreaking havoc within a tightly packed body of troops.

Steel knew all these men and their individual character-istics, from Mackay's thick-set farmer's frame and Taylor's scrawny, guttersnipe physique, to Yorkshireman Dan Cussiter's high-boned bird-like features and Thorogood's over-long arms, so effective with a grenade. He felt deep affection for most. He had fought alongside many before and was prepared to do everything he could to make sure they got through this war intact of mind and body and emerge with booty and honour. It was no less and no more than he hoped for himself.

Beyond the grenadiers, high above the Battalion Major's company, waved the silken squares of the regimental colours. One of them was tattered now, looking no more than a rag, after so long in the field. It was the Colonel's colour, red and gold above the cipher of their commander, Sir James Farquharson. The other, only recently presented, bore the new Union flag of the united kingdom of England, Scotland and Ireland, in its centre a crown. Lest anyone should be in doubt, the colour made the matter plain. Farquharson might have raised a regiment of Scottish foot who at Blenheim and

Ramillies had fought beneath the blue and white of his native country's saltire, but since last year these were Britain's infantry. British grenadiers. Proud to serve not only their Queen but their newly united nation. Steel watched the colours catch the sunlight as they rippled in the breeze.

Behind them, curving back through the marshland and up the hill towards the village of Eename, he saw the mass of the column – a polyglot force, waiting here behind Farquharson's, to step off in turn from the flimsy wooden bridges resting on tin boats. Among them, he knew, stood some of the finest infantry in the world: Lord Herbert's Foot, and with them Gibson's, Farrington's, Meredith's and Holland's. Behind them came Princess Anne's, Granville's, Clifton's and Douglas's, and those other regiments which like his own had lately made up the Scots army: the Royals, the newly christened North British Fusiliers and the Earl of Angus's Foot. All of them names that would surely be writ forever in the history of this army.

To the right of the British brigades were the Allies: the Prussians and Hessians in their distinctive blue, Hanoverians and Swiss in red, and the grey-coated Danes. Singing and swearing in a half-dozen languages, they had all come to this place on the orders of their great general. This was an encyclopedia of Europe's tribes and races: English, Irish, Scots and Welsh, pale-skinned Scandinavians, men from the Italian and German states and exiled French Huguenots.

For some time now, too many of the men had been silent. They were watching as their comrades who had arrived earlier that morning met the enemy down in the valley and gave fire and stood to take it and charged and fought and died. They were all powerless, of course. They had been ordered to wait, and increasingly there was no alternative but to watch. Steel realized with a start, however, that his own men were still far from silent and Taylor had not yet finished his song. Or perhaps he has started afresh, thought Steel, and I have not noticed, being so lost in my own daydreams. He listened now as they sang out, mid-verse:

'To be paid in the powder and rattle of the cannonballs
Wages for soldiers like Marlborough and me.'

It might, he thought, have been the song of his own life – a life paid in powder and shot. Such had been Steel's wages since the age of seventeen. He had come to this war as a lieutenant, transferred by his own request and to the dismay of his fellow officers from the Guards, and he had risen to his present rank not by purchase, as was the usual way, but by proving himself in battle.

By that, and his new-found skill as an 'intelligencer'. For Steel had become one of the new breed of officers now emerging who could act as the eyes and ears of their commander. Before Blenheim, four years ago now this summer, Steel had single-handedly foiled a conspiracy against Marlborough, designed to discredit the Duke as a Jacobite traitor and remove him from command. Then two years back he had played a key part in the clandestine taking of Ostend, now the British army's key point of contact with the home-land and conduit for vital supplies.

Steel looked at the loops of silver lace that only in the past few weeks he had been reluctantly persuaded to have sewn onto his red coat. He had once sworn that he would do every-thing he could to avoid using such blatant badges of rank. Not for the simple reason that he might make a better target for the enemy's best shots, but because he considered himself better than the preening popinjays which so many officers soon became. Steel was a fighter. Just that. What need had he of finery? But then what else could one do but acquiesce when the Queen herself presented you with your promotion?

Still he refused to conform on other points of his appearance. He would not wear the cumbersome full wig sported by other officers, but preferred to have his own hair tied back in a queue, as was the manner with the dragoons. In fact his model in this had been the man who was his inspiration as a young subaltern. Francis Hawley had been a captain in the First Foot Guards and some years Steel's senior. When Steel had purchased into the regiment, Hawley had been given command of a recently formed grenadier company. Although Hawley had transferred soon afterwards to Berkeley's Dragoons, Steel and he had kept up their friendship, and at Steenkirk in 1692, as Steel had received his baptism of fire in one of the English and Scots army's worst defeats at the hands of the French, he had watched in disbelief as Hawley had charged to his death on the bloody strand. Steel had never forgotten Hawley, and as he had grown into the army and adopted his own distinctive fashion, as all officers did, he had always sought to emulate his friend and mentor. It was through Hawley's example too that he chose not to wear gaiters and spats but preferred more comfortable and hardy half boots.

Most importantly of all, Steel cherished his weapons. Unusually for an officer, along with his sword he carried a fusil slung across his shoulder, a short-barrelled musket which in his case had originally been a fowling piece. The sword itself was far from regulation issue but a heavy cutting weapon better suited to a cavalryman, with a wicked, razor-sharp blade. Steel alone, with his advantage of height, was able to use it to similar effect. It was a Scottish Highland broadsword, basket-hilted and straight-bladed, made in Italy, that had hung on the wall of his family home in the Lowlands and which more than anything about him betrayed his origins. It had not failed him yet, and had cut a bloody swathe across the battlefields of Europe. Its weight alone was enough to cleave a man, though in Steel's hand it was as light as a feather, and those who made its acquaintance as enemies seldom lived to tell the tale.

A noise like distant rolling thunder announced the presence of artillery and made Steel turn his head. But he had already missed the flash of the shot and failed to spot the exact whereabouts of the guns. No ball had passed near them as yet, and it still seemed to him as if they might be watching a distant spectacle with the indifference of a theatre audience. But Steel knew that this was all too easy. He conjured a picture in his mind of the gunners on the opposite slope sweating at the hot barrels, stripped to their shirtsleeves, sponging out, loading, ramming home, damping down their overheated guns. He pictured the cannon bouncing back on their wooden trails with shouts of warning and saw in his mind the shot leaving the muzzle and crossing in an arc high above the battlefield to find its unlucky target. The noise of the cannon provided a bass line to the symphony of battle, the deep boom of artillery beneath the percussive rattle of musketry a sound as familiar to him as London's musical choruses were to the ear of his opera-mad wife. His hearing was attuned to the pitch of the current melody, the sound of the guns. There was no theatre here on the battlefield. These men were not actors. Yet Steel wondered when the curtain would rise on the next scene and give his men their cue.

It was, he thought, a battle unlike any he had witnessed before. For the best part of twenty years, from here in Flanders to the plains of Denmark and down among the scalding, sun-bleached rocks of the Spanish peninsula, Steel had watched as battles had begun and developed in their distinctive styles. The opening salvoes; the advance to contact; the salute from one line to the other; and then the neatly dressed lines blown into bloody raggedness and then the mêlée and the rout. But this . . . this was something new. This battle had not been the usual *mise en scène* but had rather grown piecemeal. The Allies had arrived slowly and been fed into the action as and when they had appeared. The vanguard had excelled itself in a holding action, and by the time Steel and his men had arrived here some two hours before, the fighting had been going on for four hours. Even then it had not been fully committed. It had seemed to him like two dogs circling one another in an alley, vying for possession of territory, taking tentative snaps in the air, edging closer and then backing off. But Steel knew that it was not Marlborough's intention to allow his adversary to leave this field without a serious bloodletting.

Cadogan had built his bridges and then had used them effectively to take his men – horse and foot – over the great river and deep into the ground before the enemy position. Steel had huge admiration for the Irish general. He might have been Marlborough's second-in-command with a prestigious position on the staff, but on the day of battle Cadogan could be counted on to fight like a trooper, leading from the front and giving as good an account of himself as a listed man. And his men knew it.

Steel could see Cadogan's scarlet-clad battalions now, British and Hanoverian infantry, as they clustered around the village of Eyne, eight hundred yards to their front and right. That place would surely now be his own objective, and the aim of his brigade would be to shore up the clearly ailing forces of Cadogan, thus reinforcing the entire Allied line. He looked to his right and saw that yet more Allied troops were arriving along the road from Lessines, being disposed according to Marlborough's wishes with apparent improvisation. It showed the true genius of Corporal John, who had guided them through six years of war, first in Bavaria in the great victory at Blenheim and then back up here in Flanders.

He caught another snatch of Taylor's song and again the words rang true:

'For starvation and danger it will be my destiny
To seek fresh employment with Marlborough and me.
Who'll be a soldier, who'll be a soldier . . .'

21

The singing had spread now to the other companies of the battalion and beyond to the other British regiments in the brigade who stood in line behind the grenadiers, waiting at the bridge. Waiting.

And so the afternoon wore on, and fear and frustration in their turn took hold in the minds of Steel and his men and all the others. And the men in the valley continued to die, singly at times and at times in parcels of four or six or ten, as fate directed the fall of the shot. Steel watched them as they fought in the village, in its fields and orchards and on the plain. He cursed at his commanders' inaction and wiped his brow of sweat in the sultry July sunshine that played across the scene. Yet still they were not ordered into the attack.

He called across to Hansam, as he had done at intervals throughout the day: 'Henry, what time d'you have?'

The lieutenant drew out his prized timepiece, a gold chronometer taken from the body of a dead French officer after Blenheim: 'Four o'clock and thirty minutes.'

Steel nodded his thanks, swatted a fly away from his face and tucked a finger inside the sweat-stained collar band of his shirt, which had again become home to a colony of lice. He had lost them in England and kept clean too while in Brussels, but since they had been on the march the little buggers had come back – and it seemed to Steel that they were making up for their absence. What he would give for a clean shirt, a long soak in a bath, a pitcher of ale and the chance to sleep! Above all sleep. He ran his hand across his stubbled chin. That and perhaps a shave and a chance to lie with his new wife.

He noticed that he was sweating heavily now. The day had crept up on them, and the noise from the valley seemed to amplify the heat. How much longer would they stand here? he thought. Taylor and his men had long since finished their song and silence again descended upon the ranks, letting the fears back in.

Steel drew himself up and spoke in a clear voice, intending the men to hear him: 'That was a fine piece of singing back there, Corporal Taylor. Would you mind very much if we should call upon your talents again ere long?'

Taylor grinned. 'At your disposal as always, Captain Steel, sir. Lifts the spirits, does a song. That's what I always say, sir.' And by way of an afterthought he added: 'Can't abide this waiting though, sir.'

Slaughter glared at him. But Steel was not one, as were some officers, to chide petty impertinence, particularly at such a time as this and from one of his veterans such as Taylor. He nodded. 'Nor I, Taylor. And you're right about singing. We'll hear from you again. But I dare say we'll be at them soon. Don't you worry.'

The man next to Taylor in the company's front rank, a normally dour Lowland Scot, like Steel himself, named John Mackay, spoke up: 'And we'll see 'em off today, sir, won't we? Just like we did at Ramillies, eh boys?'

'When you were still at your mother's teat,' muttered Slaughter.

There was a short hurrah from the ranks which betrayed more about their boredom and fear than it said about their confidence. Like Ramillies, thought Steel. Perhaps it would be like Ramillies. Like Bleneim too, maybe. But Marlborough's past triumphs seemed an age away now, as he stood on the bridge – almost another country after all that had happened to him since.

Before then he had not known his wife, Henrietta. Lady Henrietta Vaughan, to give her her full title. And this was the name by which she would forever be known, it seemed. He himself found it hard to imagine her as 'Lady Henrietta Steel'. Would he ever become used to it? For she was his wife of little less than a year, now safely billeted in Brussels. He had not wanted her to come out with him from England, but she had prevailed, saying that other wives did as much so why should she not follow her beloved captain?

Captain Steel. Now that was a style he had no difficulty in adopting. His part in the taking of Ostend had been rewarded at Court with the confirmation of his brevet rank as a full captaincy, by no less a person than the Queen herself. He had been paraded through the streets of London as a hero of the campaign. His praises had been sung by balladeers from Covent Garden to Holborn and talked of by old campaigners in White's, at Old Man's coffee house and the late king's new military hospital at Chelsea.

He had wondered at the time what his brother's reaction might have been had he but seen him in such pomp. His elder brother Charles, that was, who had always called him 'Jack the good for nothing', who had introduced him as 'Jack my hapless brother who will come to naught'. To him Steel would forever be the failed lawyer's clerk, a penniless soldier who had accepted the commission purchased by his mistress. What would he say now to Captain Steel, the hero of Ostend?

For a moment too he thought of his younger brother, Alexander, a professed Jacobite whose ideals had split the family – what was left of it. Alexander, the baby of the three brothers, two years his junior, who had left home to join the exiled King James at his court outside Paris. Steel had not had news of him now for five years and wondered what might have become of him. Was he still alive? Had he fought for his king? In truth Steel half expected to encounter him on a battlefield in the uniform of the 'Wild Geese', those Irish regiments in French service who fought so well for a vanquished dynasty and a conquered land. Perhaps he was wounded or maimed. Steel was overcome by melancholy and a sense of emptiness and the understanding that now, more than ever before, he had left his childhood, youth and roots far behind in Scotland when he had taken the old king's shilling and joined the Guards as a young lieutenant at his lover's behest. Now he knew that his real family were those men who stood behind him on this field – them and the pretty, headstrong

24

girl who waited for him in their small and unaffordably expensive apartment in Brussels.

Although rank and fortune were central to the plan that he had long nurtured for his career, Steel could not help but think that his real prize in the bloody affair at Ostend had been Henrietta. He had rescued her from the hands of a French privateer – no more than a pirate – in the service of the Sun King. That man had held both of them captive as together they had stared death in the face and watched a good man die horribly in an underground torture chamber. Steel had taken her out of that place, and she loved him for that. That was beyond doubt. And now, as the years went by, it would be his task to persuade her to love him for whatever else he was as a man – those virtues she had not yet seen, whatever she and her constant love had the power to make him. It was all very well to fight for yourself, to fight just to stay alive and to make a life as a soldier. But it was quite another thing to fight when you knew that back beyond the baggage lines someone was waiting. He was happy and proud that she had chosen to follow him to Flanders, though in truth he would have expected no less from her stubborn, feisty character. Marlborough's army always brought in its wake the gaggle of camp followers that came with any army – women, children, wives and lovers. But not many of those who came were attached to officers. It was one of the things he admired about Henrietta, her independent spirit that was intertwined with an unmissable sexuality. He hoped he had made the right choice for the wife of an officer of the Grenadiers. It was clear that his men had taken to her. They saw her as a natural part of the regimental family. They were aware too of what she had gone through, and respected her for it. Besides, she was Captain Steel's wife.

A captain he might be, and on the not ungenerous sum of £170 a year, but Steel was again hungry for promotion. For, as lovely as she was, Henrietta had already begun to make something more than an emotional impact on his life. Steel had not previously been aware just how expensive a woman could be. True, she had brought with her a small dowry, but it was hardly in line with her status as the eldest daughter of the Duke of Rumney, and Steel wondered whether her father, knowing his modest station and uncertain prospects, might not have deliberately held back a portion in case of some . . . unseen eventuality. In addition, a great deal more money had now been necessitated by Henrietta having insisted on bringing a maid from England and her declaration that they must live in an entire suite of rooms. Where, previously, a town billet for Steel as a bachelor officer had meant a simple bed in a tavern room, it now seemed that they must live in some style and be able to entertain. Two bedchambers, a salon, an office and a dining room were the bare minimum, according to his wife. Not to mention the maid and a share in the cook and the kitchens. Not to mention her other requirements. Steel had not known that women could accumulate such . . . stuff. His life had been transformed, and as much as he adored Henrietta, Steel found it an added burden and began to understand what Slaughter had meant when he had advised him long ago that soldiering and matrimony did not make happy bedfellows.

Nevertheless, when he lay down in their marriage bed and held her small, softly naked form, all such thoughts left Steel's mind and he was lost in such delights as he had never dreamed of. He had thought he might have grown soft during those months away from the war, nestling in the luxury of a feather bed and the arms of his wife. But in the past few weeks he had learnt that the regiment had seen little action, and he had passed up no chance of glory.

The shrill whine of a cannonball passing overhead snapped him back to the present. But even as he looked absently at the continuing battle his mind still pondered the prospect that before the year was out he would have to find some means

26

of improving his situation. Promotion to major would help, bringing in another hundred a year. However, it would, he realized, as likely as not take him from his beloved Grenadiers. Unless, of course, the regimental adjutant should come to grief in the present campaign. Steel had never liked Charles Frampton, and after that episode following Ramillies with the major's now hushed-up part in the distribution of scurrilous pamphlets against Marlborough the man was still less appealing. Naturally the business had been all but forgotten. Frampton was too good a soldier in the field to be lost. His accomplice, in truth the instigator of the scheme, had been punished and Frampton given a severe reprimand and encouraged to donate several hundred guineas to the regimental funds. Steel could hardly wish his brother officer, any officer, such ill will on the field of battle. Nevertheless, for a man in Steel's position with mounting debts and precious little money, filling dead men's shoes was the simplest way to get on. Perhaps, he thought, there might be booty. Marlborough might have forbidden any man to loot thus far on any campaign, on pain of death, but it seemed likely there would be legitimate plunder to be had if they prevailed this day and advanced into France. 'If they prevailed.' He smiled. Steel had become used to winning. But how could they win if they could not fight?

He turned to Hansam. 'Damn whoever it is that makes us wait. Aye, even Marlborough for once for his infernal caution. Surely, Henry, we must go soon? Look at the men.'

He tested the bridge with his boot. He felt the wooden timbers give and heard them creak as they swayed and strained against the ropes that lashed them to the pontoons.

Hansam spoke. 'It seems strong enough, Jack.'

'It had better be. There's an entire brigade to pass over it soon.' Very soon, he prayed. He pointed across the river. 'Look there, Henry. Down on the field. What d'you see?'

'Why, our men outnumbered by the French. That surely is why we are here.'

'But we must wait. Malborough is too clever. His plan lies in drawing out the French as quickly as possible. He shows Vendôme a part of his army as a temptation. He dares him to come and destroy Cadogan before they should arrive in force.'

'It is bold, Jack. What if the French should succeed? If they are too quick off the mark?'

'Then, my dear fellow, we shall have marched here for naught. For all will be up with our army and we shall need to double back up that hill to Lessines faster than we came. But imagine, Henry, should the plan succeed. If those men down there with Cadogan can hold off for just a little longer and draw in just enough of the French army without yielding, then here will be a moment when Marlborough can come up with the bulk of the army on his terms. Timing, you see, is everything. But that makes it no easier for us or the rest of the brigade. All we may do is watch and wait.'

There was a respectful cough at his side. 'Beggin' your pardon, sir, but when shall we go, d'you suppose? I can't hardly remember seeing the men so peevish. They're like terriers by a warren. Don't know what to do with the'selves.'

Sergeant Slaughter was with him, as he had ever been since Steel had transferred into the regiment some seven years ago. Since then the two men had shared a bond of friendship of the sort that could only be forged in battle and which transcended the usual relationship between officer and sergeant. Indeed, some of Steel's brother officers made no attempt to disguise the fact that they found it distasteful and inappropriate. But for Steel this was the way a war should be fought and the proper way for a company or a regiment to function. Hierarchy and order were vital, of course. But to share such an empathy as he had with a man like Slaughter was something rare: a bond of brotherhood that no one could know who had not been a part of it.

The French gunners on the opposite slope had changed

their trajectory now, and the balls were beginning to creep closer to Steel's brigade. A ranging shot struck the river bank and was stopped dead by the mud.

Steel turned to Slaughter. 'That's the last we'll see like that. They're just gauging our distance. The next one will strike home. Henry, time to take posts, I think.'

He had hardly finished speaking when all three men saw puffs of smoke from the enemy guns, instantly followed by the unmistakable black dots of fast-approaching cannonballs. Four ranged to their left, finding targets in the next battalion, but the remaining four came directly towards Steel and his men. There was no time to avoid them. No point. The only thing to do was to stand your ground and pray that your luck would hold. Steel watched as each black dot became a circle, then an orb, one of which, approaching him at an unthinkable speed, magically lifted at the last moment to pass over their heads, sucking the air into a vacuum as it passed. Steel breathed out audibly with relief. A few files away a sudden cry told him that others of the company had not been so lucky.

Steel turned to the sergeant again. 'I wish to God that we were gone, Jacob. I can't think the men can stand it much longer. They'll lose heart or they'll lose their edge.'

'Aye, sir, or they'll lose their heads.'

Another roundshot came perilously close to the company but thankfully veered right to carry away the head of the horse ridden by a field officer of Meredith's, together with the lower portion of the unfortunate man's leg. Steel nodded at Slaughter and noticed one of his corporals patting one of the recruits on the shoulder and placing him firmly back in the line. 'The new lads seem to be wobbling, Jacob. Will they carry it off?'

'They'll do it, sir. Don't doubt that they will. But I'm with you, sir. We must go soon.'

A ragged fanfare of bugles made them look to the left where

a great cloud of dust thrown up from the earth proclaimed the beginnings of a movement of cavalry. Both men focused their attention on the ground over to the left across the river.

Slaughter spoke. 'That's cavalry, sir. And a good lot of them. They can't surely intend to attack us, can they? Must be intended for the poor buggers on the edge of that village.'

Steel peered into the settling dust cloud, straining to see the uniforms and from where they came. 'No, they're ours, Jacob. Hanoverians. And it's none of our men they're making for. They're moving up towards the French. Thank God for that, at least. Now we'll see some sport.'

TWO

Sitting at the folding wooden table that had been set up outside a small inn on the edge of the village of Gavre, on the road to Huysse, Louis Joseph de Bourbon, Duc de Vendôme and Marshal of France, sucked the last of the meat from a chicken bone and tossed it to his dogs. He would not be parted from the two pointers that had accompanied him throughout this campaigning season and the last, and he had come to regard them as lucky talismans. Behind the Marshal the little group of French staff officers grew restless. Vendôme ignored them; said nothing; not so much as turned his head to acknowledge them, even though among their number were the Duc de Berry, the King's fat grandson, and James Francis Edward Stuart, claimant to the British throne. In fact, he mused, his own pedigree was hardly less august. He was the grandson of Henry IV of France and by right a Royal Prince himself. And what, he reasoned, could there possibly be to say to them? None of them had accepted his invitation to dine. Vendôme despaired of his generals and advisors almost as much as he did of his army. Oh, the French elements of his force of 85,000 – ninety battalions of foot and 170 squadrons of horse – were sound enough, most of them. It was the foreigners who supplemented their strength that caused him concern: the

Swiss, the Spaniards, the Walloons and mercenaries from various German states.

At least the Duke of Burgundy, son of Louis, was not among them. Vendôme was sure the Prince, apparently sent to learn the art of war, had in fact been sent to spy on him. He had not seen eye to eye with the Sun King since Italy, Louis it seemed being more inclined to take the advice of the Elector, Max Emmanuel, than the most experienced and loyal of his generals. Continuing to eat, Vendôme spat out a piece of fat. Well, he thought, soon the King would see just how expert Vendôme was at the art of war. And then he would listen.

Somewhere out there with the enemy, Vendôme's cousin, Prince Eugene of Savoy, was manoeuvring his troops with his master Marlborough, attempting to bring battle on their terms. But the Marshal was not overly concerned. Hadn't he defeated Eugene three years ago at Cassano in Italy? If only that ass Burgundy were not with the French army now, and ostensibly his equal in rank. For the first time Vendôme sensed the faintest whisker of a possibility of defeat, but dared not let it invade his mind. At fifty-four years of age and after four decades with the colours he was well aware that state of mind was everything in command. He looked down at the dogs, begging for scraps. Their luck would hold, and his generalship. He must trust to fate and experience, and think positively.

The sound of approaching hoofbeats made him look up to see a horseman, an aide-de-camp to the staff by the look of it. The man had pulled up at the inn and, on foot now, was casting around for the commander in chief.

'Marshal Vendôme?'

One of the Marshal's own aides directed the boy towards him.

'Sire, I bring an urgent request from General Biron. He is under attack, sire.'

Vendôme stared at the young man and grabbed the proffered dispatch. Wiping his greasy fingers on the tail of his grey coat, he opened the paper and began to read, muttering as he did so: 'Allied units. English . . . Prussians. Large numbers.' He paused. 'What large numbers? Overwhelmed? Overwelmed by what? By how many?'

The young man stammered: 'Why by . . . by the enemy, sire. The redcoats are there. Infantry and horse too. We are being pushed back. They have crossed the Scheldt at Oudenarde.'

Vendôme crushed the message into a small ball in the palm of his hand and muttered under his breath: 'Oudenarde. I'd have taken it in two days and avoided all this.' He frowned at the terrified aide and spoke louder. 'Biron is asking me for reinforcements, is he not? Well, you may tell General Biron that the Allied army is nowhere near us. If they are anywhere near his positions then the devil must have carried them there, for such a march is impossible.'

The aide, unsure what to do, decided magnanimously that the probable sacrifice of his military career was justified by saving thousands of French lives. He shook his head and stood his ground. 'I beg you, sire. Look again to the south. I swear to you, sire, the Allied army is there, at least a considerable part of it. A full vanguard of redcoats, sire. Foot and horse, with artillery too. They are pushing us back from Oudenarde. They have already seen off a regiment of Swiss foot and will surely be doing us more damage as we speak.'

Vendôme cursed the man under his breath, but he had not been a soldier for thirty-six years and a score of them a general not to know when it was prudent to take advice. Putting down his goblet of wine, he grabbed another chicken leg and walked across the road, past where the officers were conferring, to the crest of the hill.

What he saw on the low horizon stopped him in his tracks and nearly made him choke on his mouthful of chicken. Below him in the valley of the Scheldt a huge dust storm appeared to have arisen. Vendôme might have been confident, but he was no fool. He knew the signs of an army and of unavoidable battle when he saw them. He swore, turned quickly and walked smartly back to the messenger.

'Thank you. I'm sorry to have doubted you, Lieutenant. Yes, I do see now. Take a message to General Biron at Heurne. Tell him not to worry. He must attack the force to his front with all possible speed. I myself shall lead the cavalry to our left wing in support. Wait there a moment.' He looked across to the group of officers. 'Puységur.'

Vendôme's Chief of Staff walked across.

'Puységur, go with this officer. You're to ride to General Biron. Order him to stand where he is for the moment. We have insufficient cavalry in his vicinity to offer immediate support. He is to wait for the horse before he advances any further. And be sure to tell him that he may allow their great general Marlbrook to come across with as many of the enemy as he likes.'

Both the Chief of Staff and the courier looked askance.

Vendôme continued: 'Don't look so bemused, gentlemen. It is all part of my plan to trap the enemy. Now go.'

He called to his private secretary. 'Du Capistron. Take a message to my lord Burgundy. He must move the infantry of the entire left wing directly behind my advance with the horse.'

Vendôme crossed to the table and took a swig of the wine he had abandoned. He patted one of the dogs and smiled as he congratulated himself on his swift action. For once Marlborough had blundered. If Vendôme could act now he would trap him and a good deal of his army on the wrong side of the Scheldt. Pin him down with superior numbers and the natural obstacle of the river at his back. At the very least he would drive them back over their bridges and into the Scheldt. And all that his generals had to do was to act together. Surely that was not too much to ask of anyone? Even of that idiot Burgundy?

A large black fly had settled on a morsel of the bread on

his plate, and picking up a huge pewter ladle from the table he brought it down on the insect, squashing it into the metal. He would crush this Allied vanguard just as easily as he had killed that fly. And then, before my lord Marlbrook could reinforce his ailing line he, Vendôme, would be in command of the river and its strongpoints. Then their great British general would be routed from the field and a grateful King would surely reward his wholly forgiven and ever-faithful Marshal.

Vendôme turned to the group of officers. 'Come, gentlemen. Chevalier, if you please. D'Evreux. All of you. This is no time for lunch or gossip. Dinner is at an end. Come on. We have much work to do and a battle to win.'

There can be few more spectacular sights on any field of battle than that of a brigade of cavalry in full cry, and Steel was thankful for the diversion. With the French gunners having gauged their range, his men were beginning to suffer more than the psychological hurt of their tortured minds which had plagued them for the last few hours of waiting on this hill. Now at least there was something to offer them as amusement.

Steel and Slaughter, Hansam, Williams and as many of the company as were able to find a suitable vantage point watched, with the rest of the battalion's front rank and other regiments close to the front of the brigade, as from the Allied left wing rank upon rank of high-stepping cavalry broke out across the field. They advanced sedately at first, at a slow trot, and then, when their intention became evident to the enemy, broke into a canter and a gallop, coming on steadily towards the French right flank.

Steel looked towards their goal and saw, sitting quite still and apparently unaware across the Ghent road, a glorious body of French cavalry; dragoons and horse in elaborate blue and red coats. They seemed utterly oblivious to the men moving towards them at an increasing pace. Steel could only assume that they had been informed by their commander that the ground to their right was impassable. The Frenchmen must have seen the Hanoverian horse assembling to begin their advance. He pictured their squadron commanders, sitting high and proud on some of the finest horses to be found in France, laughing in genial conversation, although they must have been quite aware of the movement on their flank. He watched them. He too had gauged the lie of the land and had noticed the marshes that ringed the position, presuming them impassable.

He found Williams and Hansam standing at his side. 'Well, gentlemen, what d'you make of that then? Have our generals gone quite mad? First they keep us here the best part of the day, and now it seems they intend to send the best of our cavalry into a bog.'

Williams, apparently ignoring or unaware of Steel's comments, spoke with curious and undisguised reverence as he stared at the cavalry's advance. 'It's quite brilliant. Incredible.'

Steel looked at him quizzically. 'Tom? Is it catching, this madness? Don't bring it near me. What the devil are you talking about? You can see as well as I that that ground is utterly unsuited to cavalry. It's a marsh, for God's sake. Why, even the foot would be hard pressed to pass through that quagmire. It's madness.'

Williams spoke in a tone appropriate to his junior position, yet firm in its purpose. 'No, sir, it's not mad. You see, that marsh is not what it seems. I had the truth of it this morning from Harrington. I don't think you know him. He's a cornet in Hay's Dragoons, attached to the staff. Sound fellow.'

'Get on with it.'

'Sorry, sir. Fact is, though, it's firm ground. As firm as that on which we stand ourselves.' He stamped his foot. 'It merely looks like a bog from the sheen of water that it keeps on its surface. Like oil floating in a bath, if you know what I mean.'

Steel stared at him and wondered quite when the young man had taken a bath in scented oils.

Williams continued. 'Harrington says the engineers told him it could support a train of artillery and more. It's brilliant, sir. D'you see? For the French are not aware of the truth of the matter. They'll be cut to ribbons.'

Steel looked again and saw that now several of the French cavalry officers were pointing in the direction of the advancing Germans. They were laughing. He presumed that they would be mocking the decision of the Hanoverian commander to send his horse into a marsh. 'Christ almighty. You're right. Look at them, Henry. They don't know. Haven't a clue. They'll be caught off their guard. D'you see? It is brilliant. Well done, Tom.'

The Hanoverian horse were advancing at the gallop now, for, as usual on the field, the sheer weight of man and horse together did not allow them to break into a full charge. But Steel knew that they would still have more than sufficient momentum to smash into the French line with full effect. The French for their part still had not moved, even though the enemy were now apparently crossing the impassable marsh. As Steel looked on, though, he noticed some of the French officers beginning to turn their horses away from the assembly and to rejoin their squadrons and troops. Within a few moments he realized that the French would learn the salient lesson that in battle there can never be any substitute for diligent intelligence. It was a lesson that would cost many of them their lives.

He recognized the Hanoverians now, General Jørgen Rantzau's brigade of dragoons, part of Cadogan's own command, a blaze of white-uniformed German mercenaries in English pay whom he knew bore no love for the French or their Swiss allies stationed behind them, all of them mounted uniformly on huge bay horses. Eight squadrons of Hanoverian horse, some twelve hundred men. A sparkle of flashing light caught his eye, and Steel saw the sun glint off the long, straight cavalry swords which rested on their right shoulders, honed, he guessed, to an edge like a butcher's cleaver and constructed specifically so that the slightest motion exerted at the hilt might make the blade fall like a hammer on whatever lay below: flesh, bone or sinew. He looked on, horribly fascinated, as the Hanoverian horse closed with the French, who still had not moved. He watched closely and saw the final moment at which the French at last realized their peril. He kept looking as in a horrible instant there was a commotion in their still static ranks. He saw the sudden movements as the unflappable officers screamed useless commands to wheel to the right, to face the oncoming enemy. To draw sabres. But it was too little and too late to save the French, and now, as the white-coated Hanoverians on the big horses drove on relentlessly, the final act of horror unfolded before him.

A noise burst across the valley, which to the new recruits in the regiment sounded curiously like the crackle of a fire in a hearth. Steel recognized it instantly as the sound of musketry. Two hundred muskets had opened up from a battalion of French infantry arrayed in line to the right of the cantering Hanoverian dragoons. They sang out in a concerted volley, belching smoke and flame, and a few of the Hanoverians seemed to leap in the saddle as they were struck and toppled from their mounts, a fair number of which also went down in the hail of bullets. But the volley had less effect than it might have done due to the pace of the fast-moving horsemen who rode on oblivious, for such now was their fury that most did not even notice the musketry any more than one might acknowledge the annoying bite of a mosquito. Steel watched as the dragoons kept going in their headlong rush, drawing ever closer to the panic-stricken target of the French horse astride the road. This, he thought, was precisely what these men had been trained to do. This was the moment of which any horseman and dragoon dreamed but never believed would actually happen – to find an army's weakness, catch it off guard and exploit it at speed. It was textbook stuff and almost unbelievably simple, and when executed properly, as here, imbued with a savage grace.

Then Rantzau's men were up and in the French lines, scattering the enemy in all directions, moving through them like a scythe through corn, their huge blades falling relentlessly on skulls and necks and, held á point, skewering troopers where they sat helpless while the attackers' horses kicked and flared their nostrils and bit at the enemy's chargers, and even the riderless mounts of the men who had fallen still bowled into the French and added their weight and fury to the chaos and carnage of the mêlée.

Steel could hear his men cheering now as they watched the enemy in their death agonies. There was no room for mercy in war, he thought. No pity here, now. There were merely winners and losers – the dead, the dying and those who managed to remain alive for one more day. The French cavalry were lost. Twenty squadrons of them were swept to oblivion because of one man's refusal to admit that he might have been wrong. As Steel watched, the blue and red ranks simply seemed to melt away in a mayhem of screaming bodies and whinnying horses, while the great white wedge of the Hanoverians pushed further into them like a hot knife going into butter. And still the blades rose and fell, trailing gouts of blood as they went. Beneath the hooves of French cavalry that only a few minutes earlier had looked so proud and confident, patches of ground had turned to a red paste. It did not take long for Rantzau's men to push through the bloody ruin of the cavalry, then they were out and in search of fresh quarry. And to Steel's horror they did not stop.

Of course, he thought, they were dragoons, and they were only doing what dragoons did best. Get into the enemy on

39

as unequal terms as you can, and then hack them to pieces until the blood runs free. He knew Jørgen Rantzau to be a brave and experienced soldier. But however well led any cavalry might be, however fearless, how could you control such men once their blood was up? Then no amount of shouted orders, no bugle calls could stop them. So Steel watched as the inevitable happened and Rantzau's blood-crazed victors were countercharged by fresh French cavalry. The now panicked Hanoverian squadrons attempted to reform, only to be caught in the flank. Unable to stop himself, Steel stood transfixed by their nemesis.

There was a cough from his side. 'Now that's what I'd call a bloody shame, sir, if you don't mind my saying so. But that's cavalry for you. See, sir, they don't know when to stop. But what a show they put on, eh, sir? That German cavalry. Really beat up the French. We all saw it back there. Bloody marvellous.'

'Yes, bloody marvellous, Jacob. You're right there. And you're right about the cavalry. They don't know when to stop. Same with our lot, mind you. Remember Hay's dragoons after the Schellenberg? Roaring down that hill towards the town? The Danube ran red with enemy blood.' He smiled, 'But you're a fine one to talk of restraint, Sar'nt. In our day we've not been much better. After Ramillies I thought the whole bloody company was going to chase the Frenchies back to Paris.'

Slaughter grinned. 'Well, sir, sometimes you just can't hold them. Aye, and we would've done that too, if the Duke hisself hadn't stopped us. But we'll do it today, sir. Chase 'em to Paris if you tell us to. If we ever get the chance, that is. Right to the gates of bloody Paris and down that ruddy river to Versailles. And give old Louis a bleeding nose.'

He might not have been far wrong, thought Steel. France was only fifteen miles away. If they could really prevail here today, if fate was kind to them, and for the last few years the gods of

40

war certainly seemed to have been on their side, there was just the chance that some time soon he might be leading his men into Paris in a victory march. And what a day that would be. He laughed with the sergeant. 'Let's hope so, Jacob. All we can do now is hope.'

He looked again across the river. To his astonishment it appeared that the French, emboldened by their success against the repulsed Hanoverians, many of whom thankfully appeared to have managed to retire in good order to the Allied left, had begun to counterattack down the Ghent road, towards Oudenarde.

He shook his head. 'What on earth do they mean now? Can't they see we're here in force?'

Both men watched as four huge columns of pale-grey-uniformed French infantry crossed the little stream of the Diepenbeek and without any opposition took the village of the same name which lay to Cadogan's left. Steel could make out more detail among the French now. He could see their officers and sergeants quite clearly with their spear-tipped spontoons and axe-headed halberds and the frothy confections of white and silver lace in their black tricorns. The French were getting close, being drawn into Cadogan's cauldron. At once both men guessed that their time had come at last.

'Stand the men to, Sar'nt. I believe that we may be about to advance.'

It was approaching four o'clock by Hansam's pocket watch and, as he had suspected, Steel did not have long to wait. Even as Slaughter and the other company sergeants were busy herding the men back into neat files, he saw a galloper from the high command racing along the hillside, making for the towering figure of Colonel Farquharson. Finding his path impeded by the sheer volume of men waiting in the column, the rider pulled up short and Steel heard the boy's shouted words high on the breeze.

'Sir, my lord Argyle presents his compliments and would you lead the advance across the bridges forthwith.'

The ageing colonel looked somewhat put out by this ungentlemanly behaviour on a battlefield. Nevertheless, he nodded at the young man and, taking his thin sword from its scabbard with a conscious flourish so that it caught the sunlight and drew the eye, he made a half turn in the saddle. It was now the turn of his own low, gently cultivated Highland accent to ring out over their heads.

'My boys. You're luck's in at last. We've been ordered to advance.'

He waited for the cheer, and come it did, just as loud and hearty as he had expected from his men.

'Now's your chance, my lads. Do your duty and bring honour to your Queen, to your country and most important to your regiment. We fight this day for Scotland and the Union, boys. For Queen Anne and the regiment. For my regiment. For me. Now follow me to glory and fortune, lads, and I'll pay you all in beer and golden guineas. Officers, take posts. Drummers, if you please, your sticks. Major Frampton, advance the colours.'

The adjutant, Charles Frampton, stood high in his stirrups and waved his hat three times in the air. 'Three cheers for the colonel and the regiment. Hip hip, huzzah. Hip hip, huzzah . . .'

The men's voices rang out across the field and mingled with those from the other regiments in the vanguard of the brigade who at that moment were going through the same adrenaline-raising ritual. Steel turned to the Grenadiers and raised his voice.

'Stay with me, boys. Look to your sergeants. Look to your officers. But most of all look to me. When we go in we'll like as not leave the rest of the battalion standing. That's why we're here. First in, last out, lads. Stay with me. Sergeants, keep your lines straight until we close. Halt at sixty paces

42

and give fire. And if you do that for me, boys, and if you stand when the enemy fires on us, then bugger what the colonel has to offer. I'll stand any man a pitcher of rum that can beat me into the French lines.'

There was another huge cheer from the company, and then Slaughter and his sergeants and corporals were dressing the lines yet again, pushing them into attacking formation, a defile column of threes. This was the only way to cross the bridge. It was the most vulnerable formation for infantry, and looking at them standing fifteen ranks deep, spaced half open, Steel worried about the potential effect of enemy gunfire. Should a single cannonball find its mark in his advancing column it would not stop but would continue to hurtle through, taking with it heads and limbs, and killing or at the least maiming an entire file.

The drums beat up the march attack, the familiar rhythm of 'British Grenadiers'.

Steel turned back to face the front. He said quietly to Williams, 'All right, Tom? Ready for it now?'

'Fine, sir, and as ready as ever.'

'Then let's be at them.'

With Argyle riding at their head, the brigade of redcoats moved off. Steel trod firmly onto the wooden bridge and marched as steadily as he could across its creaking, swaying structure as it moved from side to side across the string of pontoons in the river. Looking to his right and his left he could see on the four other similar bridges other officers leading their men in precisely the same way. Grenadiers to the fore, the mounted colonels behind them, bringing up the battalion. It was a heart-stopping sight, and it never failed to make him puff with pride: a full brigade of British infantry marching into battle. Surprisingly, his greatest fear was unfounded, and as they were crossing no French guns found them. Evidently the gunners felt themselves unable to fire for fear of hitting their own men. Once off the bridge they began to climb a shallow slope. Soon the entire battalion was following them.

From behind he heard the adjutant taking command of the regiment: ''tallion will form line. Right about.'

Steel half-turned his head and in turn shouted an order to the company: 'Form line. Right wheel. Number two platoon mark time. Form on the left.'

Steel watched as Hansam deftly guided his half-company away from Steel's and took it to the left flank of the advancing regiment, thus ensuring that each flank was covered by half of the elite grenadiers.

Williams took up the general order, followed by Slaughter and the sergeants, and instantly Steel's Grenadiers began to wheel to the right, followed by the other eight companies of the regiment, pivoting on the right-hand man of each rank so that within seconds they were marching towards the east. Steel led them on. Sixty paces. A hundred. That would do it.

'Left wheel.'

Again the Grenadiers turned, this time moving on the left-hand man, and as if by a miracle of choreography found themselves again facing the front and the French lines. To their left the remaining eight companies of the regiment were spaced at roughly equal distances, having managed the same manoeuvre.

Steel let himself relax for an instant. That was the first task done. Slaughter went along the front of the line, dressing it with his halberd. Steel saw Colonel Farquharson ride to the front, accompanied by Major Frampton and the battalion drummer boys, ashen-faced with terror in their gorgeous gold and blue livery. Again the colonel lifted his hand in the air and brought it down towards the enemy. Then slowly he yelled the order to his regiment:

'Advance!'

Steel raised his own sword high in the air and flourished

it over his head three times. It was a little showy perhaps, slightly Frenchified even, but he had become used to the gesture and the men seemed to approve and be fired up. He shouted the command: 'Advance!' Steel lingered on the first syllable and on the last brought down the sword so that was pointing directly towards the enemy. Then he laid it gently on his shoulder. With the drums beating the steady rhythm of the Grenadiers' march, the entire line, close on five thousand men, began to climb the hill from the river. Soon they found themselves parallel with a road running across the battlefield, southwest to northeast, lined on both sides with tall poplar trees.

Steel reckoned that they were now halfway to the French lines, and as he began to calculate the distance and how long it might take them to make contact should they continue their advance the guns on the hill in front of them opened up. He called out, 'Steady!' But hardly had he said it than the first cannonball whistled into their line and cut a swathe through the Grenadiers.

'Steady, lads. With me.'

He wondered how many batteries the French had ranged against them. Cursed himself for not having counted them when he could have. Behind him the rank and file continued their advance, despite the lethal rain of shot now flying towards them. Good, he thought: words of encouragement, camaraderie and most importantly the hard pikestaffs of the sergeants were doing, had done, their job. Another fifty paces. A hundred and they were getting close enough to see the regimental facings of the enemy infantry when the drifting smoke allowed. The smell of powder invaded his nostrils and he wondered whether perhaps he shouldn't have accepted Hansam's generous offer of some snuff. Perhaps he would take it up before the next battle. It wouldn't be long now, he thought. Not long until they felt the sting of musket fire from those men on the hill. Looking to the right he could see that they were beginning to draw parallel with what remained of Cadogan's original holding force.

Suddenly, from his left three horsemen appeared. Steel recognized one of them as the Duke of Argyle. From behind he heard Frampton's shouted battalion command and a change in the drum beat: 'Wheel to your right.'

As one, the line of redcoats began to turn, and then, led by the Scottish general, continued to advance up the slope, obliquely towards the French guns.

This was new madness, thought Steel. A cannonball tossed at them now would bowl through them like ninepins. And, sure enough, the roundshot began to pour in. There was a cry from his rear and Steel turned momentarily to see the body of a Grenadier crumple to the ground minus its head and gouting blood, its gaiters still stained yellow with vomit. One of the new lads, he thought. Poor bugger. But at the same time, like any soldier under fire, he was well aware that it could as well have been him and he muttered a silent prayer to providence for sparing him – yet again.

Casting a glance to the left he saw that their place on that side of the line was gradually being taken by a mass of foreign infantry. Perhaps a score of battalions of Prussians and Hanoverians in blue and red had crossed over the pontoon bridges in their wake and were labouring up the hill before the French could turn their flank. In turning now they passed in line through the small hamlet of Schaerken, abandoned it seemed by its sensible inhabitants. It had not been much damaged in the fighting as yet, although one house had been set on fire. Thankfully, thought Steel, it was not the inn.

He pointed at the tavern sign and yelled out to anyone that might be in earshot: 'There we are, boys. Didn't I tell you if we took this field I'd buy you the best in the house? Well, there's the bloody house. Remember it. Follow me to the French and after we've won I'll wager the Duke himself will stand you to anything that's on the menu there.'

There was a cheer, but only from the veterans. The new, green troops, he noticed, although they continued to advance doggedly, said nothing.

Another cannonball crashed into their ranks and left a sea of groaning dead and wounded men. From somewhere within the confused tangle of dead, wounded and unscathed bodies a single voice began to sing. Private Coles was doing what he always did, fending off the bullets with an invocation to the Almighty. It was a song, although Steel himself would have been the first to say that it was hardly what you might have called a melody:

'Bless the Lord, O my soul,
And all that is within me
Bless his holy name.
Bless the Lord, O my soul,
And forget not all his benefits,
Who forgiveth all thine iniquities;
Who healeth all thy diseases;
Who redeemeth thy life from destruction;
Who crowneth thee with loving kindness and tender
    mercies . . .'

Clearly the man intended to continue, but as they walked on over the dead and wounded, trying in vain not to walk on living flesh, Steel heard another voice rise above the holy words. Slaughter growled out an order: 'Coles. I'll give you tender bloody mercies. There's no mercies here. Nor no benefits or kindness either. Now shut that noise.'

'But, Sarge, it's the 103rd Psalm. It's the Lord's word.'

'I don't care if it's the first bloody Psalm or if your sainted bloody mother wrote the whole of the bloody book. Shut your wailing now or you'll be on sergeant's orders for the rest of the month. That is if you live through this bloody battle, which, given your closeness to the Almighty,

I very much doubt. He must be keen to see you, Coles, you talk to him so much. But I've got no appointment with him, so shut your bleeding trap or I'll do it for you. Last thing I want on this battlefield is a bloody bible-basher. Upsets the men.'

But the God-fearing Coles was not finished: 'But they seem to like it, Sarge.'

'Coles. What is it you don't understand? Are you a fool as well as deaf? I don't care what the men like and what they don't like. Fact is, I don't like it! So shut your trap.'

'Yes, Sarge.'

For all the fire pouring in on them from the hill, Slaughter's clever outburst had broken the spell of death that had hung over the advancing company, and a few of the men were grinning now.

Then Steel heard another voice, one of the recruits: 'Bloody hell, Sarge. I mean, look, sir.'

Steel looked up to his front and peered into the clearing smoke. What met his gaze almost brought him to a standstill. It was everything he could do to carry on. For directly in front of them, at a distance of perhaps eighty yards, was an endless, unbroken line of grey-coated French infantry. As Steel looked on they levelled their muskets until he was staring down the barrel into the blackness of oblivion.

He called back: 'Steady, boys. Keep going now. Not long –' But the last syllable of his words was clipped away by the crash as the fire from four hundred muskets spat four hundred three-quarter-ounce balls that ripped holes in James Farquharson's red-coated regiment of foot. Steel looked quickly over to the left to where the colonel had been riding with the colours and drummers at his side. Miraculously Sir James appeared to be unhurt. One of the drummer boys was down and dead, and Steel saw the brass spike-tipped top of one of the flagstaffs falter, indicating that an ensign had been hit, but then the colour was raised up again. Several gaps had appeared among his own company. But this was no time to think of losses.

'Close up. Close your ranks. Keep going. With me.'

The order was repeated along the line as sergeants and corporals ran along the files.

A faint cry arose above the cacophony of drums, cries of pain, flying shot and yelling men: 'Halt.'

Major Frampton had halted the entire battalion sixty paces from the enemy – the exact prescribed distance for a volley. Steel noticed that the two sides were separated by a small stream which ran down from the top of the big hill they called the Boser Couter and along the entire Allied front line. He saw too that the French were already reloading. He barked out the command and slipped quickly between the ranks to a new position.

He found Slaughter. 'We'll give them a firefight here, Jacob. By platoons. We can do better than that ragged excuse for a volley, eh? And by God we'll give them a shock.'

By prior orders from the brigade, Steel's Grenadiers were not to be held as was the usual practice in reserve during such a firefight, but would loose off their own volleys, adding to the firepower of the battalion.

'Firing by platoon, sir?'

'Fire by platoon, Sar'nt. Three firings each of six platoons. And the only means they have of countering such a fire is to come at us, as they will, with the bayonet. And frankly, Sar'nt, I don't think they've the stomach for it today. So what will they do? Stand and fire at us? They can get off three shots a minute at the most. And I warrant they'll not manage two. And then we'll have at them.'

Slaughter nodded, knowing the grim truth in Steel's words: Farquharson's, like the other regiments in the British army, was composed of nine companies each of a field strength of around fifty men, and each of those companies was subdivided into two, including the Grenadiers. In a firefight such as this they would be 'told off' as one and two. The trick was that within each of those two platoons another six units or small platoons had also been nominated, and it was these which provided the continuous fire which the French had come to fear so much. Using this system, Farquharson's and the other British foot would be able to fire six small volleys every minute. And, Steel asked himself, what troops in all the world could stand under a volley every ten seconds?

He barked the command: 'Advance to half distance. Make ready.'

Down the line the men cocked their muskets and the front rank knelt on their right knees, placing the butt on the ground with their thumbs on the cock and their finger on the trigger. Behind them the second and third ranks closed forward.

'Sar'nt, I think that we might dress the lines. Keep the barrels down. You know the drill. The new lads might think they're on a partridge shoot.' He turned back to the line: 'Present.'

Along the length of the company and all the way down the long line of the regiment, all three ranks raised their weapons: Tower Armoury weapons, the finest that modern technology could produce, forty-six inches long, brass mounted and firing a .76 calibre ball.

Slaughter smiled and wandered off to line his pike along the levelled musket barrels until they were all pointing roughly towards the enemy's stomachs. An inaccurate musket might easily miss the killing zone of a head. But a shot that went into the torso, packed as it was with vital organs, even if it didn't kill a man, would certainly render him *hors de combat* for the rest of the action.

Steel sensed that someone was behind him, and turning found the odious adjutant, Major Frampton, looking down at him from horseback as he made his way along the flank, ordering the lines.

Frampton nodded at Steel. 'Steel. Good day. Your men look

keen. Keep them to the fore, Steel. They are Grenadiers, you know.'

He smiled, not meaning the compliment, and rode off to the other flank. Steel wondered whether he would survive. Unpopular mounted officers, and few were more unpopular than Charles Frampton, made a tempting target if you had a crack shot in the battalion. He brushed fantasy aside and turned back to the job in hand.

Frampton's voice rang out to the battalion: 'First firing. Take care . . . Fire!'

But the French had now reloaded and as the guns fired from the British line, so they did from the enemy ranks. It seemed to Steel that the air had become a storm of musket balls, and he saw men fall all along the red-coated line. But then looking across he saw through the smoke to his left that the French too had taken losses. The regimental drummers beat a short preparative tattoo which had the men at the ready.

Again Frampton's voice sang out: 'Second firing . . . fire.' The second platoon fired and more of the grey-coated infantry fell. But the slower French had not yet reloaded and were unable to return fire.

The drums beat up again. And again the command came: 'Third firing.' It was the turn of the Grenadiers this time. They cocked their weapons.

'Fire!' A deafening report was followed by billowing white smoke, and Steel knew that by now the French would be suffering badly. And all this in only thirty seconds. The theory was that it should be possible for 2,000 men to fire 10,000 rounds in a single minute. Looking down the line and all along the brigade, Steel wondered whether today might not prove the theorists right.

He shouted the command: 'Grenadiers. Reload. Make ready.'

As he did so the first firing, already reloaded, loosed off

another volley. And so it went on. Not one volley but a continuous ripple which ran up and down the Allied line. The French, now themselves reloaded, managed to fire again, and again men fell among the Grenadiers. But the storm of lead pouring out of the British ranks was just too continuous. Too relentless. Too deadly.

For fully five minutes they kept it up. Near on thirty volleys, until the barrels of the muskets began to overheat and men burnt their fingers on the metal. The smoke was chokingly dense now and there was no way to tell the condition of the enemy. Only a man on horseback, above the hell down in the ranks, might know.

Steel heard Frampton's voice: 'Cease firing.'

Now clearly what the commander had in mind was a manoeuvre agreed upon and ordered by the regiment and indeed every British brigade in the army. 'Advance by platoons.'

The adjutant's voice rang out again: 'Advance.'

Quickly the Grenadiers went forward, making sure that their pace was fast enough to ensure that when they stopped after twenty paces their rear rank was level with the front rank of the rest of the line.

Steel shouted the command to the half company: 'Halt. Ready. Present. Fire!'

The muskets sang and he knew that the same was happening with each individual platoon along the line.

'Advance.'

The platoon to his immediate left repeated the Grenadiers' move and then delivered another volley. They were nearing the French now and Steel could see the raw fear on the faces of men who had never before experienced such terrible firepower as that currently being thrown at them.

The enemy barely managed another volley. The balls rushed past Steel, most at a harmless level, and thudded into the earth as a number of the enemy turned and fled.

His blood up now, Steel half turned to his men: 'Now, boys. Into them.'

Whirling the razor-sharp Italian broadsword above his head, he ran headlong into the French line and, sweeping aside the musket and bayonet of a terrified infantryman, hit him full in the chest with his body weight. Doing so, he sensed the entire line buckle as the best part of three thousand men made contact. The man reeled back, Steel brought down the great sword and felt it judder as it made contact with the Frenchman's skull. Then he was on again, clambering over the bleeding corpse and pushing into the second rank. This man did not wait but turned and fled. To Steel's left and right men went in with the bayonet. One of the Frenchmen threw down his musket, but it was too late. He died still pleading to be spared.

There was no point in trying to take prisoners in the first rush on such a field. 'No quarter' was the only rule of war at this level when men who had been standing under cannon fire for hours and then received close-range musketry were finally given free rein. All you could do as a defender was either to stand your ground and fight, or run. Most of the French were running.

'Halt. Stand your ground.'

Steel knew that even though the enemy appeared to be retreating their victory would be short-lived. From their start position he had seen the French second and third lines up on the high ground and was well aware that as soon as the news arrived that the front line had collapsed they would counterattack.

He turned to Slaughter. 'Sar'nt, we'd better get ready to receive their attack. It's sure to come.'

Slaughter nodded and walked towards the company. 'Come on, lads. The day's not over yet. Let's give them a warm welcome when they come back.'

'D'you think they will come back, Sarge?'

It was Norris, one of the new intake, a huge costermonger's lad from Bow who had fancied his chances with an exotic-sounding Scottish regiment and whose size was not quite matched by his intellect.

'Nah, Norris. They'll not come back. But their brothers will. And they're bigger and more evil than those buggers. Twice as horrible and twice as hungry for your blood, son. So you'd better make sure that yer musket's oiled and yer bayonet's clean.'

The recruit stared at him in horror. 'Yes, Sarge.'

Another of the men spoke, one of this Scots-raised regiment's few remaining genuine Scotsmen: 'How did you manage to see them Frenchies, Sarge? You was nowhere near 'em. Same as us.'

'Second sight, Mister Macrone. Second sight. That's what I've got, isn't it? And you'd be best to remember that. Next time you take a fancy to some illicit booty.'

They walked among the dead and wounded, lifting whatever they could salvage in the way of equipment and ammunition. Unused French musket balls and cartridges were scooped up and stuffed into cartouche boxes. While the British infantry fired sixteen balls to the pound the French fired twenty-four, making each ball lighter and smaller. They might not fit the British muskets exactly, the excess 'windage' between barrel and ball causing them to fly out at erratic angles, but in the desperate moments of a long firefight, when you were down to the last few rounds a man, a few captured enemy musket balls could make all the difference between winning and losing.

Now too was the time for prisoners, though you had to be careful and it was better to poke a bayonet into a man's ribs – just to make sure – than pay for the consequences. Steel looked away and saw, down the hill, that the pontoon bridges were brimming with grey-coated infantry, Dutchmen, who were spilling off and moving up towards the Allied left wing.

The brigade was astride a stream now as it flowed down-hill and into the Scheldt, and several of the men were stooping to drink. Slaughter saw them. 'I shouldn't do that, Cussiter. You don't know what's been in it.'

Taylor echoed his advice. 'Aye, Dan. Most likely some Frenchy's pissed in it. Or worse.'

Cussiter spat and swore, and the others who had been moving to the water thought better of it.

Steel laughed. 'This is thirsty work, lads. But don't forget my promise. Anything in that inn if you take the hill, and I'm paying. Just keep the French out of the village and then send the buggers back to Paris, or send them to hell.'

THREE

Looking across the broad sweep of the battlefield, away to his right, Steel realized with an unpleasant start that the Grenadiers and a sizeable portion of the battalion companies of Farquharson's regiment had got themselves ahead of the rest of the Allied line to their flank, which here mainly consisted of Hessian and Hanoverian foot, and which appeared to have been pushed back some way by the French. It would only be a matter of minutes now, he thought, before the enemy came on again. He could see the grey-coated Frenchmen pouring through the village to his right and centre, and it seemed that if they continued their advance they might push the entire Allied line back into the Scheldt.

Hansam saw it too. 'We appear to have exceeded ourselves, Jack.'

'Quite so, Henry. And I wonder what the Duke intends to do about it. We've a marsh and the river to our rear. We cannot retire. The left certainly looks strong enough, but look over there.'

He pointed, and both men stared up the rising ground to the right where a large body of scarlet-and-gold-clad enemy horse was advancing steadily behind their infantry. Just then a commotion from some distance to their rear, followed by the crack of splintering timber and screams, made both men turn to look. At first Steel thought that the French must have succeeded in shelling the flimsy pontoon bridges, but then he realized that it was sheer weight of numbers that had brought two of them crashing down. As he and Hansam watched, hundreds of Dutch infantry were thrown into the Scheldt in full kit, losing weapons and equipment and doing their best not to be sucked under the waters. More than a few did not succeed.

Steel was thoughtful. 'Now Marlborough will have to do something, Henry. This is going to hold up his plans. We'll need to hold them here. It's my guess that he intends to turn the French right using the Dutch. But now he's going to be held up. The French need time. If they can find it and use it then they'll turn our right flank and not we theirs. D'you see, Henry?'

Hansam nodded. 'So we're going to have to make sure that they have no time. There's nothing for it but to stand – here. Against whatever the French throw at us. That lot included.'

He pointed again to where the French horse were moving steadily down the hill to their right. They had almost reached the line of the small stream that joined the one along which the battalion had taken up position. Within seconds it seemed they would be upon them.

Steel turned to to Slaughter. 'They're coming, Jacob. Prepare to receive cavalry.'

The command was echoed in shouts through and around the battalion, and Steel was aware of the horror that all infantrymen held in common of facing charging cavalry. It was the stuff of nightmares. But he knew, too, from his own experience in the Northern Wars fighting with the Swedes against the Tsar, that given the right frame of mind infantry could beat off a cavalry attack. Nor was it in his plan to use the device of forming a square. That would not be necessary and he knew that Frampton would think likewise. With the new muskets and the platoon firing system, it must surely be possible to defeat the cavalry by musketry alone. In any case the cavalry were too laden to come at them very fast. No more than a gallop usually. It would be that last crucial, critical pause in the volley firing that always did for the infantry. But firing by platoons had made that a thing of the past. All they had to do once they had fired was to make sure that they recovered their muskets sufficiently fast to charge bayonets at chest height. Then he knew they would break any cavalry.

Nevertheless, his heart trembled as he gave the command: 'Prepare for cavalry.'

Automatically the right half-company formed into three ranks as before, the front rank embedding their musket butts into the earth. It had begun to drizzle now and the earth was visibly softer. It had also become more difficult to see across the battlefield, and as he peered towards the oncoming cavalry it seemed to Steel as if they had stopped. He rubbed at his eyes and looked again, then turned to Williams.

'Tom. Look over there. Look at the enemy horse and tell me what you can see.'

There was a pause while the young lieutenant took in what lay before him. 'I see enemy cavalry, sir. A great many of them. Impossible to tell the regiment with certainty. But they look like the Maison du Roi. Louis' own horse guards. Good God, sir. They're the finest cavalry in all France.'

'Good. Well done, Tom. But tell me now, what are they doing, your fine cavalry?'

Williams looked again. 'Why, nothing, sir. They appear to have come to a halt.'

Steel stared. It was true. They had stopped. This was a new and welcome madness in a battle of big surprises. Cavalry, bearing down in vastly superior numbers upon exhausted and outgunned infantry, did not halt. They pushed on, gained whatever impetus they could, drew their swords and went hell for leather at their target. They did not stop.

He estimated their range. A hundred, perhaps a hundred and fifty yards. What the devil had stopped them? Who had given the order?

Slaughter came to his side. 'Sir, shall we give them a volley?'

'No, Sar'nt. Hold your fire. It may be a trick. They can cover that distance in just under a minute and they may think that we'll spend our firepower before they get to us. I can't fathom what they're doing. What d you think, Sar'nt?'

Slaughter grinned. 'You know me, sir. I don't think. Not unless I'm ordered to.'

'Don't be funny with me, Jacob. What d'you think they're about?'

'Well, if you really want my opinion, sir, just the same as you. That's what I was asking myself. Why stop? You've got enough men to take out a brigade, let alone our little battalion. What in hell's name's stopping them?'

It might have amused Slaughter to know that at precisely that moment the same question was being asked by the French commander in chief. For the past half hour Marshal Vendôme, sweating and filthy after having gone in himself on foot to take control of the desperate infantry fight in the centre of the French line around the village of Groenewald, had been recovering his humour on a tree stump on the edge of the village of Lede to the rear of the French position.

It was fast approaching seven o'clock when he got up and turned to his secretary.

'We're winning, du Capistron. Winning. We've pushed them out of both villages and down towards the river. I thought Marlborough was supposed to be an intellectual. To have studied the great generals. He can't have learnt much. He's got a marsh and a river to his back. He's trapped, du Capistron. We've got him. And now we must follow up. Speed

59

is everything. Lose that and we risk losing the battle. Grasp the moment and we win.'

He walked past the last few houses in the village and stood above the stream that ran along the foot of the hill. It was becoming increasingly hard to see now through the rain, but gazing down at the left wing he thought he could pick out the shapes of men and horses on the dead ground before the village of Roygem. Several squadrons of them. Presumably, Burgundy had left them as a reserve when he had attacked Marlborough's right. Vendôme continued to look, and as his eyes became accustomed to the light he saw that there were a great many more men on the plain than he had thought at first. Considerably more. He counted them off and it became evident that what he could see were not merely a few squadrons but the entire wing sitting there, drawn up in neat battle lines as they had been all day.

Vendôme shook his head in disbelief and shouted to du Capistron, who ran to join his master: 'What in God's name are they doing? Why hasn't he moved? The idiot! He should have taken them into the Allied right. I sent that order over an hour ago. Didn't Burgundy get my order? Didn't he, man? Take it again. He must attack! What are they doing there? They're not moving. Are they mad? Quick, write this down.'

But even as he was dictating the order Vendôme became instinctively aware that it was already too late. The moment had gone, and the opportunity was lost. Looking out across the valley he could see Marlborough's right wing strengthened now with two full regiments of cavalry positioned hard against his vulnerable right flank. The moment had gone.

He waved to du Capistron. 'No, no, don't bother. Don't waste your time. It's too late. That ass has missed the mark. I only hope that he hasn't lost us the battle.'

Steel and Slaughter were still staring at the motionless cavalry when another horseman appeared riding along the left of the line in a fashion so foolhardy that it proclaimed his utter inexperience on a battlefield.

Slaughter suppressed his laughter. 'Aye aye, sir. Looks like we've got company. Silly bugger'll get hisself killed, riding along a line like that. If the Frenchies don't have a pop at 'im then like as not one of our own lads will. That type of officer there's what you'd call a liability, sir. If you don't mind my saying so.'

'You'd do best to keep your thoughts to yourself, Jacob. But you're quite right. The young idiot's only going to draw their fire.'

In response, it seemed, a French gun on the hill above Schaerken opened up with a round of ball and, missing the tempting target of the horseman, sent its projectile into the ranks of a company of musketeers, killing several of them.

Slaughter sighed. 'What'd I tell you?'

The man pulled up his horse directly in front of Steel, who saw that he was a young lieutenant from Farquharson's number three company, Sir James's wife's well-provided nephew, who rather than advance at the head of a company as a battalion officer had been taken on by the colonel as his personal aide, with a view to joining the General Staff. Steel had not encountered him before, but he had heard that the young man had already run up a prodigious mess bill in attempting to win over the affections of his brother officers. It was not Steel's way, and he wondered whether the lad was really cut out for soldiering.

The lieutenant reined in, patted his horse and stared down with a supercilious air. You'd be better suited to the Royal Household, thought Steel. This battlefield is no place for a boy like you.

The lieutenant touched his hat in salute and spoke in a clipped, courtly accent. 'Sir. Lieutenant Mowbray, with a message from Colonel Farquharson. Captain Steel, the battalion is about to advance. Your company will form the van. We are ordered to take the hill.'

Steel nodded. 'Thank you, Lieutenant. I shall advance the company, and please be so good as to return my compliments to the Colonel.'

Apparently satisfied, the lieutenant turned, and as he rode back to the colonel Steel looked at Slaughter, barely managing to contain his laughter until the young man was out of earshot.

'Well, that's us told. Jacob, hold your tongue. Silly young sprat. He'd better get that head of his a sight lower if he wants to keep it attached to his body. Come on.'

Again the men changed formation and then, in a steady line, three ranks deep and two hundred men wide, the entire battalion began to advance up the hill towards the French. To their left another six battalions followed suit, while to the rear two identical lines of three ranks' depth came on at fifty-pace intervals. Argyle rode in the centre of the huge brigade column, shouting encouragement above the wind and rain.

Out in front of his half-company of Grenadiers, crossing the shallow stream of the Diepenbeek, Steel turned to Williams. 'This'll give them a surprise, eh, Tom?'

'We'll send them back to Paris, sir.'

Steel laughed and nodded, although, while he could almost see the incredulous French faces, in his heart he knew that this would be no easy victory, and he waited for the first shot to strike.

As much as Steel presumed that their assault might take the French by surprise, even he would have been astonished had he known the full extent of the trap about to be sprung on Marshal Vendôme. For while the French before them were taken aback that their hard-pressed enemy should counter-attack, it was their comrades to the right who had the greater surprise. As Argyle's brigade pressed forward, to their left from the very top of the Boser Couter down the hillside streamed battalion after battalion of grey-coated infantry with black-cuirassed cavalry protecting their flanks. They were the Danes and the Dutch. The Scandinavian cavalrymen of

Claude-Frédéric Tserclaes, Count Tilly, and sixteen Dutch battalions under the command of a Swede, Count Oxenstein. Under Marlborough's direction and the command of the young Prince of Orange fighting in his first battle, they had skirted the southwest side of the Boser Couter, hidden from French sight, and now the moment of reckoning had arrived. It was eight o'clock, and as they descended the slope, slippery from the recent rain, struggling to keep their lines dressed, Orange's men found to their intense pleasure that they were looking directly into the flank and rear of the entire French army.

But Steel was oblivious to their coming triumph. His thoughts were fixed only on the sight that lay before him: a long line of enemy infantry, with levelled muskets. The French opened fire on Farquharson's battalion at seventy paces. One of the balls struck Lieutenant James Mowbray in the right side of his jaw and passed out through his left cheekbone, shattering it and taking away half his face. As he fell from his horse his last mortal thoughts were not of the agony he might be in, for he was too shocked to feel the pain, but how much it might cost him to have his tailor make up a new coat. The same volley felled some forty men of the battalion. Not all were dead and some were only lightly wounded, but it was enough to make the company officers yell to dress the ranks and for the sergeants to push with their halberds at the reluctant redcoats, urging them on into the storm of lead. Steel, at the head of the Grenadiers, felt a musket ball touch his calf and saw that it had torn away part of the leather of his boot and grazed the skin. He swore out loud, not from having been hit, but because his imme-diate concern was where on earth in Flanders he was going to find another pair of boots as comfortable as these that had carried him down the Rhine to Blenheim and through the mud of Ramillies. Bugger the formal firefight, he thought. In for a penny, in for a pound. Another firefight might decimate the French but there were sure to be more behind, he reasoned.

The only real way to take this hill was going to be to fight for it hand to hand. He looked to his rear and yelled: 'Charge! Grenadiers, with me.'

Then they were running in. Steel sensed the momentum close behind him. There were thirty paces still to cover and the French were loading too fast. Twenty, ten more, and then they were on them just as they loosed off their volley. Steel's target was smaller than him, swarthy and moustachioed, with black hair and a gold sleeper ring in his ear. He fell on him with all his force, and as the blade of Steel's sword drove deep into the man's chest his finger tightened on the trigger of his musket and it exploded beside Steel's left ear, firing its ball high in the air and almost deafening him. Along the line it was a similar experience, most of the Grenadiers having managed to close just in time. A few unfortunates, though, were too slow and met the muzzles of the French guns at point-blank range, to be torn to pieces by the impact of the bullet, their dead flesh scorched by the flash. Steel drew his blade from the dying man and ran into the second rank. Parrying a bayonet, he cut at the man before him, and, feeling his sword find bone, moved on. The third-rank man, seeing him, turned and fled past a bewildered officer who quickly followed his example.

Now they were through the line, and apart from isolated groups of men locked in combat with Farquharson's redcoats the French unit had disintegrated. Steel saw a score of them surrendering under the merciful eye of one of the other company commanders. He looked about him to gauge his losses, but had hardly begun to make a count when he was aware of another body of men directly to their front. As Steel had feared, behind the first line lay a second, and as he watched they prepared to fire a volley at the recovering British. Steel braced himself.

'Sar'nt. Prepare the company to take fire from fifty paces front. Grenadiers, reform. Mister Williams, to me.'

As the company attempted to reassemble itself as best it could, Steel realized that across in the enemy lines all was not as it should be. He watched, intrigued, as several of the French officers stopped in the very motion of issuing their commands for musketry drill and began to look across the field to their right. He followed their gaze, and it was at that moment that he caught sight of the Danish and Dutch infantry and horse advancing down the great hill and heading directly for the French right flank. The French had seen them too, and suddenly the men who a few seconds before had been ready to take the field were thrown into confusion. Officers and sergeants shouted commands to wheel round and face the new threat. Others, though, issued orders to retreat, and soon what had been an orderly line broke into no more than a panic-stricken rabble. A few of the men, veterans who knew that often their best defence might lie in attack, stood their ground and continued to go through the motions of loading their weapons.

As Steel looked on he saw a tall Frenchman raise his musket and take careful aim directly at him. There was nothing to do but stand and hope that the man's skill was not as sound as his nerve. There was a crack and a flash and a moment later Steel felt a thump in his left arm. He knew instantly that he had been hit, and quite well. Wounds were nothing new to him but the unexpectedness and impact of this musket ball made him reel, and he fell momentarily against one of the Grenadiers, Mackay, clutching at his shoulder for support. The man turned to help him and, seeing the wound, yelled across to where Slaughter and Williams were standing staring at the unfolding drama.

'Steady there, sir. Officer down!'

Williams, breaking away from the spectacle, came running, and Steel, dazed by the shock, was just aware that the French before them, including the lucky bastard who had shot him, were turning to run, panicked by the rapid advance of the Dutch. He turned, white-faced, to the lieutenant.

'Mister Williams, follow up our attack. Get on, Tom. Get after them. Take the half-company. I'll find you. Follow up, but don't overreach yourself. And look out for their cavalry.'

Hardly had Steel got the words out before he sank down against a hedgerow. He was aware of Taylor kneeling beside him and removing his stock, trying to staunch the bleeding in his arm. Steel turned to him and babbled as the corporal tied the makeshift tourniquet, 'Taylor. Matt Taylor. Corporal Taylor. Well done, Taylor. Thank you.'

He knew that it was vitally important that he should not pass out. He waited for the pain, but still it did not come. He grabbed at Taylor's arm and pulled him down to whisper in his ear: 'Go on, Matt. Go with them. I'll find you.'

Taylor smiled at him and laid him back gently against the hedge. 'With respect, sir, I don't think you will. And if you want my opinion, sir, they'll not be needing my help.'

Steel looked towards the retreating French and saw that the slope of the Boser Couter was now awash with a sea of Dutch and Danish grey. And then the pain kicked in.

A mile and a half back from the carnage, at an inn in the village square of Huysse, on its pretty wooded hill where the alder trees grew in profusion and where on any other day than this the birds sang in their branches, Marshal Vendôme, spattered in blood and filth, paced the cobbles and kicked a loose stone across the ground. The village church clock rang the half after eight, and through the dim light of the wet evening both sun and moon hung together in the darkening sky, looking down on the rivulets of blood that coloured the twin streams of the plain of Oudenarde and flowed into the Scheldt.

A party of horsemen trotted quickly into the square, the hot breath of their winded mounts heavy against the evening air. Leaving his horse with a groom, the Duke of Burgundy walked across to the Marshal.

'We cannot hold them. The army is completely surrounded. Only the darkness can save us now. I—'

He was cut short by Vendôme. 'Why did you not execute my order? At five o'clock I sent you an order to take your wing – your entire wing, thirty thousand men – and attack the Allied right. Why did you disobey me?'

Burgundy replied, 'The Duc de Puységur informed me that the area across which I was to advance was a morass. He told me that the Allies could not advance across it and that neither should we.'

'But I told you to advance.'

'I sent word by messenger.'

'I received no such message.'

'I assure you—'

'Assure me nothing, My Lord. Your Royal Highness must not forget that you came to this army on condition that you would obey me. By what right and in what name did you ignore my order?'

Burgundy shook his head. 'Marshal Vendôme, do not forget yourself. You may be a Marshal of France but I am a Prince of the Blood.'

Vendôme fixed him with his eyes: 'But here, My Lord, it is my blood that matters. That and the blood of those men out there – dying for you and the King. We cannot now win the day, My Lord. We must retire and regroup. All that we can hope to do now is to recommence this battle tomorrow.'

There was a respectful cough. Vendôme turned towards it. 'D'Evreux?'

'Sire, if I may be so bold. I do not truly believe that the army is of sufficient strength and constitution to be in any situation to fight tomorrow. Or indeed the day after that.'

Du Capistron said, 'Sire, we have lost the battle. We have lost the army.'

Burgundy muttered, 'I didn't lose the army. It was Puységur's fault. He lost the battle.'

67

Vendôme said nothing but looked at each man for a few moments before moving on to the next. When he had done with all of them he walked alone towards one of the half-timbered houses and pressed his hand hard against the wall. Then he turned and spoke: 'This is a sad day for France. And a sad day for all of us . . . Very well, gentlemen. It would seem that you all wish to retire. So be it.' He turned to Burgundy. 'And I know that you, Monseigneur, have long wished to do so.' Before the Prince of France could give voice to his indignation, Vendôme turned back to his staff. 'Send word to what commanders we have left: *Sauve qui peut*. They are to make for the Ghent–Bruges canal. Come, gentlemen. Tonight we retire on Ghent. Why should we delay? To be sure, we have nothing else left to lose.'

Slaughter found Steel in the shade of a shattered tree, binding up the hole in his arm. 'You all right, sir? Looks nasty, that. You should have someone take a proper look at it. Someone better qualified than Matt Taylor, maybe.'

'Matt's a good physician, Jacob, as good as any London quack doctor. Don't fuss. I've had worse.' He struggled to his feet and swayed unsteadily. 'I'll be back in the fight in a moment.' He looked around himself at the field, empty save for the dead and dying and discarded weapons. 'Where the devil is the company?'

'Don't you know, sir? The Frenchies have surrendered. Battle's over. We've won.'

Steel leant backwards onto the hedge. 'Well, thank God for that, then. I don't think we could have managed that again, Jacob. So where are the men, Sar'nt?'

Slaughter produced a hand from behind his back and Steel saw that it contained a crumpled and torn piece of white and gold cloth. He reached out to touch it and felt silk and embroidery and gold wire. His face split open in a wide grin. 'Tell me that's what I think it is, Jacob.'

'It is that, sir. That's a French colour. Took it myself in the chase, with Mister Williams.'

'Does the Colonel know?'

'Not yet, sir.'

'All in good time, then. Well done, Jacob. The regiment's honour can come later. This is the Grenadiers' moment. It's their colour for now. Your colour, our colour, as much as the regiment's.' He noticed that Slaughter had a sheepish look about him. Steel recognized it of old. 'Got something else to tell me, Jacob?'

'Well, sir, you recall that as we advanced we passed a village that we'd retaken from the French and that in that village there was an inn.'

Steel looked at him. 'Yes . . . vaguely.'

'Well, sir, it wasn't.'

'What?'

'An inn, sir. It wasn't an inn.'

'Well then, what was it?'

'Well, sir, do you recall that you made a promise to the men?'

It came back to Steel. 'Ah, yes. The inn. The rum, or beer, or what you will. What was it I promised them exactly?'

Slaughter grinned. 'Well, I do remember you saying that they could 'ave anything as was on the menu in the inn, sir. That inn at least that we thought was an inn but what really wasn't an inn.'

'Yes, yes. Oh Christ. I did, didn't I?'

Slaughter nodded his head. 'That you did, sir. An' that being the case and the inn not being an inn . . .'

Slaughter was interrupted by the bizarre sight of one of the Grenadiers, an Irishman named Mulligan, chasing a woman across the battlefield. Steel and Slaughter stared at them for a moment until they vanished from sight. Then Steel spoke. 'What was that? Was that a woman?'

'Well, it's good to see that you've still got your senses, sir.'

'Jacob, you're not telling me something.'

More women appeared, a party of three this time, pursued by two red-coated musketeers. They walked arm in arm as they passed Steel and Slaughter, whom they ignored, and it was clear from their laughter that they were not entirely sober. Their faces were black with powder soot, below which it was still possible to detect traces of rouge. Their voluminous clothes hung loosely about them, in one case to the point of leaving little to the imagination.

Steel shook his head and wondered whether he was delirious. 'Jacob, what the devil are such women doing on a battlefield? This is no place for a lady.'

'But these women, sir, if you'll excuse me, they ain't no ladies. That's what I was trying to tell you, sir.'

'No, Sar'nt. Let me guess who they are and why they're here.'

'Well, it seems that we've just taken their home, sir.'

'Their home. The inn, I suppose?'

'Right first time, sir. The inn as we supposed it might be. In effect, sir, it's what you might call a house of ill repute. A bordello. Reckon that the girls must've heard that soldiers were coming and thought it might be good for their business, and then when the battle started it was too late to run, so they hid in the cellar.'

'Good God. You'd better make bloody sure that no more of the men see them.'

'Well, thing is, sir, it's a bit late for that.'

'I'll have any man who so much as handles one of those women flogged in front of the battalion.'

'Wouldn't do, sir.'

'No?'

'No, sir. Seeing as you promised the men anything that was on the menu at the "inn", so to speak.'

'I did, didn't I?'

'You did, sir.'

'Christ almighty, Jacob. The British army wins a glorious victory, and what part does my company play in it? We liberate a bloody brothel!'

'And we've taken a colour, sir.'

Steel looked a the crestfallen sergeant. He knew that there was only one way out. 'You know that I'm a man of my word, Sar'nt.'

'Loyal, sir. That's you through and through. Loyal.'

'Well, make damn sure that no one else hears about it – Major Frampton or the colonel. And before they enjoy themselves at my expense they can damn well get busy collecting weapons. God knows there are enough of them.'

'Very good, sir. The men'll be well pleased.'

'No one, Sar'nt. No one's to know. And if any of them catches the pox I'll have them out of the company. They can decide what risks they want to take.'

'Yes, sir.'

'And you'd better have Mister Williams take that colour to the rear once the men have seen it. Tell him to find Marlborough and to tell him which regiment took it. And, Jacob, be sure to tell him to say that it was Captain Steel's company.'

If Steel had thought that his trophy might have been presented to the Duke in splendid isolation, he was wrong. A little to the east and rear of the final position of Farquharson's Grenadiers, Marlborough stood at the centre of a small group of officers, flanked by Prince Eugene, who had commanded the right wing throughout the battle. They were gazing at something on the ground at the Captain General's feet: a pile of French colours to which every few minutes others were being added.

Cadogan smiled and knelt to touch the silk of one of the captured banners before standing and turning to the Duke. 'A victory, Your Grace. And, may I say, a victory like no other.

Something new for London to shout about. And what an honour for the Queen. I am informed that the enemy have lost fifteen thousand men all told, perhaps as many as twenty. Ten thousand more, they say, have deserted and run for France. On our part we have taken only three thousand casualties, perhaps a thousand killed. It was a day well won, your Grace.'

'Yes, William, it was well won, but in truth it was too damned close for my liking. Why, had you not done such a sterling job of holding the enemy at the bridgehead, allowing us time to come up piecemeal as we did, it might have had quite a different outcome.'

'But come you did, sir, and now all France lies open to us.'

Marlborough frowned. 'Aye, you're right about that. All France, ours for the taking. But how shall we exploit our victory, d'you suppose?'

Another staff officer, Overkirk, fresh from his triumph and eager for more, spoke up. 'We should pursue the French, My Lord. With the utmost vigour and quite as far as our lines permit.'

'Quite so, General Overkirk. Ordinarily, military science dictates that we should pursue the French, or at the very least divert and engage Marshal Berwick and his army. Ordinarily. But, as my friend Cadogan has pointed out, this was not an ordinary victory. France is wide open to us. Open, gentlemen. Do you realize what that means? If we are prudent we will have need of only one course of action. I know from Cadogan's spies that King Louis tires of this war. Some say that he is actually desirous of peace and it is only pride and his generals that keep him in the field. His manpower and the flower of his nation's nobility are being drained on these killing fields. Gentlemen, I have a notion.'

He beckoned to a runner who came forward and held open a map of Flanders and northern France. Marlborough traced his finger from their position at Oudenarde and took it across the map in a southwesterly direction: 'How do you think it would be if we were to march directly on Paris? To follow up this victory, not with a mere pursuit, but to leave the remnants of Vendôme's army to themselves and march for the capital?'

Overkirk spoke. 'Can we do it?'

Marlborough turned to Cadogan. 'Well, William, d'you think we can?'

Cadogan nodded. 'I do believe we can, sir. We have the men and the resources. And I know that you have a further plan.'

Marlborough went on. 'Paris is an open city. It has no defences. So confident was he of his armies that Louis opened it and demolished the walls some thirty years back. How pride will undo a man! Although in truth that is of no great concern to us. We have no need to take the place. We can encamp outside the gate and he will beg for peace – particularly when his scouts inform him that we have another army newly arrived from England and landed at Abbeville.'

'We do?'

'Not yet, but it is in my plan. Lieutenant General Erle is already embarked with his force off the Isle of Wight with an escort of naval warships. When he learns of that, as he shall, Louis will set Versailles shaking with fear. And then we shall unite with Erle at Abbeville. We shall have a hundred thousand men and supplies readily available from the coast. A swift thrust along the river Lys and we shall bypass the forts at Menin and Courtrai. Thus we avoid the bloodletting of besieging yet more of Monsieur Vauban's painstakingly strengthened fortresses, having marched past Lille and cut south' – again his finger moved sweepingly across the map – 'thus through France, direct to the capital. And so, gentlemen, Holland will be free, our men will not die needlessly, our enemies at home will be confounded and the war will be won.'

Marlborough paused and waited for a response. The generals stared open-mouthed at the map. It was the boldest plan that any of them had ever encountered – surely one of the boldest plans in all military history.

Cadogan spoke up. 'It is masterly, Your Grace. A brilliant stratagem.'

The staff nodded in assent, all save Eugene who simply stared at the map and kept his own counsel. Marlborough smiled and called for wine, and then, raising the great silver-mounted goblet made from a coconut by Queen Anne's own goldsmiths which he always brought with him on campaign, he addressed his staff: 'A toast then, gentlemen. For now I am resolved. Within the week we march on Paris.'

FOUR

Henrietta Vaughan stretched her naked body across the crumpled white cotton sheets and arched her back with a lazy grace. Then, realizing that her husband was unable to see her, she stood up unsteadily and grasped the front cross-post of the bed frame, ensuring that her nakedness was now perfectly visible in the mirror which stood against the wall at the end of the bed. Steel saw her and muttered a quiet curse.

She was indisputably the most beautiful creature he had ever seen, with the power to make him forget whatever it was he might be engaged in and to arouse in him a passion the like of which he had never known. He looked away.

Standing before the tall cheval mirror in the best bedroom of a little inn in the town of Menin, he was attempting with his one free hand to tie his cravat. His other arm was still in a sling. Although it had been almost a month since the battle his muscles were only now beginning to regain their strength and the damage to the tendons had still not fully healed. He swore again, louder this time. 'Dammit. Darling, will you please come and help? I am such a cripple that I cannot even tie my neckerchief.'

Henrietta hung by her hands from the cross-beam of the bed frame, stretching until the skin was taut across her pale body, save for the heavily rounded orbs of her breasts. Seeing her reflection, she smiled with pleasure and held the pose, and spoke to him with deliberate languor. 'Jack, I do think that you might have found us something a little less rustic than these rooms. I mean, look at this bedchamber. Did you ever see such hangings and such curtains. Simple calico? And look at the floor. Bare boards, Jack!'

Steel pretended not to have heard her and continued to struggle with his tie. But she was not to be ignored. 'Jack, can you hear me? Do you perhaps not see me? Can you see me now, Jack?'

Steel, desperately trying not to see what she might be doing to gain his attention, but conscious of it all the same, found his attention diverted from the cravat. 'Yes, I can see you, my darling. But I wish that I did not. Not now. I have to be with the Captain General. You know that.'

In fact, while he was finding it hard to look away, she had also pricked a nerve. Steel had found them a pair of mean rooms in a little inn which quite clearly was not up to Henrietta's exacting standards, particularly to judge by the opulent apartment which she had taken care to lease for them in Brussels and on which he now continued to pay the rent, even though away on campaign.

Henrietta laughed and, stepping lightly off the bed, crossed the floor to him with deliberate slowness, all the while using her body as only she could, in the full knowledge of the effect it would have on her husband. Henrietta knew that she was beautiful. Probably, she thought, the most beautiful of any woman in court circles at St James's, and certainly at present the most lovely woman in all of the Low Countries.

She stood on tiptoe to reach his tie, pushing her face deliberately close to his and her naked body against his clothes and pulling him down towards her so that his eyes were level with the nape of her neck. She smelt of lavender and musk and faintly of sweat. It was a heady mix, so much so that Steel

76

almost succumbed. He had known in his heart that it had been wrong to allow his wife to follow him here. Not merely on account of her own safety, but precisely because it would result in moments like this, when the call of duty hung in a tenuous balance with the all-too-evident temptations of the flesh.

He had not agreed at first when she had asked to come here to Menin to join him from Brussels. This was in effect the front line of the army, albeit a fortfied town held by the Allies and encircled by the entire army. But Henrietta had pleaded with him and Steel was hardly the first man to have been compelled to give in to her abundant charms. So here she was in all her nakedness, and here he was being diverted once again and already late for an appointment with the Captain General.

He snapped back to the moment. 'Darling, perhaps I had better try to tie it again myself.'

He was too late. 'There, it's done.' She stood back to survey her work, straightened the tie one last time and allowed Steel to look at her again.

He shook his head. 'I am sorry, Henrietta. You know that I must go.'

She scowled and stuck out her tongue at him.

Steel moved to the door, opened it and shouted down the hall to his soldier-servant: 'Sykes. My horse.'

Closing the door he moved across to his wife and gave her a deliberately fleeting embrace. 'I don't think that the Duke will keep me too long. And then, once I've finished, my love, we can spend all the day together.'

'All the day? Are you sure? Jack, you know how long you spend with your men and how little time with me.' Still frowning, she grabbed a gown from the bed and threw it around her shoulders. 'Oh, I hate this place.'

'Then, really, perhaps do you not think that you should return to Brussels? Or you might go to Antwerp, or Ostend.

You know that it was not my idea that you should come here.'

'And, in truth, I'm beginning to regret that I ever did and why I ever bothered.' She turned away from him but he knew that she was only shamming her grief; testing him again.

Steel put a hand about her shoulders. 'I promise that I shall make a special effort to be quick about my duties. Just for you. At least we shall have dinner together.'

She turned to him. 'It's not dinner that I want, Jack. It's you.'

'And you shall have me, my darling. Just as soon as I've seen the Duke. Now why don't you get dressed? I know for a fact that cook has a dozen oysters set aside for your breakfast. I'll see you just as soon as I return.'

He turned and opened the door, closing it quickly behind him lest he should look once more into her eyes and be diverted from his purpose. Steel walked down the dark staircase of the old house and counted himself the luckiest man in the world. A captaincy, another battle survived, a company of grenadiers and the loveliest, most devoted and doting wife in all the world.

Back in the tawdry bedroom, Henrietta sat on the edge of the bed and pulled on a silk stocking. Of course she had stopped sulking the moment Steel had left the room. She did not really care that he had gone. Jack would be back soon and then they would have as much of the day together as he could spare. Which, she thought, was probably damn little. In any case, what was there to do here in this stinkhole except make love, eat and drink? True, all three excited her, and with Jack the first was as good if not better than it had been with any of her many former lovers. But it was not enough. She craved society. And shops. Almost as much as she craved his presence in her bed. More, even. She smiled. Perhaps she would return to Brussels ere long. Campaigning was such a bore.

The army was a bore – though she would never have admitted as much to dear Jack. It seemed that he was forever on duty, attending to his men in some way or another. They were like so many children, always demanding something of their officer. She wondered that they were ever able to fight a battle.

Jack, it seemed, had so little time for her here. In Brussels at least she had the company of the other wives – what there was of them. Mrs Melville, the wife of the commander of Number 4 company and the only other wife out here with the battalion, was passably agreeable. In small doses. The two of them had agreed that when she returned to Brussels, where Mrs Melville had wisely remained, they would visit the little milliner's shop in the rue des Bouchers, where Madame Delvaux had set aside twenty yards of lace for her. It was, she had been assured, the exact same pattern lately bought by the Queen of England herself, and Henrietta was determined to have it. What matter that it might be more than seven pounds a yard? And then there was the prettiest flowered damask and an Indian stuff they called Baguzee, the like of which you never saw. She smiled to herself and rang for the maid to help her dress. Yes, she would have it all on her return. Blow the expense. In any case, Jack would be worth a great deal more in the near future if she were to have her way. Until then they would just have to exist on credit, like everyone else.

She tugged again on the tapestry bell-pull hanging on the wall to summon her maid and, as the simple girl was helping her into her clothes, placing her new-fangled, hooped petticoat over her head and over that the new ash-coloured silk quilted petticoat, she continued her musings. The maid, a timid, brainless child whose name was Maria and whom she had lately engaged in Brussels, having lost her own English maid, Bessie, to be married to a soldier, laced her in firmly into her stays and rolled her flowing blonde hair so that it

79

hung in two curled locks about her bare shoulders. All the while Henrietta pored over her plan to divert Jack away from the front line, away even from his beloved army and back to court. Somehow she knew that she would manage it. What use was he here in Flanders? What sort of life could they enjoy? Steel was a hero already, respected in London circles and praised by the Queen. But to cultivate that influence she knew that they must be back in London. True, he did not have much money. But there were ways of changing that, ways in which a man might rise in status and fortune in the City, given the right connections and the respect due to his character. Jack Steel was a national hero and she knew that he would only remain so as long as his name was spoken. The people and those in positions of power – in the mercantile and propertied classes – had all too short and fickle memories. At the moment his star was riding high, and every moment spent here in the Netherlands was an opportunity lost to Henrietta. She must do it. Not least because she was determined to prove her father wrong. Hadn't he mocked their marriage and derided her for marrying a soldier with few prospects? But hadn't that been one of the major attractions of marrying Jack? Yes, he was devilishly handsome, and for the moment a hero, but Steel also represented everything that her father had always warned about. He was the epitome of the man she had been told to avoid: penniless, reckless and out for glory. In short, Steel was the perfect opportunity to prove to her father that he had been wrong. And she was determined that he should not be allowed to win.

Making their way through the back streets of the town, Steel's horse stumbled and he looked down to see the cause. She had tripped over an outstretched leg and whinneyed in distress as the owner, who had been lying in the gutter, attempted with difficulty to rise to his feet. He wore a military red coat and an infantryman's black cocked hat, and from the state of his clothes and the smell of alcohol, sweat and vomit, Steel guessed that he had been lying there most of the night. The man was half standing now, staggering and mouthing oaths at Steel, who looked about him for a sergeant who might arrest the drunk. He quickly gave up and settled on giving him a firm shove which sent the man flying back into the gutter.

Leaving the soldier to groan and nurse his wounds, Steel rode on. The streets of Menin were crammed with soldiery, both drunk and sober, horse and foot in uniforms of all the Allied nations in a blaze of colours, although principally the trinity of British red, Prussian blue and Danish grey. For the past four weeks since the battle Marlborough had made his headquarters here, in a key position from where he was able to threaten the key citadels of Ypres, Lille and Tournai. Prince Eugene had gone east to Ath to join his own army, to which had been attached a force of twenty-five battalions and the same of squadrons of horse. In all fifty thousand men – a reasonable army by any reckoning. It was clear to anyone that something was afoot, but equally it was anyone's guess as yet as to what it might be. Steel wondered whether he might not be about to find out.

He had not been surprised to have been summoned to the commander's quarters. He had become used to doing the Captain General's business. He wondered, though, what nature of errand the Duke might now have found for him. It was a short ride from Menin to Werwicq, and save for the incident with the drunk it had been uneventful.

Steel pulled up his horse outside the town hall, which Marlborough had commandeered. Tying the reins to the wooden post provided for that purpose, he saluted the two sentries of the Foot Guards, his own old regiment, posted at the door, and walked in. The place presented the customary appearance of any temporary field headquarters, which to the layman might have appeared a form of organized chaos, with clerks and runners moving in all directions, but to Steel's eyes and those of the general staff it seemed the very picture of a well-organized military machine.

A clerk looked up from the desk. 'Yes.'

'Captain Steel to see the Captain General.'

The man, a diminutive fellow with black eyes and a face which in other times would have marked him as a Puritan, looked Steel up and down and began to fiddle self-importantly with a pile of papers. 'Captain Steel. Yes, I'm sure that I saw that order not a minute ago. Captain Steel. You're quite sure that it was today you were expected?'

From the band around his arm Steel noticed that the clerk carried the rank of captain. He wondered which of them had seniority from the date of their commission, and hoped it would not come to a matter of pulling rank. The irritating man continued: 'I cannot find you here. Your name does not appear on the list.'

'I'm quite sure of it, Captain, whether or not my name is on your list. And now, if you will allow me past, please. You'll find that Colonel Hawkins knows me.'

The clerk sniffed. 'Yes, well, I'm sure that he does, Captain Steel, but you must know that, whether or not the Colonel knows you, you cannot enter without an appointment. The Captain General is a very busy man.' He smiled irritatingly. 'You must understand, Captain. Quite apart from yourself he has a good many other officers to see and affairs of state to which he must attend. I'm very much afraid that I can't seem to place your papers at present. Perhaps you would take a seat over there.'

Steel followed the line of the man's pointing finger to the far side of the room, where on a row of chairs a dozen officers sat and slouched in various states of alertness. Two at least appeared to be asleep. Steel paused for a moment and then, his patience breaking at last, he turned on the little man. 'No, Captain, I do not intend to take a seat and wait for the workings of your petty-minded bureaucracies to catch up. I am here to see the Captain General.'

With that he pushed past the clerk and the desk and moved quickly towards the staircase, but no sooner had he done so than his way was blocked by two sergeants of the Foot Guards, both of them quite his equal in height and stature and armed with half-pikes. Steel's hand went fast for his sword hilt, but even as it did he felt another hand close over his own and stop him.

'Jack Steel. Well, here you are at last. You'd best come along with me. The Duke cannot be kept waiting.'

Steel turned to see the familiar, rubicund face of Colonel James Hawkins, his friend and contact on Marlborough's staff. Hawkins was a key advisor to the Duke, a clever, experienced soldier whose instinct and common sense had played no little part in the Duke's victories. He was also the man who these past four years had been instrumental in engineering Steel's promotion through commissioning him in the Duke's service. Hawkins pushed past the two Guardsmen who, recognizing him, stepped aside, and ushered Steel up the marble staircase.

'We were wondering what had happened to you. Don't tell me that these petty-minded idiots have been holding you up. I'll have them all on a charge. You see, this is the inevitable consequence of the Duke's reforms. To the good we have an army of professional soldiers with professional officers, well trained, well equipped and well fed. What you have just encountered is what it takes to make the army so: another army, shadowing the first, whose sole purpose is to ensure that all of Marlborough's great ideas are put into practice. Sadly, sometimes, they're just too efficient for our own good.'

Steel smiled. 'The blame does not lie entirely with them, Colonel. I was a little late in arriving.'

Hawkins smiled. 'Ever the diplomat, Jack. No matter. It's good to see you again, my boy. And you are quite well now?'

'As well as I might hope, sir.'

Hawkins laughed and clapped him on the shoulder. 'Ever a man of understatement. It is one of your most endearing qualities, Jack. Your modesty aside, of course. That and your sheer bloody-mindedness, eh? And how's your lovely wife?'

'She is quite well, sir.'

Hawkins guffawed. 'There you are again. That girl was never "quite well" in her life, Jack, and well you know it. She's radiant. And thriving. And I'll wager that it was all that you could do to drag yourself away from her to see His Grace. And who could blame you? Lucky devil. Ah, here we are.'

He opened a door and motioned Steel to enter a room abundant with carved wooden panelling, part gilded and part painted with landscape scenes of peasants working industriously in the fields of what was presumably a depiction of the surrounding countryside. Behind a huge ormolu desk in the centre of the room sat the Duke of Marlborough. To his right and left stood celebrated generals of the Allied army. Steel recognized Lord Orkney, William Cadogan and a number of others. He noted that all were British and that their Dutch allies were notable by their absence.

He turned to Hawkins. 'D'you not think it would be better if I were to wait outside, sir?'

'No, stay here. The Duke is expecting you. He will not mind. I know that you are in his thoughts.'

Marlborough, apparently oblivious to their entrance, stood up and, peering down at the map which had been spread across the leather-topped surface of the desk, cursed his allies and his health. If only he had been in better spirits, he thought, without this damned headache that returned night and day, then he might perhaps have persuaded the Dutch to accept his plan. But he was so tired. So very, very tired. Feeling his eyes begin to close, he sighed and looked up to address his generals: 'Gentlemen. I find it hard to believe that Prince Eugene, who has ever been my closest ally and truest friend, should have taken the part of the Dutch in this and forbidden our planned move on Paris.'

Steel heard the words and gazed at the Duke. So that had been his intention – to march on Paris itself. To seize the French capital. It was unthinkably bold, a master-stroke that might surely have ended the war. Why then, he wondered, had the Dutch opposed it?

Marlborough continued: 'Instead, gentlemen, His Highness, our Dutch advisor the good Herr Goslinga – fine strategist that he is' (there was a laugh from the company) – 'proposes that we should pursue the Duke of Burgundy and blockade the French in Ghent and Bruges.'

Cadogan spoke. 'His plan is not without merit, Your Grace.'

Marlborough scowled at his friend and second-in-command. 'Sadly, William, I have to confess that you are right. But it is not what we should do. On the advice of Prince Eugene I intend to compromise and take Lille. This, I perceive, will throw Louis into such a rage and terror that he may sue for peace. It should not take more than ten days' bombardment. And once the town is gained, the citadel may perhaps take as much time again. Then perhaps we shall have our march on Paris after all. I do not intend to think about going into winter quarters until we have persuaded Marshal Vendôme to quit his position at Ghent.'

Orkney spoke up. 'But do you really think that our taking of Lille will be enough to persuade Louis to treat for peace on our terms?'

'I have it on good account that as we speak the French King is of a mind to close this war. He knows that his country is being bled dry by our victories. Not for the first time, and I dare say not the last, the flower of the French nobility is being squandered on the fields of Flanders. Besides, I intend to scour northern France as we did in Bavaria.'

Orkney said, 'You'll burn Artois?'

Marlborough nodded. 'Much as it pains me to do so, as

you know that it did in Bavaria, I see no alternative. General Lumley, you will take your dragoons and as many of the Dutch horse as you can get from them and push deep into Artois and as far as you can into Picardy too. Within days I intend to have fifty squadrons along with foot and cannon deep in France. You know that we have had parties of dragoons out as far as Armentières since last week.' He pointed to the map and made a bold sweep with his hand across Picardy. 'We hold the ground and town of St Quentin, halfway from Lille to Paris. Arras and Lens too are ours for all practical purposes. Doullens and Peronne will surely follow. We have already taken French hostages, and you, Lumley, will doubtless take many more, as many as you like, but single out the dignitaries and officials. Louis will not countenance such a move. I have authorized burning and pillaging too. Houses, crops, livestock. Nothing more. No one is to be hurt without cause. It is certain to turn his hand.'

Cadogan coughed. 'We do have some disturbing reports, Your Grace, that the Dutch have already been over-zealous.'

Marlborough frowned. 'Yes. Well, we are bound to have such reports. But what else can we do if we are to bring this war to a speedy end? Ah well, gentlemen, having done all that is feasible I can do no more than submit to destiny. All that remains to be done is to take Lille and to ensure that Louis is aware of our desire to conclude a peace. Now, rejoin your units. We march on Lille.'

As the generals dispersed towards the door, at last the Duke saw Steel in the corner of the room. His face brightened and he picked up a wine glass from his desk. 'Ah, Captain Steel, welcome. You'll join me in a toast. You know what the day is?'

'Only a fool, sir, would be in this army and not know. It is Blenheim Day, Your Grace.'

'Indeed it is, Steel. And how great was your own part in that engagement? And look how far we have come since then.

You heard me speak now, did you not? You see that we are almost at the very gates of Paris.' He took a long draught from the glass as a footman filled another and handed it to Steel. 'But it seems that I am to be discouraged from such boldness. What it is, Steel, to be the commander of such an army of allies! Our allies, Steel. Allies by name. We needs must have them, but at such times as this I do wish that we did not. Perhaps not even Prince Eugene himself. Let us drink to Blenheim, then.'

Both men drained their glasses, and Marlborough spoke again. 'In truth, though, I am not much inclined to merriment. Captain Steel, forgive me. I trust that your wound is fully recovered?'

'Thank you, Your Grace. It is much better, sir. Quite healed. I have a man in the company who works wonders with herbals.'

'Then you must have him come to me when you can spare him. I am troubled still by headaches and the ague. But to business. We have a task for you. Hawkins.'

Having been standing near the door for some minutes, quaffing quietly from a goblet of wine, the colonel strode forward. 'Quite so. We have need once again of your talents, Steel. Our army might not be permitted to march on the city, but there will be a British presence in the French capital ere the week is out. You will take yourself to Paris.'

Steel guessed from their smiles that his gasp had been audible.

Marlborough said, 'Yes, I thought that might throw you, Steel. Understand, though, that we would only give such a challenge, Captain, if we thought you fully capable of succeeding. This is of the utmost importance. Tell him, Hawkins.'

'When you arrive in the city, make for the Hôtel de Boisgelou on the quai de Bourbon. I'll give you the exact directions. There you will find the house of one of our most trusted men,

87

a British officer by the name of Simpson who goes under the alias of Henri de St Colombe. Simpson is our finest spy. He is a little effete, you might suppose, and not the sort of fellow you'd expect to lead a regiment into battle. But believe me, he's unbeatable at subterfuge. He'll be expecting you. We've given him warning.'

'But I don't understand the purpose. What do you need to know? And why me, sir?'

'It's not what we need to know, Jack, it's what we need the French to know. Simpson is merely the contact. Once you're there in Paris, he will help you to make contact with a particular French officer. It is he who really holds the key to this affair.'

Again Marlborough cut in. 'Simpson has informed us that this man, a Major Charpentier, is much disaffected with the war and seeks an end to it. Explain, Hawkins, if you would.'

The colonel continued: 'It is hardly surprising. He lost a leg at Blenheim, Simpson says. In truth, though, it appears that the major is genuinely on the side of peace. He's quite disaffected with war. And you know that we wish for nothing more than a French surrender. Most importantly, Simpson has discovered that Charpentier has the ear of the King himself. Something to do with a boyhood friendship with his father. Consequently, he is held in high favour at Versailles. Simpson has alerted Charpentier that we intend to make overtures for peace – on advantageous terms to us, of course. It only stands to reason to suppose that he might persuade the royal eminence, who, if Simpson and other sources close to the court are to be believed, is already himself becoming unsure of continuing a war with England which has lasted with few breaks for some forty years of his reign.'

Steel's head was swimming with facts, and not least with the magnitude of this new mission. 'How do I find this Major Charpentier?'

'On account of his wound, Charpentier is now second-in-command at the Hôpital des Invalides, the convalescent home for Louis's soldiers on the outskirts of Paris. He has a house in the grounds, although he prefers to live as an inmate, where he can be in the company of his fellow veterans and cripples. You've heard of the place?'

'How could I not have heard of it, sir? They say it is a new wonder of the world, a haven for those ruined in battle with a gilded dome that shines out across the city, a hospital furnished with every medical advancement, a place where the poor devils can live in some comfort and security and with other soldiers. It is the greatest symbol of a monarch's gratitude to his men. I believe that it was the model for our own military hospital at Chelsea, but by all accounts it is on a much grander scale.'

'Quite so. A very haven, but twice as grand as Chelsea and three times its size. We may hope that our dear Queen might some day do the same for her own brave boys. Perhaps you will be able to advise her, Steel' – he smiled – 'being, as you will be, a former inmate of the place.'

Steel blanched. 'You want me to live in the Hôpital des Invalides? As an inmate? With the French? For how long?'

'Only a few nights. Two at the most. You must. There is no other way to meet Major Charpentier. Not only must you enter but you must take up residence there, as if you were passing through the city and had sought out the major as an old friend. No one must suspect that you are a British officer.'

Marlborough interjected, 'I am aware that it is much to ask of you, Captain Steel. You should know too that with Louis now living at Versailles the hospital has become the de facto headquarters of the French army. But we only ask you, Steel, on account of the service you have given in the past. A little more wine?'

He signed to a footman who hurried across and replenished Steel's glass. The red wine was of a local vintage, strong and pungent and packing a kick which brought home to Steel the full importance of his task. As he drank, a question came to his mind, and although he at first hesitated to ask it he ultimately could no longer resist.

He looked directly at the Duke. 'Do not be offended, sir, and please do not think that I shirk from the task, but it merely occurs to me that perhaps Simpson might treat himself with the major and tell him of your intentions?'

Marlborough replied, 'Well asked, Captain Steel. The fact is that Major Charpentier needs proof of our faith in this matter before he takes it to the King and risks his own neck.'

Hawkins continued: 'You see, Jack, he might want peace, but for obvious reasons he does not trust the English as a race. You will carry a letter to King Louis from the Duke himself. This the major, if he has faith in what you say, will convey to Versailles. It's up to you to persuade him that you are to be trusted. Besides, Simpson is precisely the sort of man he detests: a spy. He will only parlay with a brother officer, and one lately returned from the front. You are the only man for the job, Jack. Particularly since you were wounded at Oudenarde. To be honest, he'll love you.'

'But what about a disguise? An alias? What name shall I have? And how shall I get back?'

Hawkins replied, 'Choose your own alias, within reason. I suggest that from now on you will be a captain in the Irish brigade in King Louis's army. You may choose the regiment too. See the Quartermaster General and he will find you a suit of clothes. God knows we took enough to clothe a company after Oudenarde. As for returning here, Simpson has his methods. Have no worries. We shall get you back. And have no fears for Lady Henrietta's safety. We shall look after her, Jack.'

Marlborough looked up from the map over which he had been poring. 'You're quite happy with the arrangements, Captain?'

Steel nodded – and lied: 'Quite happy, sir.'

'Good. And please be assured that should you accomplish your task – as we are sure you must – we shall be most grateful.'

Steel bowed and wondered what form that gratitude would take, should he live long enough to see it. 'Thank you, Your Grace. I am honoured to be of service once again. You may trust that I shall do my utmost to ensure that Major Charpentier is convinced of our sincerity.'

'I do trust in that, Steel. And you may trust that if you succeed you will play a part in ending this war and saving a great many lives. Your own included.'

FIVE

The coach crested the hill and pulled up abruptly with a jolt, and Steel thanked God that it had. For the last five days he had travelled in this infernal machine, and even though the banquettes were upholstered after a fashion the wheels themselves lacked proper suspension, the carriage being merely hung by leather straps from the wood and metal framework, and every rock and bump in the road had been painfully amplified.

He had had only two travelling companions. For the first day he had enjoyed the company of a young captain of foot assigned temporarily to the artillery, who had been seconded from the camp to assist with the transportation of a parcel of French guns captured on the retreat of the enemy from Flanders. The two of them had played a few hands of piquet, and Steel, characteristically discarding the low cards, had taken five consecutive tricks. He had won four guineas and had teased the captain about the ruts in the road having been caused by the earlier passage of artillery. The captain, a jovial chap and a fellow career soldier driven, he said, into the army by a spendthrift father, had not seemed to mind at all and had entertained Steel with tales of the mishaps of cannon and the actual prowess of that neglected arm which would soon come to become an integral part of the army rather than contracted as Ordnance.

Sadly he had left all too soon, and Steel had been joined instead by the man who now sat facing him: a rubicund major of dragoons by the name of Cousins. The man was as tedious as Steel's previous companion had been amusing, and he wondered quite what the lumpish oaf was doing in command of anything more than a dining table. The man's entire conversation, as one might have guessed from his figure, concerned nothing save food and drink. As the hours had passed, Steel had become adept at shutting out the man's words, but somehow they now began to seep into his mind.

'Well, this is my stop and I must bid you adieu, Captain Johnson.'

For a moment Steel looked puzzled at the name, and then quickly answered to his new alias: 'And farewell to you, Major.'

'Until we meet again. I must say, Captain, I have enjoyed your company.'

Steel smiled and nodded. 'Likewise, Major, of course. And good luck with the dragoons. Be sure to keep the French busy, sir.'

The major laughed and made what Steel presumed was intended to be an impressive display of swordplay with his hand, but which instead looked merely comic. 'Oh, you may be sure of that. And good luck to you, Captain, whatever your business might be. You never did get round to telling me.' He paused by the door, as if expecting to hear now the nature of Steel's mission.

'No. I never did,' said Steel bluntly. He had done his utmost not to talk about himself, which with the garrulous major had not been difficult. He had revealed only his name, the alias of Johnson, which he had borrowed from his mother's side of the family. Steel had used it before as a cover on the

Duke's business, and it was sufficiently familiar to ensure that he would not be caught out for more than an instant should he be addressed by it. Closing the door firmly behind the major, he pointed to a group of tired-looking, red-coated horsemen sitting by a small spinney. 'Oh look, Major, your men have come to welcome you back.'

As he watched the major leave, with his attendant dragoons, Steel stretched his legs and allowed himself a few minutes' rest. He would have preferred to travel the entire way to Paris by horse, but Hawkins had insisted that he should take a carriage as far as the farthest Allied lines. Steel recalled his words: 'It is absolutely imperative that you should preserve your strength for your mission. God knows you will have need of it, Jack.' The words filled him with foreboding, but also with the thrill of the challenge that was sure to come. Soon he would be alone in enemy territory, too far from the Allied lines to rely on any help other than his own guile and that of his contact in Paris.

Taking leave of Hawkins, he had trundled out of the gates of Menin and through Flanders with an escort of a half-troop of dragoons. All the while, forty miles a day, Steel had remarked on the fact that they had seen only red-coated troops – Marlborough's men, all of them, hellbent on undertaking the Duke's work of reducing Flanders by fire. For a little of the time Steel had managed to snatch some sleep, glad to make the most of the opportunity to store up his energy, for he knew he would have need of it in the days to come. Waking, he had been conscious of the names of towns called out by the coachman, names which, once familiar as enemy strongholds, he now knew now under changed circumstances: Arras, Péronne, St Quentin. And the further they had penetrated into the heartland of northern France the more acutely aware he became of the brilliance of Marlborough's original, thwarted plan to press on to Paris, and the utter folly of the Dutch decision to prevent such a move.

Now alone, Steel ran a hand over his face and felt the stubble. He had not had the opportunity to shave these past two days, since their last stop at an inn, and without a servant there was no water to be had, hot or cold. He would have to wait till Paris to address his appearance. He cast his eyes into the distance, and from his vantage point within the carriage watched and waited until the major and the other horsemen were quite out of sight. Then, opening the door, he climbed down from the carriage and called up to the coachman: 'Matthews. My bag, if you will. And you can untie my horse.'

Matthews, a wiry Cornishman, lately a sergeant in the foot and now a driver in the personal employ of Colonel Hawkins, climbed down and handed Steel the modest carpet-bag which contained his effects. 'There you are, Captain Steel, sir. An' I don't know what it is the colonel's got you doing now, sir, but I can only say I'm damned glad it's not me as is doing it.' He shivered. 'Gives me the creeps, this does, being so deep in France. Durn't seem right.'

Steel undid the bag and took out a coat as Matthews untethered the chestnut mare that had been tied to the rear of the coach during their journey. 'Yes, you're right there, Matthews. But if my becoming better acquainted with the Frenchies is going to help win this war, then it's got to be right, somehow.'

The coachman grinned, then shrugged and grunted as Steel shook out the heavy serge coat. He removed his own Grenadier's uniform, stripped down to breeches and shirt and donned the new waistcoat, of a vivid red. It was a tight fit over his muscular form, but not wholly uncomfortable. He reached for the coat that he had handed to Matthews and drew it on. It too was scarlet in colour and faced with bright yellow rather than his own regiment's distinctive dark blue. The lace too was subtly different, stitched in the French manner, and the large gilt buttons on the cuff lay in a plain line. In contrast the edge of the coat was richly festooned with gold lace. This was not the coat of a British officer. Steel had chosen it himself with some care. It had come from a bundle of clothing lately stripped from the bodies of the dead of O'Brien's regiment of dragoons, Irishmen in the service of France originally raised by the late Lord Clare. Steel's choice had been coloured by the fact that he had known its commander when, both as young lieutenants of foot in the Guards, the two had fought side by side for King William. But Steel had also seen his erstwhile friend killed in cold blood in the village of Ramillies after surrendering to a British officer – a fellow Scot who lately had been his brigade commander at Oudenarde. Well, that was an old story. And for now the coat of poor Clare's old regiment would serve him well and he would wear it with pride, partly in memory of a brave man unjustly killed.

Matthews raised his eyebrows. 'Very handsome, sir. You look quite the Paddy officer. And hardly a mark on it, neither.'

'You recognize the coat then?'

'Could I not? Fought against Clare's at Blenheim, sir. Took off one of my fingers, the Irish bastards.' He held up his maimed left hand. 'I won't forget the bloody Paddies in a hurry. Mind you, sir, they won't forget me, neither.'

Steel laughed, and, having buckled on his sword, handed Matthews the carpet-bag into which he had placed his regimental uniform. 'I'm sure they won't. But now you shall forget me, Matthews. And that's an order. You never saw me. From this moment, for as long as it takes, Captain Jack Steel ceases to exist. Meet Captain Johnson of the Irish Brigade. And now you may take that news back to the colonel.'

Matthews nodded. 'I'll tell him, sir, just as you told me. Good luck, Captain.'

Putting his boot in the stirrup which hung at the mare's left flank, Steel swung himself up easily into the saddle and ordered his reins. He smoothed his great, broad-bladed sword in its scabbard over the saddlecloth and patted the animal lightly on the neck. Then he turned in the saddle and gave Matthews a last look and exchanged a nod before digging his knees into the horse's flanks and urging her forward into a gentle trot. He went on for some way before casting a single backward glance at the fast-disappearing coach, then he pulled the horse away from the road and onto the grassland of a hillside, speckled with alder trees. The uneven ground was a little soft under her hooves and Steel took a few minutes to relax into her easy stride after so many days in the carriage. Soon, though, he felt reborn, at one with the countryside and back in control of his destiny, as far as that was ever possible. After a few hundred yards trotting gently around the contour of the hill and away from the road, Steel pulled up and took stock of the prospect before him.

Below him stretched the plain of Picardy, a lush valley cross-hatched with a complex patchwork of fields of crops – corn and wheat, he guessed, much of it now cut for the harvest. It was good country, he thought, tended carefully by its tenants and respected by its owners for its bounties. Soon, though, he knew that it must surrender to the attentions of Marlborough's dragoons, and that even after they had passed anything spared would be trampled beneath the feet of the oncoming armies. That was the way of it in this country, long used to war. It was astonishing, he thought, that the peasants should invest so much time in their land when they must know that at any moment it would likely as not be ravaged once again by men who came from far away intent on but one thing – to win the next battle.

He reckoned that it would always be thus. Flanders and Picardy formed a fatal avenue between Catholic France and its Protestant neighbours, and Steel knew that nothing could change this flawed geography. Since Agincourt and Crécy men had come here from France and Spain and the Rhine, and from Britain, come to fight and to die, and in centuries to come they would come again when, just as the bows had surrendered to matchlock and grenade, new and more terrible weapons of destruction overtook their current armoury. For an instant his head was filled with a dreadful, blood-soaked vision of destruction. This was a truth of such epic, biblical proportions that he shuddered at the thought.

At that moment a chill breeze caught the treetops and cut through the dead Irishman's red coat, freezing Steel's blood. But it lasted only a few seconds. Bringing himself to the present, Steel clicked his tongue at the grazing mare and dug the heels of his boots into her ready flanks, and the road fell away before him. He urged her down the slope of the hill, away from the threatening form of the trees and his momentary apocalyptic vision, and within a few minutes his mood had been transformed. Steel thanked God now that he had listened to Hawkins, for despite his tedious companion and the cramped, uncomfortable coach, he knew that he had rested and was now free to feel the exhilaration of the ride. The wind felt good on his face and he knew that from now on he was on his own. In enemy territory.

He thought himself into his new persona. He was Captain Cormack Johnson, if you please. Born in Cork and raised at home by a governess, he had joined the colours at the age of seventeen and served at Neerwinden, Dixemude and Huy – all actions with which Steel himself was familiar, on occasion meeting the Irish 'Wild Geese' face to face. There would be no slip up there, certainly. Of course Steel had no Irish accent, but then he did not suppose that he would require one. Many of the Irish gentry he had come across, including poor Clare, had spoken with an anglicized tongue, and while they might have had a command of the Gaelic, which he did not have, to an untutored ear and, he presumed, to any Frenchman it would not have sounded so very dissimilar to his own Lowland Scottish accent.

He reckoned that it must by now be close to ten o'clock

in the morning, and swore once again that come the next engagement, whenever the chance presented itself, he would find as fine a timepiece as had been liberated by Hansam from the body of a French officer at Blenheim. The early chill was passing now and the sun beat down upon the countryside. He began to itch under the thick coat and scratched at his neck.

He prayed to God that the poor bugger who was the last owner of this coat had not been severely infested. No more at least than Steel himself. For all the army, officers and men alike, even up to the great commander himself, carried with them their little friends the lice, who, living in the seams of their garments, would only be destroyed if burnt or smoked out. No, thought Steel, the coat was just naturally itchy, coarser perhaps than the British model. It was a combination of that and the heat. Who knew, perhaps in Paris he might even take a bath. For a moment he revelled in the prospect. The city, so it was said, was the very seat of worldly luxury and pleasure – a cradle of vice – with such a profusion of gold ornament and decorative splendour as the world had not seen since the Roman Empire. You could, they said, get anything you desired in Paris.

Well, thought Steel, that was a hard one for a man in his position. Perhaps a year ago he might not have found it so. But now he had a beautiful wife who was in love with him, as he was with her, and thus he had no real desire for further female company. She had protested when he had announced that he must go away, but had relented with the promise of further advancement. Steel had not, of course, told her his destination, merely that he was under orders from Marlborough himself. That had been enough to calm her. He knew that she would now be content to await his return. At least she would be comfortable, even on their modest income. Although, even he admitted, perhaps a little more would not go amiss. Particularly with Henrietta's tastes. He had his health, God and the French willing. And he had his profession. What more in truth could any soldier want but rank, wealth, health and love?

He smiled, patted the horse gently on the neck and saw that he was approaching a village. It seemed a small and peaceful place, with plumes of smoke curling up into the fresh air from the crooked stone chimneys. At present, he reckoned, the people would just be entering the height of a busy morning's work. As Steel passed along the street a few of the inhabitants glanced up at him but, somewhat to his surprise, none remarked upon the presence of the tall red-coated soldier. The truth was that they had grown used to such sights. Indeed the oldest of them could still recall the day in 1643 when the Spanish invaders had come here to be met by the French under the Duc d'Enghien at a place called Rocroi and been all but annihilated. What a time that had been. The villagers had cheered their victorious troops from the windows and festooned them with garlands. But today, as this tall, solitary horseman retraced the footsteps of d'Enghien's regiments, there was no rejoicing. The people seemed sullen, and that broke his mood of contented levity. Somewhere a dog barked, and in a distant farm a cock crowed ceaselessly. Steel passed through the place without event, yet once again in open countryside he felt dejected, as if the mood of the place had sent a cloud into the sky directly above him. He could not quite place it, but he knew that in the space of minutes something had gone awry with his apparently flawless world. Nothing, of course, could ever be as perfect as it had for an instant seemed. Quite what was wrong, though, he had yet to discover.

He rode on, passing the wayside distance marker stones as they counted down the miles to Paris and listening to the church bells as they chimed his way by the hour through the French villages. He reckoned that he must be travelling at around eight miles an hour. It was not a bad speed, but if he were to keep his rendezvous he knew that he would have to make faster time, so he pushed the horse on, as gently as he could.

Soon the villages began to grow more numerous and larger, and then they became towns. At the town of Roye he rode at a careful pace below the walls of the citadel under the inquisitive eyes of the French garrison guards, but no one summoned him. No one questioned his presence. To the sentries too this man was merely another solitary soldier in an apparently friendly uniform, a messenger, perhaps, on his way back into France. The men on the battlements, seeing the sergeant of the guard wave Steel on with a cursory glance at his papers of travel (faked, of course), spat and cursed at the devil for his luck, for they all knew Marlborough and his accursed polyglot army, drawn from the gutters of Europe, might be here and upon them at any time. Tales were coming in daily of atrocities perpetrated by Lord Marlbrook's dragoons upon defenceless French civilians. Fires, it was said, rose from a thousand towns and villages of Picardy and Artois. Women, it was claimed, had been raped by the dozen, and scores of innocent suckling infants put to the sword. Had the sentries but known Steel's true identity they would have tried to string him up from a tree with no questions asked. But happily they did not know, and he was also blissfully unaware of the rumours. Confidence increasing by the hour, he made the crossroads at Conchy and took, as Hawkins had directed, the straight road to cross the Oise at Pont Ste. Maxence.

For a further half-day Steel road on. Then, as dusk began to fall and weary from two days in the saddle, he found himself on the outskirts of a dense forest. Aware that this area of the north of France was known for wild boar, and not wishing either to disturb a hunting party or to enter into an argument with one of the notoriously ferocious creatures, he decided to stay close to the edge yet sufficiently within the tree line to afford cover. Naturally, making such a circumnavigation took a good deal longer than had he plunged through the woods, and it soon began to grow dark. Steel dismounted, and having eked out the last of the stale bread and hard cheese that he had brought from the camp and washed it down with the little Tokay and brandy that remained in the two flasks that had been provided by the ever-thoughtful Colonel Hawkins, he wrapped himself in his cloak and made as good a bed as he could from the undergrowth. Sleep, as it always did when he was in the open, came to him unbidden and without much effort, and his last impression was of a canopy of trees above which the stars hung suspended in a cloudless night sky.

He was awakened shortly after dawn by a sharp cry from his front, followed by a shot. In an instant sleep was forgotten and his senses sprang into action. Instinct, which in many another man might have made him spring up and betray himself, told Steel to freeze to the spot. He pressed his taut form deep into the earth and prayed only that his horse, which, sporting an unmistakably military-style harness, was standing a few yards off, chewing happily on a patch of borage, might not yet be spotted by the intruders, whoever they might be. Cautiously and careful not to make the slightest sound, he felt to his side and found his sword. It was his most trusted weapon now. His deadly fusil he had left with the company, exchanging it unhappily for a pair of pistols, given him by Hawkins, which hung inaccessible in long leather holsters across his saddle, their ammunition held in a small leather box on a belt.

The voices sounded again, shouting clearly in French and closer now, and Steel's fevered mind began to hatch a plan. Craning his neck so that he was able to peer through a gap in the foliage, he was able to see one of the figures. The man was dressed in a uniform, but none that Steel had seen before and certainly not military in design. It was of green velveteen and ornamented with gold at the collar and cuffs. On his head he wore a skullcap of the same design, and in his hand

102

he held a long spear. Taking him at first for some courtier in a masque, Steel soon realized that he was in fact a huntsman. As he watched, another man appeared to his left, in similar dress. So that was it: he had stumbled into the middle of a boar hunt. These were the hunters, and close behind no doubt would be the quality, the gentlemen and ladies of the hunting party.

The advance party was almost upon him now. Dangerously close. Steel decided that there was nothing to do but bluff it out. Here would be a test, rather sooner than he had anticipated, of his newly assumed character. The only problem was how to make his presence known without giving the huntsmen cause to take him as their quarry and stick him with their spears. This worry, though, was quickly and violently put to flight by others of a more serious nature. Steel was already in the process of getting to his feet when his horse gave a loud whinny of distress, drawing not only his attention but that of the group of huntsmen, whose numbers had now grown to a half dozen. It was not the mare, however, but rather the cause of her alarm which now froze them all in their tracks. For not five yards away from where Steel had been asleep and where he now stood, clear in the red coat against the undergrowth, the huge form of a wild boar rose up from the dense foliage and stood utterly motionless, staring hard in his direction. Steel reckoned it must be a good five feet above the ground and in length half that of his horse. Its head was crowned by a mane of black hair, and on either side of its flat snout was a long, sharp, curved white tusk. The man nearest Steel stared too. The boar he could understand. He was a huntsman, and this was a hunt in a forest full of such creatures. But what was this other beast? This red-coated soldier who had risen from the ground was something quite unexpected. He was wise enough to know that now was not the time to question who this stranger might be – probably, he thought, a deserter or a poacher. He resolved

103

to deal with the matter in hand and whispered to Steel, in French, 'Monsieur, I beg you, do not move. Stay quite still.'

Steel nodded his head and slowly eased his right hand across his body and down towards the hilt of his sword. The boar snorted, gouts of steaming breath clouding the air from its nostrils.

As he slid the sword from its scabbard Steel was aware of the baying of hounds behind him, and seconds later a pack of hunting dogs broke into the clearing. Seeing them, the boar panicked. Steel's sword was clear now and he held it before him, as ready as he might be for the beast. But it was not at him but elsewhere that the boar's eye was fixed. The hounds were circling him now, gums drawn back and teeth bared, snarling. Not waiting, the boar lunged forward and tore through the pack, tossing one dog to one side with a razor-sharp tusk and goring it. The dogs stood back but the boar went on and hit the most forward of the green-coated huntsmen full on. The man was thrown to the ground, winded and, Steel could see, with a slight cut to his thigh from one of the tusks. The boar stood above him now, head raised, ready to push down with its full weight and skewer the man to the earth. Instinctively, Steel leapt from his position and, landing on the beast's back, plunged his blade hard into its head. But if he had thought to kill it he was wrong. The boar bellowed in agony and the huntsman rolled away before it had time to complete its attack. Steel clung on to its back and endeavoured to withdraw his sword. There was a noise, a shout as another of the men called across to the pack, and suddenly around Steel and the boar a dozen dogs were tearing at the creature's flesh. Its blood flew up in gouts, and one unlucky hound was too slow to avoid being impaled upon the boar's right tusk, where it hung, stuck through in mid-air, howling pitifully. Behind the dogs came the huntsmen. Four firm shoves from their expert pikes were all it took to finish the job. As Steel slithered off the dying creature and at last drew out the gory blade the wounded man was helped away from the scene. Steel stood recovering, and through the noise of hunting horns and shouts he heard a single voice calling desperately from behind the huntsmen.

'Let me see. Let me through. Get out of my way.'

As Steel watched a horse broke into the clearing – a huge black hunter of perhaps fifteen hands, sweating and snorting in the morning air. The green-clad figures parted and bowed in deference. Its rider pulled up before the gory, cacophonous spectacle, and looked upon the scene with an expression which to Steel's mind seemed to marry disgust with pleasure in equal measure. What made such a reaction all the more surprising and unnerving was that the newcomer was a woman.

She was of small stature, with almost the figure of an adolescent girl, and she was breathtakingly beautiful, with an aquiline nose and Cupid's bow lips. Her most remarkable feature, though, was her eyes, which were of a deep emerald green. Seeing the squealing, half-dead dog and the bleeding boar, she let out a gasp not of horror but of delight. 'Oh how splendid nature can be when at her very cruellest.'

The dog, still impaled upon the tusk, was squealing now in a madness of agony. The senior huntsman approached the woman: 'My lady. Might we –'

She brushed him away with her hand. 'Not now, François. Can't you see I'm watching?'

'But Your Ladyship, the laws of nature and all humanity dictate that we must dispatch the beast, put it out of its misery. The boar too –'

'Silence, man! I dictate what happens in my forest. Not nature, and most certainly not humanity. Don't you dare challenge me. Next time I'll have you horse-whipped.'

The man was silent.

It was then that for the first time she noticed Steel.

'Who's this? You there. Who are you, man? And what the devil are you doing on my land? Master Marin, who is this man?'

The huntsman answered, 'I do not know his name, milady, but he saved the life of young Hébert.'

Steel bowed and attempted to look as officer-like as his filthy state would allow. 'Captain Johnson, milady, of the Irish Brigade, in the service of King Louis. I travel on the King's business, milady.'

She frowned and looked at him long and hard. Steel felt the sharp green eyes searching deep into his soul, boring into his mind. He could feel, too, the sweat coursing down his back. It was as if she was deciding what to do with him, just as she might with any poacher or indeed quarry found in her forest.

At length she spoke again, with a smile. 'Well, Captain, if you are on the King's business then you had better be about it. Your uniform vouches for your story. What regiment are you?'

Steel, surprised at her interest, replied, 'Clare's, ma'am.'

'Oh yes, poor Lord Clare. You knew him?'

'Indeed, ma'am. A fine man. A damn shame that he should die in that way. Killed in cold blood – by a heathen.'

She nodded. 'I believe now that you are who you say you are, Captain. But you'd best be on your way. Thank you for saving my servant. Good men are so hard to come by these days.'

Steel was not certain as to whether he had been correct in detecting the slightly salacious edge to her last comment, but her look of parting told him that he had not been wrong.

As she turned and rode away to rejoin the gentlemen, Steel moved across to the head huntsman. 'Where are we? And who the devil was that?'

The man looked astonished and lowered his voice. 'Why,

this is the forest of Pontarmé, Captain. Biggest wild boar forest in the whole of northern France. And that was its owner. You really do not know who she is, sir? That was Her Grace the Marquise de Puy Fort Eguille. She is mistress of these lands and a good deal more.'

Yes, thought Steel, as the man went at last to dispatch the wounded hound, I'll warrant she does have a good deal more to offer. He wondered again why she had shown such an interest in his regiment, but put it down to some aristocratic connection. Seldom, though, had he seen such a display of sheer, sensual blood-lust in a woman.

His horse, though panicked, had not bolted and it did not take long for Steel to get on the road. He had thought that a grateful hunting party might have provided him with a little breakfast at least, but had been disappointed and faced the prospect of little food before he reached Paris.

At Senlis he crossed another river and shortly afterwards the road again opened up before him. Getting into his stride he urged the mare along and she cantered on the earth track leaving clouds of dust in her wake. Indeed so great was the dust that by the time he reached the village of Le Bourget early in the afternoon Steel's red coat had taken on a distinctly pinkish hue. Warily the horse climbed the slope beyond the village and Steel found himself in a small hamlet, Montmartre, where a modest church crowned the hill in the midst of a village that clung to the slopes, the pantiled houses patch-worked with vines. The sight brought on a thirst, and he was looking for an inn when he caught sight of the view away to the south.

Standing at the top of the rise and looking down into a lush valley, Steel saw the city of Paris spread before him in a jumble of spires and towers and shimmering rooftops, with smoke curling up from its countless chimneys. The snake of the river Seine curled through the centre supporting on an island the towering spires of the cathedral. He saw bridges

107

cutting across the water, the huge mass of a palace surrounded by green gardens and the domes and bell-towers of a score of churches. It was a moment he had never pictured, that he should be looking down on the capital of France, the epicentre of the civilization against which he had spent his life at war. He did not hate the French as a race. He knew them to be capable of great things in art, music and letters. But on a field of battle there was nothing to do but hate the man who was trying to kill you. He wondered whether he might ever come to befriend a Frenchman and what his contact Charpentier might be like. But such musings distracted him from his purpose, so Steel began to make his way down into the valley. It occurred to him as he went that he was riding directly into the heart of danger. His journey might soon be at an end, but his mission had not yet begun.

The city had no walls, testimony again to the beauty of Marlborough's plan and to Louis's vainglorious folly at considering his capital to be naturally impregnable without such a defence. The white-coated guardsman on the north gate gave Steel a desultory nod and took his dress at face value before waving him into the city. Steel did his best to recall Hawkins's instructions. From the gate he was to proceed east as far as the rue Réamur and then take a line southeast. He left his horse at an inn with a stables in the rue du Temple of which he had been told by Hawkins. More than likely it would not, he had been assured, be needed for his escape. His fear of being discovered quite conquered by the sort of thirst that could only be born out of battle or days in the saddle, he ordered a beer. It came, brought with a smile by a buxom serving girl. The beer was golden yellow and topped with a head of white froth, and as he wiped the foam from his stubble and swallowed deliciously, Steel supposed that he did not look out of place among the low life that appeared to constitute his fellow patrons. Nervously using his Irish persona in a crowded room in which anyone might have been a fellow 'countryman', he had given the landlord enough money to keep the horse for a week, although he wondered whether he would ever see it again.

Steel suspected, and Hawkins had confirmed, that it was best not to ride into a city such as this. It drew the wrong kind of attention and made you look as if you were not one of the natives, and that, Hawkins had told him, was vital. He knew that he must above all things look at ease. He knew the city would be tense after Marlborough's victory and the army's forays into northern France, and any foreign military gentleman in a red coat, albeit Irish, who looked lost or uneasy might arouse suspicion. The last thing that Steel wanted before he rendezvoused with his guide was an encounter with the town guard, however ineffectual they might be. He knew from past experience that such unexpected meetings generally became more troublesome than they might have seemed.

Leaving the inn, he made his way through the north of the city on foot, sticking to the wider streets and being careful not to look passers-by in the eye. These, he thought, were very different Frenchmen from those of the villages. There was something about them, a swagger and a confidence that let you know they were inhabitants of the place that boasted to be the greatest city on earth. It occurred to Steel that there might be no better way of blending in than to adopt a similar swaggering gait, and so it was that he made his way south along the rue du Temple into the Marais. In a short time he found himself at the river, the cathedral to his right, and thought for a moment how similar it was to London and the Thames, with its water-borne traffic and endless, frantic spectacle. He crossed the bridge to the island as he had been directed and found the quai de Bourbon without difficulty and the house at number 29 with its two imposing seven-foot-high painted and carved wooden doors. The Hôtel de Boisgelou had been built some seventy years earlier in the first flush of development of Louis's reign and had clearly seen better times before the majority of the nobility had followed the King out to Versailles. Above the doorway a plaque stood empty of the coat of arms it had optimistically been intended for. Nevertheless the overall effect was still imposing. Steel knocked at the door and waited.

The door was opened by a serving girl of about seventeen, a pretty lass, thought Steel, who, had he not been faithful to Henrietta, might have instantly engaged his affections. She blushed at the appearance of the handsome officer, his rugged, masculine beauty only accentuated by stubble and the filth of his journey, and, realizing his rank, made an attempt at a curtsey.

Steel again tried his French. 'Captain Johnson, to see your master, Monsieur de St Colombe.'

Simpson had adopted the false name on taking up residence in Paris three years previously, and it had served him well. Steel was unsure which if any members of his household knew his true identity. The girl nodded and smiled sweetly but seemed unsure of what to do next. Before she could do anything, however, she was swept aside by a tall, thin man with a pock-marked face of sallow complexion and a sombre expression. He was dressed in a sober, dark grey coat and breeches, and the look he gave Steel could only be construed as deeply suspicious.

He spoke, in a voice as lugubrious as his appearance. 'Oui?'

Again, Steel explained who he was. The man nodded and stood aside to admit him, before closing the door behind them. He beckoned Steel to follow, and as the maid hurried away below stairs they climbed a dark, narrow wooden staircase to the first-floor landing. The butler, for such was what Steel concluded he must be, knocked on the door facing them and was rewarded by a voice from within. Opening the door he ushered Steel in and announced him: 'Le Capitain Johnson, monsieur.'

Inside the room, before one of two leaded windows, stood a man. The light was growing dimmer by the moment and the man lit a candle at the mantelpiece. He was smaller in stature than either Steel or the servant and he had his back to them.

When he turned Steel could see that he was smiling. 'Captain Johnson. How delightful to see you again. Welcome to Paris.'

The man turned to the servant. 'Merci, Gabriel. Ça c'est bon.'

The butler nodded respectfully, turned sharply, darted Steel an unctuous smile and left, closing the door behind him.

The man spoke in a hushed tone and nodded slowly. 'My dear captain, I am at your service, but here as elsewhere in this city it is best to address me as St Colombe.'

Steel took in his surroundings. The room, like most in such private dwellings, smelled of the mutton fat used in tallow candles mixed with the scent of the dried lavender which lay around the skirting, ready to be swept daily across the boards. It was a modest house, less impressive inside than its entrance would suggest, and was furnished with just the degree of shabby opulence that one might expect from the type of educated, droll, slightly down-at-heel gentleman that Simpson pretended to be.

'You must be tired after your journey. How long have you been in the saddle?'

'Five days, if you count the coach before.'

Simpson looked him up and down and sniffed. 'Long enough for anyone. Now. For appearance's sake to further your subterfuge, we are old friends and must clearly behave as such. It will be a pleasure to become closer acquainted with you, I'm sure.' He smiled. 'Oh, I do not expect a performance as we might see at Drury Lane, Captain, merely a little play-acting of the commonest sort. You know the thing. Brotherly affection. You may embrace me from time

111

to time. A peck on the cheek as we do here in France would not go amiss. Appear to enjoy my company, even if you do not. Smile when you see me. Be courteous, affable and polite.'

Steel shook his head. 'Please, sir. I would appreciate it if you would not seek to teach me good manners. You may trust me to act accordingly.'

'My dear captain, I merely seek to persuade you to lose the look and manner of the battlefield and the barracks as quickly, I hope, as you will soon lose their smell. Gabriel will draw you a bath. Please feel free to use as much of the pomade as you will.'

Steel sighed and gritted his teeth at the insult.

Simpson, seeing his annoyance, went on. 'My apologies, Captain. I was merely attempting to ease you into my world. But I can see that you are already part of it. You will not be dismayed then if I tell you that this evening we are to attend a soirée – indeed, one of the events of the season, what is left of it with the King at Versailles and the Allies at our door. I am afraid that I have business to which I must attend. I shall meet you there. Gabriel has the address and will furnish you with directions. Be sure to take a carriage.'

Steel's patience was being sorely tried. Such details seemed trivial, and he was full of questions. 'Yes, of course. But can I not know how I meet Major Charpentier? What about the Invalides?'

'All in good time, Captain. You are to meet the major tomorrow at the hospital. I have no precise time, but he has assured me he will be waiting for you. You won't have trouble finding it, believe me, although it is beyond the city proper, surrounded by fields. I'll hire a boy to show you.' He walked to the door and, taking his leave, made one final, waspish comment. 'And my dear chap, if it's not too much to ask, do make sure that you're presentable. For a start you had better not wear those boots. They've a tear in them. You'll find some stockings and shoes in my closet. Do try to take some care with your appearance. You really don't know whom we might encounter.'

SIX

The evening was growing dark now. Outside the noise from the street had diminished, and with a heavy heart Steel realized that the time had come to leave the house. He took one last look in Simpson's looking glass. He had spent a time going through Simpson's wardrobe before he had found it: a gold brocade coat with a matching waistcoat and rich red velvet breeches. He had been forced too to abandon his comfortable bullet-torn jackboots in favour of stockings and buckled shoes. The waistcoat he wore unbuttoned to show off a fine Holland shirt. Most uncomfortable, though, was the full-length wig, which Simpson had told him was *de rigueur* in society. It was a 'Duvillier', his host had told him with pride, named after the famous French *perruquier*, and not only was it long, falling about his shoulders, but tall, rising above the crown of his head by some four inches. Made from real hair, it originated from a dozen of the city's female paupers and prostitutes for whom it had bought another day free of starvation and a night away from the attention of love-hungry clients. Steel had tucked his own hair beneath its flowing locks and set it as straight as he could, but, weighing all of fifty ounces, it sat uneasily on a head unused to wearing such aberrations. The ensemble was topped off with a low-crowned black tricorn, festooned with gold lace.

Gazing at himself in the looking glass of Simpson's bedchamber Steel had laughed out loud. He looked, he surmised, quite the part: something of a cross between a Covent Garden Molly and a player. He was a veritable beau, a fop – the sort so well caricatured by the late Mr Farquhar in his last play. Steel had seen it with Henrietta while in London and chuckled now as he recalled the lines. His reflection now portrayed him as one of the sort who in London would have been greeted in the street with cries of 'French dog', which in this case, thought Steel, was very apt. He wondered why, apart from his presumed prediliction for prettily dressed young men, Simpson had instructed him to go to such trouble and who it was, besides their hostess, they might be meeting. Nervous of venturing into the street in his new persona, he felt for his sword hilt and despaired. He had tried to wear the long Italian broadsword that he carried into battle but it had looked ridiculous with his new garb, and leaving it carefully in Simpson's garde-robe he had chosen a small day sword with a thin rapier-like blade and a steel diamond hilt adorned with a long trailing sword knot of lilac and gold. This weapon had doubtless never been drawn in anger, and Steel guessed it would break as soon as it was used. Finally he had selected a cane with an amber-crowned head and a black ribbon, and made his way gingerly down the staircase to the hall.

At the foot of the stairs he waved away an offer of help from the officious butler and took his time in opening the front doors of Simpson's house. Then, gritting his teeth, he stepped out. He had been prepared for all manner of catcalls and insults, but none came. Instead, within a few moments of setting off he felt almost at ease and found that, although his attire still seemed bizarre and must surely mark him out, hardly anyone seemed to be staring at him. Simpson had suggested, almost insisted, that he should take a carriage. Nobility and gentry did not sully their stockings with the ordure of the streets. But Steel had decided against it. He had had enough of carriages and wanted to get the lie of the land. Besides it was only a short walk from Simpson's house to his destination. He crossed the river for the second time that day and, as he rounded the turning from the rue de Birague and entered the place Royale, he knew that he would have no trouble finding the address that Simpson had given to him.

The great square shone as bright as day with the light of four score flaming torches placed at intervals around its façades. Steel stood for a moment beneath the arcade on the south side of the square and took in the scene. Around the four faces gilded and painted carriages were depositing their contents: richly dressed members of the *noblesse de robe*, the cream of Parisian society. In the grand hotels which made up Paris's most exclusive address, candlelight flickered in the windows, but one house was bathed in unparalleled light. The Hotel Camus, built originally by the secretary to Louis XIII and officially number 24 of the houses in the square, had since 1623 been occupied by successive Marshals of France. So much Steel had been told by Simpson with a wry smile before he had left. The tall building stood at the northeast corner of the square on the rue Pas de la Mule and it was to there that the crowds were now making their way across the cobbles. More burning torches had been placed directly outside the doors, and a score of liveried and bewigged servants were helping guests from their carriages.

There was a certain irony that this house should be his destination, thought Steel, for in accordance with its military tradition number 24 was currently the house of the Maréchal Duc de Boufflers. Tonight, though, Boufflers would not be their host; Steel knew that he was far from

116

home – in Lille, to be precise, besieged by the Allied army under the man whom others knew as the Duke of Marlborough but who would for Boufflers always be plain John Churchill, his old friend and comrade-in-arms from the days when the two men had been at Maestricht fighting in another siege against the Dutch in the pay of the Sun King. Bizarre, thought Steel, how wars made strange bedfellows. No, he would not encounter the Marshal in this place tonight. But God only knew what else lay in store for him.

Bouffler's residence had been hired for the evening to another aristocrat, a duchess of the royal line whose own house, a château, lay outside the city. Simpson, who apparently enjoyed her confidences as he did so many of the ladies of the court, had naturally been invited, and it seemed only right that he should bring along his Irish friend, returned from the wars. It occurred to Steel that he did not look quite the picture of a brave Irish mercenary, but he was sure that Simpson must have advised him correctly in his dress. Certainly, as he joined the throng of people outside the Boufflers house he did not feel out of place; indeed, his dress was positively understated compared with many of the creations on view among the men. One of them now came towards him. He recognized Simpson, powdered and bejewelled like the rest of them, clad in an exquisitely cut coat of palest blue silk. Simpson neared him, and before Steel could stop him had placed his right hand on his shoulder and kissed him on the cheek.

Steel drew back. Simpson smiled and shook his head. 'Why, Captain Johnson. D'ye not kiss, dear boy? It is all we men do here in Paris, whatever our persuasion. Be assured.'

Sure enough, thought Steel, around him he could see men greeting each other in such a fashion. The ladies too, of course.

Simpson went on: 'How well you improve with a bath and a change of clothes! You did take a bath?'

'Naturally. Do you not recall our conversation?'

'Every word, dear boy. But still, I sense that from head to toe you are still at heart a campaigning soldier. Your ballroom is the battlefield. You thrive in the mud and mire. D'you suppose that I was once thus? I imagine that I must have been. I can only conclude that I have grown soft living among civilians. Sometimes I truly wonder whether my alter ego has taken over. I am sure that I would not know what to do now at the head of a company of redcoats.'

Steel smiled. 'Perhaps one day you'll find out.'

'I pray not, Captain. I am more than happy doing what I do here.'

Steel, wondering exactly what that was, stared at him. 'Why have you had me dress like this? In these absurd clothes. To what purpose?'

Simpson stood back and smiled. 'Yes. I say, dear boy, I have done well, haven't I? You do look quite the beau. A beau, you know, is a Narcissus of sorts who has fallen in love with his own shadow. Look around and you will see enough of them this evening. Look at them. They hate all who do not flatter them. They scorn to condescend so low as to speak of any person beneath the dignity of a nobleman. Dukes are their cronies, from whom they derive all the secrets of the court. That, my dear captain, is why I frequent their company. And I'm very much afraid that over the years a little of it has rubbed off. I'm almost one of them. You chose well. The gold suits you. But perhaps that hat is a little *de trop*.' He giggled, annoyingly.

'You disapprove of all this?'

'Oh no. Oh no, dear boy. You will most certainly "do".'

'But you haven't answered my question. Why?'

Simpson's face grew suddenly serious. 'I have my methods, Captain, and my reasons. All I ask of you is that you trust me, and follow my words to the letter. This is my country. You are a stranger here. Now come.'

118

They walked from the main hall up a sweeping double staircase carved in pale stone and onto a landing off which rooms led to the left and right in a long enfilade lined with gilded mirrors and paintings.

Simpson took his arm. 'Come, Captain Johnson. We'll fortify ourselves before we make our entrance. Some wine and something to eat.'

They entered the room to the right, and Steel gasped. It was testimony to the time over the last decade he had spent in the field that he was unable to remember the last time he had seen such a display of wealth and entertainment. Beneath walls lined with gilded mirrors and paintings, table upon table lay heaped with all manner of food: a ragout of turkey, a fried head of lamb, roasted capons and partridge, salads, pork tongues, a duck with oysters, mussels, pies, artichokes, fresh peas – the variety was endless. Steel thought for a moment of his men and what they wouldn't have given for such a spread as this, and became aware of a woman standing beside them.

'Chéri. My dear St Colombe, you must advise me on the colour of this silk. Do you think I have made a dreadful mistake? Is it too insipid for words? Come and tell Madame de Soubise. She's being quite contrary. She will insist that it should be crimson.' She looked at Steel with vacuous eyes. 'Oh, excuse me, sir. I must borrow your friend for a moment. He is the epitome of style, the only fount of advice to *tout Paris*.'

Simpson raised his eyebrows and looked at Steel as if to ask what he could do. 'Duty calls. Two moments, Captain Johnson. Stay exactly where you are and talk to no one, unless you must.'

Steel watched him go and turned back to the room, before looking back towards the wall against which he had been standing which was hung with an exquisite oil painting of nymphs and shepherds at play around a statue of a calf.

119

Steel was staring at it, luxuriating in the depth of the colour, when there was a cough from behind him.

'I do not think that I have had the pleasure of making your acquaintance.'

It was a man's voice, and Steel turned to see a slim face set atop a well-built frame almost his equal in height. Its features, though, were obscured behind a papier-mâché mask cast in the character of a devil with a hooked nose and a bursting sun above and below the eyes.

The man spoke again. 'I am sorry, sir. As I said, I do not believe that we have been introduced.'

Steel nodded his head. 'Captain Johnson, sir. Of Clare's regiment of dragoons in the service of France.'

The man looked surprised and stood back to take in Steel's dress. 'You are a soldier?'

'I am.'

The man gazed at him long and hard. 'You will excuse me for saying so, but you do not look very much like a soldier, sir. Your dress, for example –'

Steel cut him short. 'What I choose to wear while on leave is my own business, sir. And that of no one else.'

'Indeed. But you will admit that it is hardly a soldier's dress.'

Steel spoke without thinking and instantly regretted it. 'Do you attempt to insult me, sir?'

'Not in the least. I am the last person to pick a quarrel. I merely observe.'

'Then do not observe me, sir. Or you will pay the same price as those officers who took little care to observe the reality of their situation in the late battle.'

The man froze. 'You were at Oudenarde?'

'I had that honour, sir.' Hardly had the words left him than, with an awful frisson, Steel realized that his too-clever comment on observing must have made him sound like one who had been on the winning side. He attempted to compensate.

'What I meant to say was that Marshal Vendôme did his best in an insufferable situation.'

The man smiled through his mask and Steel wondered whether he had bought the story. 'Indeed. If only he could have done more, he might have saved so many of France's sons.'

'You are against this war, monsieur?'

The man shook his head. 'I would not say that. I am against all things which cause unnecessary suffering. But be assured, monsieur, that I am in favour of all things which are right and just, and if the King declares that this is a just war then I must agree. *N'est-ce pas?*'

'Quite so.'

The man continued. 'The battle was no more than a setback, am I right? The *Paris Gazette* says that it was most indecisive, that not all of our forces were engaged. I think that the British attempt to make more of this than it merits. Sadly, however, for such a small affair, it has split the high command, to our peril. If Marlborough and his allies only knew into what disarray this business has plunged Louis and his generals they would march directly on Paris, that's for sure. And that would be an end to it.'

Steel did his best to suppress a smile. Here then was the proof of his reason for being in the French capital. It was true. The French were split and ripe for surrender. He realized that he must continue the conversation. 'So who was to blame for the defeat, do you think? Marshal Vendôme or the Duc de Burgundy?'

The man laughed, out loud this time. 'Are you serious, Captain? Why, naturally the blame must fall on Vendôme. That at least I know to be the King's opinion.'

'And you, of course, hold no opinion but that of the King?'

'Marshal Vendôme caused this catastrophe, and I have no doubt that he will suffer as a consequence. How can you doubt the guilt of a man whose own secretary had to write

121

a letter attempting to exonerate him? Such a tissue of lies. Have you read it? It has been well copied. Every café and brothel in Paris has seen it.'

Steel shook his head. 'I've seen no letter. I only know that if the French horse had not been told that the marsh was impassable then Rantzau's Hanoverians would not have been given the opportunity to start the destruction on the left wing.'

The man looked askance. 'The left wing? Surely you mean the right?'

Steel bit his tongue. In trying to be clever he had again outwitted himself. Of course his left at the battle, the Allied left, had been the enemy right wing. He shook his head and smiled. 'I'm sorry, of course. I meant the right wing. But do you not agree?'

'Sadly, I am not in a position to pass judgement. I was not on that part of the battlefield.'

Steel stared hard at the mask. 'You were at Oudenarde too? You served in a regiment?'

'Not in the field. I was with the staff. Naturally. We quartered at the mill, at Roygem. But where were you, Captain? Where exactly was Clare's regiment?'

Steel was quite confounded. It was a basic slip in his cover story. He had no idea where Clare's might have been at Oudenarde. Where in God's name had he seen Irish red in the enemy ranks? On the left, no, he meant the right. Opposite him, anyway. Or had they been Swiss? Where was the damned Irish Brigade? Had the man been playing with him all this time? Had he seen through his disguise? Was Simpson perhaps a double agent? He hit on a solution. 'I was attached to another regiment.'

'Oh, really? To which unit?'

'Lord Dorrington's.'

'Indeed. Yes. They fought on our left, did they not?'

Steel, unsure, decided to agree and pray he was right. 'Indeed, sir.'

He was finally about to ask the man whom he might be when, perhaps sensing this, the other pre-empted him: 'Naturally, being where we were, I saw little of the fight, save the glorious charge by the Prussian cavalry which did so much damage to our foot. But how sad and how stupid to use such a brave body of men in that way. Truly, I tell you, Captain, General Marlborough does not care for his soldiers.'

Steel smarted. 'They were not British soldiers, sir, but Germans.' He cursed silently. Again he found himself instinctively defending the wrong army, the wrong general.

'You're right, Captain. Perhaps I do that general a disservice. I never could work out where his loyalties lay. Whatever the case, he carried the day and then we had to leave the field. Really, Marshal Vendôme was most insolent in tone towards the Duc de Burgundy. He spoke quite out of turn.'

Steel wondered again who this man might be and was suddenly aware of the true vulnerability of his situation in an assembly where anyone might be a high-ranking French general.

The masked man suddenly pointed over his shoulder. 'Monsieur Duroc. A word.' He turned to Steel. 'Here's a man who can settle your opinion, Captain. He is the King's chamberlain. We were speaking of Oudenarde and the Marshal's predicament.'

The newcomer began to look concerned. He took a handkerchief from his waistcoat and dabbed at his head before speaking. 'The King is fully aware of the gravity of the situation. Six thousand dead and wounded, nine thousand prisoners, including 800 officers, and we appear to have simply lost fifteen thousand men somewhere in Flanders.'

The masked man waved a hand to calm him. 'There is no need to bluster, sir. We are not invaded.'

'But we have been, as near as dammit. The Allies are at

this moment scouring Artois, laying waste to every town and village, driving off the animals, burning our people from their houses, raping the women, they say, just as they did in Bavaria five years back.'

Steel felt compelled to speak. 'They do not rape, sir. Of that I can assure you.'

'How, sir, are you qualified to know?'

'I was in Bavaria, sir, and there was no rape. Of that I swear to you. No death, save that caused by others in the guise of Marlborough's men.'

He thought back to a terrible day in that extraordinary and otherwise glorious campaign when he and his men had come upon an atrocity hard to rival: a barn filled with dead civilians, done to discredit the English. They never had found the true authors of the crime, and Steel had sworn then that when they did he himself would avenge the innocent women and children of that charnel house. Remembering where he was, he wondered whether he had said too much and whether his face betrayed his emotions.

However, his companion had been further engaged by the flustered chamberlain. 'They are barely two days' march from us, sire. They will be here instantly.'

'Calm yourself, Duroc. Calm yourself.'

The little man turned to Steel. 'I tell you, Captain, Paris is on the very verge of panic. It is one thing to lose a battle in Flanders, but it is quite another to have the enemy raping and pillaging in France itself. It's unthinkable. Why, it's impertinent!'

'I assure you, sir, the British will not rape your women. I know these men. They are honourable soldiers. I have fought against them and they have treated all men well, even their enemies. They aren't barbarians. This is a civilized war.'

The taller man laughed, almost removed his mask and then thought better of it. 'A civilized war, Captain? How can war be civilized?'

124

'We must all work to make it so, sir. What would we do if war were to become a free-for-all?'

'In any case, you speak as an Irishman. You're almost one of them, aren't you?'

Steel thought on his feet, rallied all his wit. 'I am a Jacobite, sir. I do the true King's work, and yes, it's true that I've seen my countrymen cut down by Protestant bigots among their ranks. But that is not the rule, sir.'

Steel wondered what possible interest this French nobleman could have in the behaviour of the British army and its attitude to Jacobites.

'But you must agree, Captain, when a principle is at stake then surely no holds are barred?'

'No, sir. Even in the greatest cause we need some restraint, some notion of justice and morality in war.'

'Ah! I perceive that you are a man of learning as well as a fighter. You may have the look of a beau, monsieur, but you are a true savant, is that not so, Duroc?'

The smaller man smiled peevishly, while the other laughed.

Steel was again unsettled, unsure of himself. 'I make no pretence as to learning, sir, merely what I might have picked up along the way in my life as a travelling soldier.'

'And where, pray, has that taken you?'

Now Steel knew that he was in imminent peril of becoming unstuck. Of course he could recount his own campaigns of the last twenty years. Every one was etched indelibly on his psyche. But they had been fought with the armies of King William and Queen Anne. Now he must carry forward the pretence and answer as a soldier in the army of King Louis. He racked his brain for his alter ego's history. But whether it was the wine or the pressure of the moment, he could come up with none. As his fellow guest began to frown, a single word came into his head: 'Neerwinden. Yes, Neerwinden. We won that day. Won well.'

The man nodded, waiting . . . Steel decided he would have to play the fool, which did not come naturally to him. He must feign ignorance and hope for the best.

A second later someone gently took hold of his right arm. It was Simpson. Such was Steel's relief that he almost called him by name.

'Why, Captain Johnson. There you are.' Simpson turned to the masked guest. 'Ah, yes . . . I do hope that the captain has not been boring you with his tales of life on campaign. He can become so tedious.'

'Quite the contrary, monsieur . . .'

'St Colombe.'

'Quite the contrary, Monsieur de St Colombe. I fancy that he was only just about to start.'

'Then I shall whisk him away before he does. You would never forgive me, sir.' He made a low bow. 'Come, Captain. There are so many people you must meet this evening.'

Simpson ushered him slowly towards the french windows which gave onto a terrace above the house's formal garden, opened them and pushed him through with a sigh.

'Good God, Steel, please. I shall swoon if you behave thus. You must be careful here. You are here for one reason only, to give your disguise a degree of gravity and truth. No one would ever suspect that any enemy officer in his right mind would come to a soirée such as this. Do you have any idea just who is in that room?'

'As far as I can see, the biggest bunch of fops and fools in France. I've never known such hot air. And for what? What interest could such people possibly have in the life of a Jacobite officer?'

'That's not for you to reason. There's a point to your being here tonight. I intend to have you spoken about in Paris in the coming days so that you are adopted into society. Who knows, you might even obtain an audience with the King.'

Steel froze. 'I never agreed to that. Meet Louis? No. Then I really would be discovered.'

'Well, perhaps you're right. But at least allow me my subterfuge. And who knows, back in there I might find one of Louis's courtiers who speaks for peace. But whatever happens I do not want you to cause a scene. That is not the idea at all. This place is filled with spies and enemies. Know that. Now let us return to the party before we are missed.'

Steel nodded. He knew that Simpson was right. He had gone too far in his argument with the courtier. He turned to Simpson. 'Who the devil was that tedious man I was arguing with? You bowed and called him "sir".'

Simpson laughed and shook his head. 'You really don't know? That, my dear Jack, was James Francis Edward Stuart. The Pretender to the throne himself. That was the man who would be our King.'

'Good God. He told me he was at Oudenarde.'

'And that he was, I believe. On Burgundy's staff. Although in name he had command of the Irish Brigade. Well, they are his own personal troops.' He noticed Steel's ashen face. 'You must have managed to lie well enough. He seemed convinced. Good. That went as I had planned.'

Steel stared at him. 'As you planned? You knew he would be here? You planned our meeting?'

'I guessed as much. The Pretender cannot resist a rout such as this, particularly one where he is sure of being fussed over.'

'But I might have been discovered. We might both have been taken.'

'True. But we had to risk it. And now your credentials are assured.' He pressed an arm around Steel's shoulder. 'Come. Let's go back in and join the party. No point in wasting good food and wine. And this time, do have a care, dear boy.'

Steel began to wonder what else this extraordinary man might be capable of, and for the first time started to think

127

that his mission might not prove quite as straightforward as Hawkins had made out.

Back in the salon the majority of the Duchess's guests had now arrived. The room was filled with beautiful women and men in clothes similar to his own, plus a few French officers resplendent in full dress. Steel again felt vulnerable. He looked warily for the Pretender and spotted him in a far corner of the room, still masked and attended by a party of sycophants. He turned rather too abruptly in attempting to distance himself from the would-be king, and crashed into another guest, knocking her into a footman who broke her fall. Helped to her feet by another lady, the woman turned to Steel, without bothering to replace her mask.

He bowed and blurted an apology. 'I'm most dreadfully sorry, ma'am. I didn't see you.'

He looked at her and found a familiar face: the face of a huntress, the callous, sensual beauty from the forest. The Marquise de Puy Fort Eguille picked up her diamond-encrusted mask and pretended to hold it up in disguise. Again Steel was struck by her beauty, principally by the flashing green eyes, which were now mirrored in the flawless perfection of the huge emerald she wore around her neck on a gold chain. It was those eyes which now again made contact with his own. As they did so he noticed that the bow of her puckered red lips seemed to part in an unspoken word.

At length, after they had stared at each other for a few moments, she addressed him: 'We meet again, Captain . . .'

'Johnson, ma'am.'

'You appear to be in something of a hurry. Still about the King's business? Are you late for an appointment? Or perhaps you hasten to some other, more interesting diversion? I do not believe we have met on formal terms.'

She extended her hand and Steel bent to kiss it before straightening up.

'Captain Johnson, my lady. Of the Irish Dragoons. Currently on leave in Paris before returning to the front. We fight in Flanders for the King, against the tyrant Marlbrook.' He had added the last for effect, but instantly regretted it as appearing over eager.

She sighed and put on a wistful look intended to gain Steel's sympathy. 'Ah, me. My husband too fought in Flanders. He was brigaded with the Irish. Perhaps you knew him? The Marquis de Puy Fort Eguille.'

Steel shook his head. 'I am sorry, madame. I do not know him.' So, he thought, that would explain her previous interest in my regiment.

She continued. 'Nor shall you then, Captain, for he died there with his regiment. Only two years back, although it seems an eternity. And now I must wear a widow's weeds. A dreadful tragedy, wouldn't you say, for a woman just entering her prime?' She flashed another smile at Steel and parted her lips an infinitesimal distance. It was enough, and she played on the effect. 'People do say that black becomes me. What think you, Captain Johnson?'

She picked up her full skirts and slowly raised the hem until Steel was afforded a good view of a pretty ankle and calf. 'You say nothing, sir. Do they suit me? Do I make a good widow? Speak, Captain Johnson, or I shall not be pleased.'

'They are indeed most becoming, my lady, and I am very sorry to hear about your husband. I vouch that he died bravely and well fighting the damned British.'

'Thank you, but I'm afraid that he did not. Brave, yes. Of course. But in fact he died horribly.'

She was cut short by Steel's former partner in conversation, the Pretender, still masked. 'Ah, Madame la Marquise. I see that you have met our brave soldier-savant.'

'Monsieur?'

'Why, this young man is not merely a soldier but a thinker.

129

Un philosophe, to be sure. And handsome too. He would do well at your château.'

The man who would rule all Britain bowed to the marquise and turned away. Steel realized that she must have known perfectly well who he was and wondered why she had not curtsied or at least made some sign of deference. Was she so arrogant, or merely on familiar terms with James Stuart?

She clapped her hands with delight. 'What a wonderful idea! Yes. You must most certainly come to visit me in the country. Can you spare the time from your heroic ventures? I'm sure that you would find it a most pleasurable experience.'

'If you promise that I shall not again find myself face to face with a wild boar, ma'am.'

'I cannot promise anything, Captain. When you visit me you must be prepared for any eventuality. Anything might happen. I shall send my servant to find you. Give him your address. Until we meet again, Captain. I shall await your arrival with anticipation.'

As she turned and left him, Simpson hurried up to Steel. 'That woman. The Marquise de Puy Fort Eguille. What did she ask you?'

'Nothing really. My name, where I had served. Not much more. She asked me to stay with her. Why?'

'Stay away from her. At all costs. I could tell you things about her that would make you quake.'

'A woman, Simpson. Surely not. She's damned pretty, don't you think? Not your type, of course, but –'

'Don't be stupid, man. I'm serious. She's trouble. Pure evil. Just leave it at that and don't be tempted to flirt with her.'

Steel smiled and nodded, but Simpson was not sure what the young officer meant by that and whether he would keep his word.

Steel spoke. 'Oh, there is one more thing I've been meaning to ask you.'

Simpson looked grave. 'Ask me whatever you will, although I cannot promise that I shall be able to answer you.'

'Whereabouts in this city does one go about finding a pair of boots?'

Simpson laughed. 'Good God, man. You continue to surprise me. If it's boots you want, you've come to just the man.'

SEVEN

He awoke late, as the soft Parisian sunlight was flooding into his room through a small but sufficient gap in the shutters, and he instantly regretted the events of the previous evening. Turning slowly on the linen sheets and half-expecting the worst, he was relieved to see that the other side of the bed remained unoccupied and that there was no sign that anyone, male or female, had lain there during the night. Simpson of course knew that Steel did not share his sexual preferences, but you could never, thought Steel, be too sure. He trawled his memory, working backwards to the moment when sleep had taken him. Or, rather, unconsciousness. For, of the amount that he had drunk after the party there could be no doubt. Normally, Steel had the hardest of heads and reckoned that he could out-drink the best of trenchermen. But somehow last night, Simpson, damn him, for all his wiry frame and femininity, had matched him measure for measure in Tokay, claret and brandy.

Steel sat up. His head throbbed and his mouth tasted foul. The recent wounds in his leg and arm had also begun to ache and he suspected that he had not done the leg much good by hobbling around all evening in those blasted dandy's shoes. The thought reminded him that his first appointment was with the shoemaker. Simpson was right. His boots were a mess, barely adequate in the field, let alone the city. And he was damned sure that he would not borrow the man's shoes again.

He struggled from the bed, dressed quickly and poured cold water from the ewer into the ceramic bowl. Having doused his face, he found his razor and drew it roughly across his stubble, cursing as he nicked himself. Finished, he wound his cravat about his neck and drew on the heavy red coat of Clare's dragoons, and lastly buckled on the sword. The house was silent, and at first Steel thought he must have mistaken the hour. However, the gilded longcase clock in the hall chimed the quarter hour and he saw that it was past eleven. Clearly, Simpson extended his dandified persona to the very bounds of realism, sleeping well into the day. Eschewing breakfast and glad not to encounter either of the household's principal servants, Steel opened the front door and, mustering all his confidence, stepped out into the courtyard wondering where he might find the guide promised by Simpson. He did not wonder long, for directly outside the door was a small boy. He looked up at Steel and smiled, then motioned him to follow. Together they crossed the cobbles and walked out onto the street.

The day was fresh and sunny and a breeze was blowing along the Seine, which lay only a few yards before them. To their right stood the recently built bridge that he had crossed the previous evening en route to the rout. Looking to his left Steel saw the huge mass of the great cathedral of Notre Dame, its crenellated twin towers silhouetted against a brilliant blue sky. Within a few minutes the worst of his hangover had been dispelled, absorbed by all the smells, sounds and sights of a still unfamiliar city. Following the boy, Steel turned right, as he had been told to by Simpson. That much at least he thought he was able to remember. They walked quickly across the Pont Marie, in

133

the direction of the Marais, but once across the river turned abruptly to the left and began to walk along the quay above the riverbank.

Passing hurriedly along the water's edge Steel paid little attention to the people bustling about him and selling their wares from stalls. All manner of goods seemed to be on offer, from live poultry to hunting dogs, clothing, food and drink. Steel's guide stopped for no one. One thing, though, was evident. Paris seemed changed from the city of the previous evening. He no longer felt such a complete stranger, and for that he thanked Simpson. His baptism of fire had worked, even if he was still at a loss to know his exact position. He tried to get his bearings and, pausing a little way on from the huge cathedral, realized that they had made good ground, for there to his right was the palace of the Louvre, abandoned by King Louis in favour of his court at Versailles. How much easier his task might have been, he thought, had the King elected to remain in his capital city. But Steel was not hard pressed to understand why he had fled. The stench rising from the river, beautiful as it was, was almost unbearably putrid, even for one so accustomed to the stink of death as he had become these past few years. A right turn took them up and into the rue St Honoré, and the boy indicated a shoemaker's shop. Having placed his order in halting French with Simpson's bootman, and being careful to use the alias of Johnson, Steel rejoined the boy and they continued along the street. It was crammed with shops, mostly selling dress materials and such haberdashery. How Henrietta would love this, he thought. Would it be too audacious to return with a parcel for her? He imagined her eyes lighting up as she unwrapped the silks and satins. How she loved him and he her. He would return once he had accomplished his task.

Following the boy, he re-crossed the river by way of the Pont Neuf. A double carriageway ran down the centre of the bridge, and pedestrians strolled at the parapets. Midway across the river stood a huge equestrian statue of Henry IV surrounded by high iron railings, and grouped about it, facing the street, were covered booths in which merchants sold their produce. Steel motioned to the boy to stop for a moment and walked across to the wall, where he leant on the coping stones, looking west. From here it was easy to gauge the layout of the city. The river, with its endless traffic of laden barges, bisected it. To the right stood the Louvre and on the left a series of smart stone houses. Turning, he saw again the huge edifice of Notre Dame and around it the streets of the medieval city. The run of the ramparts and city walls had been transformed into wide boulevards, and nowhere in the city could Steel see an obvious area of defence. Once again he could not help but feel that had Marlborough only been granted his wish to attack then Paris would have been taken without a fight.

Then they walked on again, and as they did a carriage swept past, splashing Steel with muddy water and almost bowling into him. A footman shouted something unintelligible at him from the running board. Stupidly and instinctively, he swore in return, in English, instantly regretted it and hoped that his curse had not been heard. The boy looked at him quizzically, and the error brought him back to the danger and the matter in hand. Pushing past one of the hawkers, who tried to sell him a live songbird in a cage, Steel smiled, shook his head and carried on walking until they had reached the far bank.

There the boy paused and pointed. Steel followed his arm, and at last he saw it: a vast golden dome, its pinnacle touching the azure sky, gleaming in the distance. Steel wondered why he had not noticed it before, for it towered over all Paris. It seemed to him at first an unreal sight, as if it had been placed there by some deity. A palace for the gods. And so it was, in a sense. The Hôpital des Invalides was a building like none he had ever seen before, greater even than Wren's magnificent rebuilt church of St Paul's in the City of London with its own magnificent domed roof. This, thought Steel, was something quite different. It surely outshone all such achievements of man to date.

For fully several minutes Steel was unable to take his eye off the great gold dome. As he was looking at it, the full magnitude of what he had been commissioned to do became abundantly clear. This was his objective, as forbidding and impregnable as any he had stormed these past ten years. He was making his way directly towards the very nerve centre of France's military might. For this was not only the hospital for her wounded but the de facto seat of power of her generals and marshals. While Versailles might house the King and the ultimate High Command, it was here that strategic decisions were taken. Here you would find the highest-ranking officers. Steel stood gazing at the dome, undisturbed by and largely unaware of the hawkers and vendors, the passing gentry and the begging children at his feet. Eventually, however, when the boy tugged at his scabbard, he spun round in reaction, scattering passers-by in alarm, and knew that it was time to get on his way.

Their pace quickened now, for Steel was impatient to get to his purpose. He had no time for observations of the city, but travelled swiftly to the southwest, towards the beckoning golden dome. Impatiently he pushed through the labourers at work on a new quarter of the city and kept going towards his goal. At length, entering the newly finished rue de Varenne, he saw it close before him – not merely the dome but surrounding it a great palace of pale white stone surrounded by formal gardens. He stopped and took in the sheer scale of the place. It was as if a giant had taken up a grand country house, one of Mr Hawksmoor's creations, and transplanted it to the outskirts of this extraordinary city. They had left the crowds and hubbub behind now, and Steel reached into his pocket and gave the guide a golden coin. The boy nodded, then turned and ran off back towards the city, leaving Steel alone. There he remained for a moment, rapt in contemplation, before making his way to the outer gates.

He was walking almost in the open countryside now, leaving the city behind him. The plain of the Ile de France spread out on either side in a patchwork of farmland, making the huge neoclassical edifice with its spectacular crown all the more impressive. But Steel had no sense of space or proportion. It felt to him as if he was walking into the guns. This was as terrifying as any assault. Here, though, he would have no means of retreat. He wondered for a moment whether it might not be more prudent to abandon the peace mission and merely use his sword to do what he did best and kill as many of them as he could before he himself was cut down. But then he recalled Hawkins's words and thought better of it. He was on a particular mission. Peace was now his goal.

How ironic, he thought, that a man who had known nothing all his adult life but the making of war should now be charged with such a task. Steel the peacemaker. He wondered, if he succeeded, how he would be remembered by posterity. Would his name really figure in the histories of these wars and this time as a man of peace?

He turned right and walked through avenues of elms and poplars, along the long, low ramparts, built as if they were a plan by Vauban for the defence of a town. Another right turn and he stood before the main entrance gates to the complex: a double wrought-iron gate, flanked by pavilions bearing carved triumphs. There was a solitary white-coated guard on the gates, although Steel knew there would be more close by. The man presented his musket and asked in French for his papers.

Of course Steel had papers, a handwritten sheet in French

given him by Hawkins, which guaranteed safe passage into the Hôpital and confirmed his name, rank and unit, and also that his purpose was to see Major Charpentier while here on leave. The guard took it and read it carefully before summoning a junior officer who was lolling against a pillar, picking his teeth. The man ambled over and scanned the paper before looking at Steel.

'Irish?'

'Yes. Captain Johnson, of Clare's Dragoons.'

'To see Major Charpentier?'

'Yes, Lieutenant.'

The lieutenant stared at him again, looking closely at his clothes, then shrugged and nodded to the guard before handing Steel his paper and wandering away. The sentry snapped to attention and indicated that Steel was free to pass through the arch, but as he was about to walk on Steel wondered for a moment whether he should acknowledge the young man's evident disrespect for his superior. Was it perhaps a trap? Did the lieutenant have any reason to suspect Steel? Was that why he had been so deliberately rude? If he did not react to this apparent insult, would the lieutenant have him arrested? There was only one way to find out.

Steel spun round and called after the departing officer: 'Lieutenant. Wait a moment, if you will. D'you not salute a senior officer in this place any more?'

The young man swung round, one eyebrow raised. Steel froze. But a moment later the lieutenant smiled, bowed and murmured an apology. Steel acknowledged the salute and walked on, his confidence restored but no less aware that he had broken out in a sweat.

He crossed the wide esplanade without one glance behind him, although all the time he sensed the lieutenant's eyes boring deep into his back. At last he reached the façade and gazed up at the great entrance arch with its lofty, curved stone depicting Louis XIV in armour, seated astride a war-horse, and steadied himself as he often did when under fire. He walked quickly, but not so fast as to arouse suspicion, through the archway and found himself in a airy vestibule flanked with columns and filled with white-uniformed soldiers. As he entered, they stared at him. What they saw, though, was merely another Irish soldier, like the many who found themselves here from time to time. There were always Irish mercenaries here, just as there were Germans and Swedes and Swiss and Poles and all the others. All of them happy to serve in the armies of the great King. The Sun King. They soon turned back to their business and ignored Steel. Evidently this was the guardroom, but they would be satisfied that the red-coated newcomer's papers had been checked at the main gate.

Not wanting to delay here, Steel pushed through the vestibule and found himself in a wide courtyard, the Cour Royale. Paved with cobbles, it was all of a hundred yards long and sixty wide, and lined with galleries of arcades on two storeys. Ahead of him across the square was another elaborately sculpted and decorated vestibule which mirrored that through which he had just passed. In the tall, sloping roofs, numerous dormer windows whose stone lucarnes had been sculpted in bas-relief with what looked like trophies of arms celebrating Louis's past victories. How far he had fallen, thought Steel, their great, invincible Sun King, once so mighty and now trampled under the foot of Marlborough and his triumphant army. And how much still further he would fall, he thought with satisfaction. First, though, his mission must succeed.

The square before him was filled with men. Most were in conversation, a few standing alone. They were soldiers for the most part, the majority of them wearing the dark blue coat of the Invalides themselves. These were Louis's chosen few. These are my enemies, thought Steel, as he stared at them.

Many of them were missing limbs; some wore an eyepatch. In a few cases they needed help to walk – through blindness or maiming. These, he thought, are my enemies, the men whom I faced and vanquished in battle, the men that I killed and wounded. Bizarrely, he found himself overcome with a great and to that minute unknown sense of guilt at what he had done these last twenty years as a soldier. Steel did not keep a precise tally of how many men he might have killed in battle, although he had a rough idea. In twenty years he reckoned it at approaching four score. Of those he had wounded, however, and those left maimed for life, he had no idea whatsoever as to their numbers, and to see so many of his former foes here in such a pitiable state of ruination struck him to the core.

Within a few moments, however, guilt had been transformed to pity, and then, as he began to become inured to the wounded, his eye, with a soldier's natural instinct for survival, dwelt more on those fit to fight, the men who were still capable of doing him harm. As he entered the courtyard several of the Frenchmen paused in whatever they were doing to look at him. He pretended not to notice and was relieved when they turned away. While his progress had been relatively easy, no one as yet had offered to take him to Major Charpentier, and Steel realized that he would have to act on his own initiative.

He looked about and noticed a huge stone staircase leading away from the colonnade to the upper floors. That surely would take him to the commandant's offices. Moving carefully through the crowd, he reached the foot of the stairs. No sooner had he set foot on the bottom step, however, than he found his way barred by a pair of crossed halberds wielded by two guards, one on either side of the staircase. There was a polite cough from his rear.

'Excuse me, sir. Do I take it that you have an appointment with the commandant?'

Steel turned and met the gaze of a French officer, clad neatly in white with lilac-coloured facings and an ornately laced hat. He was immaculately turned out and could only possibly be, Steel surmised, the adjutant responsible for this place. 'You presume correctly, sir. My appointment is with Major Charpentier.' He fumbled in his pocket and produced the scrap of paper.

The officer took it and read it carefully. 'Very good. Please follow me, Captain Johnson.'

The halberds having parted, the officer led the way up the marble steps whose tall, smooth white walls were hung with tapestries depicting French victories of the past century. The man said nothing, but marched at a steady pace past nauseating images of Dutch, Spanish and British soldiers being beaten by the all-conquering French armies, to the top of the flight before turning into the left-hand colonnade. Together they walked to the end towards a tall, plain wooden door. The adjutant turned the handle and ushered Steel into an oak-lined anteroom, its walls lined with framed maps of Louis's campaigns and plans of Marshal Vauban's forts.

'Wait here, Captain. I shall announce you.'

Within the anteroom, a single sentry stood by another door. The adjutant ignored him, tapped twice and entered.

'Captain Johnson, sir. Of Clare's regiment.'

He nodded to Steel, who followed him in. Inside he found three men. One of them, that nearest to Steel, who had been poring over a map on the room's large central table, looked up.

He was in his late thirties with a round, moon-shaped face and a full brown wig. Major Charpentier left his map and went to greet Steel at the door. He walked slowly, supporting himself on a crutch, for where his right leg should have been was nothing more than a flap of blue velvet, delicately trimmed with gold braid.

141

'Captain Johnson.' He nodded briefly at Steel, who knew instantly that the man was in earnest. It was the only sign it was possible to make in acknowledgement of their real purpose, but it was enough to relieve Steel's anxiety. It seemed evident that neither of the two other men were privy to their purpose. They stood over by the window, deep in conversation above a rectangular table draped with a green baize cloth on which were arranged hundreds of small figurines. Toy soldiers. The adjutant glided from the room and Major Charpentier led Steel into the office and across to the table.

'Gentlemen, may I present Captain Johnson of Clare's regiment. Another of our Irish "Wild Geese". Captain, I have the honour to present Major Claude Malbec of the Grenadiers Rouge, recently returned from the front. Perhaps you know him. Certainly you will be acquainted with his achievements at arms. And perhaps too you will know my other guest. This is more likely, I think. He is a fellow officer in your "Wild Geese" a captain of Dillon's regiment and a fellow Irishman.'

Steel was at a loss. Charpentier knew of his mission and his cover, and the importance of preserving it. Why then, he wondered, subject him to such peril? Was it not clear to the commandant that a meeting at close quarters with a bona fide Irishman might ruin everything?

Charpentier spoke the man's name, but such was Steel's agitated state of mind that he did not hear it clearly. He was about to ask again, but by then the officer had turned to face him and it was no longer necessary. Instantly, Steel froze. The young man's eyes looked into his own and he felt himself shudder to the core. For a passing moment Steel thought that he must be imagining what he saw. Then, as in a dream, he felt quite dizzy. And only now did he hear the major's words.

'Captain Johnson, may I present Captain Alexander Steel.'

142

The man who now looked at him with a curious yet friendly smile was none other than Steel's younger brother.

Alexander Steel was perhaps two inches shorter than his older brother, but of the same athletic build, and he had the same distinctively sharp nose inherited from their mother and similarly piercing blue eyes. Fortunately for Steel, his brother favoured a long, full wig, for otherwise their striking facial resemblance might have aroused some comment among either of their two fellow officers. For a moment neither man spoke, but merely stared at the other. At length Steel sighed with relief as Alexander broke the awkward silence.

'Honoured, I'm sure, sir. You serve with Clare's? A sorry business, that which befell His Grace at Ramillies.'

'It was, Captain. A terrible thing to see.'

'You were there? With O'Brien when he died?'

'As close as I am to you now.'

Alexander smiled. 'Well, that at least is a comfort. I mean, it must have been a comfort to my lord Clare to know that he was surrounded by loyal friends and countrymen.'

It was not hard to detect the irony in his voice, and Steel hoped that it had been lost on the two Frenchmen. He stared at his younger brother, still incredulous. Had Alexander known he was coming? Was he in on the plan with Charpentier? Steel had never known him as anything other than an ardent Jacobite. Surely he had not betrayed his faith? It was not his way. Perhaps it was a trap. But then what use was he to Charpentier?

Realizing that he had said nothing for a conspicuous length of time, Steel broke away and turned to the other officer, Major Malbec. But, seeking relief, he found none, for there was something curious about the scar-faced French officer that struck a faint chord of recognition in him. Annoyingly, though, Steel was unable to place him. Thankfully, from the look on the other's face, he reasoned that he too was finding

143

it hard to recall where they might have met. Wherever it had been, Steel concluded, he was certain that it had not been in the most cordial of circumstances.

Major Charpentier, puzzled by the awkward silences, sought to defuse the tension in the room and pointed to the miniature soldiers on the table.

'What do you think to these, Captain? They have become a little passion of mine. There is not much more for an old soldier to do when he is down to one leg. They keep me amused, my little table-top warriors. The bulk of them were a gift to me from the King himself, God save the dear man. Merely a few hundred of the thousands of figures he inherited from his father when he came to the throne. He was only four years of age then, an infant thrust into kingship. But how he grew! Our generals used these figures to teach him the art of war, you know.'

Malbec spoke. 'You cannot deny that they taught him well, Major. We have been at war these forty years. And look at his victories: Cassel, Rheinfeld, Fleurus, Neerwinden. What glory, Charpentier! Even you, with your maimed leg, cannot deny that. And how many captured colours did we bring back to hang on the walls at Versailles? You know, Charpentier, perhaps if we were to fight a few exercises with these little men we might all learn a lesson or two.'

Steel winced at the major's crowing, and bit his tongue. He thought of Blenheim, of Ramillies and their recent glorious victory at Oudenarde, but naturally said nothing.

Charpentier replied, 'We certainly couldn't do any worse than we have recently. What a shambles.'

Malbec's voice turned bitter. 'There must be some way to outwit the good Lord Marlbrook. If only we could rid the world of the damned English general. If we could only defeat him, just once.'

Charpentier, who would normally have liked to add his

opinion, chose not to become involved in the rant, aware that he must maintain his bravado even though on the inside he burned with hatred for everyone and everything that stoked the flames of a war that had cost him his leg, and a great deal more. He picked up one of the soldiers, a beautifully painted dragoon, and now absorbed by his miniature universe he continued, 'Of course the King commissions new reinforcements for his little army regularly every year. I must manage whatever and whenever my meagre purse allows. Which is rarely ever at all. My figures, all but those presented by the King, are made from tin. The King's, naturally, are all cast in silver. Lead and tin are cheaper, but silver is without doubt the more beautiful, even under the paint, wouldn't you say? They're all hand-painted, of course. Two of the pensioners here do them for me. Remarkable eyesight.'

Steel looked closely at the figures. They were flat, two-dimensional models which, when looked at from the end on, all but disappeared. Now that, he thought, would be a clever trick on the battlefield. Here were tiny dragoons and hussars; miniature cannon, complete with a team of mules and a driver. All were painted in the exact uniforms of two opposing armies: one, from their colours clearly British, in scarlet coats and coloured facings, the other French in white, grey and blue. The standards which flew above their heads were also hand-painted, on silk, hung with tiny cords of gold wire. Steel recognized the Royal Foot Guards and another regiment of foot which he thought might have been supposed to be Orkney's, from its colours. On the French side he could make out grenadiers and several famliar enemy regiments from Ramillies and Blenheim.

At last he spoke. 'They're exquisite. I've never seen the like. Although I did once hear that the late King William had used similar miniatures in a room at the Horse Guards to organize the reforms of his army.'

145

Alexander responded, 'By the late King I trust that you mean the Dutch usurper, do you not?'

How stupid I am, thought Steel. 'Of course, it was merely a convenient term. He was the usurper, just as Anne now insults the throne in her turn.'

Steel found himself once again looking at Malbec. He recognized this man. He was still not sure from where, but now he was certain of it. Steel searched his mind and tried to place him, and realized that if he was now so sure then surely the man must also recognize him?

The French officer regarded him quizzically, as if thinking. Steel was certain that his cover was about to be exposed. But the officer said nothing. Malbec merely smiled and shook his head. Then he said, 'You serve with Clare's?'

'Sir.'

'Ah yes, Viscount Clare. The poor man died at Ramillies, did he not?'

'You're right, sir. He was killed in cold blood. But didn't we take two of their colours, and one of them Marlborough's own? Our colonel is now the new Lord Clare.'

'You stay here long, Captain?'

'I return in two days to the front.'

'If we still have a front, eh, Captain? After the recent débâcle with the good Marshal. I do not care for politics. I am a simple soldier. Enjoy our palace of cripples and heroes, Captain, and pray that you too do not end up like them. The major here is a fine host, but I too must return to the front soon. Perhaps we shall encounter each other on the field of battle.'

Perhaps we shall, thought Steel, but not I'll wager in the way you seem to believe. Unless you dissemble and have found me out already, in which case I may not make it back to our lines. Steel smiled and bowed. 'Perhaps, Major. It would be an honour and a pleasure to serve at your side against the invader.'

Charpentier broke in, 'Gentlemen, I hesitate to appear discourteous, but would it be too much to ask you to take your leave? Captain Johnson and I must settle the mundane business of his accommodation, and I intend to give him a tour of our establishment – although I trust that he will never have need of a longer stay.'

All of them laughed at the major's black humour.

Malbec bowed and moved towards the door. 'Charpentier, thank you for your time. My men appear to have been well received here, as ever. I have but a few more trifling questions. Perhaps tomorrow.'

'Until tomorrow, Major.'

Malbec turned to Steel. 'Captain Johnson. Until we meet again. Wherever that may be.'

Steel bowed again. 'Your servant, sir.'

As Malbec left the room, Steel's brother approached him and for a second he thought that he might give him away. But, to his relief, Alexander merely bowed.

'Major Charpentier, I shall take my leave. And thank you again for your hospitality during my convalescence. God willing I shall not have need of your establishment again.' He turned to Steel. 'Captain Johnson. No doubt we too shall meet again, very soon I hope. We Irishmen must stick together. You see, Major Charpentier, we are almost like brothers to one another in the Irish Brigade. Isn't that right, Captain?'

'Brothers indeed, Captain Steel. Until we meet again.'

Alexander Steel left the small office. Closing the door behind him, and listening to his footseps as he moved away, Charpentier eventually spoke, in a quiet tone, even though they were quite out of earshot.

'We must not be overheard. And I shall not use your real name. I do know who you are, however, and I know how you came by your fame: the captured colour at Blenheim, the saving of a regiment, the prize of Ostend, and more besides. I salute you, Captain, as a valiant fellow soldier. You recognized Major Malbec?'

'Yes. But I cannot place him.'

'He too is a hero to his country. And what of Captain Steel? You seemed to know him too for a moment? You share the same name.'

'He is my brother. You knew?'

The major smiled. 'I thought as much. And I was right in my assumption that he would not betray you. You share a certain look. But I don't think that Major Malbec suspected. It must be hard, no, having a brother who fights for the enemy? What should you do if you met him in battle?'

'I pray to God that will never come to pass, Major. It would be more than I could bear.'

'But face it, Captain, it stands to reason. As this war rages on and those who are left of the men who began it grow smaller in number by the year, then at some time, one day on a field of battle, you will encounter your brother.'

'I cannot deny the truth, sir. But perhaps we can bring about an end to the war and ensure that such an encounter can never take place.'

The major smiled again. 'I like your spirit, Captain. You remind me of a certain young captain of infantry, a man yet untainted by the scars of battle. A whole man then. Another lifetime. A world away.' For a moment he paused, lost in melancholy, until Steel roused him from it.

'I have something for you, Major. The purpose of my mission.' He reached inside his waistcoat and produced the letter from Marlborough. He handed it to Charpentier. 'A note of honour, sir, containing proof of our good intentions, delivered from the Duke of Marlborough himself. It is addressed to your King.'

The major took the letter and, pausing only to look at the handwriting, tucked it securely inside his own waistcoat.

'Thank you, Captain. I realize that you have risked much to deliver this most important document. You may rest assured that it will reach the man for whom it was intended, and let us pray that it will achieve its purpose. This war is bleeding France dry. If we allow it to continue it will kill and maim all our young men. The King has lost his way. Oh, he is still a great man, the greatest perhaps we have ever seen. But now, Captain, he is old. He does not understand what it is to make war today. He cannot know the suffering. And in what name? A greater France. Surely he has made France greater than she has ever been? What more? The throne of Spain? A worthless country. Why? Vainglory. No more. He is controlled by his generals. But perhaps when he sees this letter from his greatest adversary offering him peace on good terms, perhaps then he will call an end to this madness and you can all go home, back to your loved ones, before you are killed or end up like me, an old cripple.'

His tone was despairingly bitter, and Steel could see tears welling in his eyes. 'Have you seen them?' He indicated the courtyard. 'My children? My patients? They are young men, most of them. But they are young men with no future, Captain. They will have no families. They will father no children. They will know no joy. I hear them in the night, when I pass along the corridors. I hear them weeping.'

He paused and crossed to the window, where he picked up one of the tin soldiers. 'So I shall take this letter to the King in person, and I will tell him, Captain Steel, just who it was who delivered it to me here, in Paris. Captain Jack Steel, the hero of Britain's great army, come to meet me and offer us peace with honour. And then perhaps our King will listen to reason. That will be the measure of his greatness.'

He wiped briefly at his eyes. 'And now, as you are here,

149

captain, and you are my honoured guest, whatever your true allegiance, as one soldier to another, please allow me to extend the hospitality of the Invalides. Let me show you how a real monarch rewards those soldiers who would give their all in battle in his name and for his greater glory.'

EIGHT

The major led Steel across his office to the door and out through the anteroom into the cool of the high stone arcade which ran the length of the courtyard of Les Invalides. Looking down to the cobbles Steel saw that a company of infantry had formed up in line of threes. They wore the uniform of the Invalides: dark blue trimmed with crimson and a soft black infantry hat. The men carried a half pike and the officers swords, and they dressed their ranks as well as any he had seen, save perhaps the Foot Guards. This was made all the more remarkable by what distinguished this company from any other he had ever seen – their physical state. Most were amputees, and the greater part of these were missing a leg, its place being taken by a wooden post. Others were lacking in hands and eyes.

'You see how our men keep themselves in the military way. Sense the pride in them, Captain. They must have at least twenty years of uninterrupted military service to be considered for permanent admission here, as well as an incurable disability. These men are real heroes, Captain Johnson.'

'I do not doubt that, Major.'

Steel walked in silence beside the major, his eyes on the crippled company below, his thoughts on the legacy of the wars

151

he had fought. At length they reached the ground floor and, directed by Charpentier, he entered the refectory. Seated along the lengths of walls hung with more tapestries of French victories, some four hundred soldiers were taking their dinner. At another table in the centre of the room sat a dozen sullen-looking men.

'Why are those men separated?'

'That is the water-drinkers' table. Those men will have no wine with their food. They are being disciplined for not having respected the rules of our establishment. They must obey the rules, Captain. On that matter I am most particular.'

What a peculiarly French punishment, thought Steel, to deprive a man of his wine ration. He wondered what the equal would have been in his own army, certain that it would have involved the use of the lash.

Charpentier was explaining the rules. 'We have four sittings at every mealtime of four hundred men each. At present we accommodate some sixteen hundred hospitaliers. The men are billeted six to a room, officers two or three. They are forbidden to store any food, wine or tobacco. Officers may come and go as they please, but the men require a pass to leave the hospital. I can see that you are impressed, Captain.'

Steel nodded and smiled, but he was barely listening. He had noticed that they were being watched by two of the Invalides. One had an eye patch, the other carried himself on a crutch. Before he could move Charpentier away, the duo had approached them. The one-eyed man spoke – alarmingly, in fluent English, albeit with an Irish brogue.

'Major Charpentier, sir. We couldn't help but notice, your honour, that your friend here wears an Irish coat.' He turned to Steel and gave a short bow. 'Good day to you, Captain. It is always a pleasure to meet a fellow Irishman.'

Steel stared into his eyes and saw at once that they were filled with suspicion. 'Good day. Indeed it is. What was your regiment?'

'Well, Your Honour, I was with Bulkeley's foot. But Seamus here was with Clare's Dragoons. Which, unless I'm mistaken, would be your own regiment, sir?'

'Indeed. I serve with Clare's. Although I joined but lately, having been in Roth's these past ten years.'

'Is that right, sir? Well, that's another fine regiment. To be sure, you're a fortunate man, sir, to have served in two of the finest regiments that ever there were. And didn't Roth's fight at Cremona? What a tale that must be to tell. Wasn't it yourselves that held the gate against the Austrians? To be sure, sir, I'd like to hear your tale. And Seamus, too, to swap stories with a fellow man of Roth's. Are you here for long, Your Honour?'

'Sadly, no. I must leave tomorrow. I am afraid that I cannot see when we might have the time to speak. I shall have to forgo the pleasure.'

The Irishman smiled and bowed to Steel and Charpentier. 'Good day to you, sirs. A real pleasure meeting you, Captain.'

That, thought Steel, did not go well. To have carried himself off through the conversation at the rout and the encounter with Malbec, only to be outed by an Irish bog-trotter, seemed unjust in the extreme. Charpentier seemed oblivious.

'You see, Captain, just what heroes we have here. Truly we are united across rank and even the country of our birth. United in our pride and in our suffering.'

'He might have seen through my cover, Major.'

'Oh, I don't think so. The man's quite simple. A pleasant enough fellow, and damned brave in his time. Lost his eye at Blenheim. But he'll not trouble you, Captain. Now, shall we eat?'

It was after six when Steel stepped outside and walked down the cool colonnade towards the staircase. Having been shown his quarters he welcomed the opportunity to have some time to himself after an exhausting few hours of relentlessly

153

inhabiting his alias. He had not encountered either of the Irishmen again, for which he gave thanks. It was the one-eyed man who sprang immediately to mind, however, as, nearing the staircase, ahead of him in the twilight he caught sight of a silhouette against the wall. It was a man, certainly, standing half-seen in the shadows. A man clearly determined not to be seen. Waiting. Instinctively Steel's hand moved to his sword hilt, and as he passed the shadowy figure he prepared to draw. But the silhouette made no similar move. The man merely spoke. Just one word, but it was more than enough to disarm Steel.

'Jack.'

Steel stopped where he was and turned slowly towards the voice. He had known that his brother would find him after their first encounter, but he had not been prepared for it to happen so soon or in such a public place. As he turned, a group of pensioners walked past him and one of their number, seeing his coat, muttered a pleasant 'good day' in English. Steel turned and nodded towards them and then turned back to the shadows.

'Alexander. It is you. Thank God. We need to talk.'

Alexander Steel walked out of the shadows, and to Steel's surprise he was smiling. He embraced his brother.

'Captain Johnson! What a pleasure it is to see you again after so many years. And now you are in the service of King Louis. I must confess, I never had the slightest notion that you would join us. But tell me, why the name?'

Steel could not tell whether his brother genuinely believed that he had gone over to the Jacobite cause or whether he suspected that he was a spy. Alexander had always been a canny boy, expert with a rod and a line and as devious in his pursuit of mischief as he was of the stag. He had an enquiring, naturally cynical frame of mind, and Steel suspected that, while he might have wanted desperately to believe that his elder brother had joined the true cause to restore the

154

Stuart monarchy, he knew that Steel's real purpose here was diametrically opposed to his own. Seeing Steel's sombre expression merely confirmed his suspicions, and Alexander let go of his arm.

'Why are you here? I know you're no turncoat. Not you, Jack. Never could be. You're too simple and too true a soul to ever betray your first love.'

Steel raised an eyebrow.

'The army, Jack. And if you're not here to betray your own side, then there's only one conclusion. You're a spy.'

He studied Steel's changing expression closely and, despite all the years they had been apart, in that instant the love of a brother and his ability to see deep into the other's soul told him all he needed to know.

'Oh, good God, Jack. I'm right, aren't I? Tell me that I'm wrong. Tell me that you're not here for a reason I'm fast beginning to guess. Tell me that you wear that coat as an officer of Clare's and for no other reason.'

Steel shook his head. 'I cannot lie to you. You're too clever for me, Alexander. Always were the sharper.'

'Christ, Jack. Are you insane? Do you realize quite where you are? Do you know who that man was with me in Charpentier's rooms?'

'Major Malbec?'

'Major Claude Malbec. One of the most decorated and perhaps the most unscrupulous, most determined and certainly the most devoted officer in all King Louis's army. He hates the British with a vengeance. They killed his family, Jack. At Le Havre. Bombed them. His wife and children. Have you any idea what Malbec would do if he discovered who you really were?'

Steel sighed. 'I have a vague notion.'

'A vague notion? There'd be nothing vague about it, Jack. D'you know, it seems to me that in these past few years you must have half lost your mind. He'd kill you, Jack. No less.

And he wouldn't be too picky about the way he did it. Why the devil have you come here? No, don't answer that. I don't really want to know. God knows what I'd do with the information. You'd better just go. Go now before you're caught and it's too late.'

He shook his head and rubbed at his eyes. They looked down at the stones. Steel said nothing, but when Alexander looked at him again he could see that his brother was smiling.

'I might have known you'd do something like this. You're too bloody reckless by half. You always were a wild card, Jack. So you're not content with the battlefield, eh? Not enough danger out there for you? Not enough death?'

Steel looked hard at his brother and wondered at his faultless and undiminished ability to see into his soul. He caught his look again, a look of understanding that told him that, whatever he might have done, and to whomsoever he now had pledged his sword, his brother's love for him remained undiminished. He attempted to return the same expression.

Alexander spoke again: 'We should talk properly. You might need my help. But we cannot speak here.' He laughed. 'You do seem able to pass yourself off as an Irish officer. Perhaps we should find a tavern. Have a drink together. Like in the old days, eh? I warrant you've still the harder head.' Steel smiled as his brother went on. 'There is much I need to ask you. But only don't tell me why you're here. I don't want to know and I don't want to become involved. Heaven knows, staying alive is hard enough in this cursed war.'

'You've seen much fighting then?'

Alexander looked at him and grinned. 'Have I? Well, I'll wager that you have. Seen fighting? As I said, we have much to talk about. I know a place nearby where we shouldn't be troubled. Come now, we can pass freely through the gate. Just keep thinking in Irish, Captain Johnson, and don't look back.'

*   *   *

One hour and two bottles of claret later, two officers of Irish foot who bore an uncanny resemblance to one another were to be observed in a dark corner of a small inn on the corner of the rue Babylon and the rue du Bar. It was not exactly the venue that Steel would have chosen for a family reunion: a down-at-heel whorehouse filled with street sellers and assorted low-lifes. But it would do. Alexander had been bursting for news of the family, and Steel had given him all that he had known, which was precious little, for since his father's death he had had little to do with his elder brother back in Scotland. Carniston House, to the southwest of Edinburgh, and all the secret and precious places that the two of them had known as boys were another world to him now, so much so that he felt that he too might have taken voluntary exile.

Alexander was openly disappointed. 'I have a yearning for Carniston, Jack. I would see the old house just once more, before I die.'

'Die? Why should you die? You seem well enough to me. Hardly an Invalide.'

Alexander shrugged. 'I was only here on account of a leg wound and the fact that my colonel is an old friend of Charpentier's. It's a fine place your masters would do well to emulate. We should do honour to our soldiers, Jack, on whatever side they fight. Those wounded in battle especially. A civilized country must need have such places.'

'I meant that you hardly seem to me to be about to die, dear brother.'

Alexander stared into his goblet of wine. 'You know how it is, Jack. What this war does to a man. And you know, as all soldiers do, how fickle fate can be. She spares no one, Jack. All receive equal treatment at her hands. The dice do not know rank and privilege. Cannon shot and musketball will carry us all off some day, you and I most certainly.' He took a long drink and wiped his mouth on the back of his cuff.

'I love that old house, Jack. We should live there again. You and I. Alistair does not care for it. That I know. It is a travesty that he should have it.'

Steel glared at him. 'It's a pretty notion, but I hardly think you have any claim to Carniston. Remember that it was you left us, Alexander.'

'I followed my conscience and my faith.'

'Father lay dying and you walked out and didn't look back.'

'Jack, you know I had a duty. You of all people should know that. The King had need of me.'

'Aye, you had a duty . . . to your family. Where was your duty to your father?'

'He was an old rogue, and well you know it. He squandered away the family money. Be reasonable, Jack. I had a duty to the King.'

'The King? No King that I serve.'

'Ah well, here we are again. The rightful King, Jack. The King whom I serve. That same King to whose father and grandfather our own father was loyal throughout the civil wars. He believed in the monarchy, Jack. The God-given monarchy.'

'He believed in the monarchy, aye, but not a monarchy that betrays its people and has lost the right to power. Any monarch has the moral responsibility now embodied in our rightful Queen. My Queen is Anne, true heir to Charles Stuart.'

Alexander shook his head. 'For all her virtues, Jack, her line is not direct. You know the rightful heir to be King James. We have no doubt. I was with him several years at St Germain.'

'So while you were toadying to the King, I sat and watched as father lay dying, as he choked and coughed blood and the breath left his body. And where were you? In some gilded salon making small talk with a duchess.'

Alexander stiffened and put down his wine. 'That's a

158

calumny, Jack. I have served full ten years with the colours in the field. Take it back, or I've a mind to call you out, brother or not.'

Steel shook his head. 'This is stupid. We should not quarrel, Alexander. What would Mother say?'

'Mother was a saint.'

'Aye, that she was, a long-suffering saint. I often wonder whether had she lived we might not have become the men we are.'

He thought of their mother, who had died when he had been only fifteen, thought of her last days in the high bedroom at Carniston. Once again he was back in that dark panelled room with the scent of lavender and oranges and the terrible, heart-splitting cough of the frail, beautiful young woman whom he had loved so much. He saw again her pale, aquiline face which had still managed a smile even in her agony. And then he saw her in death, the waxy, doll-like pallor and the fixed smile of release, and he felt as if he might weep again as he had for months after. Instead, and in an effort to regain his composure, he took a long drink and saw that Alexander too had been lost in reverie.

He put down his goblet of wine. 'And what would she say to us now, Alexander? What think you on the matter? Are we to be enemies then? Surely not, brother.' Steel placed a hand gently on his brother's arm. It did not pull away.

Alexander looked him in the eye. 'Not enemies. No, Jack. But you are wrong.'

'About what?'

'About the King. He is the very model of kingship.'

Steel smiled. 'Yes, I've met him myself. He is an extra-ordinary man.'

'You've met the King?'

'Yesterday evening, in this very city. But do not ask more. You asked me not to tell you my mission. Suffice to say that it did not and does not involve your King. I have no business with that man. But tell me. Where do you live here? You are not married, but what of a mistress?'

'The army and King James's cause have been my mistress these past few years, though I happily admit that there have been women. None, though, like your own, it seems. But you know that campaigning does not marry well with love, and I shall return to the front ere long.'

'To Flanders? I wonder I have not met you on the field.'

'I too. Were you not at Blenheim? And Ramillies too? It was a strange providence that guided us through those fields of butchery without a meeting. To where do you return?'

'As usual we have not yet been told. I would not wonder if they moved us down to Spain. There is much to do on the peninsula and there are those at court who would cover the disgrace of Flanders with success elsewhere.'

'We should hope so, brother, for I am sure to remain in Belgium, and such a posting would distance our blades. Although you must then fight Peterborough's men. It cannot be an altogether pleasant feeling fighting your countrymen.'

'We managed well enough in the civil wars. The war I fight is no different from then, Jack. I fight for my King against a tyrant. I fight for the honour of Britain.'

'As do I, and let us drink to that at least.' He drained his glass and poured another. 'And what of the minute? You will stay here in Paris?'

'The regiment is billeted at St Germain. We guard the King in his court. We're kept in comfort, Jack, and I've good pay and as much as I can eat and drink. But in truth I shall be glad when we have our orders to march. I become ill-tempered in such a place as Paris. I need this war, Jack. Besides, I shall not be content until the true King sits in St James's.'

'You know I cannot share that sentiment. I used to believe that I too was driven only by war, but I've changed, Alexander, and you may do so too. You may say that now, but what if

160

you were to meet me on the field of battle? Face to face. What then? Where then would your loyalty lie?'

Alexander stared at him. 'I cannot make you out, Jack. In truth. And you are wrong about me, about the very nature of love and truth and faith. We may follow different causes, but you're still my brother.'

'And you mine. Another drink?' He turned. 'Girl, another carafe.'

Alexander shook his head. 'I still cannot believe you are here. It is the best of things. And you're married, you say, to a lady of title?'

'The Honourable Henrietta Vaughan.'

'Jack. You rogue, a title. I vow she's pretty too and that she's worth a few thousand a year.'

'You're right about the former. You never saw a girl more beautiful. But as for the latter, we are not so fortunate.'

'But her father's Lord Rumney. He's a rich man. Damned rich. He hasn't cut her off, Jack, penniless?'

'No, not that. Not as far as I'm aware. But I don't think that the dowry he settled on her proved to be quite the substantial amount she had expected. Nor that I'm quite what he had in mind as a son-in-law. Not that either matters to me more than my love for Henrietta.'

Alexander grinned. 'My, brother, you are smitten. She must be quite a girl to have pierced my brother's heart so deep. I wonder when I shall meet her. If ever I shall. Or indeed if I should ever meet my own Henrietta.'

'Have you not then? You've said nothing of women, but I guess that the court of King James is awash with pretty young things.'

Alexander smiled. 'There have been a few.'

'A few? If I know you, brother, you have taken the fancy of the prettiest girls in St Germain and broken more than a few hearts.'

'I'll admit to it. But I envy you, Jack, with your Henrietta.

How I wish that I could find such a girl. But in truth, whenever I find myself feeling an attachment, my heart tells me to pull away. A soldier is no husband for a girl. We all must die, Jack, ere long.'

Steel shook his head. 'No, I do not believe that. You and I shall make it through this war to the end, and then we shall have a happy reunion in the old house, with family and dear friends at hand. Think on that when times are dark.'

Alexander looked thoughtful and Steel knew that he must be thinking, as he was, that this meeting was all too brief. At length he looked up at Steel and spoke.

'How long do you stay in Paris? Shall we meet again?'

'I fear not. I leave at best tomorrow, unless I am discovered. In truth, my mission is fulfilled.'

'Then I am glad. Whatever it was, it was no business of mine as a soldier. I am no spy, nor would I want to be. And, Jack, it would be best for you were you not to become so again. You are a good soldier – a hero, from all that you've told me. Stay with what you know best. And now we should return to the Hôpital. It's best that we make our way back by separate routes. Take care of yourself, Jack. I shall do everything in my power to make sure you are not harmed and that you return to your regiment, but even I cannot have eyes and ears in all parts of the city. We should go.'

They settled the bill and left the inn. Outside in the street Alexander placed a hand on Jack's shoulders: 'Take care, big brother, and watch for your back. Your enemy has many different faces. Goodbye, Jack. And Godspeed.'

Steel embraced him. 'Goodbye, Alexander. Until we meet again and this war is at an end.'

With a final look, they parted, Steel walking to the left and Alexander towards the right, where the narrow streets opened out into one of the Sun King's new boulevards. Steel had not gone more than a few yards, however, when he heard footsteps behind him, quickening their pace now. With any luck it was just a prowling footpad, after a purse. His instinct told him to stand and face his would-be assailant, but in truth he had no desire for an encounter and reckoned that it would be easier to outpace the man. He was right, and in a vital split second during which he held the lead Steel ducked into a side alley as his pursuer rounded a corner. As his pursuer went past, Steel caught a glimpse of him in the moonlight and recognized the man he had met in the dining hall earlier that day: the Irishman, O'Driscoll.

Steel waited a few minutes as the man went off up the street. He listened but heard nothing over the general, distant hubbub save the few noises of the narrow street. A dog began to howl. Somewhere close by in a high tenement a baby was awake. A woman shrieked with laughter. But Steel heard no footsteps. He took a chance and darted from the alley back into the street, retracing his steps so that by his reckoning a left turn would take him again in the direction of the Hôpital. He had not gone ten paces when he heard a voice behind him.

'Captain Johnson, sir, isn't it?'

Steel kept walking.

The man tried again. His voice a little louder. 'Would you wait up there, sir. If you please, Captain. See, I've a hankering to speak with you, sir, on a matter of some urgency.'

There was no avoiding it now. Steel did not know how much O'Driscoll might have seen of his meeting with Alexander, even whether he might have overheard any of their conversation. Perhaps the man wanted to try to blackmail him. Whatever his motive, Steel knew that there was nothing for it now but to fight it out and leave him dead on the cobbles.

He stopped and turned and stared into the Irishman's face. 'Do I know you?'

'No, but I know you. At least I know what you are. Captain Johnson. Or whoever you are. You're a bloody spy.'

Steel stiffened, but played the role. 'How dare you! How dare you insult me. I'm an officer. I'm your superior.'

'Insult you, is it? Oh no, sir. Oh no. You're wrong there. See, you're the one who's done the insulting, isn't it? You're no Irish officer, sir. All your talk of Roth's men at Cremona. You betrayed yourself, sir. Wasn't it Dillon's brave lads held the gate at Cremona. Any bloody Paddy knows that. You're as Irish as the Duke of bloody Marlborough himself.'

Steel could see O'Driscoll quite plainly now, his single good eye flashing in the half-light. He saw too that the man was armed with what looked like a cavalry sabre.

Without hesitating, Steel drew his own heavy sword from its scabbard and moved quickly across the stones, cutting expertly at the Irishman's head, but the man, despite his one eye, was fast and parried the cut with the dexterity of a trooper. Steel realized he had a fight on his hands. But he had dealt with others of this type before. There was no reason for him not to prevail now. He lunged again, this time with a cut to the upper body. Again the Irishman parried and sidestepped, then with a flick caught Steel on the leg. His bad leg. Steel winced in pain and cut more blindly now, this time connecting so that the keen blade forced its way through the flesh and sinew of the Irishman's right forearm. The man gave a howl. Steel exploited the moment and brought his blade down again on the man's upper arm. It tore through the flesh and splintered the bone of the shoulder. The Irishman dropped his blade and staggered, holding his wound. Steel raised the sword and advanced. In other circumstances he would perhaps have spared the man's life and handed him over, but here and now there was only one thing that could be done. He raised the blade to the man's chest and, breathing in, prepared to thrust home. Then, conscious of a noise to

164

his rear, he half-turned to glimpse two shadows against the stone.

Steel spun round and in the same movement hacked into one of the shadows. He hit home with such force that the sword flew from his hand and clattered to the dark cobbles. At the same moment the man gave a cry and staggered backwards, clutching at his right arm, which was hanging limply, almost severed by the blow. Steel looked for his weapon and the third man took advantage of his momentary preoccupation, lunging out of the shadows with a yell, his blade pointing directly towards Steel's chest. Steel stumbled away from the sword and back against the wall of a house. With a grin of triumph the Irishman pushed his blade home and Steel waited for it to strike. Instead, though, he watched as the blade seemed to freeze in mid-air and the man's smile turned to a grimace of astonishment and agony. Then, slowly, a bright crimson flower began to spread across the man's chest and the tip of a rapier penetrated his coat. As Steel looked on, wide-eyed, the man fell to the side stone dead. Where he had been, another face appeared. Alexander Steel wiped the blood from his blade before returning it to his scabbard.

'Damned lucky for you, Jack, that I decided to follow you. I had a feeling something was up, and I was right.'

Steel bent to retrieve his sword and returned it to his side. 'I owe you my life, brother. And not for the first time.'

'Anyone would have pulled you from that loch. It just happened to be me. And any brother would have done for you what I just did.' He kicked at one of the dead Irishmen. 'Who were these ruffians anyway?'

'Never seen them before in my life.'

'Jack, I heard him call your name. Well, Johnson's name.'

Steel shook his head. 'As I said, how can I hope to deceive you, little brother? But better not to ask me again, lest you should wish to hear the full story.'

Alexander shook his head. 'I shall ask no more. For the present, though, I suggest that we might return home together. It would appear that tonight at least there is safety in numbers.'

NINE

It was a rare thing for Steel to awake in the morning without a sense of foreboding. When with his regiment, it might come in the form of anything from the mundanities of company administration to the impending action and danger of a battle. Most recently he had woken steeped in anxiety. The very fact that he was behind enemy lines was worry enough. But he could not get the face of Major Malbec from his mind.

This morning though, he had found his thoughts unclouded by any such spectres. Certainly the fight in the street with the Irishmen had brought cause for alarm. They had seen through his cover. But he hoped that he had despatched them before they had been able to communicate their knowledge. Malbec too was still a worry, but he was not a pressing matter, merely a cause for irritation.

Perhaps it had been his encounter with Alexander, the assurance that brotherly love was yet stronger than any political differences, and not least the fact that his brother had saved his life. Perhaps it was the fact that he had delivered the letter from Marlborough to Major Charpentier and had to all intents accomplished his mission. What Louis would make of the proposal remained to be seen, of course, but, as intriguing and as full of possibilities as it was, Steel knew that it was not his concern. Such things were the business of commanders. He was a soldier, not a politician. Perhaps, he thought, his mood was occasioned by the fact that he was due this day to leave Paris. For as much as the city had intrigued and delighted him, he felt a deep longing to be back with his men and a yearning too to see his wife as soon as that might be possible. He wondered how the men were surviving the siege of Lille. Any siege was a bloody affair, as he knew from experience, perhaps the bloodiest type of warfare known to man. But Lille was Vauban's showpiece, and he hoped to God they had not taken too many casualties.

He was not sure, either, how well he was suited to this deep subterfuge. Prevous missions for the Duke had been dangerous, certainly, both in Bavaria and at Ostend. But, save briefly in the latter case, he had not been compelled to adopt an alias. Certainly, his position had never seemed as perilous as it had recently been, so deep in the Sun King's capital, surrounded and quizzed by his courtiers and even a would-be monarch. No, thought Steel, he would not be sorry to leave all that behind. Men like Simpson were better suited to be spies – men who had nothing to lose, men whose everyday lives and characters were essentially duplicitous, men who revelled in an ever-present danger and for whom the knock at the door brought not apprehension but the thrill of yet another potential trial of their wits.

Deprived of his customary soldier-servant, Steel had dressed himself and now allowed himself the luxury of a few minutes looking from the window of his room onto the gardens below. He had been given a modest room on the south side of the building. Charpentier had contrived to place him on his own in a room whose previous occupant, a captain of the Mousquetaires du Roi, had only recently died, so recently in fact that as yet the room had not been reallocated and few of the inmates were aware of the vacancy. His brother was billeted in more modest accommodation in one of the side blocks of the complex, and Steel doubted that he would see him again before he returned to the front. For that reason, they had made their brief goodbyes outside the gates last night, and now as he looked down on the orange trees in the governor's garden Steel wondered when they would meet again. He prayed that it would not be across a battlefield.

There was a sudden knock at the door. Steel opened it to find a blue-clad resident of the Hôpital, a soldier-servant whom he did not recognize. The man wore neither a sword nor a hat, and when he spoke it was in a guttural, regional French accent that Steel found hard to comprehend.

'Captain Johnson, I have a message for you from Major Charpentier. He requests that you attend him in his rooms with all haste. It is a matter of some urgency.'

In an instant Steel's carefree mood had gone. What, he wondered, might denote a matter of 'some urgency'? Had they been discovered? Had someone witnessed their encounter last night with O'Driscoll and his thugs?

'Thank you. I shall come presently.'

The man coughed politely. 'I'm instructed to wait for you, sir. If you please.'

Steel grabbed his coat from the chair, flung it over his waistcoat and left in the wake of the messenger. They hurried along the corridor and passed through the anteroom of Charpentier's quarters. The servant opened the door to the governor's office and ushered Steel inside before closing it behind him. Once inside, however, Steel instantly toyed with the notion of immediately retracing his steps. For rather than Charpentier, it was Major Malbec who stood alone before him in the room, and Steel recalled his brother's warning. As before, the French officer was standing by the table in the window, where he was again examining the collection of model soldiers. Steel noticed, though, that they had been rearranged and that the table had been laid out with carved wooden miniature scenery. One half of the little figures were dressed principally in red and blue coats, and the other all in white. There must have been nigh on a thousand figures facing each other across the table.

Malbec looked up and smiled at Steel as he entered. 'Ah, Captain Johnson. Major Charpentier will not be long. He was called away on urgent business. But it is good that you are here. Perhaps until he returns you would care to join me in an exercise with his little figurines. I think you'll find it amusing.'

Steel walked across to the table and bluffed his way through his apprehension. 'You seem to have a battle in mind, Major. I see you have drawn them up in line of attack. They look splendid.'

'Don't they? Although you should see the King's collection at Versailles. This is nothing compared to that. Twenty thousand soldiers. *Quelle spectacle!* Perhaps you will join me in a little sport?'

Steel nodded. 'I should be fascinated, sir. How do we play? Is it something like chess? Or do we use cards, perhaps?'

Malbec smiled. 'Nothing quite so simple, I'm afraid, my dear captain. But for a soldier like yourself nothing could be easier. Horse, foot and guns all move a set number of inches. The firing and mêlée I shall explain as we progress. You know this is precisely how our King learnt the art of war and why for the last sixty years the forces of France have remained the unchallenged masters of the battlefield.'

Steel failed to rise to the perhaps intentional challenge, and Malbec continued. 'Now, Captain, I wonder, which side should you take? Perhaps that to match your coat would suit you best. Unless you've a mind to turn it?'

Steel stared at him and tried to smile. So, he must know. Was Malbec really playing games with him? Could he have discovered his true identity? What else to do but bluff it out?

'No. I shall say true to my colour, of course. The red coat

of Ireland will serve me as well now as it has these past ten years.'

He surveyed his troops. There were three distinct blocks of foot, brigades almost. Most were dressed in red, although those on his left flank were all in blue. Malbec's force was similar, apart from the fact that one of his regiments was made up entirely of blue-coated grenadiers, as was the fashion in France. He noticed Steel's stare.

'Captain, I see that you have spotted my unfair advantage. I have an entire battalion of grenadiers who surely must outperform all my other troops, and yours. Would you not agree that the grenadier is the king of the battlefield?'

Again, Steel, looking at the small, bearskin-capped figures, wondered whether Malbec might not be teasing him. Was it possible that he could know his true identity? Still, there was no alternative however than bluff.

'I quite agree, Major. And, yes, you are right. In that respect you do have the upper hand. But do not forget that I have an advantage in horse. Look: on my right wing an entire squadron of dragoons in superiority.'

Malbec laughed. 'Yes, you have the advantage in horse. But you are an infantry officer. Ah well. We shall see who triumphs. So, Captain, shall be begin the game? Here is a measuring stick to determine how far your troops may move. We roll dice to simulate the fog of war. Thus we determine the effect of gunfire and the outcome of mêlée, should your men ever close with mine. As my guest, you may play first, Captain. May I suggest that you open fire with your cannon? Just as was the case on the day of the real battle.'

Steel stared at him. 'The real battle.'

'Surely you recognize the terrain. Even standing as you do on the enemy positions?'

Steel looked down at the table, took in every detail. Of course. The river with its bridges, the towns and the hills

171

towering above. Malbec had set out the battlefield of Oudenarde.

'Oudenarde. Of course. How very clever of you, Major. And I am to play the hand of the Duke of Marlborough.'

'Yes. I must apologize for that dishonour. Still, it is only a game.'

Steel bristled. The absurdity of their situation merely served to increase the tension in the room. It seemed highly likely to him that this man had uncovered his mission. Thus he was in mortal danger. Yet here they were playing at death with model soldiers. More than that, this Frenchman was instructing him in the art of war.

'I am no novice, monsieur. I know the etiquette of the battle-field as well as you do. Of course I shall give you a salvo. Now what do I throw for two guns? Two dice? A three and a two. Not many casualties.'

Malbec in turn threw dice for his cannon. 'And now we move again. I shall advance my infantry towards the village.'

Steel picked up two of the tiny cavalry figures on his left flank. 'And I shall charge straight into them with a regiment of British cavalry, taking them in the flank.'

'In the flank. But we would form a defence. Back to back, or a square, in the Dutch manner.'

'You're too late, major. My cavalry are upon you while your men are still changing formation. Try the distance. And we do not stop to fire our pistols. We charge home with the sword. In the British fashion.'

Steel was transported back to Oudenarde, to the sight of the Hanoverian cavalry careering into the French infantry. He took in the glorious ranks of brightly painted toy soldiers, so neatly arrayed. And then, carnage. Here on the table, though, there was no blood as the two units closed with one another.

Malbec spoke with annoyance in his voice. 'So then, you have made contact. Very good, Captain. I admit I am taken by suprise. But let us see what fate decrees.'

172

Steel threw the dice. A five.

Malbec shook his head. 'So. What will be, will be. You have destroyed my front rank of infantry, and half of my second. You have broken through, Captain. I congratulate you. My infantry have been routed.'

'You're finished, Malbec. Your entire right flank is in disorder. You may as well surrender.'

'Perhaps. But I don't think so. You see, what can this be? I advance my fresh cavalry from behind my second line so, and charge and engage your blown and weary dragoons. You're outnumbered and outclassed, Captain Johnson. Two dice . . .' He threw two dice, a six and a five. '. . . and *voilà*! No more English dragoons. I am a ruthless opponent, am I not? I have no mercy.'

Steel stared, shook his head, and then smiled. 'Very clever. But you've walked into a trap, Major. Did you not see my cannon?' Malbec's face fell. Steel continued. 'Two batteries, firing grapeshot at fifty yards. I hardly think I need to roll the dice.'

'D'you know, Captain, I saw your guns there, but I did not think that you would do that somehow. To fire point-blank at my horse, almost in cold blood. It's not the work of an Englishman. Not someone who believes in fair play.'

Again Steel paused. An Englishman? Malbec was playing with him.

'But you forget, Major. I'm an Irishman.'

'I'm sorry. Of course. It was merely the fact that we are speaking English. And now, I shall fire my infantry at your cannon. And that will be that.'

'You can't. You'll fire through your own cavalry.'

'They have served their purpose.'

Steel stared at Malbec. 'That goes against all the principles of war.'

'Surely, Captain, you no longer fight on principle? How very English! I'm sorry, Irish.'

Steel gritted his teeth. 'It's your responsibility as a commander.'

Malbec laughed. 'Responsibility? Surely, it just goes to prove that in this game of war you must never trust a soul. Wouldn't you agree, Captain? Particularly if, as you do, you find yourself in the heart of your enemy's war machine.'

Steel stared at him and saw the smug smile of certainty which played across his face. 'How long have you known? About who I was?'

'Oh, not that long. And I have to say that I'm pleased. You see, I was troubled from the moment we met as to where I had seen you before. And as for finding your quarters, well, let's just say that we have no secrets in the Invalides.'

Thinking fast, Steel looked about the room. He still had his sword. There was a single door and a guard, he knew, outside. They were two storeys up, too high to jump without serious injury. He also presumed that Malbec would have placed further guards, and concluded quickly that if there was to be a chance of escape it was not now.

Malbec was still speaking, toying with a miniature of an ensign of French infantry. 'Where could it be? I asked myself. I went over again and again in my mind every dealing I had had with the Irish in the past few years. I wondered, were you in England, perhaps as a prisoner?'

As Malbec was speaking the door opened and Steel turned towards it, expecting and hoping to see Charpentier and perhaps a means of deliverance. Instead, however, he found himself staring into the unforgettable green eyes of the Marquise de Puy Fort Eguille.

She smiled at him and raised a single fine eyebrow. 'Captain Johnson. How delightful to see you again.' She turned to Malbec. '*Cheri*, I came as quickly as I could. Your note seemed very urgent.'

'It was of no account. The captain and I have been diverting ourselves with a game of Charpentier's tin soldiers. In fact he was doing surprisingly well. For an Englishman.'

174

Steel turned and began to speak, but Malbec cut in. 'I was just informing the captain here from where it was that I had recognized him. Don't be surprised. I was sure that I recognized you when we met, and now I know where it was. Once I learnt that you were a British officer it came back to me. You remember an incident some four years ago? How could you forget? You were, I believe, the officer in command of a party of infantry passing through a small Bavarian village. I forget the name. It's not important. There you made a most unpleasant discovery. Certain German villagers had . . . erm . . . got in the way of our plans and looked set to be a most useful means of raising the populace against you. They were . . . disposed of. Of course their bodies were not meant for you to discover, but for their own kind.'

'You? It was you and your men did that? You bastard!'

Steel made to move towards Malbec, but only now did the French officer draw his sword. Swiftly and before he could match the move the tip came to rest against Steel's throat.

'Careful, Captain. There are ladies present and I would so much regret having to spill your blood. So soon, at least. But, yes, I have to admit that it was the work of my men – a crude attempt to discredit your dragoons, who at the time, you may recall, were burning the Bavarians out of their homes as they have so recently done to the poor people of Artois. Of course I know that your Duke is as always careful not to hurt anyone. I believe that he has a standing death sentence for any soldier who rapes or kills? Well, in Bavaria we merely took things a stage further. We did the job for you. Dreadful smell, though, wasn't there? I never shall forget that.'

Steel's hand went to his sword hilt, but Malbec pushed the tip of his own weapon a fraction deeper against Steel's neck.

'You evil bastard. You murdered innocent women and children.'

Malbec shook his head. 'Murder? In time of war? Come, come. Surely you cannot believe in that? In time of war there can be no morals. The death of the villagers was merely a sad consequence of the sort of warfare that we must all fight today. So different from the neat affair on this table, no? A pity to interrupt our game. And I do believe you might have been winning.'

Still holding the sword against Steel's throat, Malbec took his left hand and swept it across the ranks of the red-coated figures, scattering them across the table. 'Ah well, you see how easily the ranks of the British fall. And that will be the way when next we meet them on the field. There was one other moment when I think I saw you. I believe that I may have encountered you briefly in the fight for Blenheim. I seldom forget a good swordsman.'

Steel nodded in acknowledgement of the compliment. So that was where he had seen the man before. It was true. Although a sword fight in the heat of battle might last for only a few minutes, there were certain faces that Steel would never forget. Mostly he saw them in his dreams, contorted into a rictus of pain as he had left them, dying. Malbec's, though, had never appeared thus, for he had managed to flee with his life. Steel wished to God now that he had been able to finish him at the time.

He wondered who might have betrayed him or guessed his true identity. For a moment he considered Simpson, but quickly thought better of it. It was impossible to think Alexander would have done so. Possibly the Irishman, O'Driscoll, had given him up before he had been killed. He decided that was the most likely explanation, but sought confirmation.

'How did you discover me? You have no way of knowing who I am.'

'No? It was really quite simple. You know this man?'

Malbec clapped his hands, and from the still open doorway another figure appeared. Steel recognized him as Simpson's butler, Gabriel.

'Monsieur Gabriel is an officer of the King. He holds the

rank of captain in the regiment of Mousquetaires, although for the past two years he has been employed as a spy – one of our best, as a matter of fact. He is currently employed as butler to a man we have suspected for some time, a man calling himself St Colombe. Clearly he is also a British spy. Soon the trap will close on him and we will bring him to justice. You, though, were an easier fish to hook. Naturally, Gabriel informed me of the arrival at the house of St Colombe of a handsome Irish captain. And when I mentioned it to the Marquise it transpired that you two had already met. You can imagine how keen she was to renew your acquaintance. She has an eye for a pretty face. But that's of no matter now. Now you are my prisoner, Captain Johnson, or whatever your real name might be. I'm sure you will tell me that in good time. You see, there is so much that you have to tell me. And sooner or later you will.'

TEN

Strapped to a carved wooden *fauteuil*, Steel tried to wrest himself free, but the thick black leather straps that bound him had been fastened so securely around the sturdy oak arms that to move at all merely caused the edge of the hide to cut into his wrist. Malbec watched his futile attempt with amusement, shaking his head.

'It is quite pointless, Captain. Consider your situation. Accept it. And ask yourself what you would do if you did free yourself. First you have me to contend with, and then there's our friend by the door, and once you're out of here you would find yourself where? In the Hôpital des Invalides. In the very heart of the French military establishment. What chance do you really think you have? No, why don't you simply tell us what we want to know and then you can go and rest. Please, Captain. And on my honour as a soldier I promise that no further harm shall befall you.'

They were in one of the rudimentary cells in the cellars of the Invalides normally used to detain miscreant inmates. Aside from the chair the furnishings consisted of a low wooden plank which served as a bed, a slop bucket and a small wooden table. The only source of natural light was a small window near the ceiling which gave out onto the cobblestones. At present the room was

178

lit by two pitch-soaked torches which flickered in their cast-iron brackets and threw moving shadows around the walls. Steel was not sure whether his present lack of clear vision was due more to the poor light or the fact that his right eye was now partly closed and bloodied on account of having been punched repeatedly by both Malbec and Gabriel, who had gone to take a break from his exertions.

By the door stood an armed sentry, a tall infantryman of Malbec's own regiment of grenadiers with a tall, bearskin cap. Another stood outside. Steel knew one thing: he was not going anywhere. Apart from the guard, Malbec and Steel, there was only one other person in the room. Steel noticed a wicked smile cross the Marquise's face.

'My dear Claude, be reasonable. You cannot really make the captain such a promise. You know my plans.'

Malbec, pretending not to hear, continued with his questions. 'Captain, we do not yet know your name, but we do know that you are a British secret agent and that you have been working with the spy Simpson who calls himself St Colombe. We have known about him for some time. In fact we have waited for just such a moment before taking him. Sadly, at the present time he has evaded us, but be assured we have a shrewd idea of his possible whereabouts. He will not leave the city and will soon be joining you. I do not know for certain the purpose of your mission here in Paris but I am sure you are intent on undermining the will of the French people to wage the war to which their King has pledged them. France shall not rest until she is victorious and Britain and her allies crushed. That is the only way it will end, however long it might take and however many lives it might cost.'

Steel spat blood from his cut mouth and spoke. 'You're insane. The people of France don't want this war any more. You've lost touch with your countrymen, Major. You think they'll follow you to death and glory, but they wouldn't follow you if you offered them the bloody moon.'

His words were cut short by the punch which the major landed hard in his stomach. Steel groaned.

Malbec stood back and shook his head. 'Don't be stupid, Captain. Save yourself unnecessary suffering. All I want to know are two things: your name, and the purpose of your mission. That's all. Nothing more than two things. What harm can there be in that? And you are an honourable man. You know it is the honourable way out. And it will save you so much pain.'

Steel stared at him through half-shut eyes and shook his head. 'Do you really think that I would ever consider betraying a confidence and my country? What code of honour do you follow, Malbec? None, I'll wager. Certainly, none that I acknowledge.'

Malbec drew closer to him so that Steel could smell his breath with its pungent, lingering aroma of garlic and spices, while the scent of lavender also hung about him. He hissed in Steel's face, spat out the words: 'I'll tell you the code of honour I follow, Captain: the code of honour that killed my wife and children in Le Havre. The code of honour of your Royal Navy. The code of honour that killed hundreds more innocent civilians at Ostend when your warships opened fire and sent their bombs raining down into its streets. That's my code of honour, Captain. Surely you recognize it? Your generals invented it.'

Malbec paused and gazed at this troublesome British officer. He had spent some months in custody in England, under house arrest in the town of York. He had hoped that he might see the true nature of the British people, that the dreadful shadow might be lifted from his mind. But what he had seen was a nation not ground down by war but enjoying the bounties of victory and prosperity. Families happy together. It had made him only more bitter and determined to avenge his family's death at every opportunity.

He whispered to Steel. 'Don't worry. By the time I've finished with you you'll be begging to tell me your name.' He turned to the Marquise. 'My dear Marquise, perhaps you should leave now. I think that this will not be a sight for such eyes as yours.'

She smiled. 'Oh, Claude, how can you think such a thing? You know that the one reason I am here is to keep a careful eye on your treatment of the captain. After all, he is mine, is he not?'

Malbec smiled. 'True. It is as we arranged. I owe you so many debts and I did swear that you could take him. Once I have finished with him.'

'And you also swore that you would leave him in good condition. Remember, Claude, a bargain is a bargain.'

Malbec shrugged, and Steel froze. So he was to be her prize. To what end, he could only imagine. Clearly their conversation was intended to be only too audible, to fill him with the terror of anticipation. She laughed.

Malbec smiled and looked at Steel. 'What exactly do you have planned for our friend?'

She turned to Steel and stared at him with a look which chilled him to the bone. He looked away and found himself staring at the huge emerald pendant which hung at her breast.

'I detest the British. So would you if you had seen your father die from the wounds he received in battle with them, blinded and unable to see his children grow up. And if you had nursed the ruin of a man, which was all they brought me of my husband. He had been reckoned one of the handsomest men in France, Captain. After the battle of Ramillies, when they brought him home, he was hideous. He had been wounded by your English dragoons. They had found him in a corner of the field, detached from his regiment and confused by a fall from his horse. There were four of them. He had surrendered, offered them his sword. It meant nothing. They still cut him down. One sabre cut slashed his face from above his right eye to his left jaw. Another

181

took off his nose. As they did it, they were laughing. Then they left him to die. But he was a strong man. His servant brought him home, back to Agen. He died in my arms sobbing like a baby.'

She was trembling now. Pausing, she looked at Malbec and then back to Steel. 'And so, Captain, I have sworn to be avenged against my husband's murderers and their fellows. With you I intend to play a game of like for like. I shall take your eyes. The rest of you, however, I intend to preserve in as perfect and beautiful a state as you are now. And then I shall think of all the delicious ways in which you can amuse me. You will stay with me at my château at Agen. At least until I tire of you.'

Here was a fate Steel had never contemplated. What was more, Malbec, a brother officer bound by a code of honour that transcended allegiances, appeared to condone her barbarity. He knew that he must escape. Perhaps, he thought, if he only played for time he might have an opportunity to find a way out. He realized, however, that he would have to endure the next stage of the major's interrogation. He wondered what now lay in store for him; something more sophisticated, no doubt, than the brutal Neanderthal pummelling he had already suffered. When, he wondered, would he lose his eyes? And how would it be done? He shuddered and tried desperately to find a means of escape.

At length Malbec broke away from his embrace with the Marquise and turned back to Steel. 'You seem surprised, Captain, that an officer should behave in such a fashion. But you forget. I gave myself up at Ostend. I had seen too much blood for one day. In England as a prisoner I had supposed that I might at last be able to understand the people who had robbed me of my most precious posses- sions, my wife and children, killed at the bombardment of Le Havre by your navy. Instead I found only hatred for an indolent and bigoted nation. It merely served to fuel my loathing for your race. So now we intend to make you pay, Captain, pay for all the injustices perpetrated by your barbarous army. But in truth I can make it easier for you. You see the influence I hold over milady. Perhaps if you were to tell me the names of your accomplices, I might be able to sway her from her unpleasant plan. At least I might be able to save your sight.'

The Marquise shook her head. 'Claude, you must not tease the poor captain. I am resolved. An eye for an eye.'

Steel was not really listening. If I can only manage to infuriate this man enough, he thought, he might just beat me into unconsciousness, and then at least they would have to wait until I was capable again of telling them Major Charpentier's name. It was worth a go, as was anything that might give him more time – time to think of a plan of escape, anything.

Steel waited until Malbec's face was close to his own, and then he spat at him, a mouthful of blood-streaked phlegm. The major recoiled and carefully wiped the muck from his cheek and mouth. Then with a sudden and unexpected swiftness he raised his arm and brought the fist crashing down upon Steel's jaw, smashing his head to one side with a ferocity which shocked and surprised him and in an instant made him wonder whether another such blow from this man might break his neck. When it did come, an instant later, it did not do anything quite so dreadful. What it did do, though, was send him and the chair crashing to the floor, and as Steel slipped gratefully from consciousness he knew that his plan had succeeded.

Steel lay in the coal-black darkness and trembled with fear. He could not see, and for a few minutes now he had been putting off the moment. Now, though, he knew that he must do it. Slowly he reached up to his face and felt for his eyes. The first touch told him what he needed to know. There rather than the empty sockets he had feared, he could feel the roundness beneath the lids which proved that he still had his sight. The Marquise could not have yet fulfilled her terrible promise. There was no pain in that part of his head, which was more than could be said for the rest of his anatomy. He moved a leg and felt a twinge across the muscle and into the bone. He ran a hand across his face and felt the dried blood and the swollen, puffy tissue. By God but they had made a mess of him. Slowly, and with the experience of a dozen battles, he felt carefully up and down first one arm and then the other and then down both his legs, checking for possible fractures. As far as he could tell there were none. Yet.

Steel thanked God that his plan had worked and that he had passed out with the pain. It came to him, though, that soon they would come for him again and that this time their method might be such that he would crack and give away the name of the major. After that he would be at the mercy of the Marquise, and that was not an option that he wanted in the least to explore. However it might be achieved, escape within the next few minutes was the only way, no matter how painful it might be and even if he died in the attempt.

He stood up and bumped his head on a low ceiling. Clearly he was no longer in the high basement cell. More than likely, he had been carried upstairs and thrown into some sort of an attic. Gradually his eyes became accustomed to the lack of light. Slowly, to his left he saw a square of light, which suggested the square outline of a small window. He walked across to it on the bare boards, listening lest they should squeak and being careful to feel his way first in case he might fall over some obstacle, but the room appeared to be empty. Reaching the wall, he felt at the window and eventually managed to lever up a small corner of what felt like a piece of wood that had been nailed into place. With a supreme effort, Steel pushed up on the wood, splintering it and cutting his hands. Instantly a shred of light flooded into the gloom and he knew that he had found a way out.

Half an hour later, his hands torn and bleeding from pulling at the rough wooden panels, Steel had managed to rip a length away, and now moonlight filled the little room through the small hole. It was a window. Cautiously he peered out and saw nothing but the sky and a rooftop perhaps some eighty yards away. He raised his head and peered down. He was, as he had surmised, in an attic room some forty feet above the ground. Directly below him lay a courtyard. He recognized it at once as the Cour Royale of the Invalides. So he was still in Paris. Thank God at least for that, he thought. Turning, he assessed his surroundings in the moonlight. The only access to the room save the window was the low door through which he must have been carried. There was no furniture to speak of, expect for a broken table and a pile of sheeting.

He walked over to the window and peered down again into the courtyard. He would have to act as fast as he could. Every moment now was precious. He pulled at the remaining slats of wood and threw them into the room to leave the window opening as wide as he could. Then, trying to remember the appearance of the roof, he eased open the window and, turning so that his back rested on the thin edge overlooking the sheer drop to the yard, he reached up with his hands to grasp the edge. The slates cut into his hands and his raw wrists, already lacerated by the leather straps, were grazed by the edge of the tiles. Making a supreme effort, Steel pulled as hard as he could and his body eased out of the window and hung above the courtyard. To anyone looking up now he knew that he would be in full view. He glanced down to check, and instantly thought better of it. His head began to swim with vertigo, and for an instant he thought he might let go of the roof.

185

Recovering, he turned back and, looking up at the slates, managed to manoeuvre so that his feet were standing on the window ledge.

Gingerly, he grasped for the pieces of carved stonework. The sill was wide, and he used the round frame to brace his body and climb onto the roof. A wolf, carved around the window frame, became a useful handhold. Pulling himself up with them, he managed to move one foot up onto the roof and searched around for a ledge of slate. Then slowly he moved on and up the roof and managed to get his other leg free of the window until he was hanging on the very edge of the slope. Little by little, tile by tile, Steel pulled himself up the steep angle of the roof until he was at the top.

He had hoped to find a chimney stack down which he might climb, but there was none here. In the centre of the roof, however, he could make out a lantern. He could see it quite plainly, some thirty feet from where he balanced, with a steep slope on either side. The only way to reach it would be along the apex of the roof itself. Steel lowered himself down until one of his legs hung on either side of the roof and slowly began to ease himself along. It was not the most comfortable of journeys and he realized that this must be what it felt like to suffer the infernal other ranks' regimental punishment of 'riding the horse' where a miscreant soldier would be made to sit astride a wooden horse, his legs weighted down. It seemed to take forever, and the further Steel went the more agonizing his progress became until he felt as if the roof would cut him in two.

At length, however, he reached the tall lantern. It was a small, domed structure of roughly his own height from the apex with six sides. Steel recalled a similar structure at his family home at Carniston which sat on the stable block allowing air in to the horses. How many times had he and Alexander used it as a means to reach their nightly rendezvous with girls from the village in the hay loft? If this lantern was built in the same way then one of the sides would have to be a door. He pushed at each of them, gingerly moving around the roof. Four of them did not yield, and then on the east side, as he pushed, it slowly creaked open. Steel pressed himself to the stonework, anxious lest the noise might have alerted someone. But, to his great relief, the courtyard below was still quite empty and no one had yet raised the alarm. Steel peered into the darkness within the lantern. A chill breeze told him that it might well be a drop of seventy feet. Carefully, he reached inside and smiled as he felt familiar handholds. It was a ventilation shaft, exactly like the one at Carniston. He climbed in and began to descend.

If Steel had thought that any other part of his escape thus far had been difficult, they seemed as naught now compared with his current situation. He reckoned that he might if lucky be halfway down the shaft within the lantern. He had no way of knowing, for it was pitch black, the only light being at the top where the door met the sky. Every step was a new danger, every rung of the slippery ladder to be carefully negotiated. And the dark was smothering him. Several times he almost panicked. He thought of his sergeant, Jacob Slaughter, with his fear of dark enclosed spaces, thought of the tunnel in the walls of Ostend where Slaughter's panic had almost cost them their lives, and thought how then he himself had steadied the sergeant. That was what ultimately drove him on, that and the knowledge that there was no way back, save to certain death.

His limbs ached – his whole frame, it seemed. Then he was aware in the blackness that the air had become somehow different and that his breathing was less hollow, somehow more audible. The only explanation must be that he was nearing the bottom of the shaft. He placed his foot on the next rung and found that it was not there. Momentary panic gave way to relief as, reaching down a little farther, the ball of his foot touched solidity. He took a few moments to get his bearings, and began cautiously to feel his way along a low tunnel. He felt with his feet, and after a few yards found an opening, or rather a hole, no more than two feet wide, in the floor. Sitting on the edge, Steel lowered himself down and found himself squatting in a tunnel. The roof was well made, of curved brick, and the floor hardened. He wondered what on earth might have been the purpose of this route originally. Whatever, that was not important now. He began to crawl along the tunnel, and after what may have been minutes or as much as a full hour, the wounds on his hands having been reopened by the surface of the floor, he began to sense the air changing and the passage becoming lighter. Then the roof of the tunnel opened up above him and another narrow shaft rose through the earth. He stood up and found that by climbing on a rudimentary staircase of rough stone, placed there for just that purpose, it was possible to touch the closure at the top. He pushed and was rewarded by movement. Taking a deep breath and praying that he would not come up directly beneath a sentry, Steel pushed harder and felt the wooden lid of the tunnel moving across grass. With a final effort he pulled himself up, and in a few moments was clambering into the fresh night air.

Steel gathered his thoughts and recovered his breath. His body felt like lead. He was bleeding badly from his hands and from the cut on his head which had reopened during his flight. He crouched on the grass and looked around in the moonlight; he could not see any sign of a sentry. His first thought was to return to Simpson's house, but then he remembered that Malbec had told him they were waiting for Simpson. The only other option in a friendless enemy city was to find his brother. Alexander had told him that he had temporary lodgings in one of the dormitory houses outside the main building – the very houses Steel now realized he must be

188

looking at. He knew that Alexander's apartment lay near the rue de Grenelle, and he tried to get his bearings. The dome rose behind him, and for a few seconds Steel stared at it before working out that he was facing east. By sheer luck he was on the right side. Now his only challenge was to find which of the three blocks housed his brother. At that instant he heard footsteps on the gravel path and a second later came the shout he had dreaded.

'*Halte! Qui va là?*'

Inspired, Steel replied in poor French, deliberately slurring his words, 'It's me. Private O'Driscoll, Your Honour. I'm a little unwell.'

The sentry approached Steel, who saw that the man had a levelled musket tipped with a bayonet pointed at his chest. 'You're drunk. And you've been in a fight. It's the guardroom for you, my Irish friend.'

Still acting the part, Steel raised his hands. 'Don't shoot, Your Honour. I'll come quietly. Yes, I may have had a drop of the hard stuff, but then we're all soldiers here, aren't we, my friend? No need for your gun. I'll come quietly. I'll do my punishment.'

The Frenchman smiled and half dropped his weapon. Steel seized the chance. Taking the man by surprise, he brought his right hand, now clenched in a fist, crashing down on the sentry's skull, knocking him to the ground. The musket, thankfully not loaded, fell to the grass. Steel picked it up and before the sentry had time to come to his senses drove it down through the darkness hard into the man's chest. He heard a brief gurgle and then the body went limp. Pulling out the bayonet, Steel quickly stripped the corpse of its white coat and slipped it on. It was a little tight, he thought, but it would do. He took the man's tricorn hat and placed it on his head. Then, picking up the musket, he positioned it in his left arm at the port and began to walk slowly and in a straight line along the gravel.

Fervently, he looked at the barrack blocks for any hint of which might be Alexander's. He was beginning to despair when he heard voices speaking in English. In an instant he recognized his brother's: 'Good night, Lieutenant, and thank you for the wine. I must return the favour.'

Walking slower now, Steel kept to the sentry's line of march and watched as a figure stepped out of the doorway and crossed his path. As the man passed him Steel brought the musket to the present and prayed that the French officer would not look too carefully in his direction. The man walked on in the direction of the main building, and as soon as he was out of earshot Steel turned and made towards the door. He turned the handle. To his surprise it opened, and there before him stood the equally astonished figure of his brother.

It was a good ten minutes before Steel was able to tell Alexander the full story, but now he did so, as they sat on a grassy verge beside the unfinished road. Alexander had taken care to dress and bind his wounds as best he could, talking much of the time in a low voice and keeping one eye on the door of his room. Then they had left, quickly and silently, walking until they were clear of the Hôpital. Still, though, Steel spoke in a hushed voice.

'So you know of the secret passage?'

'Charpentier told me. It was built by the King himself, twenty years ago, when the Hôpital was being constructed, to allow the safe passage of "unapproved" royal mistresses, those less noble girls of even lower morals who entertained him in his private quarters here.'

Steel laughed. 'So I am free on account of the great King's passion for young women? The old goat.'

'He wears promiscuity like a medal. And the whole nation emulates him.'

Steel shook his head. 'In truth, they are the strangest of

peoples. How shall we ever settle a war between two cultures?'

'Is that why you're here, Jack? To settle the war?'

'You know better than to ask me that, little brother. I'm a soldier. I told you before. Nothing more.'

'You must go. I was putting a plan together. Now we have to act faster.'

Alexander stood up, but Steel's addled mind was filled with questions.

'You knew that I'd been taken?'

'Your man, Simpson, found me.'

'But how could he know of you?'

'That I do not know. It's enough, Jack, that he did, is it not? And now, brother, we really must hurry. As I said, we have not much time. I shall take you close to safety, then I must return to the Hôpital before I am missed. Look at the sky. The night is getting brighter. We must make best use of the shadows.'

Helping Steel to his feet, Alexander indicated their direction and the two men set off eastwards, away from the Hôpital. Steel, however, was unable to resist a final look and, turning, saw the moonlight glance off the gilded dome. He thought of the empty room and the open window and anticipated the surprise and fury when Malbec discovered that his prisoner had escaped.

'Where did you say you were taking me?'

'I'm sending you, Jack. I cannot follow. They call it the "Cour des Miracles", Paris's own St Giles or Tottenham Court, if you like – a place so full of whores, cutpurses and felons that you should have no trouble fitting in.' Alexander laughed.

'Were I not as weak as a kitten I'd strike you for that.'

'Come now, brother. Deny that you're no more than a spy, and thus as guilty of deception as any who make their homes in the rookeries and tenements of Paris or London.'

Steel bristled. 'I may deceive, but I do so in the name of honour.'

'Pah! Your honour is that of the card sharp. It is the safest place for you to hide until you can leave the city. And now that's twice I've saved you. I expect as much from you one day.'

ELEVEN

They crossed the sleeping city as quickly as they could, heading first for the gardens of the Tuileries and then on to the Place des Victoires.

As they walked, Alexander told Steel as much as he could of their ultimate destination, his place of safety. 'It's a thieves' kitchen, nothing more, but a thieves' kitchen the like of which you'll never see again.'

Even at this time of night the streets around the Tuileries were remarkably well lit by thousands of candle lanterns, hung every forty feet across the street on chains. Gradually, however, as their route took them further away from the palaces and the splendid mansions, the light dimmed, and by the time they reached the Place des Victoires the candles had vanished and the only light was from the moon. Alexander took them deep into the unfashionable quartier of La Villeneuve. They took an abrupt right turn and worked their way through a tortuous series of small streets.

Alexander went on: 'The authorities have always denied its existence, and you will not find it marked on any map, but it's there all right. Of course no one in their right mind would normally go there at night, and by day only thieves and harlots. But I think you'll fit in. Have you ever wondered where they go to at night, all the beggars and rogues of Paris? Well, this is where they come to strip off their disguises.'

They walked quickly and Steel, his body racked with pain, found it hard to keep up with his athletic younger brother.

'Is it safe? I mean, why shouldn't they just kill me?'

'You'll be fine as long as you keep in with the man who rules the place. They call him the Kaiser. Don't ask me why. Simpson seems to have connections there. He's arranged it all.'

At length they stopped. Steel knew that they had come northeast. Apart from that, though, he was lost.

Alexander turned to him. 'Now, take every turning to the right and you'll find yourself at the rue St Sauveur. From there it's easy. Follow your nose. This is as far as I go. Remember, Jack. Whatever your natural instincts, in that place you're all criminals. Forget that and you're a dead man. You're on the run now, and outside the law. You must think and act like a felon. And whatever you see, do not for heaven's sake express horror or indignation. Treat it as normal behaviour.'

Steel clasped his brother by the arm. 'From the bottom of my heart, Alexander. Perhaps one day I may repay you.'

Alexander smiled. 'Who knows? Perhaps you will. And never forget, Jack, that though we fight for warring causes you and I are opposite sides of the same coin. We are still made from the same metal. Do not forget that, brother. For that we will always be. And now I must go. Not least to ease my mind about Charpentier. Do you suppose Malbec knows of his involvement with you?'

'It would seem likely. He must surely have guessed. But I swear he learnt nothing from my lips.'

Alexander smiled at him. 'I believe you, Jack. I know no one as loyal as you, brother or not. Adieu.'

He smiled one last time and then was gone. So it was that Steel found himself alone, in the last hour before the dawn, in a place with no name, off the rue St Sauveur. To his left stood the convent of the Filles-Dieu, the Daughters of God. It seemed an unlikely location for a thieves' kitchen, but then, he thought, nothing would have shocked him any more in this city of constant surprises. Following Alexander's instructions, he turned right and kept on doing so until he reached an apparent dead end. Looking more closely, he was able to discern the tiniest of passages, no wider than a single person. At the same moment he caught the smell, or stench, more like. It was as if every sewer in Paris had been opened at once. Holding his breath, Steel pushed himself through the narrow entrance and emerged in another world.

It seemed extraordinary to Steel that only a few streets away from the Sun King's vision of urban splendour you might find something as poor and unforgiving as the Cour des Miracles. Despite its name it was no more than a warren of suffocatingly narrow and badly lit alleyways and earth-floored yards that stank of urine and raw excrement. The enclave was crammed into a single block in the northeastern corner of the city's eastern extremity. This was a place where few would ever venture. But even as he cursed its foul stench, Steel thanked God that it existed.

The narrow street onto which he had emerged began to slope downwards, at first quite gently and then with a steeper gradient, so steep in fact that several times Steel thought he might lose his balance and tumble onto the cobbles.

On his left was a house – if you could call it that, for it was no more than a mud dwelling. In front of it, beside a rusty standpipe, filthy children played in rags, and their half-naked mothers, apparently oblivious to the fact that their breasts were uncovered, laughed and shouted, even revelling in their indecency. Outside of a field of battle in the aftermath of an engagement, it was without doubt the most unpleasant, most inescapably evil place Steel had ever found himself – worse even than the dungeon in Ostend where he had seen a friend tortured to death by merciless pirates, worse than the charnel house of Bavaria. For there seemed to be no end to this depravity, yet this was the place that would, apparently, be his salvation.

A figure approached him from the shadows. Steel's hand fell instinctively to his sword hilt. He drew his weapon a few inches from the scabbard.

'Who's that? Who's there? Speak your name. Why are you following me?'

'Steel. Thank God. It is you.'

Simpson walked into the low light. Steel saw that he was wearing an uncharacteristically plain coat and a more modest wig than usual. He seemed genuinely pleased to see Steel.

'By God, Jack, I'd well nigh given you up for dead. That woman is pure evil. She would have kept you at her pleasure until you died. Believe me. This is not her first encounter with a British officer.'

Simpson, it seemed, knew everything as usual. And Steel guessed from his tone of voice that he was not invited to make further enquiries for the present. However, there was a look in Simpson's eyes that spoke of a deep and lasting hurt, a lost love, even. He wondered how the Marquise had managed it, and concluded that in this strange city anything was possible.

Steel smiled. 'I was sure that you too must have been taken. And Charpentier. What of him?'

Simpson laughed. 'The major is safe. Malbec believes that he was duped by you, and Charpentier is playing along. And as for me, I'm a slippery fish to catch, dear boy. They've been closer to me than this before, and still I've eluded them. But you look as if you only just escaped with your life. Malbec and his cronies are as cruel and heartless a gang of rogues as ever set foot on the planet, Jack. And that's the only way to meet them – on equal terms. That at least is how I intend to meet them, and to dispose of them.'

Steel looked at him and saw for the first time a streak of utter ruthlessness shining in his steely-blue eyes. Yes, he thought, I believe you do and I think that you probably will.' He peered around the street, his eyes well accustomed now to the half-light.

'Now tell me, what exactly are we doing here?'

Simpson held his finger to his lips. 'Welcome to the Cour des Miracles. As your brother will have told you, nothing here is quite what it seems. It's the only place in Paris that Malbec and his bitch would never think of looking for you. But you're right. It is squalid, the realm of crime and chaos. At one time they say there were a dozen such dens in Paris. Now this is the only one.' He looked about. 'I often think it's as if the scum of all the others has risen to the top.' He brushed something which he very much hoped might merely be mud from his breeches.

Steel spoke. 'How do you know my brother?'

'A lucky encounter and a little deduction. Yours is not so common a name. At least not here. I took a gamble.'

'That we must be related?'

'That, and the probability that if that were the case and you managed to escape, then he would help you. I did not know for sure if he would do so. It might have been a dreadful mistake. I'm truly glad it wasn't.'

'Not as glad as I.'

Steel detected in Simpson's tone an honesty and a genuine friendship quite devoid of any sexual purpose, and realized that, for all his fine airs and contrary predilections, Simpson was still at heart a brother officer.

'I mean to say, thank you for being so astute as to take that risk. I should not be here had you not done so. But what concerns me now is how you intend to get me out of here. Surely the minute I set foot on the streets of the city or try to leave through any gate I'm a dead man. Or worse.'

Simpson smiled and nodded. 'Yes, I have realized that. We are here not merely to hide you until you can leave, but

197

because we must find you a disguise. And where better to look than a place where no one is what they seem?'

Steel looked around and saw that Simpson was right. For the first time he realized that as they walked other shapes had been travelling with them along the street. Now as they neared one such dark form he saw it to be a man with no legs, a cripple, pulling himself along the ground by means of a board mounted on wheels. He looked up at Steel and the light caught his face, pockmarked and haggard beneath a lace-trimmed hat of the type worn by the French foot.

'For the grace of God, sir, spare a sou.'

Steel ignored him and turned back to Simpson, but hardly had he done so than he was aware of a black shape rising on his left and flying past him along the street, cackling as it went. He turned back towards the cripple and found nothing.

Simpson laughed. 'You see what I mean?'

'That man was a sham. Not a cripple at all.'

'Exactly. But he took you in. I thought Alexander had told you.'

It occurred to Steel as he passed them that all the other dark forms making their way along the street must also be fakes, and he began to look at them as he passed: a man on crutches, a man without eyes, a woman with a dead baby, a man who addressed him in German and was wearing the uniform of a Bavarian soldier. There were men disguised as women who would lure an unsuspecting fool into a side street with the promise of sex, only to cut his throat. There were the *Francs-Mitoux*, the fakers of illness and all manner of disease. There were the *Sabouteux*, who faked epilepsy and demonic possession, writhing around on the ground to gain sympathy and alms, their mouths filled with harmless frothing sap. There were lepers covered in sores, and as he looked on the numbers seemed to grow by the moment, for they were getting close to the hub of the *quartier* now.

He turned to Simpson. 'So what are you going to turn me into? What's it to be? A cripple? A woman?'

Simpson smiled again and touched Steel affectionately on the shoulder. 'No, Jack, though I would pay dearly for the chance of seeing you in a silk gown. No, I think we're going to make you a blind beggar.'

Steel was amused by the irony of the subterfuge – to mimic a character who until lately he might indeed have been.

'But first you have to meet the Kaiser. Nothing can be done without his approval. And for God's sake show deference, or we're both dead men.'

Steel balked at the name and the arrogant audacity of such a man. 'Surely, you mean the king of thieves?'

Simpson looked alarmed. 'Sh. Do not refer to him as a thief. Never say that, if you wish to escape this place with your life. He is king here, and considered by some a magus. And every day for their protection in his city within the city he simply exacts his portion of their takings. But he's not half as scary as he seems. He knows me. We have an "arrangement".'

Steel appeared puzzled. 'You mean . . . ?'

'No. Nothing like that. He favours the ladies as much as you, dear boy. More so. No, what I mean is that should I find myself, shall we say, in a compromising position with one of my gentleman friends I simply have to get word to the Kaiser and he will arrange to make the poor fellow disappear.'

'He has your lovers killed?'

'You might want to put it that way. I suppose it does sound a trifle callous.'

'I should say it does.'

'Remember, Jack, that here in Paris, indeed as in London, to commit the act which is the ultimate expression of my love for another man remains a crime punishable by death or at least by mutilation. What else would you have me do to safeguard my position in Marlborough's employ? And in return, of course, he gets whatever riches they might have about them. I contrive to ensure that they are always carrying something precious, or a larger than usual sum of money when he turns them off. I believe he disposes of the remains in the Seine.'

Steel knew he was right. Simpson had been an invaluable asset to the Duke, a direct link to the French capital and with a previously undetected cover. What were a few stray men dumped in the Seine compared to the lives of thousands of Allied soldiers? However, it occurred to him, as it surely must have to Simpson himself, that now, with his cover blown, his usefulness was at an end. Steel wondered what lay ahead for a spy who had outlived his usefulness. A job at Horse Guards, he presumed, as an expression of the Duke's gratitude, would be all Simpson could now hope for.

The street ended abruptly, opening out into a huge square, hung with flaming torches and thronged with people.

Simpson turned to him. 'Welcome to the Cours des Miracles.'

It seemed to Steel that every beggar he had ever seen outside every church in Europe must have issued forth from this place. Certainly it was from here, he had no doubt, that the same motley band went out every morning to their day's work. But he saw through the apparent chaos. This was as well-organized an army, in regiments and companies, as ever there was. And among them, naturally, he saw the coats of the armies of France and her allies: Bavarians, Swiss and Irish. But here too were men dressed in the Allied uniforms: Danes, Prussians, Austrians and other smaller states. He wondered how many were worn for effect and how many genuine old soldiers had fallen into bad ways. In truth it was not far to drop from the rank and file to the gutter, just as it was the gutter that provided the raw material for all the armies of Europe. For the most part, though, the men and all the women here wore civilian dress, which though often of disarmingly fine cut and trim was nonetheless of another age, perhaps between ten and thirty years behind the fashion of the times. It reinforced the other-worldly aspect of the scene. For this was indeed a world within a world, the hidden, secret under-belly of Paris. The curious thing was that, quite contrary to his expectations, Steel felt safer here than he had anywhere all the time he had been in Paris.

Around the square, groups of friends huddled around open fires lit on the bare ground. Women shrieked, babies cried and dogs padded between their masters and others. The houses which framed the square were as run-down and ramshackle as their inhabitants – ancient dwellings dating, he thought, back as far as the Middle Ages. The smell of the place too was almost overpowering, the smoke from the wood fires mingling with all the sweat, ordure and aroma of cooking food in a heady *mélange* which, once trapped in the nostrils, was hard to dispel and lingered long after the original source was gone.

Simpson remarked, 'Quite a place, isn't it? The authorities cannot enter here. Whenever they do they just seem to dis-appear. But for you and me, dear Jack, spies that we are, it's a natural second home.'

They advanced into the mêlée and pushed their way across the square. Steel could see Simpson's objective. On the far side of the square, on the ground floor of one of the houses, was what looked like an inn of sorts. A dark, almost red light emanated from its windows, and the cracks and fissures in its fabric gave out a noise greater than the rest in the square. Above the door hung a sign depicting a butchered chicken and a pile of coins – French sous. Below it Steel read the slogan: '*Aux sonneurs pour les trepassés.*'

Simpson saw him staring at the words. 'A play on words, dear boy. *Sonneurs*, you see – *sous neufs*, new coins, and *pour les* – *poulets*, chickens, which also amusingly means "night-watchmen". Bribes for the night watch, the arch enemies of this place. Ah, here we are.'

They entered, and Steel was almost pushed back through the door by the stench. If the smell in the square had been stifling, then this was almost unbearable in its sheer intensity. The inn consisted of a huge circular room packed with tables, around each of which sat a number of men and women and on which tallow candles, along with the glow of a vast open fire, gave the room its flickering illumination. The patrons of this fine establishment were in various states of drunkenness. It seemed to Steel that all, well, certainly all the men, were armed with some sort of weapon, ranging from a musket to a billhook.

Seated in a prominent position at the main table was a man of immense proportions. His head was quite bald aside from the long moustaches which hung down at either side of his mouth. As Steel and Simpson walked into view he fixed them with the sort of curious yet predatory gaze that a fox might give a pair of inquisitive chickens who had blundered into his lair. He banged his hand three times on the table and the noise around him stopped, although the general hubbub of the inn continued.

'Fresh blood. I smell it. I see it. Fresh blood in the kingdom of the truants.' He squinted at them. 'St Colombe, is that you? Who's your friend? One of your boys? No need to bring him here, my friend. We'd have fixed him closer to your home.' He laughed at his own wit and was instantly mimicked by his cronies.

Simpson replied, 'My dear Kaiser. Witty as ever. But this is not one of my "boys", as you so quaintly put it. This man is a fugitive, an outcast like yourselves. He needs help that only you can give.'

The Kaiser stopped laughing and stood up. Steel was struck by his height, which outstripped his own six foot by a good few inches. He was a giant of a man, and heavily muscled, although this was countered by the size of his belly, grown fat from too many rich suppers at his victims' expense. He shook his head.

'You amuse me, St Colombe. We have a deal. You put trade my way. I dispose of your troublesome evidence. That is our deal, and it works very well. But now you come here asking for favours. You are mistaken, my friend. This is not a monastery. Is it, friends?' He turned to the assembled company, who guffawed at the thought. One man hooked his cloak up over his head like a cowl and, pressing his hands together in prayer, walked around the table singing an incantation. 'What makes you think, St Colombe, that you might be in the position to ask favours?'

'I did not say that I would not pay for such a favour. And pay well.'

Simpson brought out a bulging velvet purse from his waistcoat and dropped it onto the table. The Kaiser greedily picked it up.

'That, my dear fellow, paints a very different picture.'

Simpson continued. 'And I dare say that by the end of the month I shall have one or two young men ready to take a dip in the river. I also have a mind to put you in the way of a certain manservant of mine who has proven himself somewhat less than trustworthy. You'll need your very best men for this one. I shall direct you to him, and then the matter will be in your hands. You may be sure that you will find good pickings on him. And in this case, for once, you may be as cruel with him as you wish. I have no love for the man. Give him a good long death.'

So, thought Steel, already he begins his revenge upon Malbec and his cronies. First he deals with Gabriel, using the thieves. Not for the first time Steel saw how Simpson used the system which he had created and in which he was now trapped, at least until he should be removed to London and his due reward.

The Kaiser had noticed Steel and looked at him with

curiosity, his head on one side, as he chewed on a wad of tobacco.

'This is the man?'

'This is the man I told you of. You do not need to know his name. Merely know that he is a brave man and has suffered at the hands of the authorities. See how his hands and face have been cut and beaten. He shares your hatred of them. And now he needs to become one of you. A beggar. You have the gold. You will do what you can?'

The man nodded and leered at them. 'For you, my friend. Only for you.' He turned to Steel. 'Show yourself, friend.' Steel stepped into the light. His face still bore the marks of his beating and his shirt was stained dark red with blood. He had long lost his military coat, but retained the red waist-coat. This alone marked him out as a soldier. The Kaiser noticed it at once.

'Ah. So you're a deserter? Is that it? War got too much for you. You've taken a bit of a beating. We'll get you cleaned up. I won't ask why you're here or where you're going. This . . .' He held up Simpson's heavy purse. '. . . answers all the questions I have. But, one thing. For as long as you are with us you agree to become a member of our brotherhood. Yes?'

'Yes.'

'You swear allegiance to me and no other king?'

Steel steadied himself. 'Yes.'

'You agree to abide by the laws of the kingdom of argot? To become a true parasite, a liar, a thief, a mendicant? All these?'

'I do. All these I swear.'

'Then welcome, friend.'

He spat into the fire, making it hiss, and clapped his hands. Instantly, from behind him appeared two women of indeter-minate age and with skin like leather and manes of matted hair, which hung down upon bare shoulders and low-slung dresses that barely concealed their sagging, over-used bosoms.

The pair moved quickly towards Steel, laughing as they came. Instinctively he backed away, but they beckoned him to them.

The Kaiser laughed. 'Do not be afraid, sir. They will not harm you. But they will make you someone you are not and someone you never thought you would be. When they have finished with you, you will be unrecognizable to your own mother. They are true artists. Put yourself in their hands and I swear you will make a safe passage out of Paris. Your friend has paid for it. You're going home.'

TWELVE

Steel had watched the day break. Or, to put it better, he had seen the sun rise but, rather than shining it seemed to hang limp in the sky, an angry orange orb, obscured by mist. There was no joy in that grey dawn. Normally he would have expected to hear the chatter of songbirds in the trees, heralding the new day, but there were no birds in this place of death, just as there were no trees, only the pale orange sun and the empty muddy landscape stretching far into the horizon, the endless dull brown landscape with its unforgiving, all-consuming, every-orifice-invading mud. It seemed to Steel that the mud had sucked up the very freshness from the air and spewed it out in the inescapable fetid stench and constant noise. His head was filled with an interminable thrumming which entered the brain as readily as it did the soul. He knew exactly what that must be. It was the sound of the Allied siege guns taking up the daily rhythm of their unceasing bombardment of the city of Lille.

The army had been encamped here since the first week of September, although the first attacks had begun in August, and Steel had joined them two days ago, directly on his return from Paris. His journey through northern France had been thankfully swift – swift, that was, once Simpson and his

206

associates had secured his safe passage from the city. They had hidden him for a week and a half in the stinking piss-pot of the Cour des Miracles, and then at the end of August he had made his escape from Paris. By that time the city had been in such a state of terror occasioned by the news of the siege of Lille that the wandering progress of a blind beggar through its easternmost streets and out through the porte de Belville was nothing remarkable. Most of the populace, thought Steel, seemed to have been huddled into the city's churches praying for deliverance from the armies of the Allies, and the remnant of the city guard that had not been mobilized and sent to the front to stem the tide of Marlborough's army were too busy reorganizing the defences of this defenceless, unwalled, unmanned capital to take any notice of Steel.

Of course his horse had long since vanished from the inn at which he had lodged her almost a month previously and would not be seen again. With the *grand peur* at the imminent arrival of *le bel anglais*, as he had discovered Parisians liked to call Marlborough, the inns were almost deserted and there had been no carriage ride home. But while some people fled the city, others profited, and he had been only too thankful to pay for a new mare, without asking where she had come from or to whom by rights she belonged. On the French side, he found everywhere on his return journey through this ravaged countryside, no questions were asked of the tall unshaven man in the red military waistcoat who paid in gold and went as quickly and inexplicably as he had appeared. For no sooner had he left the city than Steel divested himself of his disguise and adopted his usual air. For too long he had walked bent over, the way he had been schooled by the Kaiser's whores.

He had begun his journey back to the lines in good spirits, but the horse, predictably, had quickly gone lame and Steel had endured a steady five-day slog on foot followed by a ride on a new horse that had taken him the best part of another week. Finally he had arrived at the Allied lines, although so vast was the undertaking of the siege that it had taken him another day and a half to regain his unit. That had been last night, and this morning's dawn was made no more welcome by the hangover brought on by the four bottles of Rhenish wine that Captain Laurent, the commander of Number 2 company, had cracked open to celebrate Steel's return to the fold – that and the not inconsiderable quantity of brandy sent down to him in the lines by the regimental mess.

Of Marlborough and Hawkins he had as yet heard nothing. It did not entirely surprise him, for, while Steel's Grenadiers, along with the remainder of Farquharson's Foot, were entrenched in the siege lines to the north of the city attached to the force of Prince Eugene, the Duke and his 'family' were encamped on the southern side with half of the army and only last week had been preparing to fight a pitched battle out in the open against Vendôme, at hideous odds. The Marshal, however, had decided not to risk all on such an engagement, and now Marlborough was back on the attack, seeking to pacify the city. Steel, frustrated, wondered whether he might not hear any news of their intrigue and the success or failure of his mission. Had Charpentier passed on the letter, as he had promised? What had been Louis's reaction? Was peace a possibility? All these questions and more were constant thoughts. All that he asked was to be told.

That and of course to be spared this stinking trench. He wondered what now would be their move. His men, he knew, would be sure to be picked for the vanguard of any attack, as likely as not for the hopeless task of storming any breach that could be found in the walls, risking their lives for fame, glory and riches. To be honest, thought Steel, at this moment I don't really care about glory and wealth. What I really want is to live and to be with Henrietta and to settle and enjoy a family. It was a disturbing thought for one whose adult life had been spent in constant danger on the battlefields of Europe, taking care of his men as one would one's own children. He was part of a sacred brotherhood. No one ever had, could, or ever would call Jack Steel a coward, and he thought the worse of himself for even contemplating not going on to serve to the end with the Grenadiers. But there was something strangely appealing about the prospect of a life of peace for one who had always considered himself a man of war. Perhaps it was only a natural reaction to his current surroundings, a desperate need to see a vision of the future as something other than this hellhole of fetid mud and dead flesh.

He knew the men were pleased to have him back, and thankfully they had suffered relatively few casualties among the old hands and the officers. In fact to date Farquharson's had fared rather better than many other regiments, although Steel knew too well how quickly that might change.

He pulled on the new boots he had bought in Paris and was fastening his waistcoat when there was a discreet cough at the door of the tented dugout that now served as home.

'Company rounds, sir. Mister Hansam and Mister Williams are ready, sir.'

Slaughter was certainly pleased to have him back, and there was no need for him to say it. Steel knew that the Grenadiers were his men and always would be. He had made them into a fighting force, and they trusted him for it – those at least who knew him, for, despite their relatively light losses, they had still been party to a new intake of replacements. As much was set out in the mountain of paperwork that had greeted Steel on his return the previous evening and which he had been putting off handling. Well, he thought, at least the company rounds would delay that chore a while longer.

'Very good, Jacob. I think we'll make a start.'

His first task was to discover which of the Grenadiers remained alive after the previous night's work, which if any had perished, and which were being treated for their wounds by the company apothecary, Matt Taylor. Please God, Steel

209

thought, let there be none with the surgeon. That sawbones was nothing more than a butcher whose trade lay in hacking off shattered limbs in an attempt to let a man live. Names were missing from the roll, some familiar, some new to him. Some of them belonged, he knew, to men who lay out there before the city which lay before them, half a mile distant. Between the trench and Lille itself lay a vast plain of churned earth, gouged with cannon-fire and littered with the bodies of the thousands of attackers not fortunate enough to have survived the numerous ill-conceived attacks which Prince Eugene had launched to date. What, wondered Steel, could be the point in having good men climb out of the trenches and advance in close order towards a fortification whose defenders had only to hold their fire until at short range their devastating firepower mowed down the attackers like corn beneath the scythe. This was not the way to wage war, and Steel felt sure it would not be the future. In years to come men would discover some other way to fight. Trenches such as this vile pit would cease to be necessary, and men would no longer climb over a parapet to certain death and uncertain glory. He surveyed the empty plain, devoid of all vegetation now. Of course the first action of the besiegers had been to sweep the area clear of all crops and possible sources of forage. What the dragoons had begun the showers of cannon-fire had finished. And when this was over, he thought, when the crops once again came to be planted outside the walls of Lille, they would most certainly grow well, for the soil would be made all the richer by dead men's blood and bones. That would be their sad legacy.

Steel looked down at his boots and wondered how long they would stand up to these conditions. Long, he hoped, for they were uncommonly comfortable and there was not much prospect of commissioning anther pair in the near future – unless, of course, they were to march into Paris in triumph after Louis's surrender. He had no idea whether his mission, which had almost cost him his life, had been a success or a failure. He had sent a runner to the Duke on his return with the simple message that the mission – the delivery, at least – had been accomplished. Nothing more. As yet he had received no reply. He had not expected to. His role in the affair was over, he presumed. He waited for the next assignment and wondered what plan the Duke might now have up his sleeve. If only, he thought, the bloody Dutch had not put paid to his plan to take Paris. Steel knew it had been achievable, and better surely than this living hell. He stared at the bottom of the trench in which he was standing, ankle-deep in mud. The water table was high in this part of Flanders, and in some places the trench was no more than four feet deep. The difference between this and the height of a man was in general made up by placing gabions, wicker baskets filled with stones and earth, on top of the parapet to a height of three feet. For the most part this worked admirably, a firestep being all that was needed for the attackers to oppose any sally from the city. In the case of Steel and the Grenadiers, however, their height became for once a disadvantage, often making them very nearly level with the top of the gabions. With caution now, Steel mounted the firestep and, crouching, peered over the parapet. It was as well that he did. Directly to their front through the morning mist he saw a sudden bright orange flash, and then another and another. He knew the sight only too well. Knew what to expect.

Not waiting for any further prompting, Steel leapt from the firestep, ducked down into the trench and yelled, 'Ware cannon. To you front.'

With a shriek the first cannonball flew high above his head and screamed away into the rear of the besieging army, followed by a second, a third and the others of the salvo as the French within the citadel sent over their first response of the new day to the Allied bombardment. Steel waited, counted to twenty, and then got up again and brushed off the mud

211

which had clung to his breeches. He was aware that Sergeant Slaughter was watching him.

'They seem to be getting closer, sir, don't you think? Perhaps they've seen you.'

'Don't flatter me, Jacob. It doesn't suit you. Besides, I hardly think the shot are too particular as to whom they land on.'

'You're right there, sir. One of them took away poor young Harrison last week. Silly bugger. Took his head clean off at the shoulders. Had to throw his coat away. New issue too. Shame. Not that any of the men would have wanted it anyways. He never was very particular about his personal matters.'

'Stank to high hell, Jacob, is what you mean to say.'

'More than the rest of them, sir. We used to say you could put him in a casemate and he'd clear it of rats quicker than any terrier. Poor bugger. Won't miss the bloody smell, though. A walking sewer, 'e was.'

Steel and Hansam laughed. Williams managed a smile. It was the sort of graveyard humour that now permeated the company and all the men of the Allied army who had lived in these trenches for the last month. And it was not badly meant. Harrison was gone now, and nothing could save him or any of the others, and if a light-hearted joke at his expense could bring some relief to their condition, then what did it matter? And who would hear them? Certainly no kin of Harrison's. Wherever they might be, thought Steel.

There was another whizzing sound in the air above them.

'Heads down, lads. Here they come again.'

It had become a familiar routine. The Allies would start their barrage before dawn, the gunners stripped to the waist sweating in the night to send shots raining into the city, causing as much confusion and panic as possible. And then, when they paused, the enemy would reply. Generally, the French fired three bursts before settling down for the business of the day in which they would maintain a steady, if

212

somewhat weak, fire for hours on end. Their timings were predictable, and it was quite possible for the Allied troops to avoid being hit if they only remembered when to expect them. What troubled Steel was how on earth the French might be finding the ammunition to keep up such a rate of fire. As far as he was aware the Allied army completely surrounded Lille. There was surely no way supplies could be got in. Either, he concluded, the French had a huge underground storehouse of ammunition, which given Marshal Vauban's ingenuity in his siegeworks was not beyond possibility, or there was a breach in the attackers' entrenchments.

Steel and his small party walked along the line of the trench looking at his men as they sat against the parapet. Most had removed their ornate mitre caps for fear they might be shot off or present too tempting a target for the French gunners, and instead they had adopted plain black or red skullcaps, often worn over a small inner cap of steel. Their scarlet coats, already faded to brick red, were now covered in dried mud which turned them a strange shade of brown, and to a man they looked more like a crowd of farm labourers than a company of grenadiers. But Steel knew that their fighting spirit had not dimmed. They were still his men, even if they would rather be anywhere else on earth than in this stinking ditch in Flanders.

He turned to one of the men, half asleep and propped against the trench wall. 'Good morning, Mackay. Catching up on your sleep?'

The man roused himself to attention and was rewarded by a glare from Slaughter. 'Yes, sir. That is, no, sir. I was, er, inspecting my musket, sir.'

Steel smiled. 'Inspecting your musket, were you? Well, see it doesn't get mud down the barrel, or if the Frenchies come over that parapet you'll find yourself sleeping a sleep from which you'll never wake.'

213

The others laughed and walked on behind him as Slaughter shook his head at Mackay.

Steel turned to Hansam. 'D'you see, Henry. In another regiment, indeed any company other than our own, I'll wager that the commander would have placed that man on a charge for being asleep at his post. But I do not intend to do that, and you may ask me why. I'll tell you. Respect. That man, Mackay, has been with me since before Blenheim, Henry and I respect him, and he does likewise for me. Did you hear that, Sar'nt? Be sure that you do not place Mackay on company orders, if you please.'

The sergeant shook his head and wondered whether his captain, the man he counted not only as a superior officer but a faithful friend, had grown soft in the head or just soft with married life. He had known others go the same way. But surely not Captain Steel?

Hansam knew that the lecture was for show. There was a time and a place for the harsh discipline that the army demanded, and a man such as Mackay would not benefit from the lashes that might have been summarily meted out in other units. It was true, as with other men in the company, they had a mutual respect, born from five years of campaigning together against the French. Besides, it was clear to anyone that any attack launched from the citadel would be seen long before it would wake Mackay.

The mist was beginning to clear now.

Slaughter said, 'I hate sieges. If you want to know, sir, I can't be doing with them at all. Cooped up in these bloody stinking trenches. When do we get to fight?'

Lieutenant Hansam offered a reply. 'That is the very nature of the beast, Sar'nt. Your siege is what is known as "static warfare". Never a pleasant experience for either side.'

'You're right there, sir. Nastiest place on this earth, if you ask me.'

While at any other time he would readily have agreed, at

214

present Steel did not share their sentiments. He knew of at least one other place that offered a worse prospect than this: a small cell in Paris, where a wooden chair still bore traces of his own blood. But now was hardly the time to mention that.

'Unless, like Mister Williams here, you are able to find yourself your own cosy citadel and get on with the important business of life, eh, Tom?'

Williams nodded, for he was unable to speak. He was sitting in a small embrasure cut into the forward face of the trench and covered above with a piece of taut canvas. As they found him he was gnawing on a roasted bird, lately taken from a still revolving spit which stood close by, bearing four more fowl, and being turned by one of the drummer boys. He grinned and swallowed.

'Fair forage, sir. It was sanctioned by the Duke himself, for the duration of the siege, at least. Two of the men brought them in this morning. Three brace of French partridge. Good eating, sir. The lieutenant has already marked his share. Would you join us?'

Steel shook his head. 'Thank you Tom, but I have to be about company business.' He noticed that the ensign's cheeks were caked in grey mud and that his breeches and gaiters too were covered in the stuff. 'I shouldn't go on parade like that, Tom. Get yourself cleaned up if you can find any water. You were out last night?'

'I led the patrol, sir. We went out with the miners and were seeking a mine ourselves. But we found none.' He paused to tear at another piece of partridge. 'Though we did bring in one prisoner. A Walloon. Surly fellow. He's being questioned now.'

'Well done for that.'

Williams was learning well, thought Steel. How he had changed in the four years since he had come to them as a green ensign, fresh from Eton. He was now a seasoned officer, as good as any in Steel's eyes and better than most. Mining parties were among the toughest assignments in this war. Leading out a party of men armed mostly with picks and spades, sharpened as weapons in the case of an encounter with the enemy, was perilous work that sharpened the wits. Williams had done well.

Steel continued, 'The more we know of their defences, the sooner we'll be in. And I'm sure we shall know of their mine soon enough. At least, should it explode beneath us we shall in fact know nothing of it. Eh, gentlemen? For we shall all be blown to eternity.'

They laughed, and Williams, who had finished his breakfast, said, 'There's talk of an attack tonight, sir. Is there any truth in it, d'you suppose?'

'Well, Tom. There's always talk of an attack in the trenches on account of the fact that the men would do anything to be out of them. Or at least they think they would, until they get out there. But the truth of the matter is anyone's guess.'

It was true, he thought. You could see it in their faces, worn and grey with stress. Rumour upon rumour confounded their minds. The trouble with this type of warfare was that there was just too much time to think. And thinking, as any officer would readily inform you, was not something in which the common soldier should ever be encouraged.

'Don't worry, Tom. I'll let you know as soon as I hear anything more. Now, please do go and get your servant to clean you up. If the colonel sees you like that I'm just as likely to be for the high jump as you.'

It was only five hours later that Steel remembered his promise to Williams. And by then it was too late to matter.

At about one o'clock in the afternoon he noticed that the seven batteries of heavy siege cannon directly behind their position had begun to play upon the rising ramparts of the star fort which encircled the city. The effect, he could see from the trench, was to send a party of the enemy who had been engaged in making repairs to previous damage scurrying back into the fortress. After they had gone, the barrage continued. Ten minutes later a messenger arrived, panting, having run from the support trench.

'Captain Steel, sir. Colonel Farquharson's compliments, sir, and you're to stand the men to. You're to prepare to advance on the enemy.'

As the man left, breaking into a run, Steel shouted to Slaughter: 'Stand them to, Sar'nt. Officers, take posts. Check grenades and fuses. Light your tapers.'

The sergeant took up the commands. 'Check your muskets, lads, and your bayonets. We're going to attack.'

However, it was not for another five hours, at almost six o'clock in the evening, that they finally received the order to make ready to advance. The messenger was followed by another, a young lieutenant, barely sixteen, Steel guessed, from Sir James's battalion staff. Steel knew that he would tell him what he needed to know, and sure enough the boy's boiling excitement spilled out.

'The regiment is to be part of a grand assault, sir. We're to go in at seven o'clock this evening. A great column, sir. Sixteen full battalions. Fifteen thousand men in all, d'you know.'

Steel heard his calm assurance that their target, the St Andrew and St Magdalen sectors, would have been softened up by cannon-fire from the great siege batteries which had been assembled to their rear on the high ground. They would advance at walking pace into the assault and engage the enemy through the breaches in his defences. This would not be a forlorn hope, or so the generals were confident. As grenadiers, Steel's company would form the vanguard of the advance. So, he thought, a frontal assault on a heavily defended position. There might be no forlorn hope, per se, but Steel knew that in truth the grenadiers were just that – an impossibly outnumbered strike force being sent right into the mouth

217

of hell, whatever the generals thought of the invincible power of their great guns. Steel had seen it before, too many times. He sighed and, drawing the great sword from his side, ran his thumb gently down the razor-sharp blade.

A drum roll came from the left.

Steel looked to Hansam. 'What time d'ye have, Henry?'

Hansam looked at his coveted French timepiece. 'I have thirty minutes past the hour, Jack. It's time.'

Steel nodded. Well then, this was it. One more time for luck. All for nothing and good Queen Anne.

'Here we go, boys. And remember, keep low, duck your heads as if you were advancing into a snowstorm, and try to work in pairs like I taught you. Some of us will fall, boys. But most of us, I promise you, will get through, and then we'll show the Frenchies what we can do, and we'll take this bloody town. We're going to kick King Louis's arse and chase his Grand Marshal back to Paris.'

A ragged cheer rippled down the ranks. The drums beat again, more urgently now. One of the orderlies was passing through the ranks with the customary tot of rum for each man before an assault. All took it hungrily, and those who refused soon found their shares taken up by neighbours only too happy to be advancing into the enemy fire with less of their wits about them. Someone, one of the younger men, vomited his rum ration and the remains of his breakfast onto the floor of the trench.

Slaughter swore. 'What a bloody waste of good rum. Cochrane, you dirty little man, I'm going to make you clean up that mess there when we get back.'

'Yes, Sarge. Thank you, Sarge.'

There was a ripple of laughter from the ranks.

'Sergeant to you, Cochrane. That's enough. Look to your front. Officer present.'

Steel nodded to the men and Slaughter. 'Ready, Sar'nt?'

'As ever will be, sir. I hope those guns 'ave done their work.'

218

'The generals seem to think so, and in whom else can we trust?'

Suddenly the earth was rocked by a huge explosion. Instinctively the men ducked, and then just as quickly rose again to survey the result. Far off across the mud, in the outer wall of the first ravelin, a cloud of dust was climbing into the sky.

One of them said, 'Bloody hell, Sergeant. What was that?'

'That, my lad, was a bloody great mine exploding. One of ours, luckily. Take a look, Hooper. You're a lucky boy to see that. And mark it well, for that's where we're headed.'

The men craned their necks to see over the parapet. Steel, reckoning that there was little chance that the French artillery would open up after such a shock, climbed onto the firestep and said nothing. Slowly the smoke and dust cleared to reveal a huge V-shaped gap blown in the wall of the ravelin. Around it was utter devastation. Flames crackled on the wall and in the mud and scorched debris: stones, wood and what had been men smoked and crackled wherever the eye could see.

Steel turned to Slaughter. 'That's it, Sar'nt. They've done it. We're going in.' He looked towards the men. 'See that hole in the wall there? That's your target, lads. Come on, with me. Before the Frenchies come to their senses.'

Another of the men spoke. Steel did not see who it was. 'God's blood, Sarge. It looks like the bloody gates of hell itself. Oh bloody hell. We're not going in there, are we?'

With a single step Steel crested the trench and stood on the parapet. Instantly the remainder of the company were with him, and all along the line now to the left and right they could see men standing above the trench line.

Slaughter gave the command: 'Form up. Line of attack. Steady now. Wait for it . . . Wait for it now. Stand steady there, I said.'

Steel drew his sword and held it high above his head.

'The Grenadiers will advance with me. For the regiment and for Queen Anne. Forward. Let's take that bugger.'

With a cheer they set out across the mud at the normal walking pace of an attack: 'as fast as foot could fall'. They could all see it now, the huge breach blown in the defences by a mine that had been two weeks in the making, a mine that had been tunnelled out by sweating, naked men from Yorkshire, Nottingham and Cornwall who had advanced underground through a long, thin, claustrophobic shaft to lay tons of explosive at the foot of Vauban's masterwork. This was their achievement, and Steel was determined that they should not have worked in vain. He urged himself on through the mud and looked around, saw Hansam, Williams, Slaughter and the others.

He shouted back to them, 'Come on. Were nearly there. Not far, boys.'

He was aware of Williams mouthing some words at him and pointing with the tip of his sword towards the fort, but the cacophony of the Allied guns and not least the sound of his own breathing made them unintelligible. He followed the line of Williams's sword, and then he saw what was worrying the junior officer. For there, pouring out at them from the very breach itself, the very mouth of hell, was a great body of white-clad infantry. And they didn't look as if they intended to surrender.

Steel gasped. 'Oh Christ in heaven. How in hell's name?'

He didn't have to say anything more. The beleaguered garrison was making a sortie against the attack. It was any besieging soldier's worst nightmare. The enemy allowed you to expose yourself in the open, picked off as many as he could, then, feeling sufficiently confident, counterattacked in strength.

Continuing to advance, and followed steadily by his men, Steel watched as the white flood built to battalion strength, then as still more came on. There must be thousands of them, he thought, enough to easily outnumber the attackers.

'Keep going, lads. We can take them. They're just putting on a show. They know they're beaten.'

In truth he did not believe his own words. The best the British could now hope for would be to stand their ground and trust that the French counterattack petered out. Otherwise, even if they escaped with their lives, they would surely lose all the gains that they had made in the last few minutes and for which many men had died. It was madness, but there was no alternative.

Steel chose his moment with great care. 'Halt. Make ready.'

They would meet the French attack head on with a solid volley. He was aware that the other five companies of the regiment would still be advancing in their wake but trusted that when they saw the turn of events they too would stop. Indeed if the adjutant or Colonel Farquharson had enough nous they might even be able to join the Grenadiers in the line and give the enemy a really bloody nose before they had a chance to close. For now, though, during the all-important first volleys his men and the Grenadiers from the other regiments to his right and left would be on their own. Slowly the gap between the advancing lines of red- and white-clad soldiers grew less and less. At fifty paces they stopped.

'Make ready. Fire by platoons.' He paused. 'Present. Fire.'

The first of the volleys rang out from the British ranks, followed by another and then another along the line. It was met almost simultaneously by an explosion of fire from the French, which although more instantly murderous was soon over, while the red ranks continued to pour it on. Steel saw white-clad Frenchmen fall in numbers but was also aware of gaps appearing in his own line. Slaughter pushed and pulled at the men, and the drummers dragged out the dead. Another French volley, and the rippling fire of the Grenadiers continued. The French did not break and run, as Steel had hoped they would, and as the smoke cleared he saw why. Behind the two ranks of the enemy regiment to his front, in which there were now significant gaps, another unit had appeared to reinforce it, and as he watched the front regiment split in four and allowed the sections of the fresh unit to come through and form a new and untarnished front line.

Christ, he thought, they've got us. He realized that there was no way to win this firefight. It galled Steel that it had happened so quickly, but if there was one lesson he had learnt in this war it was to know when the time had come to concede. And that time was now. There were just too many of them.

'Sar'nt, have the men retire. Fall back. Fall back to the trench, lads.'

Slaughter intoned in turn, 'Steady. Keep it steady now. Don't turn your backs to them. I'll shoot any man I see turning away from the enemy. Fall back, slowly.'

They had reached the parapet now, and the French had halted some fifty paces away. Now they in turn were falling back towards the city. Every few paces they would loose off a ragged volley, but the bullets made little impact. One of the Grenadiers was caught on the cheek and cursed as he wiped away the blood. But just as the last few of his men were climbing down after him into the trench, Steel was aware of a more powerful volley.

There was a cry. 'Man down.'

Steel looked around. He saw Hansam clutching a wounded arm, Williams panting with exhaustion and Slaughter counting in the men. He peered over the parapet and saw that the French had turned now and were marching at double time back towards their defences. All the men were back in the trench now and the unlucky last-minute casualty had been dragged in with them.

'Sarnt, who is it? See if Matt Taylor can patch him up.'

Slaughter shook his head: ''Fraid he can't, sir. It *is* Taylor, sir. He's dead.'

*   *   *

The week following the attack passed slowly. Surely, thought Steel, there must be some end to this stalemate? He had been astonished by what had happened – their failure to get as far as the breach and the apparently unaffected French. He had been dismayed too by their casualties. The company had lost a score killed and wounded in the brief fight, including Matt Taylor. His loss was sorely felt throughout the company. He had been hugely popular, not only for his skill with wounds, but for his cheerful good humour and sound good sense. For Steel in particular it was a dreadful loss. Taylor had been one of his originals, with him in this war since the outbreak. Indispensable, apparently immortal. Steel had lost not only one of his men, he had lost a friend and a soul mate.

With spirits low, it was vital to raise morale. The men spent three days when not fighting in games of cricket organized by Tom Williams. Steel himself took a part in one. It was not a great success, as the mud was still soft and the ball had no bounce. Still, it kept morale higher than it might have been, and it was always good for the men to see him at play. Particularly with them. But such distractions were not always possible.

On the sixth day after the attack Steel could be found sitting in a damp hollow within the trench. The rain was falling in sheets and he had wrapped himself in his cloak and had his hat pulled down hard on his head. Beside him sat Hansam, similarly clad. The Grenadiers lay about the trench in various attitudes. Some were asleep. Some could not sleep, despite their evident state of exhaustion. A few played cards. All were wet, cold and miserable. All were impatient for action. Having been sitting with his eyes shut for some minutes, at last Steel spoke.

'It would not be so bad if we were given some notion of when we might go in again. The problem, Henry, always lies in the not knowing. Don't you agree?'

'Yes. Always. But, Jack, surely too much information is a

bad thing. Tell the men too much, tell them the facts, and we'd have a mutiny on our hands. Still, it would be nice to know how long we have.'

There was nothing worse for a soldier, thought Steel, than boredom. It ate into the soul and gnawed away at the sub-conscious fears they all harboured, fears of death and mutilation. And a siege was the very worst place for such fears. Every day the same routine. Missiles flying overhead from both sides reminding you that the instruments of your potential destruction were always close at hand, that any day might be your last. He would rather have led a forlorn hope than sit here, like this, day after day, hour on hour, waiting for death. Attempting to divert his mind, he had given much thought to the matter of his mission in Paris. Had relived every moment, from his arrival in the city to his ignominious departure. He did not linger, however, over the memory of his terrifying interview with Malbec and the Marquise. He wondered how Simpson had got on, whether the odious Gabriel had been 'disposed of' by the Kaiser's men, and not least where his brother might now be and whether anyone had discovered his complicity in Steel's escape.

Chiefly, though, his mind was occupied with the wish to know whether he had succeeded, and it was on this that he was thinking when he was roused by the sound of approaching footsteps, or rather splashes, for the mud in the bottom of the trench had turned to filthy slurry as it filled up with water as the level within the ground grew daily. Most of the tunnels had been flooded, and the mining activities had been temporarily suspended on both sides. Which, he felt, was a blessing. At least they would not all be blown sky high without notice. Steel looked up to see who their visitor might be and was greeted by the sight of a young officer. The man's cloak and hat hid both rank and unit, but Steel guessed from his fresh demeanour and step that he must be a runner from the brigade command.

He stopped and greeted Steel with a smart bow. Steel struggled to his feet and turned away to shake the rain from his clothes.

'Orders, sir, from General Webb. Your men are to become part of a converged battalion of grenadiers to accompany the general as part of a force to escort a wagon train of supplies.'

Steel knew Webb. He was a sound commander who had led a brigade at Blenheim and now had command of a division. This seemed a curious task for such a man.

'Supplies? From where? Brussels?'

'No, sir. Road's cut. Supplies from Ostend, sir. You are to march out with the general and escort the supply convoy from Ostend. You won't be alone. He has twenty-four battalions and twenty-six squadrons of horse.'

A sizeable force, thought Steel. 'How bad is it? How far have the French got?'

'Word is, sir, that while we've been sitting here the French have occupied a line along the Scheldt from Lille to Ghent. In some force, it seems. In effect they've cut us off from Brussels. We still hold the port and are connected to it by the road through Menin and Thourout, although in parts it's no more than a causeway and it's flanked by the French at Nieuport and Ypres. At this moment Sir General Erle is proceeding in convoy from the port towards our camp with munitions and other supplies.'

Steel blanched. Henrietta was in Brussels. He had sent her there for her safety, and now it seemed that all he had done was to deliver her into captivity.

'We've lost Brussels?'

'Not lost, sir. Cut off.'

'Quite. Yes, thank you, cornet, you may go. Tell General Webb we shall make ready to move.'

Steel turned away from the man as he took his leave. Hansam looked at him, read his thoughts.

'Don't worry yourself, Jack. She'll be fine. She's sure to

have got away, in either direction. She survived Ostend, so surely this will be little trouble.'

'Little trouble? A French army stands between me and my wife and you call it "little trouble"? Have a care, Henry.'

'I'm sorry, Jack. That was insensitive of me. But it is true. Besides, what can you do to help? Nothing.'

They both knew he was right. They had been commanded to march by the brigade general, and nothing could stop that happening. At least they were not going directly to Ostend itself. The name hung low in Steel's mind, forever associated with death and horrid carnage. It was the place where he had seen a friend butchered in cold blood and where he had almost lost his own life. But it was the place, too, where he had first seen his dear Henrietta.

While Steel was apprehensive, Slaughter was jubilant. 'Thank God for that, I say. We'll finally get shot of this bloody trench. I'll tell the men, sir. They'll be that glad of it.'

'Thank you, Sar'nt. So am I, for that matter.'

Williams came running into the fire-bay. 'Sir, have you heard? We're to march with General Webb and a whole battalion of grenadiers drawn from the division. I met young Bellows on the way here. Told me everything. Isn't it terrific?'

'I don't suppose you thought to ask your friend where we're to rendezvous with the column? It quite slipped my mind.'

Willliams looked pleased with himself. 'As a matter of fact I did, sir. We're to meet at a place called Wynendael. He reckons we won't see any action, but it will be good to be away from here, sir, won't it?'

'Aye, Tom, that it will.'

As the grenadiers prepared to take leave of their trench, handing over their squalid billets to a company of disgruntled dragoons, none of them was aware that their fate was being decided some miles away in a tent pitched in a field on the southern outskirts of Bruges.

226

Marshal Vendôme stretched his fingers out across a map of the Low Countries and settled the tips on a junction in the road just southwest of the city.

'General de la Motte, you will take your division, twenty thousand men, and advance to this crossroads at Thourout. We have intelligence that the Allies are sending a relief column from Ostend to supply their army besieging Lille. You will meet the enemy column here, between Thourout and Wynendael, and seize it for France. At all costs it must not be allowed to get through to their lines at Lille. I do not anticipate that you will encounter any problem whatsoever. According to our intelligence, the escort consists of only some seven thousand men. They are mostly British, I grant you, but you will have an advantage of some three to one in your favour. Marlborough has sent a dozen more battalions to reinforce them, but we do not believe that they have yet arrived. Even if they have, however, you will still enjoy a considerable advantage. There is no excuse for failure, de la Motte. No excuse whatsoever. Take the column and return with it to me. That is all I ask. You lost us Ostend. Now you can at least save Lille.'

THIRTEEN

Riding at the head of the small column, Major General John Webb reflected upon the task that lay ahead of him. He did not know if they would win the day, nor even if he would escape with his life. What he did know, though, at least what he had been told by Marlborough, was that he faced a force numbering certainly twice his own column strength of six thousand infantry, and that the enemy force would doubtless be of all arms, infantry, cavalry and artillery.

Webb was too seasoned a soldier to suppose that he could fight a straightforward pitched battle at such a disadvantage. The lack of cavalry, for one thing, would put his men at peril of being outflanked and ridden down. Worse still was his utter lack of artillery. He saw the reason for it. For one thing, his role was to be a mobile unit, to escort the convoy. For another, the Duke he knew did not have any medium guns to spare, all of them being employed against Lille. He would not have expected artillery. But the French would have it, that he knew, and his men would have to stand and take the shot for just as long as the French could sustain their fire, or until they became bored with knocking men down like ninepins and decided to close the action with an infantry attack. All the initiative lay with the enemy, and to say that his options were limited would have been an understatement. But Webb knew that there was no turning back. If he failed in his defence of the supply column, then Marlborough would raise the siege. As a soldier his duty was to keep the French at bay, and die at his post if he must. As a man, though, his inclination was quite otherwise, and as he rode along towards the enemy he ruminated on the situation.

He did not care much for Marlborough. Wasn't his own cousin the Member of Parliament Henry St John, Tory leader at Westminster and directly opposed to the Duke? Webb had even served as a close ally of St John as an MP himself for three years in the late 1690s. He regretted the duel which had forced him out of his seat and back into the field in the army of King William.

If the truth be told, which he hoped it never would be, he was more of a Jacobite than most people would ever know. It irked him to be fighting in the field shoulder to shoulder with the Dutch, in particular, who had perverted the course of the British bloodline. Queen Anne was reasonable enough, indeed he had even had a position in her husband's household. But she was too easily led, and at present still in thrall to Marlborough's conniving, courtly wife, Sarah Churchill. And when Anne died, what would happen then? The Queen was barren. Thirteen miscarriages, they said, and the poor Duke of Gloucester dead at eleven. At the age of forty-three it looked unlikely she would now produce an heir. Webb was concerned that the throne might pass over the Channel to the Dutch again, or worse still one of the German princes. The Act of Settlement had named the Electress of Hanover, and that could not be allowed to happen. He knew that others in Britain shared his worries. He was the last man to wish another bloody civil war on his country. He had been born just seven years after the end of the last. Yet it was clear that something would have to be done. In the meantime, though, there was another more pressing problem facing him.

In fact, thought Webb, it would suit him very well to be beaten off by the French and for the siege to be a failure. Before any action could be taken to restore the proper Stuart line, Marlborough would have to be discredited. But defeat was not in Webb's nature, and it was perhaps because of that fact and the conflict of emotions in which he now found himself that the shrewd Marlborough had given him this troublesome command. No, there was only one thing to do, and that was to forget politics and beat the bloody French. Duty demanded it and his conscience demanded it. Besides, what would his fellow generals say if he turned tail and ran? Moreover, he was a man of honour who abided by his word.

Webb had accepted the command with thanks, and with it Marlborough's selection of the units which should form it, down to the minutest detail. Why, the Duke had even gone so far as to suggest that he should appoint a particular captain to the command of the converged grenadier battalion. Arguably, in this skeleton force, the grenadiers were the most important element. The man sounded solid enough – a hero, by all accounts, decorated and promoted at Blenheim and Ramillies and newly married to Rumney's eldest daughter, which in itself, knowing that family as he did, he could see would be a demanding undertaking. Webb hoped that the captain would prove himself capable of leading a battalion in the coming fight, for all their sakes.

Steel stood with the eleven other battalion commanders in Webb's makeshift field headquarters, a clearing in a copse at the edge of the road from Roulers and Courtrai. They had slogged up here from Lille over three days, and Steel recognized the road from the previous year's campaigning, for it was up here that they had marched towards Ostend. The name chilled him to the bone ... and now here they were again in a country ravaged by war. Many of the villages had been deserted, he noticed, most only recently. It was often thus in this war and those which had preceded it: soldiers constantly retracing their own footsteps. How, wondered Steel, can you really tell who's winning or losing? It didn't seem to make sense. Towns fell and were recaptured time and again, and men died in their name. Eventually the villagers would leave, sick of the fighting. After a while they would return to turn over the bloody fields and repair the broken houses and start again.

The rain had not let up until this morning, and they were grateful for the time to dry out before the engagement. They were a typically assorted force for this war of nations, thought Steel, looking around at his fellow officers: apart from his own composite grenadier battalion, there were Hanoverians, Prussians, Dutch and Danish and, importantly for him, four battalions of Scots. He noticed that Webb was speaking.

'Count Loudenburg, I want you and your Prussians on the left here, if you please. The Hanoverians on the right wing. Your Danes would do best in the centre of the line. The Scottish brigade I will position here too, in the centre, closest to me. We shall form up in three lines of battle, each of four battalions, for that is all we have. And we must face facts, gentlemen. As you know I have pushed on the cavalry, and by their report we are heavily outnumbered and by all arms. What we need is a miracle, gentlemen – some means by which we can counter that superiority by stealth and surprise. I have positioned us between two woods. That at least will have the effect of funnelling the French towards us, for the woods, I believe, are quite impassable. The French commander has stretched his line between two woods, a gap of a thousand yards. Comte de la Motte may attempt to flank us. Heaven knows he has enough men.' Far more than I was advised by the Duke, he thought. 'But in truth that may not be possible, and I certainly believe so. To our right lies the Château de Wynendael, making it impossible for infantry to manoeuvre in line and with hedges which would impede his cavalry. To the left the wood becomes a tangled coppice, quite impassable. I have selected this position with care. Formed two deep in three lines we shall be able to deploy maximum firepower while forcing his numbers into a tighter gap than he would have wished – a tunnel of fire, if you like. But that may not be enough. We need some means of amplifying the effect of our firepower.'

One of the Prussians spoke up. 'We will be using your method of platoon fire, General? My men are quite conversant with this procedure. I believe it would work admirably.'

'Yes, Captain Becker. It is my intention to do so, and I am equally certain that it will prove effective. But we must search for some other element.'

Steel had a sudden thought. 'Sir.'

Webb looked at him. 'Who are you, sir? Introduce yourself to the company.'

'Captain Steel, sir, late of Farquharson's Foot. I have the honour to command your Grenadier battalion.'

Webb looked at Steel long and hard. 'So, you are the great Captain Steel. Well, I admire your candour and your bravery, sir. Your fame precedes you. You're a Scot, are you not?'

'Sir.'

'A Highlander?'

'No, sir. My family home lies southwest of Edinburgh.'

'You're no Covenanter then?'

'Sir?'

'Did your people come out against King Charles in the late civil war? Where did your sympathies lie?'

'My family came out for the King, sir. That was my father's wish. But we are as loyal to the present regime as we were to the last. Whoever is the rightful monarch as decreed by lineage and by Parliament.'

Webb laughed. 'So you are a politician as well as a soldier, Captain.'

Steel thought of his brother and how he too would have laughed at their conversation. 'No, sir. I try to stay away from politics as much as I can. I am a simple soldier.'

'One thing I suspect you are not, Steel, is simple. You wished to make a comment on my plan of battle?'

'Of course I agree with you, sir, that the woods are impassable to infantry and cavalry in formation. But I have walked them this past hour, General, and men can pass through them quite easily, if unformed.'

Webb laughed. 'That may be, Captain, but what difference will that make to the French? An unformed unit can be of no threat to us, surely, any more than we can use the woods to attack the French?'

'I was not thinking about the French passing through the woods, but our own men, sir. I ask you to place half of my Grenadiers on the left wing, concealed within the woods, and below them a unit of Prussians, the Brunswick Erbprinz regiment perhaps. And on the right place the remainder of the Grenadiers and another battalion, equally capable of such a manoeuvre.' He indicated one of the Dutch commanders. 'Might I suggest the Heukelom regiment under Colonel de Villegas here. They were first recruited, I believe, mostly from country men from Zealand. They would do well in such conditions.'

Webb looked interested. Steel went on. 'In fact the woods are sufficiently dense to conceal both bodies of men. My plan is that the men of both units should hide themselves as best they can in the undergrowth so that the French have no idea that they exist. Then we play out the battle according to your orders, sir. Following the bombardment the fire-fight will commence and the French will advance towards our position, coming to halt with their flanks each resting on one of the woods. That is our moment, sir. At a given signal, the Prussians and my own Grenadiers on the left and the other half of the Grenadiers and the Dutch on the right will rise up and pour volley after volley into the French flanks. We wait, of course, until they are in thirty or forty yards from our line, and then the trap is sprung.'

Webb stood back and nodded, and there was a general murmur of approval. Eventually the general spoke. 'Captain Steel, your plan is bizarre and not a trifle haphazard, and certainly not within the rules of war. But it seems to me that it is our only hope against such odds and with precious little horse and no cannon. If the Danes agree, then you may carry out your strategy.'

He looked towards Colonel Carlsen, who was nodding in approval.

'Very well then. But do not forget that you are gambling with two precious battalions, a sixth of my force. If anything untoward should occur, I shall hold you personally responsible as the originator of the plan. Do you understand?'

'Perfectly, sir. And thank you.'

Steel stood with half of his new battalion at their start line on a track which ran through the woods to the left of the position. Around him he had gathered a small knot of officers. Three of them were foreigners from the other contingents which made up his converged battalion, and the other two were familiar faces: Hansam and Tom Williams.

He looked over his temporary command. In the front he could see his own company in their familiar red coats and mitre caps, worn since leaving the siege lines at Lille. Behind them came the other detachments, Danes, Prussians and Dutchmen mostly. They would not, he supposed, for the most part understand what he was about to say to his own men. But they might at least feel the spirit in which the words were said and through that his intention and the extent of his resolution to stand their ground.

He began. 'We are to occupy the left wing of the position. This ground –' He stamped his boot. '– right here.' He sensed a stirring in the ranks and knew why. 'No, men. I grant you that it is not our usual way to stand on the left of the line and that some of you may feel that is a dishonour. But let me tell you now, it is my doing and mine alone that we are here. I do not often take you into my confidence, but this time I shall. I intend to hold this position to the death. We are heavily outnumbered. I won't pretend that we're not. We have no artillery, and precious few cavalry, a hundred and fifty sabres in all. But we have something that the Frenchies never had. We have spirit. We can win, lads, just as we did at Blenheim and Ramillies and Oudenarde. And that we should win here today is vital, not only to the convoy but to the siege of Lille and, yes, to the entire war. If this convoy is taken then we may have to withdraw our lines at Lille and yield it to the French. But it's not going to be taken. And we're not going to yield. We're going to fight in a new way today, lads. We'll be fighting dirty and we'll be fighting to the death. For one thing, we're not going to show ourselves. Do not think the worse of any of this. It is still an honourable matter. But surprise is everything today. It is our task to take the enemy completely unawares.'

One of the men spoke up, Steel was not sure who. 'An ambuscade then, sir.'

'Well done, that man. An ambuscade indeed. Who's a countryman here? A son of the soil. You, Macfarlane. You're a farmer's boy, aren't you? Peebles, isn't it?'

'Aye, sir.'

'Well then, you'll know what I mean when I tell you to dig out forms. Use your bayonets for it. Make the sort of shallow hide that a hare would use. They don't need to be too deep, but they need to fit your body. About half your girth. And that shouldn't be a problem for most of you. I can't see any man here who hasn't lost a few pounds over the last few weeks.'

There was a short burst of laughter from those who could understand.

'It's the Duke's new rations, sir.'

Slaughter growled, 'Quiet, Stevens.'

Steel ignored the comment and those that followed it. 'So you know what to do. Now be about it before the Frenchies come and spot us.'

Hardly had the men begun to dig themselves in than the French cannon opened up. Hansam's watch showed two o'clock. Steel tried to count the guns from the individual shots and got to twenty before he gave up. Twenty cannon were more than enough when your own force was utterly lacking in artillery.

The guns hammered away again, but the Grenadiers, snug in their forms, remained unscathed.

Steel looked at the carnage on the open ground between the two woods.

Slaughter summed up his thoughts. 'Poor buggers. He should have 'em lie down.'

Williams said, 'Christ, how many times is that now?'

No one made a reply. He hadn't expected one.

Another voice spoke, a Londoner: 'We was happy to come away from Lille and the trenches and all that, but this ain't any better, is it? I mean, just look at the poor sods.'

The voice came from one of the Grenadiers, crouching behind a laurel bush. Steel followed his line of sight and watched as a salvo of cannonballs rained down upon the infantry exposed in the centre of the position, cutting in half one man and bouncing on to disembowel another. At the same time another shot took off the moustachioed head of a Prussian musketeer and then the hindquarters of his commanding officer's horse. Steel looked away.

'Doesn't do any good to complain, whoever said that. We're all here to do a job. Your turn will come soon enough.'

Slaughter's response came in a whisper: 'That man there, you're on a charge. And now shut it, Black. Think yourself lucky you're not standing out there under that bloody barrage getting your bollocks shot away, and are nice and tucked up here instead. Get back in your hole.'

One of the men joined in. 'That's right, Chalky. Do what Captain Steel said. Imagine you're a hare.'

'And you, Wilson. I'll give you bloody hare. Any more of your cheek and I'll bloody well skin you alive meself.'

Black spoke again, his voice filled with fear. 'They're coming, Sar'nt. I can see them.'

Steel ordered, 'Silence now. Quiet there, you men.'

It was five o'clock. Evening was falling fast now and it was clear that the French, having sustained their bombardment for some three hours, were keen to exploit the shock their guns had administered to the battered Allies.

Steel whispered to Williams, 'Pass the word down the lines, Tom. Silent order till I give the command. Dead silent.'

The French came at them out of the twilight, the Walloons first, spectral forms in their off-white uniforms, their muskets held at the ready, advancing into a foe they presumed had been shattered by their artillery. Their drums were beating, and with their colours to the fore they came on down the side of the wood. And Steel waited. Waited until they were fifty, forty, thirty paces from the Allied lines. Until their front ranks were fully past him.

Steel stood up and peered into the darkness, and then, at last, he gave the command: 'Now boys. Rise up, the Grenadiers! Present. Fire.'

As one, three hundred muskets opened fire from either side of the gap in the woods, into the French flanks.

Steel yelled, 'Pour it on, boys. Let them have it. Reload. Present. Fire.'

Again the guns crashed out. The thick white smoke added to the confusion of the twilight. But there was no real need to see what was going on. The terrible shrieks of the French infantry told their own story.

Musketry lit up the night, and in the brightest of the flashes he could glimpse the enemy now. Line after line of them, six or ten of infantry, with squadrons of cavalry massed to their rear. But it was what he saw at the front of their lines that made his heart leap. The space between the woods had been turned into a pile of dead and dying men.

The French were bewildered, caught in a murderous cross-fire from spectral and unseen figures in the woods on both flanks. They began to panic. Steel watched as men turned in all directions before being spun round dead by a bullet. The next man would then take up the infectious error, and so it spread until a whole battalion was running, and then another. Weapons were being thrown away, packs torn off in the scramble to escape the relentless, faceless musket fire.

Steel looked to his left and heard, before he saw, the jingle of harness that told him that a body of horse was advancing behind the Allied lines. For a terrible moment he imagined that it must be de la Motte's cavalry which had got round their flank, but then he saw the guidon of a regiment of English horse and knew that these were not the enemy but reinforcements sent by Marlborough from the main army, and that the day was theirs. The Allied infantry began to cheer and then the silver sabres were slashing down again and again on the men in the white coats. The French retreat turned into a rout.

At the head of the troopers Steel glimpsed the figure of

Cadogan, and wondered to which general Marlborough would ascribe the victory, his friend the Irishman or the Jacobite Webb.

Steel knew that it had been yet another demonstration of the power of Marlborough's infantry. Having stood their ground under the French bombardment, the Prussians and Hanoverians had taken up the Dutch and British form of platoon firing, and that surely had been the initial cause of victory. But, he thought, more than this had won the day. Their triumph had been assured by the grenadiers, and through their use of unorthodox tactics. It was a lesson in the art of war, not least for himself.

Over and above all this, Steel had achieved a personal goal. He had commanded an entire battalion in action. It had felt good, as if it might have been the job he had been made for. Indeed, if he thought about it, he had actually commanded a brigade, for his plan had involved three battalions. The Prussians he had never doubted, and he wondered how the Dutch had fared on the left and prayed that they had not come to grief. He wondered whether he might ever have such an opportunity again – whether perhaps one day he might be Colonel Steel? He was still unsure where his future might lie, and the last few days had only muddled his head still further. On the one hand, there was the thrill of the encounter, and nothing could ever vie with the unique exhilaration of winning an engagement, particularly one such as this.

He had still heard nothing from either Marlborough or Hawkins about the success or failure of the Paris operation, but he presumed that he must not be entirely out of favour with the command, having been appointed to direct the converged Grenadiers.

He walked through the woods, sharing the occasional word or two with one of the men. Tarling had been shot and lost a finger, but it was on his left hand and not vital. He would fight again, thought Steel. Others had been scratched by ricocheting bullets, and one man's leg was punctured by a piece of flying wood, blown off a tree by a French musket-ball. For the most part, though, they were in good spirits, savouring the pleasure in being alive that always follows a fight. He found Slaughter standing over one of the dead.

'What are our losses, Sar'nt?'

'Well, I reckon the General's lost some nine hundred men all told, sir. As for us, our half of the battalion has lost thirty men killed, wounded and missing.'

'What of our own company?'

'I count four dead and six wounded, one of them as won't last the night.'

'Who's gone?'

'Connolly, sir, and Patterson. And young Wilson.'

New blood, all of them.

'That's a shame, Sar'nt.'

'Aye, sir.'

'You were fond of him, weren't you?'

'Wouldn't put it that strong, sir. Thought he might have had the makings of a good 'un, though. Pity.'

Behind them the English dragoons were still going about their grisly business, and the night echoed to sporadic gunshots and the cries of wounded men. To Steel's right a Prussian band had started up, playing a victory march, and in the dead centre of the field a Dutch regiment had ordered their arms and were singing a psalm.

Steel took off his hat and scratched his head, wiping the powder smoke from around his eyes. 'I've said it before, and no doubt you'll catch me saying it again, Jacob, but there's few stranger places on this earth than a battlefield.' The psalmists' voices rose to a crescendo and Steel grimaced and shook his head. 'I never could stand that caterwauling.'

Slaughter peered into the night. 'D'you suppose that

convoy had more than powder on board? I've a terrible thirst on me.'

Steel laughed. 'You're not alone there, Jacob. But you won't catch it now. It's three days' march back to Lille. Come on. We've a company to find.'

FOURTEEN

It had always been one of Steel's basic tenets as an officer that he should share in all the hardships which his men had to endure. Surely if they enjoyed the glories of victory together, they should also be as one in moments of adversity. And today he knew was one of those moments. He was standing with Sergeant Slaughter in the forward trench before the defences of Lille. It was shortly after noon and the enemy had only recently ceased their morning bombardment. It had become customary during the lull for the company to take the opportunity to find their dinner, and Slaughter and Steel were staring disconsolately into the bottom of a small black metal cauldron.

The sergeant was unusually agitated. 'D'you see what I mean, sir? How can the lads be expected to eat that? I ask you. That there's nothing more than a few stewed potatoes and turnip heads. Cattle feed, that is, sir. No good for nowt but cattle and pigs.'

Steel peered into the thin, unappetizing broth. He lifted a ladle of it out and sniffed at it, before letting it trickle back into the pot. 'Yes, Sar'nt, I do see what you mean. Well, I also know that serving up such swill is not something that the Duke would do willingly, Jacob. I can only think that we must have a problem with supply.'

'I thought we'd sorted that, sir. The fight in the woods and all that. Those Frenchies were fair beat, weren't they? The supply column got through here, didn't it?'

'It did, Jacob, and we beat the French all the way back to Bruges. But remember, that was over a week ago. And d'you know what was in that column? It may have had enough powder and shells to supply our guns for a month, but you may be sure that the space they occupied on the wagons had to be at the expense of other provisions. In truth I suspected that this might happen. The Duke has always been careful with our food and drink. But why d'you think you've all been getting extra pay these past few weeks? Mr Williams had a word with me yesterday. In the place of vittles. That's the answer. The Commissary's been instructed to compensate the men with money for the shortage of food. You might say that was admirable of the Duke, and you'd be right. He's one of the fairest men I know. But battalion stores are running dangerously low in all things, and I can only suppose it must be because the French have again cut our lines. For now all we can do is accept it and make do.'

'Oh, I know that, sir. You know I do. I'm the first one to draw in my belt. An' I don't need rum to fight the Frenchies. But I don't speak for myself, Captain. It's the men. You know as well as I do that their bellies need to be filled for a fight.' He paused. 'And they were complaining last night about there being no rum.'

Steel looked alarmed. 'No rum? That's a different matter. That's serious. Any officer, from the Duke downwards, knows that no matter how brave they might be, and they are, Jacob, it's rum that gives the men the spirit to climb from the trenches and take the fight to the enemy. It's rum that makes them stand. No matter what I tell them about Queen and country. By Christ, Jacob, no rum! Give it a few days and we'll have a mutiny on our hands.'

243

'Aye, sir. I'm with you there, an' all. Seen it before. Ugly business. Waste of good men at the end. Oh, I dare say most of our lads are sound enough. But I can't speak for the other battalions in the line, nor even for the other companies of the battalion, aside from our own.'

'Leave it with me, Sar'nt. I'll see what can be done.'

Steel now knew what had to be done. For some days now, since they had returned from Wynendael, he had been toying with the idea of going to see Colonel Hawkins at headquarters, principally with the intention of asking him if he had any news from Paris. But he had wondered whether it was his place to be so forward with his superior and mentor. This new crisis, however, had provided the excuse he needed. He would visit Hawkins to ask after the rum and in passing enquire as to the fate of the letter to Louis.

For several weeks Steel had felt a growing sense of bitterness the like of which he had not known. He was dissatisfied, not with his men or with himself – both of those things, though rare, were nothing new – but with those who controlled him. What he had said to Slaughter was true. He had long considered the Duke one of the fairest and most even-handed men alive. Yet, although he had delivered his report to Marlborough and Hawkins immediately on his return from the French capital, he had still heard nothing about the success or failure of the plan to coerce a French surrender or at least an armistice. And he had a nagging need to know. Previously, he might have let it be, but since his marriage to Henrietta, Steel was aware that he had changed within himself. The future, which before he had allowed to take care of itself, living every day as it came, within reason, providing he had made provision for his men, now seemed to be altogether more immediate. His head was filled with new and undreamt-of plans and possibilities.

Perhaps the biggest of these was the question as to whether he would always remain a soldier. Seen through newly domesticated eyes, the world suddenly seemed a much larger place. But before he could decide which course to take, he had to know the fate of the war. And there were too many other loose ends in his life which compounded the problem. What, he did not cease to wonder, had been Simpson's fate? And what of Major Charpentier? Of his brother, of course, his superiors could know nothing – unless Simpson had discovered anything new. He wondered whether Alexander's complicity in his escape had been discovered by the French, and in particular by Malbec. If Alexander were dead then the blame would lie with Steel, and for that alone his conscience demanded satisfaction. And there was more. He burned with the need to settle his account with Malbec and the Marquise. Steel knew that, whatever he might decide to do in his life with Henrietta, in the immediate future he would have no rest until both the French major and his woman were dead.

'O'Brien.'

Steel's servant came hurrying up. He was a young Irishman, only recently transferred to Farquharson's from a now defunct regiment of foot, disbanded through heavy casualties and the loss of their colonel, and he seemed willing enough. Steel had only taken him on since the last engagement when his last lad had been wounded.

'O'Brien, my horse if you please. I've an appointment with the Captain General.'

As Steel rode away from the support trench and up towards the lines of command and the wagon park, complex feelings had begun to take hold within him. By the time he crested the hill they had risen almost to boiling point. Realizing what was happening, he reined in and gave himself a moment's pause. There would be no point in seeking an audience with the commander in chief in such a frame of mind. He would have to be lucid in his arguments and

245

reasoned in his indignation. It was not Steel's manner to be insubordinate, and it would serve no purpose.

He turned his horse so that he was facing back down the hill. She was a good, sound animal but not a patch on Meg, the pretty little bay mare that he had lost in Paris. He thought about how such change seemed inevitable, how he clung on to everyday things and resented that which interfered with routine, even though in his heart he detested the mundanities of company book-keeping. He supposed that it was natural in a world where any moment your life might be snatched away. There was a reassurance in familiar faces and simple rituals. That was how the army worked, in a sense. It gave you the routine, got you used to it, so that when your world fell apart, when your friends were blasted to atoms, the bones of a structure would still be there. Looking down on the siege lines, the truth of this thought was laid out before him.

From up here it seemed that so many ants had built their colonies and were busy about their daily chores. The fields, what was left of them, were criss-crossed with trenches and saps, zig-zagging their distinctive way through the shattered land. He saw the lines of circumvallation and the parallels, curved around the extent of the city, mimicking its boundaries. They were connected by communication trenches dug in short, angled sections to ensure that if a trench were taken its occupants could not be enfiladed. Everywhere there was frantic activity, from the labourers filling fresh wicker gabions with earth to the officers sighting cannon, infantry at drill and the normally unseen, unsung sinews of the army driving on to their common goal. It was an impressive sight and one that could only have been seen in Marlborough's army. This, thought Steel, was the sum of what the Duke had achieved: the ability to work together, fast and efficiently, to counter the might and manpower of France with an unprecedented professionalism. This was what won the

Duke his battles. This, Steel hoped, was what would bring them Lille.

However, no amount of pride could divert his feelings. He continued to brood on the command's apparent disregard for his interest, and by the time he had arrived in the tent lines around the Allied headquarters, much against his will, his sense of injustice had risen to a crescendo.

He rode up to the large blue-and-white striped marquee marked out with a fluttering Union flag, which served as the Duke's field headquarters. He dismounted and tethered his horse to a small rail, which had been erected for the purpose close by. Then on foot he walked towards the entrance. Two sentries snapped to attention and then levelled their muskets in the present. Steel stopped at the muzzles.

'Where's the officer of the guard? Find me whoever's in charge.'

A lieutenant came hurrying out of a small white bell tent pitched close to that of the commander in chief, cramming his hat on to his head. From within the tent came the sound of laughter and the chink of glasses. The lieutenant stopped beside one of the sentries, who had not dropped their muskets.

'What's going on, Sar'nt Baker?'

'This officer here, sir. Says he wants to speak to you, sir.'

The young man straightened up and then, taking in Steel's rank, bowed. 'Lieutenant Trevenning, sir. Her Majesty's Foot Guards. May I ask your business here, Captain . . . ?'

'Steel, Lieutenant. Captain Jack Steel, of Farquharson's. I would see the Captain General on a matter of some urgency.'

The lieutenant, recognizing Steel's name, eyed him with interest, but did not move. 'Might I enquire as to what that matter might be, sir?'

'No you may not, sir. Merely tell His Grace that Captain Steel wishes to speak to him. And if you encounter any difficulty in doing so, you might find me Colonel Hawkins. In fact you may do so in any case, while you're about it.'

The young man bristled. Hero or no hero, Steel's manner was almost too much to bear. Besides, as a lieutenant in the Guards he ranked equal with any captain of a line regiment. But he realized, from all the accounts he had heard of the captain, that this was not the man to call out on a matter of honour – if, that was, he wanted to come away with his life. Instead he smiled.

'I shall go and enquire, Captain, but I shouldn't get your hopes up too high. The commander in chief is far too busy a man to deal with an unarranged appearance by any field officer. Wait where you are, Captain Steel, if you please. I shan't be a moment.' He nodded to the sentries to maintain their 'present' and entered the striped tent. When he emerged a few minutes later he wore a peeved expression, and he was not alone.

Colonel James Hawkins greeted Steel with a beaming smile. 'Jack, m'boy. You have long been on my mind. Come in, come away in. Thank you, Lieutenant. That will be all.'

Leaving the young man to fume, they went into the tent and Steel saw at once that they were alone.

Hawkins explained: 'Marlborough's at a meeting with the brigade commanders, observing the lines. He's not in the best of tempers. But he won't be long. You'll take a glass, Jack?'

Steel stiffened. 'Please.'

Hawkins summoned a servant and turned to Steel, cutting him short. 'Now, Jack. I'm sure that you've been thinking to yourself, Why the devil haven't they sent for me? You would like, no doubt, a report on whether fat King Louis swallowed the bait. And indeed as to whether the war will end. I'm sure you're filled with questions.'

'Well, yes, sir. I –'

Hawkins waved a hand at him. 'Of course you are, and well you might be. By God, if I were sent on a dangerous mission behind the lines and then heard nothing more of it wouldn't I be as angry as you are now, Jack? You are angry?'

He handed Steel a brimming goblet of the local red wine and took one for himself. 'Your health, Jack, and may I say how glad I am to see you back here in one piece after that affair with General Webb. A triumph, I would call it. He mentioned you, you know. The general. Spoke very highly of your ability. Battalion commander, you were for the day? Eh, Jack? How did that feel? Good, I'll bet.' Hawkins winked at him.

Steel was at a loss for words. Hawkins had completely disarmed him. Was he now toying with his ambitions? Or was there some substance to the hint that one day Steel might have his own battalion?

'And now, Jack, to business. What would you like to know first?'

As he spoke the tent flap flew back and Marlborough entered, accompanied by a servant who took his hat and cloak. Rubbing at his temples, he strode across the room towards a large table upon which lay a map of the region.

'Hawkins, a drink, if you please. My head throbs and my mind aches with it. All I seem to hear is prattle about this siege. Our lines of curcumvallation are overlong. I know that. The trenches are flooded. I know that too, only too well. I have generals reminding me of schedules. Reminding me! I know the dictates of siege warfare only too well. Twenty-five days and you must have built your walls, opened the trenches and reached the covered way and the demilune. Another week and the latter should be taken, and a breach then created. Then and only then are you to cross the ditch and breach the main defences. Given another week the enterprise must be complete. Forty-eight days, Hawkins. That is the prescribed time in which to complete a siege from the start to the capitulation. And how many days now have we been here? You know the answer. Too long. Two and one half months. Three weeks beyond the time. We have seen an

249

enemy army come and go with no battle given and five thousand men, five thousand of our own men, fall in one day attempting to storm the damned place. I tell you, Hawkins, I should be the happiest man alive were this the last siege I ever see.'

He took a draught of wine and continued, apparently oblivious to Steel's presence. 'At least they know that when we take their precious town we shall not hang them from the ramparts as was formerly the custom. We fight a civilized war, do we not?'

'If any war can be considered civilized.'

'A war fought with the purpose of preserving civilization is surely civilized by its very nature.'

'But is it just?'

'Can there ever be a just war, Your Grace?' It was Steel who spoke.

'Ah, Captain Steel. What brings you here? Hawkins, did I ask for Captain Steel?'

'You did not, Your Grace. But . . . I did. We do owe him a report, sir, on the talks with the French. After all, he was instrumental in their introduction.'

Marlborough's face clouded and Steel suspected the worst. 'Ah yes. A bad business, I'm afraid, Steel.'

'I take it then, sir, that the letter I delivered was of no avail. That the French King will not sue for peace?'

Marlborough nodded. 'Show him, Hawkins.'

Hawkins produced a letter and began to read: '"The King desires peace . . . The appearance of the Allies, though most brilliant, cannot prevent those who have experience of war . . ." It's from the Duke of Berwick.'

Marlborough glared. 'Berwick, my own cousin. Best general they have. Wasted, though. Quite wasted. And that he should have written this to me! "Experience of war!" I have more experience of war than that bloated monarch, for all his years.'

Hawkins continued: '". . . those who have experience of

war, from perceiving that it is strained in all sorts of ways and may at any moment be so transformed that even if you were to take the citadel of Lille you might be thrown into extremities which would destroy your armies and put it out of your power to supply with munitions and food the strong places you occupy beyond the Scheldt . . ."'

'It is nothing less than an affront, Steel. A rebuke. Well, if that is what the King wants that is what he shall have. Let no one ever say that I did not attempt a reasonable peace. From here on I shall only desire to crush France beneath my heel.'

Hawkins explained. 'Fact is, Steel, while Louis might have wanted peace, we've been trumped at the game. We believed that we might catch the ear of the King direct, but it's the generals now who have the upper hand in France. In matters of the war it seems that the King is no more than a puppet. He's an old man now, too old to realize that that letter was meant for his eyes alone and not for those at his court whom he likes to trust but should not. He's lost his grip, and there's too much at stake for them. If they give up now all of France's hard-won prestige will be lost. The Sun King's glory will be tarnished forever. They cannot allow it, and it seems they have turned his mind. I am truly sorry. But your work was not wasted. Thanks to you we know now who betrayed so many of our agents.'

'The man Gabriel. You caught him?'

'He, er, met with an unfortunate accident. It seems his body was found floating in the Seine.'

Steel smiled. 'And Simpson?'

'Captain Simpson is fine, although he is no longer in Paris. We have not yet decided how best to employ him. He's a marked man now.'

'And what of the others? The French agents? Have you news of them?'

'Sadly, no. They appear to have gone to ground.'

251

Marlborough took a long drink and Hawkins continued, 'There is something else, Jack.'

Steel stiffened. What more might there be? Surely they had not had news of Alexander. He waited for the worst.

'It's Henrietta, Jack. We've had word.'

'She's not . . . dead?'

Hawkins smiled and placed a hand on Steel's shoulder. 'No, no, Jack. She's not dead. Nor yet a prisoner. But she is trapped, in Ostend. She cannot get out. The French have flooded the fields to prevent supplies coming through, ten miles around the city and further afield, from Bruges out to Oudenburg and down the coast past Nieuport. It's completely cut off. What's more, if we leave Ostend without attempting to retake it then there's no saying that the French might not take it back themselves.'

Steel shook his head. 'Good God. This is my doing. I sent her there, from Brussels. For safety.'

He thought of his wife, cut off in the city in which only last year she had been held captive and from which he had rescued her. Hawkins, for once, said nothing, but merely patted Steel on the shoulder.

Marlborough, who had been gazing at the map, spoke, apparently oblivious to their talk of Henrietta. 'To lose Ostend again is unthinkable. What's more, we need powder and shot now, for this damned siege, if we're ever to take Lille. Salt, too, for the men's food.'

Steel, although his mind was filled with images of Henrietta, heard the commander and remembered another of his errands. 'And we do need rum, sir. We've none left to speak of.'

'No rum? Hawkins, is that right?'

'I'm very much afraid it is, Your Grace. Quartermasters are aware. Rum's held up in Ostend. We've had to cut all rations.'

'Well then, find something else. Give them brandy. Anything. Get the dragoons out. Scour the local inns. Give 'em wine if needs be. The men must have their grog. Can't have them in the trenches sober. No one could stand sober under that rain of death and remain sane. Isn't that so, Steel?'

'Quite so, Your Grace.'

The flap of the tent lifted and the Earl of Cadogan, Marlborough's right-hand man and closest friend, entered. The Duke turned to him.

'We were just saying, Cadogan, how vital it is that the men should always have their rum ration. Do you not agree?'

'Utterly, sir. Without question. And that is why it is imperative that we restore the line of supply with Ostend.'

Steel harnessed what was left of his anger and his indignation, which was precious little, and decided to stake his all on a bold request. He looked at Marlborough. 'Sir, may I have your permission to take myself and a few chosen men off to Ostend, to rescue my wife?'

Hawkins interjected. 'Out of the question, I'm afraid. I'm sorry, Jack. All such ideas are out of the question. We need every man we can get at present.'

The Duke went on: 'I intend to find Marshal Vendôme and defeat him in a pitched battle. Only then can we hope to repair the dykes and drain the region.'

Hawkins added, 'In the meantime we still have the more immediate problem of getting provisions, in particular the rum, through to the men.'

Cadogan said, 'On which subject, Your Grace, I have an idea. We could use a system of carts and barges, sir. General Erle is at Nieuport on the northernmost extremity of the inundation, with its canal to the sea. He has the craft and the seamen to hand to man them. I took it upon myself to amass a quantity of large wheeled carts, high enough to pass over the waters without making their contents too wet. We can use these in the shallows to move supplies from the barges and into smaller carts on dry land.'

Marlborough nodded. 'That seems an admirable plan. What d'you say, Hawkins? Will it work?'

'I see no real reason why it should not, although may I point out, General Cadogan, with respect, that as soon as we begin this flotilla you can be sure the French will assemble something similar and attack the convoy while it's on the water.'

Marlborough thought. 'You're right. We must provide some form of escort or deterrent. Cadogan?'

Steel saw his chance. 'If I may suggest something, sir. Why not detach a portion of the barges for such a duty, and man them with water-borne troops?'

'Would the troops take to it? Fighting on water? They're not trained for such warfare. And we have no time now to summon Colonel Killigrew's new marine infantry force from England.'

Steel smiled. 'My men could carry it off, sir. I'm sure of it. We can certainly try. Our muskets are shorter than those of the centre companies, and we have our bombs which might be of some effect against the craft themselves.'

Marlborough pointed to the map. 'Very well, Captain Steel. March with the army as far as Roulers, here, and then take your men across and up to Dixmude, in the south of the flood. Cadogan, you appear to have command of the situation. Have General Erle detach some barges from his force. How many men are you, Steel?'

'I have Sir James's Grenadier company, sir. We number some fifty men at present.'

'No, no, man. I mean your new command, the converged Grenadiers whom you led under General Webb. You will form that battalion again. What did you have? Prussians, Danes, Dutch? Take them into the waters. They did well at Wynendael.

Show me that you can do as well again and I swear that I'll be of a mind to give you your own battalion. They'd all be British, mind you. I tell you, Steel, open the route to Ostend and you'll come back a colonel.'

Hawkins smiled at him and, bending over to refill his wine glass, whispered in Steel's ear, 'And, what's more, Jack, you'll come back with your wife.'

FIFTEEN

'Boats, sir? Us fighting on boats? On the water? You're having a joke, sir. Aren't you?' Slaughter shook his head.

Steel was adamant. 'No joke, Jacob. I'm quite serious, and set on it. We're all to be sea soldiers. Marines.'

Hansam, who had been standing close by wearing a smile, interjected, 'I presume, Jack, that by "marines" you refer to that fine regiment raised by Sir William Killigrew forty years ago. I believe they number six battalions today.'

'The very same, Henry. As you will recall, they took Gibraltar four years back, when we were all down in Germany at a place called Blenheim.'

'Both were famous victories. And they held it against the French after that. Nine weeks.'

'Well, we shan't be called on to do that, I'm sure. All we have to do is escort a convoy of barges from Ostend back down here. If the French do spot us, God knows how they'll get to us, short of calling in their own navy, and I hardly think they'll have the time to do that.'

Williams was excited. 'Well, I think it's a capital idea. I've a cousin in the navy. Wait till he hears of this.'

Slaughter was mumbling, half to himself, but clearly wanting an audience. 'Course I've heard that there are

256

soldiers serving on ships of the line. But I'm not equipped to fight at sea, sir. And most of the lads can't swim. Nor I for that matter. We'll all be drowned, Captain.'

Steel laughed. 'I thought it was enclosed spaces you had a fear of, Jacob, not water. Christ, man, you've more worries than the Duke himself. We're not going to sea, man. We still fight on land.'

'In a boat? Nah, sir, I don't see it. How can that be?'

'The French have opened the sluices in the dykes across Flanders and flooded the farmland. How many times must I explain? We are to act as a waterborne escort for the supplies. We do not travel by schooner or rigger or sloop. We are to make our way by barge, Jacob. Though I can't vouch for the condition of our vessels.'

But Slaughter was still speaking to himself. 'They wear yeller coats, them marines, don't they? Can't trust no one as wears a yeller coat. Red's the only colour for a British soldier's coat. Yeller. Huh.'

'Oh, calm down, Jacob. The marines are quite as brave as we are. In fact I wish we had some of them to fight with us here, rather than this foreign hotch-potch. They could tell us the tricks of the trade. There is doubtless a skill to being a soldier aboard a boat. We shall just have to learn it.'

Hansam continued, 'They are the Duke's old regiment, Sar'nt. We mustn't speak ill of them. Besides, the yellow was done away with long ago. Now they're in red, just like us.'

Steel said, 'If you can call it red.'

He was looking about him at the men resting by the roadside on the outskirts of the little town. He was right. Months of campaigning without the opportunity to acquire a change of coat, years in some cases, including his own, had done much to transform the scarlet uniforms of the infantry. Still, he thought, there was no mistaking his men as anything other than British infantry. They had a certain cut about

257

them, a certain gait. A certain way with women and drink too, some would have said. His were true British soldiers. Two years ago he would have called them Scots, but since the union of the parliaments, and following their heavy losses at Ramillies and Oudenarde, not to mention the numerous actions between, most of his original fellow Scots were gone from the ranks of Farquharson's. His company was a motley bunch now, a mix of Scots and Geordies, men from Yorkshire, Somerset and Northumberland, Cockneys – many of those – and farming men from the mid shires and the Weald of Kent, and of course the normal scattering of Irishmen. Slaughter and his fellow sergeants did well to keep them in order. Steel wondered how they and he himself would cope with the new command, for as promised by the Duke he found himself again at the head of the converged Grenadier battalion that he had led at Wynendael.

Steel was content with his lot this October morning. His mind, so troubled these last few weeks, had finally settled on a plan for the future. He knew that if he could succeed in this venture his promotion was secured. The Duke had given his word on it. Major Steel. It had a good ring to it. Perhaps even Colonel. And all seemed well with Henrietta. Brussels was again under threat from Marshal Berwick, but she was at Ostend now, and Hawkins had sent word there by messenger that she should leave with the convoy. Steel would meet her en route. She would be his greatest incentive in this operation, and once he had pulled it off and gained his promotion they would be together.

Cadogan had arranged for Erle to provide the Grenadiers with a dozen flat-bottomed barges, canal boats, commandeered at Ostend. They were simple craft, equipped with a single sail, and with provision if necessary to be powered by oarsmen. They had been commandeered by Cadogan in a remarkably swift operation. That man was extraordinary, thought Steel. Whatever might be said of his self-interest, he was apparently capable of whistling up anything on command.

Their Dutch crews had been paid off, and English and Dutch naval ratings had sailed them from the Allied-held ports and quickly refitted them from cargo carriers to being able to take a force of infantry. Their experienced crews had guided the barges quite expertly from the open sea across the flooded plains to the little Flanders town of Gistel.

Steel and his battalion had come here, eight miles north-west of the site of their victory in the woods, having first marched with Marlborough's larger force in the direction of the French army, which appeared to be spoiling for a fight. The Duke at least seemed to think so and was determined to give battle should the opportunity present itself. At Tourhout, Steel had parted from the main column, heading north. Having not had time to do so before the engagement at Wynendael, he had made it his business while on the march from Lille to spend some time becoming more familiar with his new subordinates.

The battalion was made up of grenadiers drawn from six other regiments. Most familiar to him were the Scots who had come from Lord Orkney's own regiment. As with the others, there were some fifty of them under a captain and a lieutenant. The captain he had recognized at once. Charles Murray had known Steel since they had been boys, and although Jack had known that he was an officer with Marlborough, for some reason their paths had not often crossed. Now here they were at last serving in the same command, albeit with Steel as its overall leader. Murray's second-in-command was a callow youth in his twentieth year, a younger son of the manse from Perthshire named Ian Donald. According to Tom Williams, who had attempted to befriend him on the march north, although a thoroughly amiable sort, he said very little and preferred to keep his own company, spending much time poring over a dog-eared copy of Thucydides' *Peloponnesian War*. Murray, however, swore that he was a tiger in a fight, and Steel could hardly wait to see the transformation for himself.

Then there were the foreign elements of the battalion. First, thought Steel, in order of precedence, he would have placed the Dutch. Their captain, van Heemskerk, was a grizzled old campaigner with skin like leather, some ten years Steel's senior, who clearly thought he should have been considered for command of the battalion. His men were similarly experienced, although not as long in the tooth, and Steel elected to station them on the right of the line in any fight. That honour at least would have the effect of placating their commander. The Prussians, of course, looked as if they had walked off a parade ground. Steel wondered how, when it came to the march attack, he would coordinate their deliberately high-cadence step with the more relaxed amble of his own men and the others. They were led by a thin young man with a waxed moustache. His name was Emsdorf, and he reminded Steel of the poor Prussian officer he had served alongside at Blenheim and who had ended up face down on that bloody field, felled by the sabres of ten French life guardsmen. From that poor devil, at least, Steel had learnt that as far as the Prussians were concerned retreat was never an option. The Hanoverians were an altogether less reliable-looking bunch, he thought. Their officer was something of a dandy. And lastly, in Steel's eyes, came the Danes. Their officer was a lanky youth with straw-coloured hair, and despite their countrymen's sound reputation they did not seem of the same calibre as the others.

These were the men that he hoped would provide a crack fighting force, if needed, over the coming few days. It was a lot to ask – a force capable not only of holding their own on a field of battle, but also of fighting from the deck of a ship riding the inland sea. In effect they were a microcosm of the Duke's army, and Steel was well aware of the difficulties their commander had encountered in coordinating their actions. He preferred to think of them now as a distillation of talent, all elite as they were.

He turned to Slaughter. 'Like it or not, Jacob, you and I have got to work with this lot as a single fighting unit, and a force that can and will operate on board ship. Speaking of which, I think it may be time to inspect our transports. Form the men up, Sar'nt, and let's give it some swagger. We don't want to be upstaged by a bunch of foreigners.'

'Nor by Lord Orkney's men neither, eh, sir?'

The Grenadiers carried no drums, but they had fifers aplenty, so it was to the strains of 'Lillibulero' that Steel's little force entered the town by the southern road. Marching over the little bridge that spanned the Grootgeleed stream, swollen by the influx of water, Steel noticed a flour mill over the watercourse. He carried on up the main street towards the rendezvous point with Erle's sailors. Hardly had they entered the market square, though, when Steel was almost stopped in his tracks. For there, where the town should have ended in another road leading onto fields and hedges, lay nothing but an expanse of water as far as the eye could see.

With Slaughter at his side, Steel stared out across it. Perhaps after all his sergeant had not been far wrong when he had spoken of a sea, for the entire country now lay under water, with houses, windmills and the tops of trees protruding from the surface of the floods. Close to the town it was clear that some progress might still be made on horse or in a wide-wheeled wagon. But at a distance of perhaps a mile the waters seemed to be deeper as the land sloped away to the coast.

'There you are, Jacob. There's your sea.'

'Should've sent in the cavalry, sir, or dragoons more like.

261

If you had a horse yourself, Captain, you'd be able to reach that church there at least.'

As the commander of a battalion Steel knew that he should have been on a horse, but he had refused to take one. He would make too easy a target for enemy sharpshooters, he had argued, and besides this type of fighting would not make for horsed warfare. If there was one thing seafaring soldiers were not, it was cavalry. Nevertheless Slaughter was still cross. It went against the grain that the commander of any regiment should walk on foot.

'Yes, Jacob, I know your thoughts. But it would not have been enough. We need to get all the way up to the convoy, almost to Ostend, and the only way is by boat. Now once and for all stop your bloody grumbling and let's get on with the job in hand and get to these boats.'

They found them some hundred yards away, tied up to the horse posts of what had until recently been an inn on a road that curved uphill and into the town from the north and which was now submerged. Beside them stood a company of sailors from the Royal Navy and a few officers in that arm's distinctive blue coats. Steel approached them.

'Gentlemen, I believe that we are your passengers. Captain Jack Steel, of the Grenadiers.'

One of the officers, the most senior to judge from the amount of gold braid he wore, walked to meet Steel.

'Captain Cassels. Good to have you aboard, Captain. We're under orders to set sail as soon as we find you. There's no time to waste. We must reach the convoy before the French.'

'The French? Are you expecting trouble?'

The officer looked askance. 'Why, most certainly. Do you not know? The French have brought in a fleet of galleys from Brest. They're manned by privateers and are intent on taking the convoy. We'll have to hurry if all is not to be lost. You may have a battle on your hands, Captain.'

* * *

262

The little flotilla moved slowly across the dark waters. To right and left they passed the tops of houses and the upper parts of churches. Trees stuck out like islands, and here and there cattle stood disconsolate, surreally isolated on flat roofs. It looked to Steel like some artist's vision of hell in which the world had been turned upside down. A day of revelation. Dead bodies floated around them. They were mostly livestock, sheep, cattle and swine, but here and there they encountered the bloated corpse of a man or woman who had not been quick enough to escape the inundation when the French had opened the sluices of the dykes.

Two of Steel's men hung over the side, vomiting into the water. Slaughter, although not physically sick, had a horribly pale complexion that reflected the colour of the waters.

'I told you, sir. Don't agree with me, this water soldiering. Nor with many of the men.'

'Nonsense. You're just a little seasick. And God knows why! The water is like a mill pond.'

They were in twelve barges, long vessels of about thirty-five feet in length and ten wide. *Skutsjes*, the Dutch called them. They were powered by a single sail and a number of oars on either side. Fortunately for the flotilla a light wind had come up and the barges were now skimming the waters at around ten miles an hour. They were remarkably stable craft, even when fully laden, and the shallow draught ensured that they did not collide with the many obstacles that lurked just below the surface of the flood waters.

Each was capable of taking a half-company, and Steel had obviously taken his own half-company of Farquharson's men. He looked across the water towards the remainder of the company and could see a few Grenadiers hanging over the edge. Most of the men, though, appeared to be content if not comfortable, clinging to whatever came to hand to steady themselves.

The naval officer he had met on shore, Captain Edmund

Cassels, approached him. 'Well, Captain Steel, we should espy the convoy soon. Shouldn't be long. Your men all coping with being at sea?'

'We've taken a few casualties.' He pointed to the unfortunates at the side.

'Funny, being afloat will take some men that way. Myself, I've never been troubled by it, which is just as well really. This is like a sailing pond. I'm used to three-masters. Glad to get this mission. Ah, that looks like our lads now.'

Steel followed his line of sight and on the far horizon picked out a number of sailing vessels approaching their own. Straining his eyes, he could see that from several of their mast-tops fluttered the Union flag. And somewhere there, with them, was Henrietta.

There must have been close on fifty vessels, Dutch barges like their own mostly, and as they closed he could see that they were laden with case after case of hemp-wrapped provisions. Slowly the two groups of boats approached each other until Steel was able to make out the figures on deck. There was a shout from the leading boat, and within seconds the captain of Steel's barge had leapt aboard the other and was in conversation with its commander, who might have been his Doppelgänger, in both clothing and stature. Then together the two men stepped back onto the deck of the transport with an ease that Steel knew he could never have hoped to master.

Cassels said, 'May I present Captain Hugh Cassels of the Royal Navy. Captain Jack Steel, commanding the escort.'

'You're brothers?'

'Near identical twins, in fact. Yes. Extraordinary, isn't it, that we should both pitch up in the Navy? And both of the same rank.'

His brother continued, 'Commissioned in point of fact on the same day of the same month. Though Edmund's the finest sailor I know.'

'Hugh, you exaggerate. I'm no better than you.'

Hugh Cassels turned to Steel. 'Captain Steel, a word with you. I intend to take the lead with the convoy. Follow on behind us, Captain, if you please. I think that will be the most effective way of getting on, and time is of the essence, as you are aware.'

Steel frowned. 'If you will pardon me, sir, I would beg to differ. Such an arrangement goes against all the tenets of battle. Surely, if the French do come upon us they would be more deterred if you were flanked by the escort rather than if the escort were to follow on. That way if you were attacked they would have a chance of taking some of you off before we could reach you.'

'Ye. I had thought of that, but it is a risk I'm willing to take in the interest of speed. Or would you have the provisions delayed further?'

Steel stiffened. 'That is not my intention, Captain. I am merely concerned for your safety and that of the convoy. We shall follow your wishes. I have said my piece. I shall say no more on't.' He paused, only deflected from further argument by the knowledge that he had need of retaining the captain's good favour. 'I do believe, though, that you may be able to help me on another matter. You have with you, on one of the convoy transports, a young woman. She is my wife, Lady Henrietta Steel. I wonder if you might get word to her that I am arrived and shall shortly be escorting her back to dry land.'

'Your wife, sir? Point of fact, I don't think we have any civilians left aboard. We did certainly have a party of several ladies, and I dare say that among them may have been your wife. I do recall a lady of title. But they all diverted to Leffinghe before we met you, under their own escort. Yes, now I think on it, I do believe that she may have been with them.'

Steel shook his head. 'You must be mistaken, Captain.

My wife was under specific instruction to meet me with the convoy.'

Cassels was growing annoyed. 'Sir, I cannot vouch for the actions of your wife. But I do know that we have no females travelling with us now, and those as we did have are in Leffinghe. It was felt to be more prudent by the officer and escort that was with them. That place is held by the Allies. I suggest you go to Leffinghe to find your wife, for she is surely there. She'll be perfectly safe there, Captain Steel. Their escorting officer assured me of it. No Frenchies for miles, and all in good hands. Oficer of the Foot Guards, Captain. The very best.'

Steel, of course, could do nothing else but agree.

An hour passed and another. The convoy, now set on its course back to Gistel, made good time, much to Steel's annoyance, proving Cassel's brother right. But with the onset of evening a thin mist descended fast upon the barges, making it all but impossible to see beyond the vessel directly in front and obscuring those to port and starboard. The sailors, however, lit lanthorns and hung them from the masts, giving the impression of lights bobbing about to left and right.

Slaughter said, 'I don't like this, sir. Not at all. It's like so many will-o'-the-wisps. Them that come to lead you astray. Unquiet souls.'

Steel laughed. 'Jacob! Really I don't think I've ever seen you so unnerved as on this expedition. They're the lights of our own boats.'

'You say what you like, sir. I tell you it's not right. They keep coming and going and I swear there's more there than there was.'

'Don't be ridiculous.'

But Steel was still peering at the lights, trying to count them, when Edmund Cassels found him.

'Pretty sight, ain't it? Didn't know we had so many boats.'

'We don't.'

As the words left Steel's lips both men turned, their attention caught by a sudden orange glow that rose on the starboard bow. And such was their shared experience of war on land and sea that both knew to duck. A second later a whooshing sound announced the passing over their lowered heads of a round shot. It passed over the barge without effect.

Steel was the first to recover. 'To arms. Stand to.'

This was what they had all feared. Slaughter had not been wrong about the lights. Whoever was attacking them had come up under cover of the mist, masquerading as other barges. Steel watched as the night around them was lit up with further flashes. Cannon shot came crashing in, and through the mist the noise of metal against wood testified that all the vessels had not been so lucky as their own. Their attackers seemed to be coming at them from all sides.

Steel yelled at the Grenadiers, who had assembled in two ranks, 'Fix bayonets!'

Cassels set his men to the oars. 'Row, for all you're worth.'

Up ahead it seemed that battle had already been joined. Cries from the convoy revealed that the transports had been boarded. Steel swore.

Cassels shouted at the oarsmen, 'Row, damn you.'

Steel joined him. 'Can't you get this thing to go any faster? We need to save the convoy, or what's left of it.'

His words were drowned in a cacophony of shot and cries, and then the enemy were upon them. There was a sudden thud as the keel of the attacking vessel crashed into the hull of the barge. Seconds later the deck was filled with armed men.

Steel, standing behind the Grenadiers, gave the order: 'Present. Fire.'

A volley crashed out and sent the first wave of attackers to the deck, killing and wounding a score of them in the confined space. He looked at them and knew their type at once. Pirates. Privateers at least, in French pay. He had met their like before, and knew their fury and the full extent of their brutality. They would give no quarter. They wore no single uniform but a collection of tatters and finery. Here was the coat of a French dragoon, over there that of a Dutch officer. One of the bigger men, dead now, was dressed in a captured British red coat. Steel had no time to stare, for the second wave was in. He knew he must meet them now on equal terms.

'Bayonets. No quarter. Give no quarter.'

His men lunged, and steel pierced flesh as another ten pirates fell. Some of the Grenadiers who had already reloaded fired off at point-blank range. Steel saw one of the Frenchmen staggering, groping at a huge blackened wound that had taken away half his abdomen. More pirates leapt on to the deck of the barge, but there were fewer this time.

Not waiting to see if more were to come, Steel took his chance. 'Come on, lads. Let's finish them.'

With a cheer the half-company rushed towards the boarding party, followed by the sailors, and with Steel at their head, sword in hand. He brought the great blade hard down on the head of a stocky, dark-skinned attacker, cutting it clean in half. Stepping over the corpse he drew back the sword and, parrying a cutlass, riposted with a lunge towards his assailant's chest. He felt the steel slide in slickly, and then withdrew it and spun round to face a man he had sensed was behind him. The fellow had a billhook, but before he could use it on Steel one of the Grenadiers had run the man through his side.

And then they were gone, as suddenly as they had come. Their ship, a long, low war galley, was slipping away from the side of the barge.

Cut off by the mist and the night Steel could only wonder how the others had fared. He turned to find Cassels.

'Can you take us into the convoy?'

The captain yelled and his crew, back at the oars, struck out hard, and soon the ship was heading into the thick of the flotilla. Up ahead Steel could still hear gunfire, which suggested that the affair was not over. But as they approached it ceased, and at the same moment the mist began to lift and the moon revealed itself, lighting up a scene of devastation. It was hard at first to tell the one from the other, but after a while it became clear that the escort had managed to beat off the attackers with relatively little loss. The bulk of the carnage was made up of debris from the pirate ships and the convoy. A good half dozen of the transporters were damaged beyond repair; another six could be towed in. They had lost twenty grenadiers in the fight, mostly the hapless Danes, and the same number again of Cassels's seamen.

As his men helped to throw the bodies of the dead overboard and move the precious cargo from the beleaguered vessels, Steel knew that it was now time to speak up. He found Hugh Cassels staring at a dead sailor.

'We should find a mooring for the night.'

'Impossible. We must head on. Time is everything –'

Steel cut him off. 'Do you see what has happened here? We have lost men and matériel. They were playing with us, and if we go on they will come again. I command the escort here, sir, and I am now taking command. Our only course is to tie up, man a defensive line and wait for morning. Then at least we shall have a sporting chance.'

And as for myself, he thought, I can sit down and try to understand why the devil Henrietta should have taken herself off to Leffinghe.

Lying on a divan in the finest room that Leffinghe's only inn had to offer, Henrietta Vaughan looked up into the eyes of the man she loved and sighed contentedly. How strange it was, she thought, that she could be in such physical danger,

269

here on the very front line of a war, and yet feel so perfectly happy.

Of course, there would be a scandal. But after the tittle-tattle had died away and once she and Jack had divorced and she and Lachlan were married she knew that her father, pleased with a proper match, would settle on her the proper portion of his wealth which she had never had with Captain Steel.

Poor Jack, she thought. But she had always known that their marriage would never work. He was just not quite in her league – charming, brave and lovely, of course, but somehow not quite right.

Lachlan Maclean spoke with a contented sigh and immersed himself a little further in the bath of hot water that he had coaxed from the landlady. 'I think that I shall sell m' commission. I have concerns in London. Money matters. It will occupy all of my time. Save for you of course, my darling. I shall always make time for you.'

Henrietta smiled. 'How clever of you to bring me here.'

'You admit that I was right, then. It's so very much more sensible to stay here with me than go on to Lille.' He paused, thinking. 'You're quite decided about your husband? No second thoughts?'

'None. How could there be? It was so clever of you to find me in Brussels and gather me up.'

'No more than any man would do for the prettiest girl alive, who seemed to have lost her way.'

'Yes. I had lost my way, hadn't I? For longer than you know, I think. And you were so kind . . . and so very generous.'

She stretched out her arm and admired the two sapphire and diamond bracelets that now adorned it.

'As I said, no more than any man would do.'

'But you are not just any man, are you?'

'As you keep on telling me, my love. I cannot think why.'

'Then come here and I'll show you.'

He did not need to be asked twice, and as she felt his body against hers, his breath hot and sweet against her lips, Henrietta realized that there was something deliciously wicked about doing this with one of Jack's comrades and felt a frisson she had not known before. And then the guns began.

SIXTEEN

It was not until the following morning that the convoy reached Gistel. As Steel had ordered, they had found a quiet, makeshift mooring, tethered to the tops of the trees of a submerged copse, and he corralled the supply vessels inside a loose circle of barges manned by the grenadiers who had taken turns of the watch by platoon. As he had predicted, the privateers had not returned, and starting out at dawn for the south the convoy had made good time.

The little town was not quite as they had left it. The waters still lapped around the northernmost houses and had not yet reached the centre, but there was a sense of agitation. It did not take him long to discover why.

'Leffinghe is besieged? Surely not. It's no more than ten miles from here. Surely we would be aware of such a state of affairs? It may, I grant you, have been raided by the same privateers who attacked our convoy yesterday evening. But surely, Major, the French do not have a force of sufficient size or the transports to ferry them to Leffinghe?'

He was standing with his back to the fireplace in a large first-floor room of the town hall which had been commandeered by the Allied commander in the area, a jovial major of the Buffs by the name of Meddowes.

'I'm afraid they do, Captain Steel. We have no reason to doubt the news. It came to me from a most reliable source. The officer arrived here this morning, direct from Leffinghe. They have, he says, a battery that maintains a constant fire upon the place from a nearby hill. Part of the town has been set afire, and God knows the fate of the poor inhabitants. But they are holding out. I have sent to the Duke for re-inforcements.' He paused. 'Oh, I almost forgot. When I told the officer who brought the news that you were escorting the convoy he embraced me. Most odd behaviour. It seems that he knows you. He was most anxious to see you on your arrival.'

So it was that within the hour Steel was sitting in the town's most opulent tavern, sharing a bottle of its finest claret with Captain James Simpson.

Simpson smiled. 'So you see, dear boy, here I am. Safe and sound, in good health and as keen as mustard.'

'Well, thank God you are. I was certain you'd be taken.'

'I told you before, my dear chap, it takes more than your usual *crapaud français* to snare James Simpson. And now it is my turn to be the hunter.'

'Meaning?'

'Meaning that I want blood, Steel. I've tasted it and it has whetted my appetite. I mean to finish the job.'

'Finish the job?'

'Disposing of Malbec and his whore. Oh, I neglected to tell you, didn't I?'

He delved into his waistcoat pocket and pulled some-thing out, then holding his hand out to Steel he slowly folded back his fingers. There in his palm lay a piece of jewellery, a gold chain from which was suspended a single, brilliant emerald.

Steel gasped. 'Good God. You killed her.'

'Well observed, dear chap. Most satisfactory, and a fitting end for such a woman. I told you, dear boy. Matter of honour.

Loss of a dear friend and so on. She had to atone for her actions, and that she did, in full.'

'How did you manage it?'

'With great ease, actually. Far less trouble than I'd thought. After your escape they were in quite a flap, blaming each other. Charpentier was questioned but escaped with his life, though only thanks to the intervention of the King. Malbec led a search for you. Scoured all Paris. And in the meantime the Marquise sat in her apartments in the Place Royale and waited for news. That is where I found her.'

Steel grew cold. 'How did you do it?'

'Oh, I was merciful. By her standards, at least. Although I did make her sweat a little. There's nothing like the anticipation of an event to bring out the heat. I'm sure that you know that.'

'Only too well. Go on.'

'I waited until the house was abed and then I entered through an upper window. D'you know, Steel, if I hadn't been a soldier I think I'd have made a very good picklock. So there I was, staring down at her in her bed, a vision of nipples and lace. Exquisite creature. Shame about her character.'

Steel nodded, remembering.

'I placed my hand over her mouth and woke her. Imagine the look of terror in her eyes when she saw me. Of course the bitch tried to bite me, but I soon put a stop to that. Then I gagged her with one of her own silk stockings and bound her hands behind her. My God, she struggled! But a few sharp jabs with my knife and she soon stopped that. And then, d'you know, her expression turned from anger to terror. She was afraid. And that Steel, although I am ashamed to admit it, made me the happiest man alive. I wanted her to know fear, so I kept her like that for a good four hours. Of course I talked to her all the while, telling her what I was going to do to her, how exactly I intended to kill her. In the most minute of detail. And from time to time I would give her just

274

the most subtle of cuts with my knife. Ever so thin. Just wherever it took my fancy. On the arm or on the thigh. Or anywhere really. Tiny, tiny cuts. But I think it was the words that affected her most vividly, rather than the cuts and the sight of all that blood. Interesting, don't you think, how tiny cuts can call forth so much blood? At one point I was sure she was going to faint. Well, of course, I wasn't having any of that. You know there's nothing like a pitcher of ice-cold water to waken a girl, eh? So I went on with the detail and her eyes grew wider and wider and finally she began to shake with terror.' He laughed at the memory. 'Shake, dammit! By that time the dawn was coming up, so then I took her other stocking and wound it around and around her beautiful little neck and pulled it very very tight. And then, puff, she was gone. Snuffed out. But just to make absolutely certain I slit her throat from ear to pretty ear. But not before retrieving this.'

Again he held out the pendant, before putting it away again in his pocket. Steel felt drained by the account. He took a long drink.

'It was well done, Simpson. But tell me, why the devil are you here? Has the Duke no further use for his spies?'

'Alas, it is I for whom the spies have no use. My face is too well known, you see, my cover blown quite asunder. Of course, Gabriel was drowned. The Kaiser's work. But there are others still in Paris who know me. In fact that is why I came to Leffinghe. Had to leave France by boat. Only way, dear boy. Patrols everywhere. So up the coast to Ostend I go. And I may tell you that I stank of fish for days.' He sniffed at his coat. 'Tell me that I do not now.'

Steel laughed and shook his head. 'No, Simpson, you do not stink. At least not of fish.'

Simpson smiled and went on. 'Well, when I heard the convoy was off to Lille I managed to contrive passage for myself. And when the party detached to Leffinghe, suffice it to say that a certain Jack tar among the crew had taken my fancy and that he just happened to be among the sailors ordered off with them.' He frowned. 'So, as you see, I have returned to the front. A soldier once again, dear boy. I march to the sound of the guns. "Lillibulero" is my anthem, Mars my patron saint. It was all that I could do not to stay and fight at Leffinghe.'

'Are you sure about the French? I mean, that the place is actually besieged? Are you certain?'

'As certain, dear boy, as I am that the King of France is an ass. And of that you should make no mistake. To have allowed his generals to dissuade him from the Duke's generous offer of peace that you bore to Paris was utter folly. He will rue the day. He has grown old, Steel. He no longer deserves the throne.'

But Steel's mind was still in Leffinghe. 'They were not privateers that you saw? You're sure that they're infantry? They wore white coats?'

'Regular, common-or-garden, good-for-nothing Frenchies as ever there were in their dirty donkey grey.'

'They didn't come in pirate galleys?'

'Barges and galleys, rather, and with some guns too. But they mean business. The guns they positioned on a nearby knoll. It had been a hill, you know, until the waters. Quite firm ground, though. Good for guns. Well chosen. They had gabions too and were digging out earthworks on the main island when I saw them. You know Leffinghe is on a hill. Hence it's being spared the floods.'

'I know it is the key to this whole game.'

'You mean the question of resupply? Yes, I can see that. It is precisely in the centre of the floods. He who holds Leffinghe has complete control of all the comings and goings of our boats from Ostend down to here and hence to Lille. Doubtless the French too have seen that. Which may explain what I have just told you.'

'How many men did they have?'

276

'Oh, I should say three, perhaps five thousand. Two brigades at the very least.'

'And the garrison?'

'No more than a thousand at most. Bit of a mixed bag. Dutch mostly, an under-strength battalion of English foot and, after we had made land, a few dragoons.'

Steel bit his lip and thought hard. 'You know that my wife is there.'

Simpson managed a smile, but only just. He stared down at the table, unable to look Steel in the eye. 'Yes. I did know that. What do you know of her situation?'

'What d'you mean? Is she wounded?'

'No, dear boy. It's just that . . .'

'What? Tell me, man.'

'It's merely that there's talk.'

'Talk?'

'About her.'

'She is the subject of gossip?'

'I'm afraid so. But I'm sure it is merely idle rumour. You know how women get when on campaign. The most ridiculous tales. Why I knew a major's wife in Tangiers who swore blind that her sister –'

'Shut up, Simpson, and stop trying to divert me. What are the rumours?'

'They are saying that she has been seeing another man.'

Steel fell silent, looked away. This was impossible. Henrietta would never do such a thing. She loved only him. He was sure of it. Her eyes said it all. He turned on Simpson and stood up.

'You're lying.'

Simpson shook his head and stayed in his chair. 'Unfortunately, for once, I'm not lying. There is merely a rumour, nothing more, that she is conducting an affair with another man. Another British officer.'

'Who? Who is it?'

'I'm not at liberty to tell you that. It would perhaps not be in your best interest to know.'

'Tell me, damn you.'

'I'm afraid that I shall not tell, dear boy.'

Steel sat down, shaking his head. 'Never mind. I shall seek him out when we relieve the town.'

'You? Relieve Leffinghe? But Major Meddowes has summoned a relief force from the Duke's main body –'

'Well then they will be glad of another battalion to swell their ranks, will they not? Moreover a battalion of veteran grenadiers, with its own amphibious transports.'

'I presume that you would be going against your orders, which must be only to provide escort for the convoys. You might be court-martialled.'

'I suppose I might. What of it?'

Simpson laughed and raised his glass in a toast. 'Jack Steel, you are truly an independent spirit. I raise my glass to your ambition.' He drank. 'But do be careful, dear boy. You may discover this man's identity, but do not then do anything foolish. If it is who they say, and if there is any truth in the rumour – which I trust and pray there is not – do not be rash. He has influence, Steel. Court martial or not, he could sink you.'

'I'll take my chances. I do not give in so easily.'

'Well, I have warned you. And it occurs to me now that perhaps you will need someone to watch out for you in Leffinghe. Someone who knows the place. I volunteer.'

'Don't be ridiculous. Of course, I'm flattered, Simpson, but you're hardly front-line material at present. You haven't fought for years.'

'Don't insult me, Steel. I may have resorted to strangulation with the Marquise, but I can still handle a blade with the best of them. Besides, I have a particular reason to want to come with you.'

'The sailor-boy?'

'Oh, no! What do you take me for? No, no, not the Jack tar. Though jolly he was. Malbec, of course. I have good reason to believe that he is among the besieging troops. At least I know that his regiment is there. The Grenadiers Rouges.'

'How do you plan to kill him?'

'I have no precise plan as yet. But he must die. He was the other assassin of the pair that slaughtered my friend. First the bitch dies, and now the dog. I rather thought that I might kill him in battle. Be a little more sporting than I was with his whore. And it seems to me that if anyone is going to be in the thick of it in that fight, and if anyone has the power to draw Malbec to him, it must be the brave, bold Captain Steel.'

Steel laughed. 'You will be rusty, Simpson. I'll have one of my men look after you. Just in case.'

He turned to Williams, who, with Hansam and several other officers from the grenadier battalion, was sitting at a neighbouring table. 'Tom, look here. Take care of Captain Simpson in the battle tomorrow, will you? He's not used to this sort of fighting. I dare say he's good with a sword, but strictly on a one-to-one basis. Look out for his back in particular.'

'It'll be a pleasure, sir. Though I didn't actually know there was to be a battle. Are we to attack?'

'Oh yes. We are to attack, Tom. You see, we have a bead drawn on our enemies. That's for sure. Now it is merely a question of being able to find them.'

SEVENTEEN

The boats came in under cover of darkness with their sails down and muffled oars. It was the best way. Steel had only once taken part in a amphibious assault, in Spain three years ago, and that had been a fiasco. The defenders had seen them coming a mile off and had thrown everything they could at them. Their little boats had been blown out of the water in a welter of foam, blood and flying debris. A third of their attacking strength had been lost before they had reached the shore. This time Steel was determined that it would be different. The darkness at least would give them some degree of cover and they would need every last bit of surprise if they were to have any chance at all of getting into the town.

They were coming in from the southeast. According to Simpson, the town was built around one main street running directly north–south. The defending British and Allied soldiers had thrown up barricades across the width of the outermost streets, while the French on their part had wasted no time in establishing a bridgehead near the shore. In a part of Europe renowned for its flatness, Leffinghe had been built on one of the land's few hilltops and thus now occupied an island. To the south, left of Steel's approach, a neighbouring knoll, now also an island, served the French as their battery position, and from there for the last three days their cannon had been raking the town with fire – shell and roundshot. As Steel's men approached, the guns opened up again, sending more shells into the houses. He watched as they burst and, seeing one catch fire, instantly thought of Henrietta.

She had not been far from his thoughts since his conversation the previous evening with Simpson. He wondered whether there could be any truth in the rumour. His initial reaction had been to dismiss it as jealous chatter. But slowly an invidious suspicion had crept into his mind, and try as he might he could not rid himself of it. Perhaps, he thought, it was because Louisa, the pretty Bavarian girl he had taken home to England after Blenheim and whom he had thought that one day would become his wife, had also run off with a fellow officer. But he kept persuading himself that such things did not happen twice to the same man. He was sure it must be gossip. Nevertheless, Steel knew that as soon as he got into the town his first priority would be to find Henrietta. Just to make sure she was safe . . . be sure. Malbec, for the time being at least, he was content to leave to Simpson.

The little boat containing his half-company chopped its way through the water, the Royal Navy ratings pulling for shore with all their might. It was heading directly for the east side of the town and flanked by eleven similar craft, carrying the entire battalion, less the casualties they had left in Gistel.

Slaughter, predictably, was no happier now than he had been when they had first embarked. 'These boats aren't made for this work, sir. They're for carrying grain, see, not taking soldiers into the attack. By the time we get off they'll have seen us and then there'll be merry hell.'

'Well they haven't seen us yet, Sar'nt, and we've only a couple of hundred yards to go. Have the men make ready.'

Steel's plan was to land on the right flank of the attackers. That way, when they were seen, it would only be by a few of the French, and by the time word of their arrival had reached the enemy commanders they would be formed up on the beach and ready to engage the French line. His prime goal, of course, was not to get into a prolonged firefight. That would be suicide, outnumbered as he expected to be by at least ten to one. Rather he intended to get as many men as he could into the town. Clearly Marlborough would have despatched the larger relieving force proper by now, but Steel knew that they might take anything as long as another day to arrive. What was needed now was more guns inside the walls to help the defenders hold out until the relief column turned up. And that was what Steel intended to give them.

Slaughter reported in. 'They're ready, sir. Ready as they'll ever be. But it still doesn't feel right.'

'If the marines can do it then so can we, Jacob. Don't mind getting your feet wet, do you?'

There was no moon, but as the barges grew closer to the shore the flashes from the cannon and the flames of the burning houses cast an unwelcome light in their direction. At fifty paces out Steel heard the cry he had been expecting.

'*Aux armes! A droit.*'

He knew these now were the crucial moments. Timing was everything. The first of the barges beached against the hillside, and then the second. Steel felt his own vessel strike land and held tight to the side as it stopped. Then he was off, jumping down from the prow into the shallow water above the sodden grass, sword in hand, calf-deep, aware that his men were close behind. He heard Slaughter curse and then they were all splashing through the shallows and onto the hill. All down the length of the shoreline he could see that the other barges had made landfall and were now disgorging their own passengers.

He turned briefly. 'Form up. To me. All of you, rally on me.'

As he spoke, Steel heard the first muskets crackle at them from the French ranks. They were too far off to be effective.

But if they were to make it to the defences without being cut down Steel knew he would have to deal with them first.

'Sar'nt, form the men up here. Line of battle.'

Within seconds the grenadiers were formed. Steel's half-company had been joined by their comrades. Behind them a second line was formed by the Prussians, then came the Dutch. He stood for a moment, savouring the experience of looking over a battalion-sized command. Then, drawing his sword, he gave the order:

'Advance.'

With Steel walking, sword flat against his shoulder, on the left flank of the company, the battalion began to move along the shoreline towards the French. At thirty paces the enemy opened fire for a second time. Steel braced himself and watched as two of his own men were hit and fell, to be passed over by the following ranks.

'Steady. Keep going. Sar'nt Slaughter, halt at twenty paces. Fire by platoons.'

At twenty paces they stopped.

Again the French loosed off another volley. This time four men fell in the British ranks. It was a gamble, he thought, but if it paid off it would win them the shore and with it the time to get into the town. In a prearranged manoeuvre, the Prussian second rank moved at double time and split either side of Steel's own stationary men, thus giving a two-company frontage in three ranks. He prayed that it would work.

'First platoons, make ready. Present. Fire.'

One third of the muskets fired and thirty one-ounce lead balls flew towards the French, six of them finding their mark.

Hansam took up the command. 'Second platoons, present. Fire.'

Another thirty guns spat flame, and another seven Frenchmen fell as they were still reloading. The echo had not stopped when the third platoon volley crashed out, felling more of the white-coated infantry. Then the first platoons were firing again. And so it went on. The French fired off a single, mass volley, but you could not really call it that, for now almost thirty Frenchmen were lying dead and wounded on the wet grass, slick with their blood, officers and sergeants among them, and those who were left in the three ranks were beginning to falter. Again the British and the Prussians fired their rolling volleys, and again the French failed to return fire. Then Steel saw two of the French infantry turn and run. That was all it took. Two men. Within seconds others had followed, and soon the battalion was streaming away from them down along the shoreline, their officers yelling for them to return, or joining in the rout themselves.

Steel turned to the Grenadiers. 'Cease firing. Stand steady.' Many of them, he could see, were eager to be after the enemy with the bayonet. He shouted, lest they should take the opportunity for glory, 'No. Not this time, my boys. You'll soon have time to complete your victory. Now, with me. Into the town.'

Turning back the way they had come, Steel was preparing to run to the head of the company when he felt a heavy blow on his left arm as if he had been hit with a hammer. Knowing instantly what it was, he spun round and, clutching at his shoulder, felt the blood and swore. The wound, he supposed, must have been around two inches above the one he had collected at Oudenarde, and it was probably not as bad, by half. Through the smoke he could make out the figure of a French officer, but the man, holding a still-smoking musket, turned and ran with his men before Steel had a chance to retaliate.

Slaughter came to his side. 'You hit, sir?'

'Yes. The damned coward shot me in the back. Ran away, damn him.'

'Got no manners, these Frenchies, have they, sir? Here, let me have a look.' Slaughter gently took Steel's injured shoulder and peeled away the red cloth, now stained with blood: 'You're lucky, sir. Passed clean through, just under the bone. Nasty hole, though. Looks sore, too.'

Steel gritted his teeth: 'It is, Sar'nt, a little, and too damn near the hit I took at Oudenarde.'

Between the two of them they contrived a dressing from a piece of shirting, and Steel walked to the head of the company, which had turned sharply and formed into a column of threes. He turned to them and, having sheathed his sword, raised his hat in the air. 'With me, men. Into the town.'

In double time they raced up the hill towards a road he had spotted when they had landed, yelling all the time, 'Hello, up there. In the town. Hold your fire. We're British. Hold your fire.'

He could hear cheering now, and soon saw a group of the defenders, grey and red coats among them, with their arms and weapons held up over their heads. Evidently they had seen the firefight, and as the Grenadiers approached their makeshift barricade of furniture, barrels and flotsam they began to pull it apart to make a gap through which Steel's men could pass. Steel was the first, clapped on the back by the defenders and cheered with loud huzzahs. He found a sergeant of English infantry, his face blackened with powder scorches.

'By God, sir. It's good to see you. Where are the others?'

'It's just us for the time being, I'm afraid, Sar'nt. But we're better than nothing, wouldn't you say? There's more on their way. Where's your officer?'

The sergeant pointed to the right. 'Major Kidd's two streets along that way, sir, and the officer commanding's in the main square, up there.'

Steel decided to make for the overall commander and set off up the street, followed by his half-company. All about them lay the debris of a siege. The street was littered with stones, cobbles, bricks, broken window frames, possessions blown or thrown from houses, and the occasional corpse of a dead soldier or civilian. It was Ostend all over again, and he hoped that Henrietta, wherever she was, was not too scared or touched by the memories of that place.

He arrived at the town square and walked into a vision of hell. On two sides were dead bodies: soldiers, men, women and children had been laid out in stiff rows. On the other two sides lay the wounded. Some of the townswomen were attempting to tend their wounds, but Steel could see that there was little they could do. Off to the left a small group of officers in red and grey coats stood in conversation. He hurried across and introduced himself.

'Captain Steel. To whom do I have the honour to report?'

One of the redcoats looked up. He was a good-looking young man of about Steel's own age with an angular, chiselled jaw and jet black hair which he wore drawn back in a queue as did Steel, although in this man's case it was less an idiosyncrasy than accepted fashion, on account of his being in the dragoons.

'I command here. Maclean. Major, Hay's Dragoons. You are most welcome, Captain Steel. You are the advance guard?'

'In a manner of speaking, Major. I command an independent combined battalion of grenadiers. We were in Gistel when we heard of your predicament. We are thus not, so to speak, with the relieving force, but I do know that they will be here soon.'

The major frowned. 'Ah well, better some than none at all. How many are you?'

'All told, with casualties, we number some three hundred muskets. All grenadiers, sir.'

As he said it a roundshot came howling in over high their heads and buried itself in a timber-framed building at the back of the square, carrying away a good portion of the first-storey wall and windows. Instinctively the men ducked, save Steel and Maclean who carried on speaking quite calmly.

'I would ask you to split your force, Captain. You will move half of your men to the left flank, where you came in. The remainder I would place to the south. It is there that the French clearly plan to make their main attack.' He noticed Steel's wound. 'You're hit. It's not bad?'

'Nothing, sir. I'll live.'

'Fine. Divide yourselves now as you will. Good day to you, Captain.' And with that he turned back to the Dutch officer to whom he had been speaking on Steel's arrival.

Steel, impressed by the man's sang-froid, although bemused by his apparent indifference, turned to the Prussian captain who was standing with him.

'Captain Emsdorf, take your company together with the Danes and the Dutch to the east, near where we beached. I shall be fighting with the remainder of the battalion on the south side of the town. Good luck.'

The Prussian clicked to attention and hurried away. Steel was about to assemble the three other companies when above the sound of the guns to the south another noise rent the night.

'What the devil was that?'

The officers stared in the direction from which the noise had come, to the northwest, and as they did so it came again. All recognized it.

'Muskets,' said Steel. 'Christ almighty, they've got round to the rear of the town.'

Maclean barked an order and pointed to the direction of the firing. 'Sar'nt Davidson, get your men over there. Hurry, man. Steel, you'd best follow him.'

A half-troop of dragoons ran across the square and vanished down a side alley towards the guns. Steel's first thought was for Henrietta. Maclean, believing that an order given was an order obeyed, did not bother to check whether Steel was carrying out his command, and Steel made use of the moment. Looking across the square he saw Simpson standing with Williams. He ran over to him.

'Simpson, you must tell me where my wife is. I beg you. Now, man. She will need my help.'

'Very well, but where d'you suppose I will find Malbec?'

'It's my guess that he's either down at the south entrance with the main body of the enemy or that it's him who's making all that bloody noise over there. Probably the latter.' He pointed in the direction of the new musketry, to the north-west. 'You might try either. He'll be with his regiment. You can tell them by their fur caps. Take Williams and a half-company of my men. Now, where is she?'

'She has rooms in a tavern in the north of the town. The Swan. And Jack, remember what I said. Be careful. I say, you're hit.'

'Don't worry about me. Just find Malbec. I'll join you when I can. Save some of him for me if you can bear it.' He turned to Hansam. 'Henry, you have the company. I'm taking Sar'nt Slaughter and Number 1 platoon off on an errand. I don't suppose we shall be long. And Henry, make sure Williams stays with Captain Simpson. Let's try to keep him alive.'

Maclean had still not realized that Steel had not done as ordered, but just to make sure that he wasn't disturbed Steel set off with the platoon across the square towards the guns, before doubling back up a side street towards the north. He found the inn in a back street, almost at the water line. From his left he could hear the sound of isolated musketry, and it was getting closer. The Swan was hardly salubrious, and certainly, he thought, not up to his wife's demanding stand-ards. He pushed open the door and, peering into the smoky fug, was surprised to find townspeople drinking, apparently oblivious to the battle raging around their homes. Or more likely, it struck him, drinking to escape it. He saw a staircase in the corner and turned to Slaughter.

'Jacob, stay here with the men. Don't hesitate to shoot if there's any trouble. I'll be as quick as I can.'

Pushing his way with his good arm through the half-drunken

288

crowd, Steel climbed quickly to the first floor. It was his experience that the finest rooms in such a place always lay at the far end of the corridor, and sure enough, moving quickly down its length, he pushed open the final door to reveal a simple sitting room with a settle, two chairs and a table on which lay the remains of the morning's breakfast. Henrietta's simple young maid Maria was standing in the corner rummaging through the contents of a tapestry bag. As he entered she looked up in alarm. Steel walked across to the inner door, leading to the bedroom.

'Wait a minute. You can't go in there. That's Lady Henrietta's bedroom. And she's alone.'

'So much the better. Marie, d'you not recognize me? It's Captain Steel, girl. I'm her husband.'

The maid nodded and stared. Then thought again. 'But, sir, you are not the man . . . her man. I . . .'

Steel's heart sank. The stupid girl had told him what Simpson could not. It was true, then. No idle gossip. He pushed open the bedroom door. Henrietta was sitting with her back to him at a small dressing table, combing her hair in the mirror. She was naked. As he entered she screamed, then turning and seeing his face reached for the gown which lay on the bed and covered herself.

'Oh, Jack. Good God.'

'You did not expect me?'

'No. How could I?'

'You thought that I might be someone else, perhaps?'

She saw it in his eyes. 'You know? Oh Jack, I am so very, very sorry. I did not intend it to be this way.'

'You thought you'd escape back to England and send me a message?'

'Yes. No. I mean, I did not intend for you to find me here.'

'Clearly. Why, Henrietta? How could you? What of our marriage vows? Do they mean nothing to you? You swore to love me. That you loved me. What of that, Henrietta? Is that for nothing? How could this happen?'

She looked down at the floor, said nothing for a moment, then: 'I, I don't really know. It just happened. He found me in Brussels and I was lonely. And you were gone and I was lonely. And . . .'

'And so you climbed into his bed. Is that it? From boredom?'

'No. Not at all.'

'Well, deny it then. Deny that you slept with him when I can see the evidence of it only too clearly.'

He looked down at the crumpled clothes that lay strewn across the floor: an officer's cotton shirt, a petticoat, silk stockings and garters, clearly discarded in haste.

'Jack, do not leap to assumptions. You're wounded. Let me help.'

He stepped away from her. 'No. It's nothing. Assumptions?' He picked up the shirt on the tip of his sword and flung it on the bed. 'I don't need assumptions. There is no leap to make.'

She saw how deeply he was hurt, and knew it was hopeless. So she moved to the offensive. 'Well, what else could I do? He was so kind and you had been gone so long and I was frightened.'

'And fear, as we all know, breeds betrayal. Who is he? Tell me his name.'

'He's a major, if you must know. You will know all soon enough anyway. I'm going to divorce you, Jack. I intend to marry him.'

Steel said nothing but was quietly thoughtful. 'You're sure. Of that? I mean? Perhaps –'

'No. You and I know that you don't mean that, Jack. It's over.'

Steel turned away and walked across to the window. He looked out into the darkness, his mind addled with shattered dreams, confused with the suddness. After a few moments he turned back to her. 'Very well. If that is truly your desire.'

Unable to meet his eyes, she continued to stare at the floor.

After a while she spoke. 'His name is Maclean. Lachlan Maclean.'

Steel nodded. 'I've met him. He commands the defences. He seems a good enough soldier. A brave man, certainly. Do you love him?'

'Yes. At least, I think so.'

Steel laughed. 'As you once thought you loved me?'

She looked away. 'Jack, please don't be like this. How can I answer that? I know it's hard for you.'

Steel did not reply. Instead he moved towards the door and then turned. 'I'd better go now before I do or say anything foolish. But I should like to talk to you again. Stay here, and if you hear anything try to hide yourself. I'll send someone to protect you as soon as I can.'

Steel left the room and gently closed the door, and as Marie watched him, terrified, he walked down the corridor. Nothing had changed in the inn, and he could see that Slaughter and the men still stood by the door. But in those few minutes in that room something had changed within Steel and it seemed wrong that the world should not mirror that transformation. He felt curiously numb, as if his universe had been frozen in time and yet at the same time as if it had fragmented, blown into so many tiny pieces, as if some gigantic shell-burst had ripped out his heart and scattered it to the winds.

Hs shoulder was starting to throb now. He prayed that it was not infected with a fragment of cloth from his coat, as so often happened. Well, that was for later. Now he had other business in hand. Instinctively, he knew what to do. He ran down the staircase, pushed across to Slaughter and nodded to one of the men.

'You. Macdonald. Up there, in the back room. My wife's in there. Keep a watch on her. I'll be back later. Come on, Jacob. We've got a battle to win.'

*　　*　　*

291

Tom Williams was not enjoying his new role babysitting Simpson. The man might, as Steel had said, be out of practice with a sword, but, thought Williams, he was no stranger to bravery. It was almost as if he wanted to die, and in the last few minutes Williams had saved his life three times. Simpson would insist on throwing himself into the hottest areas of the combat, there to be engulfed by Frenchmen. With Hansam's half-company and the men of Orkney's regiment that had come ashore with them, they were defending the barricade on the southernmost street of the town. It seemed clear that Major Maclean had been right. The moon had slipped out now from behind the cloud which had covered it earlier and shone down on the prospect of more than two thousand French infantry advancing steadily up the slope towards them. Williams calculated the odds against them and wondered where Steel might be. He would know what to do. It was not that Hansam was not a good officer. Williams had the utmost respect for him. It was simply that Steel had a knack of knowing what might get them out of a scrape. Mind you, this was beginning to look like something more than a scrape. He heard an officer's voice.

'Here they come again. Officers take posts. Look to your front.'

Major Maclean was with them now, along with four of his dragoons. He seemed to Williams to have something of Steel about him – a coolness in battle that he himself could only hope one day to possess.

As they watched the French advance, Hansam gave the order: 'Make ready. Present.'

As the guns opened fire Williams saw the major talking to his sergeant and by chance caught a few words: 'Milady . . . danger . . . inn.' As he watched, the major yelled something at his men and then turned and ran away up one of the back lanes which led off the street. Williams was intrigued. Surely such a man was no coward? He could only conjecture what his behaviour might mean. Finding Simpson standing waiting for the French, he realized that his agile mind might shed some light on the matter and began to tell him what he had just heard.

Simpson had known that Steel would be right. He might not have made the best of spies, and his courtly manners left a little to be desired, but on a battlefield it did not take much to realize that Steel was your man. Simpson had taken his advice and marched to the sound of the guns, and there he had found Malbec. It was almost as if the man wanted to show himself.

And so he did. For the truth was that Malbec had already spotted Simpson. At first he could not quite believe it. For two weeks he and his men had sought the spy with no success. They had tracked him through the back streets of Paris, had even raided the Cour des Miracles and barely escaped with their lives. Then his posting had come through and he had returned to his regiment, but he had known Simpson was out there somewhere. The other British spy was out there too, the Irish officer. He had sworn that some day he would find them. But this – this was too good to be true, an opportunity not to be wasted. The problem was how to get the spy where he wanted him. And the answer was a trick as old as time. He would use himself as bait to lure him in. All that was needed was a little bravado.

Close by, to the left of the attackers, two houses were burning, set afire by French shells, casting a lurid orange glow over the scene. His head framed against the leaping flames, Malbec stood high on the makeshift ramparts of the town's west entrance road and waved his sword around his head, yelling encouragement to his men: 'On, on, children of France. On for your King and for glory.'

A musket ball flew past his right ear and another touched his hat, making a neat round hole. He jumped down onto the cobbles and found himself confronted by a Dutch infantryman who attempted to impale him on a bayonet, but Malbec was too fast for him and, parrying away the thrust, pressed home with a counter-thrust which pierced the man's heart. He looked up and was pleased to see, some twenty yards away, that Simpson had not moved and was engaged in a fight with three of his grenadiers. He was fighting alongside a group of British grenadiers, and as Malbec watched he saw one of them, a young ensign, shout something in Simpson's ear. Within seconds the spy had turned and was running back up the street away from the fight. Malbec did not stop to wonder why, but leaving his men in the care of his second-in-command he fought his way out of the mêlée and ducked up a side street in pursuit.

Steel and Slaughter had not gone four hundred yards when they found Major Maclean and his men hurrying towards them. Steel shouted to them across the din, 'What's up, sir? Are the French behind us?'

Maclean, seeing who it was, pulled up, confused. 'No, Captain. I mean yes. Rather, I was told that they might have gone round to the north and thought to take a look.'

Steel smiled: 'I've just come from there, sir, and I can tell you there's no Frenchies up there. None whatsoever.'

'All the same, perhaps I'll just make certain for myself.'

Maclean began to advance. Steel said nothing but just stared at him. Then he placed his hand upon the pommel of his sword and Maclean knew instantly what was in his mind. Steel spoke again, more deliberately.

'I swear to you, sir, there are no French to the north. And you have nothing to fear . . . When I left her, Lady Henrietta was quite well. Should we not return, d'you think, to the fight?'

Maclean looked at him and knew that he was beaten. Steel was right, of course. It was their duty to fight and beat the French, whatever affairs of the heart lay unanswered. For an instant he was filled with admiration for his lover's husband,

294

and then, almost at once, he felt belittled. He knew that it was true after all what they said about this man, that he was the very epitome of honour, a true soldier who placed his duty to his men above all else. There was only one possible course of action.

Maclean nodded at Steel. 'We should go back, Captain Steel. Of course, we must. Come. With me. Let us give the French a bloody nose they'll not forget, and let us pray that Marlborough comes in time to save us all.' He paused. 'But should we not, d'you think, send a man to check? It would be prudent.'

Steel replied, 'Of course, sir.' He turned to Slaughter. 'Sar'nt, take two men and check the north of the town again. Then report back to me, at the double.'

Slaughter saluted and the three of them doubled off back up the street. Steel turned to Maclean: 'Now, Major. Shall we go? It would not do to give the Duke all the glory.'

Simpson ran as if his very life depended on it. There was only one thought in his mind: he must at all costs prevent Steel from encountering Major Maclean. Williams had sent his mind into a spin. The major, it seemed, had left the fight muttering that he had an urgent matter to attend to, a matter of a lady's safety. Simpson had no doubt as to his destination. What if Steel was still with his wife when Maclean arrived? He could not bear to see Steel killed by Maclean, and if it went the other way then surely Steel would face a court martial. Fate was cruel, but Malbec would have to wait.

He rounded a street corer and at last found himself outside the inn. The street was curiously empty. Simpson pushed at the door and entered. The drinkers were quieter now and there were fewer of them than there had been. He walked across to the staircase and went up, taking two at a time, to the first floor, dreading what he might find. The door at the end of the corridor was shut, and Simpson opened it.

Inside, Lady Henrietta Steel was talking to her maid while a red-coated Grenadier stood by.

Simpson sighed with relief. 'Oh, thank God.'

'Captain Simpson? What a pleasant surprise. Are you come to guard me too? How very gallant.'

Simpson shook his head. 'No, my lady, I am come merely to warn you. Both your husband and Major Maclean are on their way here. They must not meet.' She began to protest her innocence, but Simpson put up his hand. 'My lady, please. I know all. Such after all was until recently my business. Might I suggest that you come with me and avoid any confrontation?'

'I am afraid, Captain, that you are in part too late. My husband, Captain Steel, has already paid me a visit. He is aware of my situation. Not so, however, Major Maclean who must it seems arrive forthwith. So, you see, your fears are quite unfounded. I am quite safe.'

At that moment the room shook to the sound of a single gunshot and the Grenadier, who during their conversation had been gazing lustily at Marie, fell dead to the floor, a hole through his temple, his brains spattered over the wall behind. The maid stared for a second, then passed out in a faint. Simpson and Henrietta looked in the direction of the door and saw through the drifting powder-smoke the smiling face of Claude Malbec.

The Frenchman spoke: 'Captain Simpson, at last we meet. I am honoured to make your acquaintance, although I suspect that ours will be an all-too-fleeting friendship.'

Simpson smiled and noticed that in his left hand Malbec held a second pistol, the pair of the one with which he had killed the Grenadier. It was trained directly at his head.

'Major Malbec. And I had thought you lost. You have simply no idea how hard I have been trying to find you. You do me a favour, sir. I am much in your debt.'

Malbec shook his head. 'How I love your English

296

bravado. No matter how long I know the English, I shall never understand them. At heart, though, they are still a nation of heartless sons of whores.'

'Come come, Major. You allow your emotions to run away with you, sir. You should take care with your insults. After all, there is a lady present.'

'You seem to forget, Captain Simpson, that I hold the only pistol and that it is currently pointing at your head.'

For the first time Henrietta spoke. 'And you seem to forget, sir, that you have only one bullet and there are two of us.'

Malbec laughed. 'How brave! I'm sorry to mock you, madame, but I hardly think you are a threat to me. After I dispatch the captain here I may merely slit your throat with my sword.'

Simpson said with a smile, 'Ah, what exquisite irony! To suffer the same fate as your own dear lady.'

'What? What are you talking about?'

Simpson reached into his pocket and Malbec cocked the trigger of the pistol.

'No, no, Major, do not worry. I have no hidden weapons. Merely this.' Slowly, gauging Malbec's reaction, he brought out the emerald pendant.

Malbec gasped and very nearly dropped the pistol. Gazing at the pendant his hand trembled, and Henrietta saw her only chance. With a single swift movement she raised her hand and threw its contents, a pot of white foundation powder, straight into Malbec's face. Half blinded, the Frenchman screamed and instinctively pulled the trigger. The shot hit Henrietta in the chest and penetrated her heart, killing her instantly. Her body slumped to the floor. Malbec dropped the pistol and rubbed at his eyes, and as he did so Simpson thrust with his sword and cut the major on his forearm, drawing blood in a long line. Malbec groaned, but, managing now to see sufficiently to draw his own weapon, quickly parried Simpson's next and potentially lethal thrust to his groin and

297

riposted to his adversary's thigh. The Englishman recoiled with an oath as a trickle of blood began to flow down his breeches. Looking up, he could see the hate in Malbec's eyes now, and in that second he knew that, as Steel had said, his swordsmanship could easily be outmatched. His only chance was in pitting wit against brute force. He came *en garde* and the two men circled each other in the small room.

Simpson took the initiative. 'Major, come come. Shall we not settle this like gentlemen? Shall we allow ourselves a little more air?'

Malbec shrugged. 'Why not? It makes no difference to me where you die, as long as I can make your death long and exquisitely painful.'

Simpson shivered and gradually, as if by mutual agreement, the two men edged out of the door and along the corridor until they stood at the top of the staircase. The tavern was deserted now, cleared by the shot from Malbec's pistol.

'Does this suit you better, Captain? Is this a good enough place to die?'

Simpson lunged. It was a competent enough move, but the French officer parried it easily, before riposting with a deep lunge. The spy stepped back and brought up his blade in what he had hoped would be a neat counterattack, but Malbec had anticipated him and extended his arm so that Simpson simply walked onto the blade, embedding it deep in his side. He gasped, wide-eyed, as Malbec withdrew it.

'Don't worry, Captain. That was not a lethal thrust. Nor is this.'

Before Simpson had a chance to recover, Malbec was on him again, this time aiming for his head. He cut him across the left eye, cutting into the retina and blinding it. Simpson screamed and, clasping his left hand to the bloody wound, slashed at the Frenchman. But Malbec stepped back and manoeuvred neatly, without making a hit, deciding where to make the next cut.

He's playing with me, thought Simpson. The pain was beginning to kick in now. *He's killing me inch by bloody inch.* Summoning all his strength, he lunged again, but Malbec easily tipped his blade away with the lightest of touches and, extending his boot, kicked him hard in the groin so that with a yell Simpson fell backwards and went tumbling down the staircase. Malbec stood at the top for a few moments, looking down at him. Simpson could not move. He knew that something bad had happened to his leg during the fall and, quite apart from the excruciating pain in his eye and that in his side, that something was very wrong.

Malbec began to descend the staircase, taking his time, smiling and swishing his blade from side to side as he went. 'You sad little man. Did you really think you could win against me? You think I am heartbroken about the Marquise? Well, I will tell you, I have no love left in me for that. You British killed all the love in me years ago. I'm sad for her, yes. She was a good woman. But not for me. And what was it for? Because we killed your little popsy? Was that why? Revenge? I know all about revenge, Captain. Let me show you how nicely it can be taken.'

Simpson thrashed about on the floor, but try as he might he could not move his legs. He made a supreme effort and raised his sword towards Malbec. The Frenchman roared with laughter and walked a few paces more until he was standing directly over Simpson. He brought the tip of his blade down until it rested at Simpson's throat and said nothing, but looked down into his enemy's eyes. It seemed to Simpson that the gaze lasted forever, and that was Malbec's intention, although it was not as long as he would have liked. Suddenly his attention was distracted by a noise from outside the inn: gunfire, closer and in greater quantity than previously. Sensing that the battle was reaching its climax, he gazed down at Simpson.

'Oh dear. Our time is over, Captain. Unless, of course, you'd care to beg.'

Simpson shook his head and made another pathetic attempt to hit Malbec with his blade. The Frenchman kicked the sword aside and was distracted again by the sound of gunfire, closer now. He shook his head, shrugged and smiled, and then slowly leant down on his own weapon which was still poised over Simpson's throat until he felt its tip pierce flesh and bone and embed itself in the floor of the inn. Then, equally slowly, he drew out the blade and, wiping it against the dead man's breeches, slipped it back into his scabbard and made for the door.

The southern barricade of Leffinghe was a butcher's block of dead and dying flesh. The bodies of French, British, Danes and Prussians lay draped across its top and sides, and above their lifeless forms the battle raged on. The noise was deafening, but by now, after three long hours, it seemed to those involved to be as natural as birdsong. Standing on a broken upturned chair, keeping his balance with his left hand, Steel thrust again with his sword and, parrying the bayonet of a French grenadier, struck home. The man fell back with a look of astonishment, clutching desperately at his stomach, while to his right another of his comrades was struck down by a cut from Hansam's sword.

The lieutenant recovered his weapon and spoke to Steel without turning, coming to the ready for the next attacker: 'Hot work, Jack. Where the devil is the Duke? Any longer and we'll all be dead.'

'He'll come, Henry, just as soon as he can. Have patience. Just kill the buggers.'

It seemed that they were faced by an endless white tide of French infantry. As quickly as they managed to cut one man down another would spring up in his place. It was clear that the French must prevail by sheer force of numbers if Marlborough did not come soon. Steel lunged up with his sword and dealt another French infantryman a fatal blow through the chin.

Slaughter was at his side now. Momentarily without an enemy directly to his front, Steel turned to him. 'Jacob. All well?'

The sergeant looked at him and did not move, and Steel saw a look in his eyes that he had not often seen, but was able to recognize: fear mixed with unaccountable grief.

'I'm sorry, sir. I'm truly sorry.'

'My wife?'

'Sir. And Mister Simpson, sir. I'm sorry.'

Steel staggered from the barricade and took a few moments to recover his bearing. 'How?'

'Shot, sir, and Macdonald with her. Clean, sir. She can't have known about it. Mister Simpson's a bit of a mess, though. All carved up, he is. Killed in cold blood, by the look of it. Killed slow, sir.'

Steel knew at once. Malbec was here. Instinctively, he turned back to the oncoming French. They were cresting the barricades now, and all around him the thin ranks of red-, grey- and blue-coated men were falling back towards the town. There was no question about it: the Allies were losing. But fear was dispelled in Steel's mind by another emotion. A red mist seemed to cloud his vision as the hate boiled up inside him, masking sadness too and any thoughts of pity.

He turned to Slaughter. 'Ten guineas for any man who can find me the French major.'

'Sir?'

'Malbec. He commands the Grenadiers Rouges. Find them and you'll find him now. He's done what he came to do. Ten guineas.'

Slaughter looked at him with concern. He had never seen Steel like this – irrational, caught up in rage, his reason clouded. This was not the officer he had known for the last six years.

'I'll tell them, sir. But don't you think we should attend to all the French first? There's a fair few of them. More than just a major.'

Steel snapped at him, 'What business is it of yours who I choose to kill? I'll kill who I like. Malbec, his whore, their bloody king and all his blessed generals, and the damned Pretender too. It's all madness, Jacob. War. Love. Loyalty. All that's left is death. There's no virtue. No justice. Only death and blood.'

As he spoke, Steel ranged around in the rear of the ranks, seemingly unable to decide where he should place himself. Slaughter stared at him. He wondered for a moment whether he was fit to command, whether he should inform Hansam.

But the lieutenant had already seen for himself. He placed a gentle hand on Steel's shoulder. 'Jack. Steady. You must command. We must fall back into the town, to the second line. Maclean is hit, and Kidd's dead. We need your help, Jack. The men need you. Your battalion needs you. For Christ's sake, listen to me, Jack. Your battalion.'

Steel spun round on him and Hansam, seeing the hate in his eyes, let go and took a pace back.

For an instant both Hansam and Slaughter wondered what might happen, and then, almost as suddenly as it had come upon him, the mood left Steel. He looked at both of them in turn.

'Well, what are you looking at? Pull the men back to the second line. Where's Maclean, d'you say?'

'He's in a house. Second road on the right. He's hit bad, Jack. Might not make it.'

Steel nodded. 'Jacob, I want an orderly withdrawal, in two ranks, bayonets fixed. Withdraw by platoon. Second platoons to keep up a covering fire. Alternate movement by platoon. Clear?'

The sergeant nodded. 'Clear, sir.'

But as Slaughter turned to go, Steel added a coda: 'And don't forget about the ten guineas. I meant it. Henry, we'll fight the battalion by company. Keep the companies independent. I want what's left of the best men: us, the Prussians and the Danes on this side, the south. All of them here with me. The others can form a third defensive line to the north, with the wounded. And then we just pray for Marlborough.'

Drunk with the elation of killing Simpson, Malbec had skirted the north of the town along the shoreline and come round to the south by way of the west. Now, he thought, to complete this perfect day he would lead his men across the barricades, finish the English and take the town for a grateful King. He could see his regiment now, at the front of the battle, pushing on at the defences. Malbec ran the last few yards and, drawing his sword, placed himself on their left flank. And that was where Steel saw him.

For a single moment their eyes met, and it was enough. Steel grabbed a musket from the man to his right. Within seconds, despite his painful wound, he had its butt up and at his good shoulder, the weapon cradled in his left hand, cocked and ready to fire. His right index finger caressed the trigger and squeezed. But as it did so the smoke from new volleys clouded the target and he lost the Frenchman in its white mist. Cursing, Steel returned the musket to its owner and drew his sword. The early morning mist had combined with the powder smoke now, and the mêlée around them was no less than mayhem, a tangled mass of men, unsure as to who was on which side.

Steel plunged in and made towards the spot where he had seen Malbec. Another volley rang out from their left as the second platoon attempted to disengage from the enemy. Steel heard Slaughter's voice ordering the men to reload, and at the same moment he glimpsed a fleeting form to his front. It was as if a ghost had crossed his path, but he was certain of what he had seen. Certain enough at least to shout after it: 'Malbec.'

The shape stopped and turned, and again their eyes met.

Steel came *en garde* and the Frenchman rushed at him through the smoke, sword raised. Their blades met with a fury that sent a jolt up Steel's arm. He turned his wrist and deflected Malbec's sword, managing a riposte that just connected with his shin. Malbec stepped back and, disentangling his blade, attempted another cut. Again Steel parried but was slower than before and his stroke aimed at Malbec's arm fell short, so that his sword hung in the air. Malbec reacted quickly, with a short lunge, and whipped his blade along Steel's left side, tearing a gash through the red coat.

Another volley ripped the morning air, and with it came a different sound. It was the unmistakable whistle and rat-a-tat of fife and drum, and both men had no doubt what it meant. They circled each other, neither of them attempting another attack.

Steel watched Malbec for a few moments longer before shouting to him above the din, 'You're finished, Malbec. D'you hear that? Those drums? They're playing your funeral march. Those are Marlborough's men, come to take back this place. The convoy's safe, Malbec. Lille's a doomed city, and you're a dead man.'

A ragged cheer from the mists confirmed the truth of his words. It was enough. Malbec lunged wildly at Steel's chest and Steel parried the blade, anticipating its direction so that Malbec's sword pointed into the smoke. And then, with all his force, Steel thrust hard towards Malbec's chest. The well-tempered Italian blade slid easily below the Frenchman's breastbone and he stared at Steel in disbelief. He gasped a word, but nothing came from his mouth but a trickle of blood. Steel slid the blade clear of his body and the tall Frenchman stood motionless, his sword hanging at his side, limp in his weakened grasp. He began to sway from front to back and as he did so his head began to nod, giving him the appearance of a grotesque marionette. And then he gave Steel a smile that he was never to forget. For with it, from Malbec's clouding eyes, came a look not of hatred, but of thanks. Then it was gone and Steel was standing over Malbec's body.

He bent down and, plucking the major's cravat from round his neck, used it to wipe his blade clean of gore before returning it to its scabbard.

Then, throwing the bloody rag to the ground, he turned and began a slow walk up through the little Flemish town to find his wife and take her home.

HISTORICAL NOTE

The battle of Oudenarde was a pivotal point in the war. It had an instant effect on the morale of both armies . The French were forced back into France and never really recovered. It was the end of Louis' great Imperial dream.

It gave the Duke of Marlborough an unprecedented opportunity to invade France. As detailed in *Brothers in Arms*, he was opposed by the Dutch and unusually by Eugene of Savoy, thus losing the chance to end the war. Had he managed to do so, the conclusion would undoubtedly have been a very different one to the eventual peace and the history of Europe might also have been changed. Instead he harried northern France much to Louis' chagrin and provoked widespread panic in Paris.

In fact, Marlborough's initial concept of the siege of Lille was that it should be taken quickly, as a prelude to an invasion of France which under such circumstances the Dutch could not oppose.

Lille however, became a whirlpool of death more akin to the prolonged trench warfare of the Great War than any conflict seen to date. Notably, the battle for France's second city caused in one single day the same number of allied casualties as had been suffered at the battle of Oudenarde. Nevertheless, the siege of Lille has been unjustly ignored.

The battle of Wynendael is also one of the most fascinating smaller actions of the wars and General Webb a largely unsung British hero.

Converged grenadier battalions, such as that commanded by Steel, were not uncommon, thus giving a large body of elite troops. Certainly one was present at Wynendael and may have played a large part in Webb's victory which was so essential in sustaining the siege.

The Earl of Cadogan appears to have taken much of the credit for this triumph and Marlborough's opponents at home were to accused him of favouring his friend in his initial dispatch. Webb however subsequently received full credit and the thanks of Parliament for the action, and the following year he was promoted to Lieutenant-General. Nevertheless, from this point onwards Webb became the centre of Tory agitation against Marlborough.

The overtures of peace made to Louis are based on truth. Marlborough and Cadogan had established an extensive espionage network throughout Europe which kept them fed with information about French moves and plans. Independently of this however, we know that in May 1708 a Dutchman, Herman van Petkum, had visited Paris to negotiate a peace but that his demands were thought excessive. The Duke had himself made overtures to his nephew, the Duke of Berwick, one of Louis' generals. But Louis preferred to deal with the Dutch. Ultimately the King and his generals could not bear to humble themselves before Marlborough.

The story of the blockade and the flooding of northern Flanders is wholly factual as is the use of barges by both sides in water-borne warfare. Leffinghe is another of those battles consigned to the margins of the history books, which played an important part in securing the allied lines. It lay in what Churchill terms 'an archipelago of villages and unsubmerged hillocks', of which it was the key. Following the relief of the garrison by Marlborough on 24th October, the relieving troops celebrated so well that they were surprised quite drunk by a French night assault and the village retaken. By that time though the precious convoy had been secured.

Steel of course had also left the village behind him and was en route to Lille.

Now, shaken by the deaths of his wife and his friend, he stands on the brink of Marlborough's greatest and bloodiest campaign. Promised command of a full battalion, he is an independent man once more, all the more determined to further his career, having learnt that, while the life of a spy might hold its own dangers and rewards, he is better suited to that of a soldier, leading his men as he has always done, into the very heart of battle.

ACKNOWLEDGEMENTS

As always, I have relied where possible upon first hand accounts and this time in particular on the memoirs of the Duc de St Simon. My chief secondary sources once again were Trevelyan's history of England in the reign of Queen Anne and Sir Winston Churchill's history of his ancestor, the Duke of Marlborough. Of more recent works, apart from the indispensable David Chandler, James Faulkner's recent book on Marlborough's sieges was very useful, as were Andrew Trout's masterly 'City on the Seine' and Andrew Hussey's history of Paris. Charles S. Grant's two volumes on uniforms of the wars were, as usual, invaluable.

Lille, like much of Flanders, is changed today, although it is still possible to discern important elements of the fortifications. Vauban's astonishing models of his forts are on view in Lille and in Paris at the Musée de l'Armée. Steel's Paris is now mostly gone, a victim of the great Haussman rebuilding of the nineteenth century. However, the Place Royale, now the Place des Vosges, still exists and it is possible to find the historic house where Steel attended the soiree with Simpson.

This book was written during a very difficult period and countless people were extraordinarily kind and generous with their time and tangible help. Of these I would like in

311

particular to thank Caroline Barty for her unstinting hospitality at Nerac (Puy Fort Eguile) and also in France, David and Kate November and Carly-Ann Montariol. A huge thank you is due to those in Edinburgh who rallied round when the going got tough, in particular Susie Usher, Kate and David Oram, Polly Lambert, Catriona and Henry MacDermot, Tom and Kitty Bruce-Gardyne, Robin Gaze, Liza Stewart, Richard and Florence Ingleby and Patrick Barty. And last but not least an enormous thank you to my indefatigable editor, Susan Watt at HarperCollins, who understands only too well just how hard such times can be.

Last but far from least, a percentage of the royalties from this book is being donated to Help for Heroes, an apolitical UK-based charity which helps service men and women from current conflicts. I write about battles of the past , but I am acutely aware that wars never cease and this is an important chance for me to give something back . Over the past year and a half the charity has raised £16 million and by pure coincidence its annual sponsored bicycle ride through the Normandy battlefields is named 'Brothers in Arms'. You can find more information about Help for Heroes at www.helpforheros.org.uk